SECRETS OF THE DEAD

Recent Titles by Simon Clark from Severn House

LONDON UNDER MIDNIGHT
THE MIDNIGHT MAN
VENGEANCE CHILD
WHITBY VAMPYRRHIC
HIS VAMPYRRHIC BRIDE
HER VAMPYRRHIC HEART
SECRETS OF THE DEAD

SECRETS OF THE DEAD

DEAD

Simon Clark

Severn House Large Print
London & New York

This first large print edition published 2016
in Great Britain and the USA by
SEVERN HOUSE PUBLISHERS LTD of
19 Cedar Road, Sutton, Surrey, England, SM2 5DA.
First world regular print edition published 2014 by
Severn House Publishers Ltd., London and New York.

British Library Cataloguing in Publication Data

Clark, Simon, 1958- author.
  Secrets of the dead.
  1. Mummies–Egypt–Fiction. 2. Castles–England–
  Devon–Fiction. 3. Horror tales. 4. Large type books.
  I. Title
  823.9'2-dc23

ISBN-13: 9780727870049

Severn House Publishers support the Forest Stewardship Council™
[FSC™], the leading international forest certification organisation. All
our titles that are printed on FSC certified paper carry the FSC logo.

One

Thirty years ago. The night the horror began . . .

DANGER! KEEP OUT!

The two boys ignored the sign on the ancient door. After the tallest of the pair unlocked it, they passed through to the other side. This part of the castle was so dark that John Tolworth bumped his face by walking into a wall. Softly, he swore under his breath as he rubbed the sore tip of his nose.

Philip was eleven – one year older than John – and he always took charge. 'John, stand still, or you'll fall down a bloody hole or something . . . Wait a sec. Ah, found it.'

The light switch gave a loud click. Immediately, a yellow glow revealed the stone steps that gave access to one of Baverstock Castle's formidable towers.

Philip Kemmis began to climb the spiral staircase. Philip was amazing – absolutely amazing. John Tolworth had never met another human being like him. Of course, that could be because Philip was the son of a genuine English lord. His physical appearance was astonishingly different to other boys. He had blond curly hair that framed an unusually white face: its paleness made the freckles stand out so much that it seemed as if tiny spiders were running across his cheeks and his nose.

What made Philip even more striking were his

1

eyes. Those blue eyes of his were humongous. Gigantic! When they'd first met, Philip laughingly introduced himself as 'The Incredible Bug-Eyed Boy'. What had astonished John even more were the portraits of Philip's ancestors in the huge entrance hall downstairs. Some posed regally in crimson robes; others wore armour and carried swords. To a man, they possessed those same massive blue eyes. *All the family's got the bug-eyed chromosome,* John had told himself in awe. *Every single one!*

Philip Arthur Gordon Kemmis also talked posh. Very posh. If anyone talked as posh as that at John's school the other kids would marmalize them.

In polished, elegant tones Philip announced, 'You're so scared, you could shit.'

'I'm not scared.'

'You were the one who begged to see our family's mummy collection.'

'I still do.'

'Turn back if you want. I won't tell anyone that you were frightened.'

'I'm not frightened of the mummies. I just don't want to get told off by your dad.'

'Mother and Father are fast asleep.' Philip offered this statement as he sauntered up the steps. 'Dead to the world they are.'

'You're sure?'

'After all that champers, a keg of bloody dynamite wouldn't rouse them.'

Philip had such a funny way with words – comically funny, that is – and despite the boys' social backgrounds being poles apart they were genuinely good friends.

John laughed. 'They're always drinking champagne. I thought your family were skint?'

'Skint? Ah, colloquial for "broke". Indeed they are "skint", John. There's no dosh to repair this Gothic heap. Ceilings are falling in; the moat's run dry; ravens nest in the attic. My parents, however, prefer to describe their financial state as "genteel poverty".'

'They still drink loads of champagne.'

'Must keep up appearances, old boy. Can't let the locals think that the British aristocracy are falling on hard times. Ah . . . here we are. The mummy chamber.'

Philip switched on another light, revealing a wooden door covered in iron studs. John decided that this is how a door should be in a castle: as powerfully solid as those thick stone walls. John watched as Philip selected a rusty key from other keys on a ring.

'You're still free to go back, John.' Even though Philip was eleven he could sound so grown-up. Almost fatherly. 'We could watch a film instead.'

'I've heard about these mummies. I want to see 'em myself.' At that moment it was incredibly important to prove how brave he was. He didn't want Philip to think he was just some cowardly little kid.

Philip pushed the key into the keyhole. 'I need you to understand some important facts here. Egyptian mummies are dead people. Have you seen a human corpse before?'

'No.'

'Then prepare to be frightened. You'll be looking at dead people's faces. Three thousand years in a tomb has a ruinous effect on one's complexion.' Philip had a habit of invoking these funny turns of phrase. 'I don't want you haunted by nightmares.'

'I'm alright.'

'You're trembling.'

'It's cold up here.'

'Be warned. There are significantly horrifying corpses behind that door.'

'*Open it! Open it now!*'

Such a strange energy blazed through John. Yes, he was scared. He was excited, too. This was the thrill of doing something forbidden. In all his ten years he'd never experienced anything that seemed as ferociously dangerous as this.

'OK, your funeral.' Philip pushed open the door.

John shoved by his friend so he could rush into the room first.

Blackness. Silence. A jail cell of a place that imprisoned the dark rather than criminals. John Tolworth wanted to yell out. To shout something – shout *anything*. He ached to break the silence. Because that total absence of sound was like thick glue that gummed up his ears.

'The mummies are in this room,' Philip intoned from somewhere behind him. 'Nobody's been here in years.'

'I want to see them.' But at that moment John was screaming inside: I DON'T WANT TO SEE THEM! I WANT OUT OF HERE! The darkness turned ominous. It pressed against his eyes; there was a suffocating quality about that wall of black. He felt panicky, short of breath; his heart pounded so hard it hurt.

WHOOSH! John told himself that when Philip flicked the switch and the light blazed it really had made that dramatic sound. What's more, its brilliance ripped the darkness to shreds and flung what was left beneath the tables and chairs to become lurking shadows. Patches of wet slime oozed on the walls. Cobwebs hung from the ceiling. A jagged hole in the floorboards, which made John think of a hungry, gaping mouth, exposed a dark cavity: possibly the room below this one. A misstep would have sent John plunging down into that blackness to smash his bones and leave him in agony. Meanwhile, the stink of decay haunted this cold, neglected chamber.

John stood there panting with shock. He saw everything . . . yet bizarrely he saw nothing. He'd expected bandaged people lying in coffins. Instead, there were mystery objects covered by dustsheets. One sheet had slipped away, revealing the statue of a black dog – or something resembling a dog, with sharp ears pointing upwards from an ebony head. The animal lay on its stomach, its eyes staring forward, alert to trespassers.

'Anubis,' Philip announced, coming forward. 'Sacred jackal of the Egyptians.' He patted the creature's back. 'Carved from wood. Three thousand years old.'

'Show me the mummies.' John's heart raced. He felt bad through and through. Really bad, as if he demanded to be shown something dirty. Like sexy pictures of naked women. *'I want to see them!'*

'The mummified dead are all around you.'

John stared hard at those worrying oblong

boxes beneath their white sheets. At the far side of the room, an object beneath yet another sheet made him look twice. Someone appeared to be sitting on a chair beneath a dusty shroud. John burned with excitement. Yet he felt dizzy and sick at the same time.

He knew he shouldn't – he mustn't – but . . .

'Which one's the pharaoh?' His lips were hot and gritty.

'The gent on the throne. Do you want to see him first?'

John nodded. His heart got ready to explode.

Philip did that posh, sauntering walk across the room. John watched, hardly daring to breathe. Because, yes, beneath that sheet sat an Egyptian king who'd died three thousand years ago. *Bones and skin, bones and dust! And the eyes! What do eyes look like after three thousand years? Will they be open or shut? What if the eyes stare at me?*

His friend didn't hurry. But Philip never behaved like a regular eleven year old. 'My ancestor found these remains in the Gold Tomb in Egypt. That was a century ago. Lord Gordon Kemmis was so obsessed with royal mummies that he spent his every last ruddy pound finding this chap.'

The moment that John had both dreaded and eagerly wanted came. Philip swished back the sheet.

That's the instant the light failed.

John could not prevent himself from yelling. Even though he yelled at the top of his voice, as he was plunged into darkness, he could hear another scream: this one even louder than John's.

Philip yelled, '*JOHN! GET OUT!*'

John desperately scrambled across the room.

He could see nothing. Objects smacked against him as he ran. Chairs? Tables? Mummy coffins? Who knows? He simply concentrated on reaching the door. By chance, he avoided that yawning hole in the floorboards. Somehow he found the handle in the dark. Behind him, Philip's screams went on and on. Something was hurting the boy. Those were pain screams.

The stairway corkscrewed downwards forever. Or so it seemed to John. Down, down, down! He ran as fast as he could; his heart pounded with terror. Getting out of the tower dominated his mind . . . and getting away from those shocking screams. Reaching the bottom of the steps, he hurtled through the doorway into the residential part of the castle. The part that Philip and his family called home.

A corridor stretched away in front of him. Suits of armour flanked the walkway. There were soft carpets, bright lights. The faint aroma of the pizza they'd eaten for supper still lingered. As John ran, brittle thoughts clamoured: *I'll go back to my bedroom. Lock the door. Hide. I'll be safe there.*

But what was he running from? *And why did I leave Philip behind?* He made himself stop dead. *You don't run out on a friend. You stick together.* John turned around so that he faced the entrance to the tower. He stared into cold shadows that accumulated there.

As he watched, something awful happened. A figure lumbered through the doorway. Its legs were oddly stiff. The apparition found it difficult balancing on limbs that were as rigid as wooden poles.

7

The disturbing creature spoke. 'John . . .' Its voice was flat . . . dead . . .

John took a breath to steady his nerves, and after rubbing his eyes with his palms he finally realized that the figure was his friend, Philip Kemmis. The boy lurched along the corridor, his eyes glassy. For some reason, Philip held a red cloth that was all shredded and raggy. The cloth was wet – sopping wet. Red stuff dripped on to the floor. Then John understood that he wasn't seeing a red cloth at all. Those were shreds of skin that swung loosely.

'Philip! What happened to your hand?'

But no. The question should have been: WHERE IS YOUR HAND?

Philip still walked as if his legs were sticks. He held out the ruined arm towards his friend. His face had gone slack. No expression. Those uncannily large eyes of his were dead. He stared without blinking, and though he continued walking he never seemed to get any closer.

And he kept repeating over and over: 'John . . . John . . . John . . .'

Two

Thirty years later. Horror returning . . .

'John . . . John.' His wife called him again, 'John. The tea's arrived. Don't let it get cold.'

John Tolworth stood on a grassy mound that

overlooked the sunlit patio of the quaint Devonshire tearoom. His family already sat at the table, where they watched him with some bemusement.

'John, what are you doing up there?' Ingrid wafted a bee away from the scones.

'I can see it.'

'See what, Dad?' Eleven-year-old Oliver Tolworth stood up, ready to dash up the hill.

'No, Oliver. Sit. We're going to eat.' The boy's mother pointed at the chair.

'What have you found?' called Vicki.

'Baverstock Castle. I can see it from here.'

Vicki gave him that disdainful look that sixteen-year-old girls manage so adroitly. 'If we're that close, why did we bother stopping here? I'm hot, I'm fed-up, I want a shower.'

John heard Ingrid say, 'Vicki, your dad wanted to treat you to something nice.'

'Cream teas are weird. I'm not eating anything.'

Oliver detected a promise of extra food. 'I'll have yours, then. Can I, Mum?'

'No. Vicki will eat to please her father . . . won't you, Vicki?'

John didn't want the cream tea he'd been looking forward to so much ruined by an argument between mother and daughter, so, as he walked down from the mound, he decided to play peacemaker to the best of his ability.

His wife, Ingrid, wore a plain white T-shirt with jeans. She'd had her black hair cut shorter than usual, which coincided with her promotion to year-head at the school. Half-jokingly, she referred to the new hairstyle as a 'power cut'.

9

On one brown wrist she wore the exquisite replica of a Celtic gold bracelet that he'd presented to her on their wedding anniversary last week. Daughter Vicki shared her mother's exotic, almond-shaped eyes and shiny black hair, although hers reached halfway down her back. Genetic potluck had gifted Oliver with John's paler colouring and blue eyes. Oliver possessed the same hair-type as his father, too: light brown and so bristly that it defied the toughest of combs to tame it.

John took his place at the table and, being mindful of his role as peacemaker, tried to distract mother and daughter from arguing by being pleasantly chatty. Sometimes it worked . . . occasionally . . . or, to be completely honest with himself, rarely. He tried anyway.

'I used to come here with your grandma and grandad when I was Ollie's age. There's a pond over there that's full of carp. Huge, they are. Monsters. Leviathans.' He pretended his arms were jaws and clamped them on to Oliver's shoulders. 'Man-eaters. Aaarrr!'

'No fighting at the table.' Ingrid smiled. 'I'm supposed to be relaxing, and already I'm having to scold the pair of you.' Jokingly, she assumed firm schoolmistress tones. 'Behave, boys, I won't tell you again.'

'Or what?' Oliver chuckled, his eyes twinkling with mischief.

'Behave,' she said, 'or I'll chuck both of you in the pond and those monsters will gobble you up.'

Ingrid's good-humoured threat to feed her husband and son to the fish made even Vicki laugh. John's smile was one of relief as he spooned clotted cream on to his plate. His daughter never used to have inhibitions about being openly affectionate or joining in family fun. However, she'd now reached that awkward age when children scowl at their father's jokes instead of laughing; her expression always remained stuck to 'Very Serious' mode. John knew she was passing through that prickly borderland between being a child and becoming an adult. He loved his daughter. Though she could be trying sometimes. So BLOODY trying. Lately, the arguments that erupted between Vicki and her mother could be so fiery. Ingrid had wisely explained to John that Vicki's actions were normal in the decidedly abnormal world of adolescence. Ingrid had said, 'Vicki's testing our affections. It's as if she's saying: "If I behave like a total bitch to my parents, will they still love me?"' Testing that love almost to the point of destruction had become immensely important to their daughter.

Happily, there were no symptoms of a fresh argument now though. Vicki and her mother were chatting about a new pair of sandals that Vicki had bought in Ilfracombe on the way here. Oliver had transformed his scone into something that resembled a snow-topped mountain, there was so much clotted cream on the thing, and was devouring the confection with utter bliss. There was peace. There was tranquillity. *Happy families*, John thought, smiling. *I hope it lasts. I really do.*

After sucking his spoon clean, Oliver fixed his bright eyes on John. 'Tell me about Baverstock Castle again.'

'OK. It's a medieval fortress standing on a hilltop between the moor and the sea.'

'Were there any battles there?'

'Lots. When Lord Kemmis defeated the Earl of Boscombe in 1426 he cut off the Earl's head, then he stuck it on a big iron spike on the battlements.'

'Brilliant!'

John continued, 'In the English Civil War, the castle was pounded with cannon balls. The worst damage occurred to the place was when some idiot walked into the gunpowder store, lit a candle and . . . *boom*.'

'And you really lived in the castle when you were my age, Dad?'

'To be accurate, we lived in a cottage nearby. Back then, Baverstock Castle had lots of tenants that farmed its land. Because the place is so remote it became a little self-contained world in its own right. The Kemmis family made the rules, told people what to do, and they also built a school. That's where my parents – your grand-parents – were teachers.'

Ingrid sipped her tea. 'Sounds feudal. The king of the castle ruling the peasants.'

'It might have been dictatorial hundreds of years ago,' John said. 'When we lived there Lord Kemmis really cared about his tenants. He was a nice guy, too.'

Vicki fluttered her fingers in the air. 'Now, years later, you're mysteriously drawn back to the castle. Ooooh . . . spooky.'

'Is it haunted, Dad?' Oliver's eyes were wide. 'Did you ever see anything weird?'

'No, Ollie. There's no such thing as ghosts.'

Ingrid distracted Oliver from notions of haunted turrets and phantom-plagued dungeons by offering him half her scone. Oliver was boisterous, mischievous – a typical eleven year old. But there'd been a spell recently when he'd had nightmares about 'faces in the bedroom wall'. Now, John and Ingrid thought it wise to steer their son away from topics of conversation that involved the supernatural.

So why am I going back to the castle? John had been pondering that question a lot over the past few days. His return had a rational explanation, of course. John had specialist skills in archaeological photography. Utilizing a state-of-the-art camera, he photographed damaged or incomplete artefacts that had emerged from excavations. Then he used computer software to construct images of the shattered Viking bowl or mangled Roman brooch, or whatever the object was. That was his day job, and being self-employed gave him a freedom that he loved.

By chance, he'd seen a news item about experts restoring a neglected collection of ancient Egyptian artefacts. The story had immediately interested him, and his heart had leapt when he saw that the collection was housed in Baverstock Castle in Devon: the very place he'd lived near as a child. On checking the castle's website he'd learnt that the restoration team required the services of a specialist to work on damaged papyrus documents. Reassembling those ancient texts electronically would be much simpler than the incredibly fiddly process of gluing together

13

thousands of fragments of ancient paper. The work was scheduled to last four weeks.

John Tolworth applied there-and-then online; fortunately, he had an impressive CV and glowing testimonials from museums to support his job application. Within hours, he'd received an email from the head of the restoration team, informing him he was hired. Naturally, he'd then had to convince his family that his impulsive decision had been a sound one. His sales pitch ran something along the lines of: 'Baverstock Castle is in a beautiful part of the world. School? No, don't worry about that. The job's in August during the school holidays. It's perfect down there, and it's so near the coast. We get a free cottage for the month, too.'

Persuading his family to move away from the comforts of city living hadn't been that easy, however. Nevertheless, he'd found a way in the end – even if it *had* required a judicious bribe here and there to get the children to agree. Ingrid was a teacher, so had the time off anyway during the long summer holiday, and John hadn't worried too much about convincing her. In the event, she'd only offered token resistance. If anything, she was intrigued about discovering where John had spent three years of his childhood. He'd always described his stay in Devon in such a wistful way, as if describing a piece of heaven on earth.

After they'd finished their cream teas, John and his family climbed the mound to catch a glimpse of Baverstock Castle in the distance. Its solid stone walls rippled in that mystifying way you get on a hot summer's day. The ancient fortress appeared to be in the process of changing its shape and transforming its battlements and towers into something else entirely, as if in the power of a magic spell.

'Dad.' Vicki sounded alarmed. 'There's nothing there. It's wilderness.'

'Beautiful, scenic countryside,' John corrected.

'No! Wilderness – as in the middle of nowhere.'

'It'll be relaxing.' Ingrid's smile appeared to mask her own doubts about the place.

Vicki's expression darkened. 'I've got a bad feeling about that castle. There'll be nothing to do except die of boredom.'

Oliver chipped in: 'Dad, were you bored when you lived there?'

'No. I was friends with Lord Kemmis's son.'

Vicki giggled. 'Every time you met him did you have to curtsy?'

'Nothing of the sort. I liked Philip a lot. We had a great time together.'

Oliver asked the next question so bluntly that it took John by surprise. 'Why aren't you friends now?'

'We lost touch when he went to secondary school.'

'I still see my friends when they go to different schools.'

'Ah, but Philip was sent to a boarding school in another country.'

'Why?'

'Sons and daughters of aristocrats have to do things like that.'

'So Philip never came home?' Being condemned to a foreign school forever was clearly a worrying notion for Oliver. 'That stinks.'

15

'I suppose he came home for holidays.' John shrugged and frowned. For some reason, even though the hot sun blazed down, he suddenly went cold. In fact, icy cold, as if snow was being packed inside his chest. 'I never saw Philip again.'

Ingrid studied his face. 'Are you alright, John?'

'Fine.'

'You don't look fine. In fact, you look terrible.'

Vicki stood back. 'Shit. Dad's going to puke his guts up.'

'No, I'm not.' Though at that moment John felt he was going to do exactly that. Nausea stirred the contents of his stomach. His blood ran even colder. Shivers prickled across his skin. 'It's just that . . .'

'What?' asked Ingrid. She was worried now.

'I've gone and remembered something. It's so strange . . . I'd forgotten about it completely. Something happened to Philip.'

'Oh?' Ingrid became uneasy.

'I've just remembered the last time I saw him. I was ten, so Philip would have been eleven. I'd been at a sleepover at the castle, and we'd gone exploring after everyone was asleep.' John's heart started to pound. 'We went into one of the towers. We shouldn't have done, because it was so dangerous. The place was falling apart.' He frowned as he struggled to recall details of what happened. 'Then Philip got injured. His arm . . . or his hand. You know, this sounds odd, but I'd forgotten all about it. Philip hurt his arm, and I never saw him again after that.'

'Is he still alive?' asked Oliver.

'I suppose so.' John tried to shake off the strange sensation of cold liquid flushing through

16

his body. 'He's probably doing what the sons of lords do – whatever that is.' He smiled, trying to prove to his family that everything was fine so they shouldn't worry.

As if telepathically sensing the uncanny chill gripping her father, though, Vicki shivered. 'The castle's a death trap? Why don't we turn round and go home?'

'That was years ago. You'll love it there.' *Why do I feel as if I'm lying through my teeth?* John wondered. 'There's nothing to worry about.'

They headed towards the car park. A steady stream of vehicles, filled with holidaymakers, rumbled along the main road in the direction of the coastal resort of Lynmouth. Vicki and Oliver climbed into the back of the car. John hung back. For an unsettling reason he couldn't explain, he found himself reluctant to complete the journey. Although the nausea had left him, those shivers of cold had not. The 'someone's just trodden on my grave' sensation remained with him. *Why did I forget about Philip hurting his arm? Why's the memory so hazy? It's like I'm remembering a dream . . . or a nightmare.*

Ingrid slipped her arm around his waist. 'Maybe seeing the castle again made you remember what happened to your friend?'

'Maybe. I was only ten at the time.'

'You can turn back, if you want?'

Her words made John flinch. Suddenly, he remembered Philip using that exact sentence when they entered the tower. There was something else, too. In that polished voice of his, the boy had said: '*You're so scared you could shit.*' Philip uttering

17

that line came back so vividly as John stood by the car. But why was the rest of the visit to the tower so blurry? *Something about mummies . . . about seeing the mummy collection. Something about . . .*

'John. John?'

'Philip. What's happened to your hand?'

'John, what's wrong? Why did you say that?'

His forehead ran with sweat. 'I didn't say anything, did I?' He attempted a smile. The way Ingrid recoiled suggested that smile must have looked like the snarl of a frightened dog. 'I've been sitting in the sun too much, haven't I? And it's been a long drive.'

She gently squeezed his arm. 'When we get to the castle you're going to have a couple of days relaxing. You don't start work until after the weekend, so take it easy.' She glanced round to make sure nobody else could hear, then gave him a sexy smile. 'We're going to have *Us-Time*. We're going to spend time in bed together when the children are out. And not sleeping. We're going to catch up on making love. Plenty of love. OK?'

'OK.'

Still smiling, his beautiful, dark-haired wife kissed him on the lips. 'Come on, there's a castle waiting for the Tolworths. We're going to inject some life into the place.' She gave his bottom a cheeky squeeze. 'There are those Egyptian mummies as well. So, Mr Tolworth, show me some mummy bones and I'll show you some willing lady flesh. Get my meaning?'

John laughed. He dismissed the memory-ghosts of the past as things that couldn't hurt him or his family, or poison their future happiness. *Watch out, Baverstock Castle! Here we come – and everything's going to turn out fine.*

Three

John Tolworth felt exciting tingles of recognition as he drove his family through picturesque Devonshire villages that he'd not seen since he was a child. Here were pleasant inns that dated back centuries and ancient churches that had stood tall for a thousand years. The last part of the journey, which had begun six hours ago in London, was along a private road. This took them through wilder realms of the Baverstock Castle estate. From rugged hillsides, strange fingers of black rock pointed at the sky.

Oliver leaned forwards from the car's backseat. 'Those stones are ace,' he exclaimed as his bright eyes eagerly devoured what he saw. 'They look like loads of soldiers, don't they?'

'They're just a bunch of rocks.' His sister yawned. 'Are we nearly there yet?'

'Five minutes,' John told her before adding: 'When I lived here those rocks always made me think of legions of dark knights on the march.'

'Dark knights? Really?' Ingrid smiled. 'You must have been an imaginative child.'

Vicki shook her head. 'You're certifiably peculiar, Dad.'

Oliver studied the pinnacles of rock as they drove by. 'Who put 'em there?'

19

'No one. They're natural.'

'Will we see the lord today?'

'You mean Lord Kemmis?' John shook his head. 'No, the Kemmis family couldn't afford the upkeep of the castle so they sold it. The company that owns it now are doing the restoration. They're the same people who hired me to work on those old Egyptian documents.'

Ingrid eyed the terrain with growing unease. 'The place is more isolated than I expected – and more barren.'

Vicki ruthlessly got to the point: 'It's a bloody wilderness! There's nothing but rocks, grass and sheep.'

'And sheep poo,' Oliver added with a gleeful chuckle.

John eased the car along the road where it passed between two massive outcrops of rock: monstrous granite jaws that swallowed the Tolworth family in one go.

'There it is,' John almost shouted with excitement. 'Baverstock Castle.'

The castle appeared to have ferociously bludgeoned the crown of the hill in order to give it a level platform on which to sit. From this lofty position that muscular thug of a building, with battlements, buttresses and formidable towers, glared down upon the surrounding countryside.

Sight of the fortress brought out the schoolteacher in Ingrid. 'Castles weren't just built for defence. They were statements of power. Castles sent out a clear signal to local people that disobedience would be ruthlessly crushed.'

20

John nodded. 'The architectural equivalent of pointing a gun at someone's head.'

Oliver was impressed. 'It's great! I can't wait to see inside!'

The emotion that flowed through John at that moment astonished him. He'd never expected to be so moved at seeing the place again after all these years. His entire body grew tense, and he felt butterflies in his stomach. *This is such an odd sensation*, he thought. *It's as if this area is hugely important to me. Like I'm coming home to see family.* But his parents now lived in quiet retirement on the other side of the country, and his sister lived in Tasmania. Yet the landscape he drove through triggered powerful emotions he couldn't explain or even properly identify. *Strange.*

His wife and children were busily commenting on what they saw. He, however, had been drawn into a remote oasis of the past. He visualized himself riding his bike along this road when he was ten. As likely as not, in one hand he'd be carrying a glass jar that teemed with tiny, silver fish he'd caught in the tarn.

John slowed as he approached the gatehouse. The castle lay half a mile beyond that Gothic archway.

'What on earth is that man doing?' asked Ingrid in surprise as she stared at a figure emerging from a line of bushes.

Vicki laughed. 'Well, someone's pleased to see us.'

The man, aged forty or so, wore a billowing green dressing-gown over a black T-shirt and tracksuit bottoms. He fixed the car with a hard stare. Dark rings were etched deep in the delicate skin beneath his bulging eyes. However, it was what this striking individual was doing that caused John to reduce his speed to a crawl. The man was applauding. He clapped his hands together with a slow, calculating rhythm. His applause for the new arrivals became more impassioned as those bulging eyes locked on to John's face.

Ingrid became alarmed. 'John, keep going, don't stop.'

The stranger lunged towards the car and started pounding at the windows. Inside, there was thunderous banging as he slammed a fist against the glass.

Vicki screamed in horror when the man opened the back door.

'No, you don't,' snarled Ingrid. She reached back, caught the handle, and tugged the door shut. 'John! Go on! Faster! *Put your foot down!*'

John floored the pedal. The car roared away. In the rear-view mirror, he caught sight of a second figure, pushing a wheelbarrow. Clearly, he'd seen what had occurred. Within seconds, this man, who was sixtyish with white hair, had caught hold of the berserk Car-Hater. Firmly, yet gently, the white-haired man guided their attacker back towards the bushes.

'Damn it!' Ingrid took deep breaths to steady her nerves. 'That's a welcome we won't forget in a hurry.'

John's heart pounded. 'You kids OK in the back?'

Vicki nodded. 'We're both alright.'

John found it touching the way his daughter gripped Oliver's hand to reassure him. Oliver, meanwhile, twisted his head around to stare at the stranger in the green dressing gown. 'Why did he punch our car, Dad?' He sounded frightened.

'I don't know, Ollie.'

'My God, what a psycho.' Ingrid shook her head in amazement. 'Why the hell is he allowed to roam about by himself?'

John drove along the final stretch of driveway to the castle. His mouth turned dry as a revelation struck home. For a moment, he struggled to put into words what was troubling him. 'Ingrid . . . that man back there.'

'The psycho?'

'I'm sure it's Philip Kemmis.'

'Your friend from when you lived here?'

John nodded. He was certain he recognized Philip even though he was now an adult. What's more, he was absolutely certain that Philip had realized that it was his childhood friend, John Tolworth, driving towards the castle.

Which begged the most significant of questions: *what had made Philip Kemmis so angry? Why did he try to attack us? And what* really *happened to him in the tower all those years ago?*

Four

A man wearing a white shirt, a vivid blue necktie and formal grey trousers strode out of the castle to meet them.

Oliver Tolworth watched his dad talk to the

23

stranger. Dad pointed back along the drive; he did a lot of gesturing, no doubt describing how they'd been attacked by Psycho-Nut in the green dressing gown.

'Did you notice,' Oliver began thoughtfully, 'that even though it's blazing hot he was wearing gloves?'

'You mean the lunatic back there?' His sister scowled. 'As long as he's tied up in a straight-jacket now he could've been wearing a ballerina's tutu for all I care.' She shuddered. 'What if he'd pulled me out of the car, Mum? He might have—'

'Well, he didn't,' Mum said gently. 'We're safe. That's all that matters.'

'But why gloves? Big, thick gloves?' Oliver persisted. The lunatic with the glaring eyes had scared him. Oliver fully expected to see him bounding up the drive, waving an axe, screaming his head off, wanting blood.

'I'm sure he won't bother us again,' Mum said. 'Ah, here comes Dad.'

The man in the office clothes came, too. Smiling, he bent down at the windows so he could talk to them.

'Hello. My name's Greg Foster, head of admin. I'll be looking after you while you're here. Did you have a good journey?'

'We were almost murdered.' Oliver felt panicky again. 'Someone started bashing the car.'

His mother reached back to squeeze his hand. 'Don't worry, he's gone now.'

'Your mother's right. Everything's under control.' Greg's smile was enormous. 'I've picked out one of our most beautiful cottages for you.

It's a lovely old place: oak beams, stone floors, and a garden with its own stream. Right, if you follow me, John, I'll show you the way.'

The man in the white shirt and impeccable blue tie collected a bicycle that was propped against the castle wall. Soon they were driving along after him as he smartly pedalled down the lane. Moments later, they arrived at a clutch of houses built from stones that were the colour of oatmeal.

Everything seemed to get back to normal after that. Oliver soon put the drama of the Car-Hater's attack out of his mind. He was excited about the bedroom he'd been given, which filled the entire attic of the house. Straightaway, he loved the sloping ceilings and the big windows that had views of the wild moorland, with their masses of strange boulders. He remembered what his father had said about imagining the rocks were dark knights on the march. *Stone ghosts, alien invaders, man-hunters* . . . Oliver's own imagination kicked in. Already, he wondered how he'd react if he woke up one morning to discover that those dark sentinels had crept up to his home during the night and were shuffling closer to the door. A potentially frightening image indeed; however, he was too busy to get obsessive about it.

All the family joined in to help unpack the car. After they'd finished, Vicki stalked about the house trying to find a signal on her phone. Oliver knew that his sister had gone crazy for boys – in fact, one boy in particular – so she'd be pining for a text from Lee. Meanwhile, his mother and father were pleased to find the fridge packed with food; they shone broad smiles at one another when they noticed a bottle of white wine cooling on the bottom shelf.

'I'm sure we're going to love it here,' said his mother happily and kissed Dad on the lips.

Those contented words put Oliver at ease. His adventurous nature was returning. This faraway place excited him. He wanted to see the suits of armour and Egyptian mummies that his dad had told him were in the castle. There'd be dungeons, too, wouldn't there? Maybe swords and maces and shields – yeah, all kinds of cool stuff. He just knew this was going to be amazing.

Oliver Tolworth explored the garden, testing low branches for his signature monkey-swing. Then he headed down the lawn to inspect the stream. From there he could make out more cottages, which stood beside the lane. Beyond those were trees and broad meadows before the land rose up towards the moor.

Nobody else was in sight. There were no sounds other than bees going buzz-buzz amongst the flowers and birds singing in the trees. Oliver allowed his imagination to flow. In no time at all, he pictured himself as Lord of the Castle. In his mind's eye, he wore shiny armour with a steel helmet. Happily, he picked up a stick as barbarian warriors in the form of stinging nettles launched their ferocious attack on him.

'Dush! Wha! Splat! Die, die, die!' He hacked the tall plants down with heroic swipes of the stick. 'Drive them back into the sea . . . Save the maiden . . . Die!'

So often, when he was alone, Oliver slipped

into a dream-world that could easily seem more real than the one everyone else inhabited. Of course, he enjoyed the company of friends. Being alone, however, was special. Being alone with your dreams was a magical place – there were worlds of wonder, adventure and excitement.

'Who are you?'

The male voice startled him. *Crazy-man*, thought Oliver in panic. *Crazy-man's going to get me!* He spun round to find a figure walking alongside the stream. Oliver expected to see the fierce psycho in the dressing gown; those ominous hands in leather gloves reaching out.

Instead, a boy approached who didn't seem a great deal older than Oliver. The stranger wore jeans and a red polo shirt. He had black hair and big, bristly eyebrows that formed black arches above his eyes. Oliver stared at him, saying nothing. After the psycho's attack on the car, Oliver was wary of anyone new in this place. After all, the countryside here could be crawling with weirdos eager to do him harm.

The boy used stepping stones to cross the stream. He stopped five paces from Oliver and stared at him. 'I'm Fletcher Brown. I'm twelve.' The boy's voice was loud and strangely emphatic. 'My dad's the caretaker. We live in the gatehouse. My mother's in hospital, dying.'

Oliver continued to eye the visitor with a large dollop of suspicion. This boy wasn't like any kid he'd ever met before. Even at eleven years old, Oliver realized that there was something not quite right about Fletcher Brown. After all, the boy had declared that his mother was dying in such a matter-of-fact way that he could have been telling Oliver that she'd just popped to the supermarket.

'What's your name?' the strange boy asked.

'Oliver Tolworth.'

'You're new here.'

Oliver nodded.

Fletcher continued in that blunt manner: 'I was born here. I know all about the castle and the moor. I know secrets. Big secrets. Secrets you wouldn't believe until you see them with your own eyes. Are your parents still alive?'

'I've got to go. My mother wants me.'

'Not yet.'

Oliver flinched. *He's not going to let me go.* 'I've got to go home,' he said, trying to keep calm. He mustn't reveal he was scared. Bullies smell fear – and fear provokes bullies to do their worst.

'Stay here. I want to show you something.' The unsettling stranger drew an object from his pocket. 'My phone's fantastic. It'll be miles better than yours.'

Oliver nodded, while making a grunt that sounded vaguely complimentary.

Fletcher gave a self-satisfied nod. 'Do you know, if I was on the Moon and phoned you it would take one point three seconds for the signal to reach here? If I called you from the Sun it'd take over eight minutes. If I phoned from the centre of the galaxy you'd never hear what I had to say, because you'd be dead. Even though my voice would be travelling at the speed of light, it would take twenty-five-thousand years to reach the Earth. You'd be in your grave – just bones and teeth and shit. Oliver, I've decided something important about you.'

Oliver's blood ran cold. 'Decided what?'

'I've decided to make you my friend.'

Fletcher offered his hand. In the circumstances, it seemed wisest to play along, so Oliver shook it.

'Oliver. Do you want to see secret things?'

He's going to take me away. Thoughts of being led to a place where nobody could hear his screams sent a flurry of panic through him.

Fletcher moved closer. 'See? I took photos with my phone. I wasn't allowed, but I took them anyway. They're secret, so don't you dare tell anyone.'

Without thinking, Oliver reached out to take the phone.

'Ah! Ah!' Fletcher tugged the phone away. 'Look with your eyes, not with your fingers.'

Oliver found himself staring at a photograph of a sign reading: 'DANGER! KEEP OUT!' The buzz of insects seemed to grow louder, as if to emphasize how alone Oliver was here by the stream. If Fletcher decided to hurt him, he knew he could do nothing to stop it. The boy was a lot bigger than Oliver; certainly stronger. Nor would his shouts bring anyone quickly enough to save him. This was a big garden, and the house seemed a long way away. *Best play it cool. Show an interest in the photos – after that, get back to Mum and Dad as fast as you can.*

Fletcher gave Oliver a searching look, as if hunting for indications of treachery. 'I'm showing

29

you these private photos because you're my friend. If my dad knew I'd climbed into the mummy room, he'd kill me.'

'I have to go home.'

'No!' Fletcher grabbed Oliver's arm. 'You haven't seen the best ones yet. Look.' He pointed at the screen. 'Death mask.'

Oliver found himself staring at a smooth, gold face with wide, lifelike eyes and a solemn mouth.

Fletcher revealed the next image. 'Without death mask.'

The whisper of the stream and hum of insects vanished. The sounds of the garden seemed to be stolen away by the face on-screen. If the gold death mask had been the essence of serenity, then this horror was its absolute reverse. Open cracks in the mummified flesh formed veins of shadow that wormed from forehead to jaw. The upper lip had shrivelled back into a snarl. Gaping eye-sockets glared with violent anger. That's what Oliver was sensing right now. He understood with frightening certainty that he'd crossed a line. Although he couldn't articulate the emotion, he knew with all his heart that he shouldn't have seen the picture of the mummy. The cruel voice of childhood premonition warned him there'd be consequences . . . That meant punishment, revenge and suffering. Oliver was being blamed for looking. Blamed for gawping at naked bone, which poked through broken skin. There was rage in the face of that ancient corpse. Out-and-out murderous rage.

Oliver's heart thudded as he stared Death in the face.

30

Then Fletcher leaned forward to whisper these chilling words: 'When people sleep, that's when the mummies wake up.'

Five

Philip Kemmis had seen the car arrive. Instantly, he'd recognized his childhood friend, John Tolworth, even though they hadn't met since that fateful night thirty years ago.

He had seen terrible things in the car with John – three figures bound in the wrappings of mummified corpses. Their withered faces were a mass of ugly, cracked flesh, while their eyes had stared out through the car's windows in hatred. The three mummies were evil things. Somehow they'd tricked their way into the vehicle. Why hadn't John seen them for what they were? They were hideous things that had died three thousand years ago. Why hadn't his old friend known that loathsome Egyptian mummies rode in the car with him?

Philip had tried to warn John. He'd pounded on the car's windows. He'd desperately attempted to pull open the back door so he could drag at least one of the vicious creatures out. To his shame, he'd failed. John had driven away, not realizing that he carried a cargo of death with him: three grotesque figures, clad in the wrappings of the grave. They would destroy John, just as they'd destroyed Philip's life all those years ago.

31

Philip sat on a bed in the gatehouse apartment that had been his home for twenty years. Through the window he glimpsed Baverstock Castle in the distance. Figures moved behind windows in the tower. He knew what those shapes were. His enemy was stirring.

At that moment, the bedroom door opened. A husk of a man stood there. One covered with a criss-cross pattern of bandages. The tar-like odours of bitumen that had been used to help preserve the corpse all those years ago in Egypt flooded the room. He stared in horror at the grim totem as it lurched towards him.

'Philip . . . It's alright, it's me.'

The grim apparition of the mummified man vanished, and Philip sighed with relief. He realized he was mistaken . . . a trick of light, or perhaps the shock of seeing his old friend again in the company of those *things*.

The white-haired man was David Brown. He occupied the other apartment in the gatehouse with his wife and son. The wife, though . . . Something bad had happened to her. Philip struggled to remember. *Yes, that's it. She's in hospital – the mummies from the castle must have hurt her in some way. Perhaps poisoned her food . . . or even infected her with microbes that oozed from their bones.*

'Philip.' David's voice was sympathetic. 'You've not taken your pills again, have you?'

Philip's entire body twitched in a single convulsive spasm. He hated the medication. It robbed him of his senses.

David continued, 'I can tell, you know? You're

32

agitated. And you must have scared that family half to death when you ran after their car like that.'

'Family? Did you see what was in the car with John? I did. I've got to tell him before they hurt him.'

'Here, Philip. Take your pills. You don't want to go back into hospital again, do you?' The white-haired man spoke kindly. 'Here, let me help. Hold out your hand.' He picked up the blister pack from a table and pushed two pills through the foil into Philip's palm.

'My friend's come back. I should talk to him as soon as I possibly can.'

'Of course, Philip. Take the pills first. Here's a glass of water.'

'He needs me. He's in danger.'

'Swallow the pills. Don't get yourself all worked up again.'

Philip washed the pills down with a gulp of water. 'Did I tell you what happened to me, David?' He lifted his arm to show the stump that ended at the wrist. 'Did I tell you how I lost my hand?'

'Yes, Philip. You told me. Now lie back, give the pills chance to work.'

Philip put his head down on the pillow. His heart thudded loudly. He was thinking how he could save his friend, and how he'd destroy those three obscenities that John Tolworth had unwittingly carried in his car.

Six

Eleven-year-old Oliver Tolworth walked across the lawn in the direction of the house he'd be living in for the next four weeks. The strange boy, Fletcher Brown, mooched along with him with his hands clasped behind his back, humming to himself. Oliver had been shocked when Fletcher showed him photographs of the mummy's face. The face had been ghastly. Oliver had been ready to run away from this peculiar child who had so casually claimed that his mother was dying in hospital. However, Fletcher had put the phone back in his pocket and pointed out a roe deer that had come out of the woods to drink at the stream. Seeing the animal had amazed Oliver so much that it had driven the image of the gruesome face from his mind. Fletcher had then told Oliver about foxes and badgers that could be seen prowling the area at night. After a while, Oliver had begun to relax in the boy's company. He didn't seem so strange after all . . . OK, a bit strange, but Oliver was tolerant of eccentric children. Didn't one of his best friends always keep at least two live mice in his coat pocket? Some kids did funny things, for sure. That didn't make them nasty, just different.

As they walked, Fletcher said, 'There are lots of secrets around here. I know what they are.'

'Like what?' Oliver was interested.

'There's secret stuff about the graveyard.'

'What is it?'

'I won't tell you . . .' Fletcher gave a funny half smile. 'I'll show you.'

At that moment, Oliver's father appeared at the patio doors. 'Ollie? Want to give me a hand unpacking?'

'Who's that?' asked Fletcher.

'That's my dad.'

'What's his secret?'

Oliver shook his head, puzzled. 'He doesn't have any secrets. He's just my dad.'

'Everyone has secrets, Oliver. Everyone.'

Oliver's father smiled at Fletcher. He always welcomed Oliver's friends and was probably the easiest-going dad in the world. That's what Oliver told himself, anyway. However, before he could say, '*This is Fletcher. He's my new friend,*' Fletcher had slipped quietly away. Oliver merely shrugged. Maybe his new friend was shy?

'Who was that, Ollie?' asked his dad.

'Oh, just a kid. He's going to show me where some foxes live.'

'Ah, getting to know the locals. Good idea, Ollie. I'm glad you found a friend so quickly. What's he called?'

'Fletcher.'

'Can you give me a hand? Mum wants to put the clothes away before we have something to eat.'

'Yeah, OK.'

Before Oliver reached the house, the man in the shirt and tie, who'd shown them the way to the cottage earlier, pedalled up the drive on his bicycle.

35

'Hello,' the man said pleasantly. 'Are you settling in?'

Oliver's dad smiled. 'Yes . . . we're getting there. It's a lovely cottage, by the way. Those views of the moor are amazing. And Oliver here has already found a new friend.'

'Good, good. He'll be entertained, then. Is it Mark Oldfield from next door? His mother's our bones expert.'

'No, it isn't,' Oliver told him. 'He's Fletcher Brown.'

'Oh.' Just for a moment the man sitting astride the bicycle looked uneasy, as if he'd heard bad news. 'Well . . . I'm sure . . . uhm . . . Anyway.' He flashed a smile. 'I popped down to ask you if you'd like a tour of the castle. All the family's invited, John. I thought you'd like to see the lie of the land, as it were, before you start work on Monday?'

'That sounds great. What time would be best?'

'Seven would be ideal. It'll give you time to get yourselves sorted and have something to eat.'

'Seven it is. Thanks.' His father smiled. 'You want to see inside the castle, don't you, Oliver?'

The man turned the bike round, ready for the off. 'Cheerio.'

'Bye.' His dad waved as the man pedalled away down the drive.

Oliver remembered the mummy photographs that Fletcher had shown him on the phone. In a couple of hours, Oliver would walk into the castle where the mummies were kept; his heart began to beat that bit faster, because he recalled what Fletcher had told him: *When people sleep, that's when the mummies wake up.*

36

Seven

When Philip Kemmis stepped through the door that led from the entrance of his apartment in the gatehouse, he saw David Brown with his son, Fletcher. The white-haired man and the boy were heading towards where David parked his car. It was late afternoon, and the sun still burned down on the Devonshire landscape.

David waited until his son had climbed into the passenger seat before walking across to Philip and asking, 'Feeling any better?'

'Much better, thank you. Sorry about earlier. I'd forgotten to take my medication.'

'Not to worry, Philip.' The man smiled in a friendly way. 'You must get sick of swallowing pills. I know how it is with Mary. She takes so many she rattles when she walks.'

Philip knew that the man was putting a brave face on things. His wife was seriously ill in hospital.

'How is Mary?' Philip asked.

'Oh . . . shouldn't complain in the circumstances. She's comfortable. That's all we can hope for.' He took a deep breath. 'Well, I best get on. I'm taking Fletcher to see her now. Can't be late for visiting, or she'll worry.'

'Will you pass on my best wishes to Mary? Tell her I'm thinking about her.'

'I will, Philip. Thank you. It'll mean a lot to her.'

David climbed behind the wheel of the car and started the engine. The man's son stared back at Philip as they left.

Fletcher, you're an oddball, Philip thought. *You and me both. We're* both *oddballs. Then, it's hardly surprising. Those things in the castle have a knack of reaching out and touching minds here – anyone sensitive enough . . . or vulnerable enough . . . can fall prey to those things lying in the mummy cases.*

Just visualizing those ancient, dry-as-dust bodies in the castle put Philip on edge again. Even though he'd taken the pills that were prescribed to dampen down his anxiety and quell hallucinations, they were never powerful enough. Even with those chemicals oozing through his veins, making him infuriatingly dull-witted, it didn't take much to conjure up images that flashed with the savagery of lightning. Of that time in the castle tower when John Tolworth was there . . . when they were in the chamber with the Egyptian mummies and the lights went out. He remembered . . . yes, he remembered. His heart began to pound. Blood roared like thunder in his ears.

Philip breathed deeply, trying to dispel the images that haunted him day and night. He began to walk at a furious pace. Sometimes exercise helped. He struck off from the drive, following the path to the church built by his ancestors. This was their private place of worship on the estate. Though the castle had been sold, only the Kemmis family and their remaining staff were permitted through its doors. He walked through the gate into the graveyard. Ahead of him, the church, built from black stone, sat in the forest clearing. All around were tombstones that bore his surname: KEMMIS. All those dozens of people that shared his blood lay six feet down in their graves. Like insects trapped in amber, his ancestors were trapped in the silence of the tomb. Fixed there for eternity. Bones in long boxes. Leaving nothing but their names etched into cold stone.

Philip walked faster, trying to shake off the sense of foreboding that wrapped itself around his heart in the same way a python wraps itself around a lamb.

'Stop it,' he hissed at himself. 'Don't let these thoughts control you.'

Just then his right hand began to hurt, a sensation of hot metal spikes being driven into the ends of the fingers. He looked down at the hand. Even though this was a hot summer's day he wore a black leather glove there. He grimaced as the pain grew worse. A groan escaped from his lips.

'This isn't fair . . .!'

A savage jolt of pain in the hand nearly brought him to his knees. As he stopped to gulp in a lungful of air, he looked at the graves of his cousins, uncles, aunts and grandparents, who had all once lived in Baverstock Castle. Just for a moment, the soil became transparent. In each and every coffin lay a dried, wrinkled corpse wrapped in strips of linen, a criss-cross pattern of bandages across each chest. Faces with shrivelled lips and withered eyes.

The mummified bodies in the castle were responsible for this grisly spectacle – he was certain of it. Even so, he recalled those long talks with his psychiatrist. '*John, you must remember that these visions of the mummies are nothing more than a dream. They can't hurt you any more than having a nightmare about drowning in a river can kill you. There is a chemical imbalance in your brain, that's all. The chemical imbalance is producing these images you see of Egyptian mummies . . . The medication will make them vanish.*'

He gasped. 'Dear God, I wish the pills would work . . . They're useless . . . bloody useless.'

Inside the leather glove on his right hand he felt a sensation of something wet sliding across his skin. Like an extremely slimy tongue being run across the palm of his hand. In disgust, he tore off the leather glove. Beneath the glove was the artificial hand. A lifeless thing made of plastic and steel.

'But why can I still feel sensation there?' He stared at the prosthetic in horror. The fingers hurt, while the sensation continued of a tongue lapping the sensitive skin of his palm. He twisted the artificial hand, removing it from the connection fixed to the wrist stump. It didn't make the pain go away. When he looked into the forest beyond the churchyard wall he saw mummies standing there – sentinels that watched him and took pleasure in his agony.

Thirty years ago, he'd entered the chamber in the castle tower. The collection of mummies had been there since his ancestor brought them back to England all those years ago. He'd entered the chamber with his friend, John Tolworth. The lights had gone out.

In the darkness he'd felt them: teeth closing

over his wrist. Due to the absence of light he hadn't seen what happened next. But he'd felt . . . oh, yes, he'd felt that dreadful, soul-destroying bite that changed his life forever.

Eight

John Tolworth approached the castle's main entrance. He felt tingles of anticipation, wondering what it would be like after all these years. The last time he'd stepped through those massive timber doors was thirty years ago when he was ten years old. His wife and children gazed up at the massive walls, topped with battlements. Towers soared up towards clouds blowing in on the evening breeze from the ocean.

The head of admin, still wearing his white shirt and blue tie, greeted them warmly. John wondered if Greg Foster ever went off duty. *Perhaps he sleeps in the shirt and tie, always 'on', always ready to serve the company.* He immediately regretted the flippant thought. *The man's only trying to make us feel welcome,* John told himself. *And he does seem likeable.*

Greg smiled. 'All settled in at the cottage? Beautiful setting, isn't it? You have the forest, the meadows; all those wild flowers. This could be the Garden of Eden.'

Ingrid smiled back, appreciating his efforts to make them welcome. 'Thank you, Mr Foster. The cottage is lovely. I'm sure we'll enjoy staying there.'

'There's a stream at the bottom of the garden,' Oliver said. 'I really like that.'

Sixteen-year-old Vicki held up her phone. 'I bet you could get a signal in the Garden of Eden. I can't get one here.'

Greg laughed. 'Baverstock Castle is rather remote. You should see it in winter; snows are positively arctic.'

John smiled, too. 'I'll be more than happy if the sun keeps shining. We're looking forward to lots of barbecues in the garden.'

'Absolutely.' Greg rubbed his hands together. 'Right. Everyone ready for the tour?'

John followed Greg into the impressive entrance hall. He was pleased that his children looked around them in an interested way, rather than the bored manner they could adopt when the mood took them. A massive staircase swept up to the next floor. Tapestries hung from the stone walls. Oliver was fascinated by suits of armour that flanked the staircase.

'Don't touch.' Ingrid caught Oliver's hand as it closed around the handle of a sword that lay on a table.

'This way,' said Greg. 'We're still doing renovation work, so keep clear of scaffolding and cables.'

John caught the distinctive scent of fresh paint. The last time he was here the place was still owned by the Kemmis family. Back then, the odours filling the ancient building had been ones of damp and decay. He recalled how plaster had been sloughing from the walls like a snake sheds its skin. Every door had squealed on its corroding hinges. Many of the windowpanes were cracked or roughly repaired with pieces of wood. Now, corridors were pristine. Rooms contained beautifully restored furniture. Everywhere he looked there was renewal and repair.

'We've still plenty to do,' Greg told them. 'All being well, however, we'll open to the public next year. Ah, in this part of the castle we have the Egyptian artefacts that Lord Kemmis brought back from his expeditions.'

They entered a room that contained jars made from creamy alabaster. There were foot-high figures of men and women made from clay. They all seemed to be busy with some job or other, whether grinding corn, making clothes, or playing musical instruments.

Greg indicated the figures. 'These clay people were found in a tomb. It was thought that in the next life they'd serve their dead master and mistress.'

Oliver asked, 'When can we see the mummies?'

'They're in the lab upstairs,' Greg told him. 'We're still carrying out scientific tests on them to determine their age, and what kind of food they ate, and whether they suffered from disease.'

'Can we see them now?'

John noticed that Oliver's eyes had gone big and round. His son was excited about seeing the mummies. However, he was nervous, too.

Ingrid flashed John a warning look, then she cleared her throat. 'I don't think we'll have time tonight.'

Greg beamed. 'Oh, I'm sure there'll be plenty of time.'

Oliver had been troubled by frightening

nightmares recently, so seeing dried-out corpses would undoubtedly trigger another bout of night terrors. 'Maybe another time,' John said while catching Greg's eye in such a way that he hoped the man would understand. 'We've had a long day travelling. Oliver's tired.'

'I'm not tired,' Oliver said crossly.

Greg, thankfully, changed the subject from mummies. 'I'll show you the woodworking tools found in the Nile Delta. You won't believe the excellent state of preservation.'

'Oh, great!' Vicki exclaimed. 'I've got a signal on my phone.' She beamed with delight. 'There's a text from Lee.'

Vicki was more focused on her phone than the tour of Baverstock Castle. She texted her boyfriend as she walked along. John glanced out of a window. Huge slabs of black cloud had taken the place of blue sky. The moorland had now become a gloomy wasteland as the light faded. Ingrid listened with interest as Greg described how the castle had been converted from a fortress to an aristocrat's residence in the nineteenth century. The rooms here had been restored to how they would have been in the 1850s. Oliver repeatedly yawned. At least they'd managed to avoid him viewing the Egyptian mummies, John thought. He didn't doubt for a moment that gazing at the faces of what, when all's said and done, were dead human beings would unleash another spate of nightmares. Perhaps Oliver had reached that age when he had begun to understand what death really was.

Greg, meanwhile, explained how the antique

upholstery had been cleaned. 'The sofa cushions are supposed to be stuffed with wool, but when the fabric was removed it was found that someone had actually re-stuffed the cushions with old shirts. Dozens of them.'

Ingrid politely laughed at the notion of repairing furniture with clothing. 'Necessity is the mother of invention,' she said.

John glanced along the corridor. He recognized the door that led to the spiral staircase. Oddly, a strange taste flooded his mouth – it was almost like when you touch battery terminals with your tongue. A weird, tingling, *electric* taste. He found his eyes were repeatedly flicking towards that timber door with iron studs, as if he expected someone to burst through the doorway at any moment. A muscle began to twitch in his eyelid. Damn it, he must be overtired. It had been a long drive to Devon from London.

Greg Foster opened a cabinet that contained willow pattern plates.

John felt Oliver tapping his arm. 'Anything wrong, Ollie?'

Oliver whispered, 'What do you think Mr Foster's secret is?'

John looked at his son in surprise. 'His secret?' He spoke so that Greg wouldn't hear. 'What makes you say a thing like that?'

'Everyone has secrets. That's what my new friend says. What's your secret, Dad?'

This question took John aback. However, he masked his surprise with a smile. 'These hands.' He held them up. 'These are strangling hands.' He pretended to throttle his son.

45

Laughing, Oliver dodged back, knocking into an antique sideboard as he did so, making vases sway perilously.

'Behave, you two.' Ingrid automatically adopted schoolteacher mode.

'Yes, behave,' murmured Vicki without taking her eyes from the screen. 'He's gone bowling with his friends.' Her eyes narrowed. 'I hope that Susan Cranshaw isn't there. She was all over Lee at his birthday party.'

Greg evidently realized that the time had come to bring the tour to an end. 'We'll go along the corridor,' he said, 'and use the stairs in the east wing. That's the oldest part of the castle. Almost a thousand years old, or so the archaeologists tell us.'

They walked along the corridor, passing the formidable door that sealed off the spiral staircase to the tower. John Tolworth remembered running up and down the corridor with Philip Kemmis, the son of the lord that owned the castle back then. Perhaps it was those memories from so long ago that made him feel strange and sort of jittery inside. He wondered whether he should ask Greg about Philip. After all, it had been his old friend who'd launched himself at the car earlier and beaten the windows with his fists. John couldn't possibly know what had actually befallen Philip in the intervening years. He could make an accurate guess, however. *The man's clearly not well. Something psychological. It has to be. Why would a grown man wear a dressing gown outdoors in the middle of the day and hurl himself at passing cars?*

'John?' He felt a hand touch his back. 'What's wrong?'

'Hmm?'

'You're staring at that door like it's going to bite you.' His wife smiled as she tried to make light of it. She did look worried, though.

'Oh . . . I was just remembering the time I was here.'

Greg took an interest. 'You've been here before?'

'A long time ago. My parents were teachers at the local school. I lived here for about three years. In fact, we had a cottage near to the one we're occupying now.'

'So you'll know all about our famous mummies from the Gold Tomb.'

'Hardly *all*.'

Oliver said, 'I really want to see the mummies.'

Ingrid spoke firmly. 'Not tonight, Oliver.'

'There are five mummies.' Greg was proud of the castle's unusual residents. 'Archaeologists believe it's a family – a mother and father along with three children. One would be about Oliver's age . . . ahm . . .' Greg realized that was perhaps too much detail to give a child. 'Of course, John, you'll soon be busy restoring the papyrus. Reassembling the fragments has defeated the experts for a century or so, but we're confident that you're the man for the job.'

Vicki took an interest in the conversation again – well, at least she wasn't actually texting as she spoke. 'What exactly is your job here, Dad?'

'Greg's company have asked me to put the pieces of an old Egyptian book together that's made from papyrus, which is an early kind of paper.'

'Is that all?'

Greg smiled. 'Oh, it's going to be an extremely complex task. You see, hieroglyphs are a form of—'

'Writing, yes, I know,' said Vicki, a tad too sharply for John's liking.

'Anyway, these ancient documents are very important.' Greg didn't let his smile falter. 'It might reveal if the father mummy – if that isn't a too seemingly contradictory phrase – is the lost pharaoh Akhenaten.'

Ingrid added, 'The pharaoh Akhenaten radically changed the religion of the ancient Egyptians. They used to worship dozens of gods and goddesses. Akhenaten decided they should worship only one god, the sun god called the Aten.'

'Indeed,' said Greg. 'Our family of mummies had been buried in an underground chamber called the Gold Tomb. In the next chamber were the papyrus documents. At some point individuals broke into the chamber and ripped the documents into tiny pieces.'

'Why?' asked Oliver.

'Because,' John explained, 'the Egyptian priests told everyone that Akhenaten was evil after he died. They smashed up his statues and chiselled his name off monuments so people later wouldn't know that he'd ever existed. They might have ripped up the papyrus for the same reason. Now it's in thousands of fragments. I'm going to put it back together so archaeologists can read what's written there. Perhaps it will solve the mystery of who the mummies really are.'

Greg took up the story with enthusiasm. 'You see, Oliver, if ancient Egyptians didn't like people

48

who'd died, they'd open up the tombs and destroy the bodies.'

'Oh?' Oliver's eyes went wide as he imagined such a thing.

'It seems to be a quirk of human nature,' Greg explained. 'Sometimes the living try and get their revenge on people who've died by attacking their remains. In effect, they're trying to kill someone who is already dead.'

'Then I shouldn't be surprised if it happens the other way around.' Vicki kept her eyes on the phone's screen as she talked. 'Sometimes dead people will be so angry with the living that they get back at them, too. Revenge from the grave. Vengeance from the tomb.'

Everyone stared at Vicki after she'd made that bizarre statement.

The sixteen year old shrugged. 'That's my opinion . . . I'm entitled to have an opinion aren't I?' She read an incoming text. Her eyes narrowed with anger. 'Susan Cranshaw's gone bowling with Lee and his friends! I knew I shouldn't have come to this dump.'

Nine

The last minute before sleep . . .

'And I thought you were too tired to make love,' Ingrid said, sighing with pleasure.

'I hope I'll never be too tired for that.' John

49

Tolworth smiled, although his wife wouldn't have seen his contentment in the dark.

Outside the breeze had picked up, making a soft roaring sound that slowly rose and fell. *Such haunting music*, he thought, feeling drowsy and completely relaxed.

'I'm looking forward to staying here,' she murmured. 'It'll make a change from the town, all that traffic, bustle, noise. You know something?'

'What?'

'I'm going to immerse myself in nature, relax, read books, and enjoy being a mum with her family for a change.'

'Sounds a good idea.'

She sighed happily again. 'Do you want to cuddle into my back?'

'I'd love to.'

She turned over. He moved closer until he pressed softly against her bare back, and he felt the curve of her bottom deliciously in contact with his skin.

He slipped his arm over her. 'Do you know what Oliver said earlier?'

'Hmm?'

'He says his new friend told him that everyone has secrets.'

'Of course, they do; it's human nature.'

'Ingrid, what's your secret?'

She chuckled. 'Wouldn't be a secret if I told you, would it?'

John never even heard her evasive answer. His body had acquired that heavy sensation, as if sinking deeper into the mattress. Within seconds he was dreaming. The castle doors swung open.

He was ten years old again and going to meet his friend, who would show him the secrets of the chamber in the castle tower . . .

Vicki's phone lay on the bedside table. She stared at it, wishing with all her heart that a text would arrive from Lee. Vicki knew that Susan – the witch! – had somehow tagged along with Lee and his friends to play bowling tonight. Fiery images zinged through her mind of Susan laughing and flirting with Lee, and of them eating hamburgers after the game. And after that?

After that . . . well, that's when Vicki's imagination went red hot. All kinds of images flickered inside her head. Horrible ones that made her so angry she wanted to scream at the walls of this stupid house that was miles from anywhere. She checked the phone. At least she had a signal now. Perhaps it was something to do with the weather? Had it made reception better? It meant there was a chance, just a chance, that Lee might text, or even call. The sound of his voice would tell her if everything was OK between them.

'I'm going to stay awake all night, if I have to,' she murmured.

Yet a moment later her head sank back into the pillow. Her breathing became slower, more rhythmic, as she fell into a deep, dreamless blackness.

Oliver Tolworth had been woken by sounds coming from his parent's bedroom below his. He occupied the attic room, which faced that mysterious expanse of moorland. He sat up in bed, looking through the window. The world was black

51

out there. The breeze made ghostly sounds in the trees . . . the sound of ghost creatures, he decided. Usually, such images of phantom monsters running through his head would keep him awake; however, he was tired after the long journey from London today. Oliver lay down and soon fell asleep, lulled by the sounds of the breeze in the forest.

Fletcher Brown had been to see his mother in hospital. He sat on his bed and drew a picture of her: tubes coming out of her arms, dark rings under her eyes, those machines bleeping by the side of her bed. He sketched a coffin standing against the wall next to her bed. The coffin hadn't been there in real life, but the twelve year old decided it should go into the picture anyway as a vision, as it were, of things to come. He drew a grave, too. He wrote the line: *The grave worms are hungry, Mother.*

Fletcher put the paper and pencil down on the floor beside his bed. Resting his head down on the pillow, he said quite loudly to himself, 'That's it. I'm going to the Land of Nod.'

In no time at all he was there.

Philip Arthur Gordon Kemmis sat in the armchair next to his bedroom window. He'd taken more pills than he should have done. These were the ones that were supposed to damp down his anxiety and fend off hallucinations. They didn't always work. Sometimes, even though his mind was swimmy and unfocused by the drug, he saw figures walking from the castle to the gatehouse where he lived. He looked out of the window into the darkness. Yes, not too dark to see. A shadow moved with such an ominous intent towards the gatehouse. *That's the body language of a murderer*, he told himself. *An assassin moves like that when they're closing in for the kill.*

Philip told himself to stay awake. The safety of those who lived in the castle grounds depended on him tonight. It was his duty to protect them. He decided he should warn David Brown in the neighbouring apartment that a menacing figure approached the gatehouse. He attempted to rise from the chair. His limbs felt so heavy . . . The pills had dissolved into his bloodstream and were melting consciousness away.

'Don't you come here!' He directed the order at the figure on the driveway. 'Don't you dare . . .'

His eyes closed, and his head rolled back as he sat there in the chair. Philip's breathing wasn't relaxed. It made a crackling sound in his throat. What's more, his body twitched as he slept.

The walker approached the gatehouse. The shape of Philip Kemmis's head was visible as he slept in the armchair. The figure passed by in the darkness. At one window it glanced in to see the sleeping boy. A picture of a woman lying in a bed was on the floor. Words were visible on the drawing: *The grave worms are hungry, Mother.*

The walker continued. It passed a line of cottages between the forest and the meadow. Midnight was long gone now. Only foxes, badgers and the other night creatures were awake. They darted away from the walker. It was as if an oppressive force had descended on to the landscape. Animals retreated to their burrows. Bats deserted the area as if alarmed by an unseen predator. Stars vanished as thick cloud flooded the sky. And the breeze gave a ghostly cry as it died away.

Ten

The rainfall of the previous night had been heavy. The trees that spread their massive branches over the lane, as if trying to imitate a green tunnel, dripped water on to John Tolworth. He held a plastic file over his head to prevent his hair getting soaked. The time was coming up to ten on that Saturday morning. Even though he didn't start work until Monday, he decided to visit the lab where he'd be based. This was in the castle itself. He was looking forward to his month's tenure here. The work on the Egyptian artefacts interested him in its own right. What's more, this was a beautiful part of England; there'd be plenty of free time to spend with his family, either relaxing at home, or walking through the countryside, or visiting the beach, which was no more than fifteen minutes away by car. He felt good: yes, he was going to like it here.

He even relished the commute to work. This would involve a ten-minute stroll from the cottage, following this lane for a couple of hundred yards, before taking a path that led uphill to Baverstock Castle. There'd be no battling through crowded stations to find there were no vacant seats on the train.

'This, as the saying goes,' he murmured to himself, 'is the life.'

Rabbits hopped across the lane. Even though water dripped on to him from saturated leaves, he glimpsed blue sky through the branches. The weather was improving. Perhaps they'd have a barbecue on the lawn later.

John noticed the oddity straight away when it presented itself there, in a patch of soft mud, at the side of the road. A footprint. A bare footprint. He clearly saw individual toes splayed out. *That's strange*, he thought. *It's summer, but would anyone walk barefoot along a road, even a private road like this one?* He raised his eyes, following the line of footprints. The footprints stopped at a pair of bare feet. Startled, John looked up and found a pair of bright eyes glaring at him.

John immediately recognized the man standing there. 'Philip? Philip Kemmis?'

The man flinched back as if expecting John to scream abuse, or even to attack him.

John's scalp prickled; the man's frightened reaction unsettled him. 'Philip, it's me, John Tolworth. You remember me, don't you? We knew each other when we were boys.'

Philip Kemmis stepped out of the gloom. He wore a black sweater with black jeans. His feet were bare. Red lines ran across the top of the pale skin of his feet. *Scratches from brambles and thorns*, John surmised. *He's hurt himself walking around barefoot.* Philip bared his teeth – John believed the man was trying to smile,

55

only he was so frightened that the expression became a snarl.

Taking another step closer, Philip suddenly said, 'Yes, yes, I remember you, John. I was eleven the last time I saw you . . . You would have been . . .'

'Ten.' John lowered the plastic file that he'd been using to shield his head against the dripping branches. 'How are you?' Yes, a polite thing to ask, and perfectly normal, as a rule.

However, Philip made a sound that seemed like a failed attempt at laughter. 'Mixed fortunes. Had to sell the castle. Falling down around my ears it was. I'm still "Lord" Kemmis, though. Couldn't sell the title. Oh . . . and I lost this, too.' He held up an arm.

John saw that the hand ended at a bare stump. The wrist tapered to a point; its flesh was puckered with scars.

Philip tried to smile. 'Believe me, old boy, their bite is definitely worse than their bark.'

John decided he couldn't let yesterday's incident pass without raising it now he was face-to-face with Philip. 'When I arrived here yesterday you ran at the car and started hitting it. What was all that about? Did I do something to make you angry when we were children?'

'Far from it. You were my friend, John. I was trying to help . . . I saw them in the car with you.'

'My family?'

'No, you wouldn't have seen what they really were. No one does.'

'I'm sorry, Philip, I don't understand what you mean. Who did you see in the car?'

'Ha. Who did I see in the car? *What* did I see?'

John felt a degree of confusion along with increasing anger. He remembered how much this man had frightened his son and daughter when he pounded the windows with his fist. Then he'd been wearing black gloves, no doubt to conceal the fact that one of his hands was artificial.

John took a step forwards. 'You really did scare my family. Why did you do that?'

'Even though I haven't seen you in thirty years, I still consider you to be my friend. You were the closest friend I'd ever had.' The barefooted man became even more jittery. 'That night . . . everything went wrong. This happened.' Once more he brandished the shocking stump of a wrist. 'Since then, I've been trapped in a living hell. Pills, nightmares! I try to hold it together, but I know I'm losing the battle. They'll win in the end!'

With that, he turned and sped away through the trees. John could have believed he was watching a wild animal flee in terror. He shook his head, both baffled and shocked by this strange meeting. *'They'll win in the end.'* The man's statement was a peculiar one; disturbing, too, as if he was locked in a battle with an implacable enemy.

The bizarre encounter left John shaken, even a little sick to his stomach, if truth be told. His old friend seemed such a tragic figure. John could only conclude that Lord Philip Kemmis had been affected by some mental illness. The man's peculiar statements, including, *'I saw them in the car with you,'* reinforced John's opinion that Philip was unstable. John was still thinking about his childhood friend when he arrived at the castle.

Greg Foster, attired in a white shirt, blue tie and grey trousers, held a ladder while a man worked on a CCTV camera above the main door. John told Greg that he planned to take a look at the lab where he'd be working before he started on Monday morning.

'Good idea.' Greg beamed happily. 'Take the main staircase to the next floor, turn left and you'll see signs marked "Technical Laboratory". You can't miss it.'

'Thanks, Greg.'

'Oh, and you'll find Samantha Oldfield there, our osteoarchaeologist. Can I ask you to introduce yourself? I'm going to be tied up here. I'm chief ladder holder. Are you OK up there, Alan?'

'If you can just keep your foot pressed down on the bottom rung of the ladder. She's sliding a bit.'

'Oh, yes, sorry.' Greg placed his foot on the rung. 'Only another twenty-two cameras to go. See you later, John.'

John headed upstairs, as directed, and found the lab without any trouble. The Technical Laboratory, as it was described on the door, had been formed from a large room with views over the driveway to the gatehouse. There were long tables that appeared to be covered with objects; however, these were shrouded with white sheets so John couldn't tell what was there. He supposed they'd be various historical artefacts waiting to be cleaned-up and restored before going back on display in time for the castle being opened to the paying public. He noted the usual array of equipment that would be found in a lab like this – microscopes, computers, storage trays, shelves of files, display boards full of photographs, charts, printouts of emails, an invitation to a barbecue (today's date, and: *'Bring bottles, cans, cake.'*). There were also the usual notices written by exasperated members of staff that hinted at past lapses in lab etiquette: 'DO NOT BRING SANDWICHES INTO THE LAB **PLEASE!!!**' 'BREADCRUMBS CONTAMINATE RESULTS.' 'HANDLING ARTEFACTS? THEN WEAR GLOVES – ALWAYS, ALWAYS!!!'

A female voice breezily sang out from across the room: 'There's no CCTV going in here, and let me know when you start drilling the walls in the corridor. I don't want comparatively modern dust getting mixed up with my ancient dust. That ancient dust is my life's work.'

John turned to see a woman of around forty with blond hair striding towards him, carrying a mug of coffee. She wore a white lab coat, yet John could tell she had an amazing athletic build. She was tall, too, and reminded him of Greek statues of Diana the huntress. He could just picture her in a forest hunting down a stag with a bow and arrow.

'Your ancient dust is safe.' He smiled. 'I'm not the CCTV man.'

'Oh?'

'I'm John Tolworth.'

'Oh, the papyrus man? You've been hired to do the impossible, haven't you? Gosh, have you seen the state of the papyri? They must have been ripped into a million pieces.'

'Me and my computer software have achieved the impossible before.'

'Sorry, should introduce myself, shouldn't I? Osteoarchaeologists, such as *moi*, spend so much time with the dead that we forget how to be socially polite with the living. I'm Samantha Oldfield.' She thrust out her hand. 'We'll be neighbours as well as colleagues.'

He shook her hand. 'Pleased to meet you, Samantha.'

'Of course, I shouldn't be here, we're not obliged to work weekends, but this work is compulsive. It's like having an unfinished jigsaw. I can't resist popping in and tinkering. Besides, I'm waiting for DNA test results on my specimens.'

'From the mummies?'

'Indeed so. I'm excited as a wee child waiting for Christmas Day. I think my family of mummies here will spring amazing surprises. Coffee?'

'No, thanks. I had one just before I came out.'

'You will come to our barbecue this afternoon? We're convening at three, and there will be food and drink, plenty of drink. My husband is on a mission this morning to buy kegs of cider, that potent stuff they brew on farms here.'

'Thank you, yes, that'd be great.'

'Of course, bring the family. I've got two sons. My youngest is pining for someone of his own age to talk about computer games and air rifles and all that boy-stuff.'

'We've got wine and beer. I'll bring that over.'

'Super.' She beamed cheerfully. 'Just a warning, though. If my husband invites you into his recording studio, make any excuse you can and stay away.'

'Oh?'

'He composes music using the Found Sound Process.' She pushed her blond hair from her eyes. 'Do you know what Found Sound is?'

'Not really, other than I guess it's found.'

'Exactly.' She gave a pretend shudder of horror. 'Tom records sounds in the environment – car engines, wind in the trees, dogs' barking, you name it, then he processes the sound, slows it down, speeds it up, and generally manipulates the hell out of it, then he puts all those weird noises together to form music – of sorts. Tom is a lovely man, but if you find yourself in his studio he'll talk about Found Sound until you surrender the will to live.'

'I'm sure his music is interesting.'

'Consider yourself warned. Ah . . . did Greg explain everything? About what we're doing here?'

'Pretty much, but I didn't get chance to see where I'd be working when we came up to the castle last night.'

'OK. I can deliver my standard compact-sized lecture that I give to visitors. It'll outline our purpose here . . . though I should say "our mission", which is probably more accurate, as we hope to solve one of ancient Egypt's great mysteries. Stop me if you've heard this before.'

'Fire away. It'll be useful to hear about the work from someone in the front line.'

'Nicely put, John. Well, here goes.' She used the coffee cup to point at a plan on the wall.

'That's a diagram showing the Gold Tomb in Egypt. Over a hundred years ago, Lord Kemmis blew his family's fortune searching for the lost tomb of the Pharaoh Akhenaten. He believed he did find the tomb of the pharaoh, which also contained some members of his family. The problem is that there are no names in the tomb to prove who is buried there. The mummies were left in what is essentially an unmarked grave. Lord Kemmis seems to have made a leap of faith when it came to identifying the male mummy as the Pharaoh Akhenaten. What we're aiming to do is ID the gent found in the tomb. We can do that by examining his DNA and comparing that with the boy king Tutankhamen, as it's now widely believed that Akhenaten was King Tut's father. That's where you come in, John. If you can put the tiny fragments of papyrus documents together again, then those, with luck, might tell us who is in the tomb.'

John nodded. 'If it can be proved that the adult male in the tomb is King Akhenaten then it will be the biggest discovery in Egyptology since the discovery of Tutankhamen.'

'Exactly. It will be immensely valuable in historical terms.' She dropped her voice as if revealing a secret. 'It also means our employers, the new owners of the castle and the mummy collection, will make millions from photographic rights and souvenirs. People will be queuing down that drive to pay to see the lost pharaoh and his family.'

John was sceptical. 'But you don't even know if the mummies are related. And there are no clues to suggest that the adult male really is Akhenaten.'

'But we're hot on the trail now, John. DNA results could link our mummies with King Tut. And if you restore the papyrus to a point we can read the hieroglyphs . . . well, if it says something like, "Here lies the mortal remains of Pharaoh Akhenaten," then we're going to collect the biggest cash bonuses of our lives.' She smiled. 'As well as put our names in the history books. Fame and fortune, John. It's not often that an archaeologist can enjoy success like that.'

John turned his attention to the drawing of the ancient tomb. 'So, there are two chambers. One was trashed by tomb robbers, or whoever got into the tomb thousands of years ago, so it makes you wonder why they left the second chamber intact, especially as that's where the mummies were, and grave goods like jewellery and the gold statues.'

Samantha took a sip of her coffee. 'Ah, just one of the many mysteries. The first chamber, which we call the Library, on account of the papyrus books that it contained, was attacked with incredible ferocity. Every document wasn't just torn apart but shredded to tiny fragments. What we also found, when we sieved the debris, were fragments of human bone. There's speculation now that whoever broke into the tomb was killed, and then they were pulverized to fragments themselves.'

'Gruesome.'

'It also explains why the tomb raiders didn't make it into the second chamber, which is simply linked by an unlocked door. The second chamber is painted yellow, hence the name Gold Tomb.

The bodies were found in coffins, with the exception of the adult male who sits on a chair. It might be the throne-like chair that suggested to Lord Kemmis that he was in the presence of a king.'

'And there's no writing whatsoever on the coffins, or walls of the tomb?'

'No. Totally anonymous.' She moved to one of the tables covered with a white sheet. 'Right . . . if you wish, John, I can introduce you to one of the occupants of the tomb.'

John shivered, recalling the night three decades ago when Philip told him he would see mummies in the tower. Now here he was, about to see one for the first time.

'Say hello to Isis, as we've named her.' Samantha tugged away the sheet.

The three-thousand-year old corpse of a woman lay on its back on the table. Its eyes, or more accurately the shrivelled remains of them, stared up at the ceiling. The body was still bound in strips of linen in the typical 'mummy wrapped in bandages' style. The head had been freed of bindings, leaving the face completely exposed. Samantha explained that the head had been unwrapped almost a century ago, and that no self-respecting Egyptologist today would do such a thing – removing a mummy's bandages would, as she phrased it, 'degrade the integrity of the body, thus compromising its scientific value'. Isis's skin was a reddish brown in colour. Lips were slightly parted, exposing the teeth.

John had been taken by surprise at the sudden unveiling, as it were, of the mummy; he hadn't expected Samantha to do that. Now his surprise turned to keen interest. 'The hair . . . it's remarkable. I've never seen such beautiful hair on a mummy.'

'Looks as if she's just come from the stylist.' Samantha nodded. 'In the right conditions, hair is almost indestructible. Isis's hair is beautiful, isn't it? It must have been her pride and joy. Of course, this adds to the mystery.'

'Oh?'

'Egyptian men and women, and children for that matter, usually shaved off all their hair and wore wigs. This is natural hair that grew from her scalp. See the length of it? It would have swished around her waist; a cascade of glossy, raven-black locks. You can just imagine this striking woman lounging on cushions in the palace, while a slave girl brushes her wonderful tresses.'

John examined the face, which had a papery quality. He noted the high cheekbones and smooth forehead. 'I wonder, what was her secret?'

'Secret? What makes you say that?'

'Oh, my son repeated something his new friend told him. His friend said, "Everyone has secrets."'

'What a wise statement.' Samantha gave a surprisingly erotic wink. 'We all do harbour secrets, don't we, John?'

'That's what makes humans interesting.' He laughed. 'The fingernails, too: an amazing state of preservation.'

'Thank goodness the thieves who vandalized the papyrus documents didn't get their hands on the mummies in the next chamber – they'd have ripped them apart, looking for jewellery wrapped up with the bodies.' She shone a penlight into the mouth of the corpse. 'Has your son made friends already, then?'

'A boy of around twelve.'

'Local?'

'He must be. His name's . . . let's see . . . ah, Fletcher, that's it, Fletcher.'

'Fletcher Brown. Oh dear.'

'Anything I should be concerned about?'

She thought for a moment, perhaps choosing a diplomatic description. 'Fletcher lives with his mother and father in the gatehouse, though I believe the mother's in a bad way in hospital. Fletcher is . . . how can I put it nicely? Different. He has a tendency to say peculiar things.'

'Perhaps I should have a chat with my son about him.'

'Fletcher isn't unpleasant, or a bully, or anything like that.' She bent over to shine the light at the teeth in the back of the mummy's mouth. 'It's just that my son won't have anything to do with him. I think Mark finds Fletcher a bit frightening. He even described Fletcher as being "other-worldly", but then Mark does have good vocabulary.'

John moved in closer to see the state of the cadaver's teeth. 'Would you say that Fletcher has learning difficulties?'

'Just the opposite.'

Samantha's decidedly attractive face was just inches from his. John even felt her warm breath on his skin. John realized that the woman did have an erotic power; what's more, he knew full well that *she* knew it, too. He suspected she enjoyed flirting and took pleasure in encouraging men to do likewise. He moved to the other side of the table.

'There's another mystery about Isis,' he said. 'Her teeth.'

'Ah, smart man, you've noticed. She has wonderful teeth. I'd call them movie star teeth.'

'And generally ancient Egyptians had rotten teeth?'

'Absolutely. They often lost their teeth at a young age. The millstones used to grind corn into flour left gritty particles in the bread. In effect, the bread was like sandpaper. Gradually, it wore down molars to stumps.'

'This lady avoided that fate.' John studied the face. 'She's what? Thirties? Her teeth would get a whistle of approval from a modern dentist.'

'Nicely put, John.'

'Are the rest of the mummies in such a good state of preservation?'

'Yes, our king and queen, and their children, are all damn near perfect.'

She circled the table to be on the same side as John. He moved to the head of the table to examine the mummy's scalp. He still maintained an air of being relaxed in Samantha's company, even though he knew she was being teasingly sexy with him. Probably harmless fun, and perhaps testing boundaries with a new work colleague, but John wished she'd ease off on the femme fatale act.

'Do you know her cause of death?'

'There are puncture wounds in the torso of this

body and in the other bodies, suggesting they were stabbed with a knife or sword.'

'Murder?'

'Apparently so. An entire family slain, comprising of a mature adult man and woman, a youth in his late teens, a girl of sixteen or so, and a boy of around eleven.' She may have been annoyed by the way he kept his distance from her, because in a sharp voice she said, 'In fact, John, they're the same ages as you and your wife and your own children. Or as near as damn it.'

'Not quite. I don't have a son in his late teens.' John turned away, as if to admire the view of the moors through the window. He recalled the words of his son's new friend, Fletcher; the boy had said: '*Everyone has secrets.*' John's secret was that he had fathered a boy almost twenty years ago. He'd kept the secret well and intended never to reveal the truth; he certainly would never reveal it to someone as emotionally manipulative as Samantha Oldfield.

Fletcher Brown acted strange. It wasn't funny ha-ha strange, it was worryingly strange. Oliver Tolworth didn't like the older boy's behaviour one little bit. In fact, Oliver was starting to feel frightened.

If Fletcher had been strange right from the start this morning, when they met up by chance in the lane, Oliver would have gone home. But Fletcher had been friendly, and pleasant, and . . . well . . . normal. Fletcher had taken him to see deer grazing in the meadow. The twelve year old had then shown him big carp gliding just below the surface of the pond. Fletcher had also allowed Oliver to use his penknife to score his initials in a tree trunk. Fletcher said that's what kids did in the olden days before they had TV and computer games to entertain them. Oliver wasn't allowed to own a penknife, so it had been exciting to handle that sharp blade. Oliver decided to buy a penknife then find a hiding place for it in his bedroom so his mother and father wouldn't find it.

All in all, Oliver Tolworth had had a really enjoyable Saturday morning. What's more, there was the prospect of an enjoyable afternoon too. When he'd stopped by the house earlier he'd discovered that his dad had phoned his mother to say that they'd been invited to a barbecue. But now the day was being spoilt because Fletcher had got into a weird mood. He seemed determined to frighten Oliver. Oliver thought of the word 'sadist' and wondered if it applied to the twelve year old. They were now in a graveyard that surrounded a little church. There were no houses nearby. Neither were there any other people in sight.

Fletcher danced amongst the graves. 'There are two hundred dead people's names written on these gravestones. I know because I've counted them all.' He picked up a length of plastic pipe from the grass. How it had come to be there Oliver couldn't guess; perhaps Fletcher had planned something and left it there earlier. In any event, Fletcher slashed the pipe through the air as if it was a sword and he was beheading invisible men. The pipe, about a yard long, and of the type used in plumbing, made a buzzing sound as he swung it left and then right.

Oliver said nervously, 'Careful, don't hit me with that thing.'

'I'm not going to. It's a scientific instrument. I'm going to use it like a stethoscope.'

'A stethoscope?' Oliver was baffled by the strange behaviour. 'How?'

'You'll see, and you won't be able to believe your ears.' Fletcher used the plastic pipe to knock the heads off wild flowers that grew in the grave-yard. 'Just imagine,' he said, 'if there were electronic buttons on the gravestones and you could press them, and then . . . *whirr, buzz, clunk* . . . a hoist mechanism lifted coffins up to the surface.' He pretended to press buttons on a tomb slab that lay flat on the ground. Inscribed there: *Joshua Alfred Kemmis. Born 1822. Departed this life 1856. Drowned in Kelp Bay.* The boy made sound effects of a mechanism: '*Whirr, buzz, clunk, chugger-chugger.* The coffin rises up out of the ground. We grab the lid . . .' He made a screeching sound. 'We open it up. What would we see inside? Imagine how Joshua Alfred Kemmis would look after being eaten by worms for over a hundred and fifty years.'

'Stop it.'

'A family of mice would live inside his skull.'

'They wouldn't.'

'Would, too. Baby mice all nibbling what's left of his brain like it's stinky cheese.'

'Shut up.'

'Scared?'

'No.' Oliver's face burned. He felt angry rather than scared.

'Just imagine – you lean forward to look at

70

Joshua's skull. Suddenly, he reaches up and grabs you, and pulls you into his coffin. Whoosh . . . you look into the eye sockets and see mice staring back at you.'

'You're stupid.'

'Am not.' Fletcher swished the pipe through the air. 'Don't you believe the dead can come back to life?'

'No, I don't.'

'I do. I've seen them.'

'You haven't.'

'Have.'

The boy was older than Oliver, but now he sounded like a spoilt little kid. An eight year old, maybe. Oliver was tempted to go home and have nothing more to do with him. But it had been fun this morning. And Fletcher had let Oliver use the penknife. Oliver found himself reluctant to stop being friends with him. Perhaps Fletcher would soon stop talking about coffins coming out of the ground, and maybe he'd let Oliver use the penknife again. There must be a million uses for a knife like that.

Oliver tried to change the subject (sometimes that worked when his sister was being cranky). 'I'm going to a barbecue this afternoon.'

'Where?'

'At a house near where I live. There's going to be lots of burgers, sausages and stuff.'

'My dad doesn't have time for barbecues. He's always visiting my mother in hospital.' The situation clearly annoyed Fletcher. 'I told you about my mother, didn't I? She's dying. Nearly dead, in fact.'

Oliver didn't know how to react to such a

statement so he didn't even try to respond. 'You could come too, Fletcher. To the barbecue?'

'Nah, they won't want me there. People around here don't like me.'

'I like you, Fletcher.'

'You don't like me talking about coffins coming up to the surface.' He pressed another imaginary button on a gravestone. '*Buzz. Click!* Oooh, look, Oliver, this woman died of leprosy. She's got a face like a bowl of bubbly yogurt.'

Oliver realized, at last, that this was Fletcher's strange sense of humour. Even so, Fletcher's expression remained deadly serious. Oliver, however, started to laugh. 'Yogurt face. Ha-ha.'

'Death yogurt. Post-mortem yogurt. Yogurt of the grave.' Fletcher put the pipe to his lips and started making ghostly sounds through it. His sombre expression gave way to a wicked grin. 'Attack of the yogurt-faced woman.' He lurched forward, a hand extended to Oliver, zombie-style. 'Fatal leprosy wasn't the end . . . it was the stepping stone to becoming one of the living dead.'

'The juicy, gooey living dead. Can I borrow your penknife again, Fletcher?'

'Later.'

'Go on, I won't bust it.'

'Later. I want to show you this.'

'What is it?'

Fletcher reached a grave that took the form of a stone oblong box about six feet long. The sides of the stone box were covered by inscriptions. 'This gentleman,' Fletcher began with a strange formality, 'is the cause of all the trouble at Baverstock Castle.'

'What did he do? Burn it down?'

'Probably would have been better if he had.' Fletcher tapped the stone box with the pipe. 'Lying dead in this sarcophagus is Lord Kemmis. He died in 1916 after spending all his money looking for tombs in Egypt. He found the mummies that are in the castle now.'

'My dad's going to be working on them, and some old-fashioned paper called papyrus. It's what the Egyptians wrote on.'

'He's going to be with the mummies? Then God in all His mercy spare him.'

Oliver scowled. 'What do you mean? Are you saying my dad might get hurt?'

'Might? There's no "might" about it, Oliver. Those mummies are evil. Ask Philip Kemmis.'

Oliver didn't like the suggestion that his father might be in danger. 'It's not nice to say that people are going to get hurt. He's my dad.'

Fletcher was pleased with himself. He pointed at a hole in the side of the box-like tomb. 'See? The weather did that. Erosion.' He thrust one end of the plastic tube through the aperture and into the grave. 'Oliver, the tube's now a stethoscope. Put your ear to this end. You can hear the dead man crying because he made his family broke and brought the evil mummies here.'

'You listen yourself, you idiot.'

Fletcher put his nose to the end of the tube. 'You can smell his mouldy bones . . . phawww!' Fletcher had that evil gleam in his eye. He liked frightening Oliver.

This made Oliver angry again. 'I told you I liked you, but you don't like me.'

'Yesterday, I promised to show you secrets. That's what I'm doing. You're my friend.'

'Well, I don't like it.' Oliver backed away.

'Sniff the tube, Ollie-bollie, you can smell His Lordship's rotten face. Smells like the fish-burgers your mother's frying for your dinner.'

'Sicko. I'm going.'

'Wait. I'm going to tell you more secrets.'

'You're just trying to scare me.'

'Did you know, if you go into the castle at night, and look through the keyhole into the room where the mummies are kept, you'll see a shriv-elled eye looking back at you?'

'Bugger off!'

Oliver ran in the direction of the cemetery's gate. He'd had enough; this was bullying, and he was going home.

The boy called after him, 'You didn't give me a chance to warn you about the mummies. They kill people! They hurt my mother! She's dying and it's the mummies fault. Do you hear?' Fletcher wasn't saying these things as a joke now. He screamed, 'The mummies are bad! They hurt people. They'll hurt your dad! They're going to kill you!'

The barbecue was a full-blown party. John Tolworth realized that his neighbours had invited pretty much everyone that lived in the castle's extensive grounds. *Come to think of it*, John told himself, *nearly everyone here would be employed by the owners of Baverstock Castle, or be related to someone that was.* One person he didn't see was Philip Kemmis, which was a relief. Clearly, his childhood friend had led a troubled life and was, frankly, mentally ill, as well as suffering the loss of his hand. John hadn't time to dwell on it, because as soon as he and his family arrived, he quickly became recruited to help out with refreshments. Samantha Oldfield's husband, Tom, a pleasant man, with a shaved head, and wearing a Black Sabbath tour shirt and Bermuda shorts, asked John to help him unload the cider from his car. The cider was in plastic kegs. Each one required two men to carry it.

John made conversation as they hefted these monster barrels on to trestle tables on the lawn. 'Samantha told me you're a musician.'

'That's right. I'll show you my studio later. I converted the garage.'

John remembered Samantha's dire warning about being taken to the studio, but he decided he could withstand hearing about 'Found Sound' in the name of neighbourly friendship. Samantha had come on strong in a flirtatious way earlier in the lab, but now she expertly played the role of hostess. Perhaps the woman's display of come-hither sexiness had been merely a playful welcome. *I'm probably flattering myself if I believe she was really trying to seduce me*, he told himself.

'Shall we try some?' Tom slapped one of the kegs that were now lined up on the table, which, it must be said, sagged under the weight. 'We've worked up a thirst.'

'Thanks. Don't mind if I do.'

Tom pulled plastic glasses from a box under the table. 'This cider is brewed by a local farmer, using his own apples and a cider press that's over two hundred years old.' Tom operated a tap to release a stream of golden liquid into a glass. 'It looks like a urine sample, and it has a taste that's . . . shall we say, interesting? But it'd power a rocket to the moon. Cheers.'

'Cheers.' John gasped. 'Phew. I best pace myself with this stuff, it's strong.'

Tom laughed as he began pouring out more glasses of cider for the guests. Greg Foster was there, and without the tie for once. He wore his white shirt open at the neck.

'Chin-chin,' Greg said, and downed the cider in one go.

As Tom and John handed out drinks on the ever more crowded lawn, Tom murmured, 'If it's anything like last time, Greg will be swinging through the trees like Tarzan after he's had a couple more pints of this stuff.'

John noticed Ingrid chatting to a couple of women that he didn't recognize, while Oliver hung on a rope swing. Samantha's son was pushing him. Both boys were laughing, clearly having a good time. Meanwhile, Vicki, who had arrived in one of her grade-A sulks, insisting she'd be bored, had struck up a conversation with Samantha's eldest son, Jason. He was about seventeen or so. Vicki smiled, playing with her hair, as he explained something to her that required big arm gestures. John had a feeling that his daughter was already smitten.

'John.' Tom pointed at the barbecue. 'Would you do me a favour? Fire up the beast, would you? All you need do is light the gas.'

76

John said that he would. He walked across to the barbecue – a regular behemoth that looked as if it would be capable of roasting half a cow. At that moment, the chatter and laughter stopped dead. It was as sudden as someone hitting a mute button.

A figure stood at the garden gate. John recognized the boy. It was Fletcher, his son's new friend. The expressions on the faces of the other guests said loud and clear that they weren't pleased to see him. In fact, there were scowls as people exchanged glances that seemed to say, *Here comes trouble.*

Fletcher announced, in an oddly emphatic way, 'I've come to the barbecue. Oliver Tolworth said it would be alright.'

'I don't want Fletcher Brown here. I don't like him.'

John overheard the Oldfields' youngest son, Mark, saying this to his parents. Fletcher stood at the gate with an air of solid immovability. John began to appreciate why the Oldfield family regarded the boy as being a bit peculiar. The twelve year old had a bovine quality.

Samantha whispered something in her son's ear, perhaps reminding him to be polite. Samantha adopted an artificial smile. Turning to the still-as-the-proverbial-statue boy, she said, 'Come on in, Fletcher. Of course you can join the party.' She opened the gate. 'There are soft drinks on the table over there. Burgers and hot dogs are under the gazebo. Help yourself.'

Fletcher could have been an alien creature from another world, the way the crowd on the lawn fell silent and parted to allow him to pass through to the drinks table.

Ingrid touched John with her elbow and murmured so no-one else would hear, 'Reminds me of Quasimodo in that old film *The Hunchback of Notre Dame*. The people react like that poor boy's some kind of ugly monster. It's not right, is it?'

'They say he's odd.'

'Being odd doesn't entitle us to mark a child out as a social outcast. Look, they avoid him as if he's got an infectious disease.'

'Not our problem, Ingrid.' He topped up her glass with white wine.

'It should be everyone's problem.' She watched Fletcher open a can of coke. 'Prejudice is like a virus that mutates. It can change from dislike of a person's skin colour to rejecting a person on account of physical handicap, or if they behave a little bit differently from other people. Prejudice is always hungry for more victims.'

'I'm glad I married you.' He smiled. 'You're the wisest person I've ever met.'

She smiled back. 'Thank you. You say the nicest things.'

He appreciated that Ingrid's duties at the school where she worked included explaining to pupils what was right and wrong, and carefully instilling moral values. All of which meant that she'd quickly identified that prejudice probably lay at the root of people here disliking Fletcher.

John's phone signalled a call coming through.

'John.' Ingrid raised her eyebrows. 'It's a party. Are you going to switch that off?'

'I had an email to say the three-D printer's in stock. The courier's going to ring me when it's on its way. I need to get it up and running before I start work on Monday. S'cuse a mo.' He grinned at her as he took the call. The courier told him that he'd deliver the 3D printer between four and five. The device cost a heck of a lot, yet it would be a useful asset for his business.

The moment he finished the call with the courier, his son raced across the lawn, shouting excitedly, 'Water fight! Water fight!'

'What water fight?'

'Parents versus kids.'

'Buckets?'

'Water blasters!' Oliver laughed with delight. 'Parents are going to take on the kids. We're gonna have a water war!'

Mark produced an entire arsenal of formidable water weaponry. These were brightly coloured plastic rifles with large reservoirs that contained a couple of pints of water. A pump compressed air in a canister attached to the rifle. The result was, when the shooter pulled the trigger, a high-pressure blast of water would drench the target. Children laughed and shouted as they collected their guns. Mothers, on the whole, wisely excused themselves from the battle. It was the dads who accepted the challenge; they removed watches along with anything else that would suffer from a soaking, while exchanging slightly embarrassed grins.

Those not involved with the contest quickly moved clear of the lawn. John noticed that Fletcher hadn't been invited to take part, and he stood by the barbecue, eating a hamburger. There was something disconcertingly mechanical about the boy's movements. His face was completely blank, not the tiniest indication whether he was enjoying the party or thought it was the most dreadful afternoon of his life.

John selected his weapon of choice: a bright-pink bazooka-style water blaster. He pumped the handle. Bubbles fizzed in the reservoir of water. 'Unleash the dogs of war,' John said to nobody in particular. He chuckled, though, a mixture of high spirits and the cider that was so potently rich in alcohol.

'Before you unleash any dogs of war,' Ingrid told him, 'you best give me your phone.'

'You're right, I doubt if it would survive a squirting.' He handed the phone to her. 'Best keep it switched on. The courier might have to change the delivery time.'

'Will do, soldier.' She saluted. 'Now, go and be my hero.' Her dark eyes twinkled with mischief. 'Something tells me you'll look good in a wet T-shirt.'

The atmosphere brimmed with good-natured fun. The children formed a line at one side of the lawn, while the adults exchanged banter as they familiarized themselves with these unusual aquatic weapons.

Tom Oldfield armed himself with a pair of water pistols. 'OK, listen up,' he announced to the two opposing armies. 'The battle commences when I've reached the count of ten. Right? No firing until I say "ten" – it's a rule of the Geneva Convention.' He took a deep breath. 'One, two, three, four—'

80

The children didn't wait any longer. They fired into his mouth as he uttered the word 'five' – such is war.

The battle of the Oldfields' garden raged. No mercy given, no prisoners taken. Torrents of high-pressure water blasted friend and foe alike. The sun that shone through blasts of spray painted rainbows.

John staggered, half blinded by jets that stung his face. *Dear God, these water blasters are powerful*. He wiped away water from his eyes just in time to see Fletcher take a direct hit. Fletcher hadn't been part of the war. As a bystander, he'd been standing quietly eating the hamburger. However, Mark Oldfield took the opportunity to target the boy he disliked so much. The force of the water blasted tomato ketchup from the burger into Fletcher's face, making it look as if he'd been spattered with blood. He didn't react like any other boy of twelve – there was neither anger nor laughter. His face remained expressionless.

Instead, he uttered in a flat voice, 'Mark Oldfield. I've seen them at night looking in through your bedroom window when you're asleep. They're coming to get you. And there's nothing you can do to stop it.'

Mark ran up to Fletcher, pushing him hard in the chest. Fletcher, the bigger of the two, pushed back, sending Mark falling on to his backside.

'I'll get you!' Mark scrambled to his feet, ready to start punching.

Tom pounced first. He caught hold of his furious son and pulled him aside. Fletcher took

81

a step forwards. John Tolworth wasn't sure if Fletcher would attack Mark, so he grabbed hold of Fletcher's arm; however, the boy appeared strangely impassive.

'I'm going home,' Fletcher stated.

'You don't have to go,' John told him. 'Look, we'll get you cleaned up.' He scooped up a roll of kitchen tissue from the table. 'Here, dry your face. Then I'll get you another burger.' He glanced at Ingrid, who nodded her approval. She was pleased her husband hadn't ignored the boy who was being treated like a social outcast. 'See, no harm done,' he said. 'It's just a bit of water and tomato sauce.'

Oliver ran across the lawn to Fletcher, the water blaster still gripped in his hands. 'That wasn't fair what Mark did,' Oliver said. 'You weren't armed.' He held out the gun. 'Want a go?'

Fletcher shook his head. 'I'm going to eat a burger. Are you going to have one?'

'OK.'

'Just a moment,' John said to Fletcher. 'Let me wipe your hair. You've got onion stuck to your head. Believe me, that's not a fashionable look.'

The joke bypassed the stone-like Fletcher. John cleaned the onion from the boy's hair. As he did so, he heard his phone again.

Ingrid pulled the phone from her pocket. 'I'll get it for you.'

'It'll be the courier again,' he said. 'Make sure he confirms the delivery time.'

Ingrid nodded as she answered. 'Hello, John Tolworth's phone. Pardon . . . what was that?' Her expression changed from one of bemusement to concern. 'You're calling from the hospital? Yes, John Tolworth does have a son. Why . . . who wants to know? Sorry, I don't understand. You say John's son has been injured in an accident?' Now she was smiling with relief. 'Sorry, you must have the wrong John Tolworth. I'm Mrs Tolworth . . . Yes, we have a son. I'm looking at him right now. He's standing in front of me.' She began to sound exasperated. 'No, my husband doesn't have another son. Look . . . who is this exactly? A friend of Ben Darrington? I don't know any Ben Darrington. Yes, alright.' Her eyes fixed on John in a very direct way. 'You should talk to my husband. He's right here.' Ingrid held out the phone. 'John. I think you should speak to this person. Someone called Ben Darrington's been hurt in an accident. They've told me that Ben is your son.'

Philip Kemmis watched the party from a distance. Smoke rose from a barbecue where a man flipped burgers. Children and adults alike towelled themselves dry after the water fight. John Tolworth spoke into a phone, while his wife stared at him, arms folded. Fletcher Brown stood alone, holding a plateful of food. The boy wasn't eating. He stared into space, seemingly unaware that he was in the middle of a crowd who were chatting and laughing, while consuming plenty of beer, wine and cider.

Philip kept to the shadows beneath the tree. His hand itched furiously. He'd have loved to dig his fingernails into the skin and scratch as hard as he could. The problem was, there was no actual hand. However, the phantom pains, aches and endless

83

itching still plagued him. It wasn't unusual, of course, for people who'd lost limbs to still have sensation in the missing flesh. However, he'd endured thirty years of this – his fingers on his right hand stung, even though he had no fingers. His palm prickled, even though the flesh had long gone. Knuckles continued to ache, even though the hand would have been burnt to ashes in a hospital incinerator. Part of him had been cremated long ago. Yet it still seemed as if he was haunted by the ghost of his dead hand.

Philip studied the faces of the people enjoying the party. Every so often those faces were transformed. They became masks of dried-out skin. Eyes shrivelled to nothing in the socket, leaving empty voids. Clothes became the linen strips that wrapped corpses in ancient Egyptian tombs. Just for a moment, an Egyptian mummy raised a glass of wine to its withered lips. A rotted paw of a hand picked up a slice of watermelon. Laughter pealed from a woman who was nothing more than a dead husk.

When he saw these monstrous things, Philip wanted to believe that they were hallucinations. He no longer could reassure himself that they were, however. The medication didn't help like it should. He lived in a world where humans became walking mummies. He watched as children playing on a rope swing morphed into dead things wrapped in bandages that fluttered in the breeze.

He must destroy the mummies. He must smash them to pieces, burn them, annihilate them – and do it soon.

Eleven

Saturday evening after the barbecue. Empty cardboard boxes stood against one wall. The 3D printer, the size of a refrigerator and made from cream-coloured plastic, stood on a table in a back room of the cottage. John read the instruction manual: printing three-dimensional objects was straightforward, it reassured him, providing he carefully followed this step-by-step guide. *Thank goodness I didn't have too much cider*, he told himself. *I'm going to need a clear head for this*.

Ingrid walked into the room. Instantly, there was an air of tension that was nothing less than electric.

He glanced up, smiling. 'How's the headache?'

'Not too bad now, thanks. How's the printer?'

'It's all set up. I'm going to give it a trial run.'

'Tonight?'

'The printhead gradually builds up a plastic replica of whatever you want to duplicate. It can take hours.'

'Oh.'

He glanced again at his wife. Her face seemed strained. 'Samantha Oldfield gave me a memory stick,' he told her. 'There's data on there of a detailed CAT scan made of one of the mummies. I'm going to attempt to print the head.'

'This machine will actually produce a three-dimensional copy of the head?'

85

'All that and more. A conservator used a computer program to repair the damage and shrinkage to the girl mummy's face. When the printer's finished making the model we should have a copy of a human head as it was in life . . . not after lying dead in a tomb for three thousand years.'

'In that case . . .' Ingrid rested her hand on top of the printer. 'I hereby rename you the Resurrection Machine.'

He plugged in the machine and switched on. Lights on a control panel lit up. 'Success,' he said.

'We have to talk, don't we?' Ingrid said.

He felt his muscles tense. A confrontation loomed . . . but Ingrid remained in control of her emotions. She wasn't icily cold; she was concerned, understanding and perfectly reasonable, which John found even harder to deal with.

'Let me get this straight, John. You have a nineteen-year-old son called Ben Darrington?'

'Yes.'

'Why didn't you tell me?'

'It didn't seem necessary.'

'John, if the situation was reversed and I had a son from an earlier relationship, how would you feel if I hadn't told you?'

'I'd be surprised, and . . . well, curious.'

'That's how I feel. I'd add the words "in shock", though. After all, the first I heard that he existed was when I answered your phone and someone told me that a stranger by the name of Ben Darrington had been hurt in an accident, and that Ben was your son! Which means, of course, that our children have a half-brother they knew nothing about.'

Ben sighed. His wife remained calm and clear-headed. He knew she'd continue to interrogate him in a methodical way. She'd listen carefully to his answers, while studying his body language. Ingrid could read her pupils like a book; she could read him like a book as well. He knew how she ticked. She'd never get angry. However, she'd continue her forensic dissection of his answers with meticulous care.

'It was a long time ago, Ingrid,' he said, trying to be as open as possible. 'Ben was born before I met you.'

'It would help me deal with this, John, if you explained as fully as you can what happened.' Her voice was gentle, even compassionate.

'Once upon a time . . .' He tried to lighten the mood. Not a good idea. 'Sorry, this has come as a shock to me, too. I never thought I'd hear about him again. Well, here goes . . . I was twenty years old and living away from home at university. I met a girl who played in a band. She was called Carol Darrington. You could say she was a party animal, whereas I was quiet back then, and really shy. Awkwardly shy. She took me under her wing. I think she saw me as a project; she decided to turn me from an introvert to an extrovert. Carol stopped up all night drinking and partying, always the centre of attention and making people laugh. We had a relationship, but it was an odd one. She'd vanish for days on end. I thought she might have been seeing other men. I later discovered she went on drink and drug binges – it soon became obvious that this wasn't just a young, fun-loving girl having a good time. Carol was, I guess, going off the rails. Sometimes she'd be fun to be with for a while, then she'd become this violent wildcat. I'd been seeing her for three or four months when I tried to persuade her to get help about the drink and drugs. She just went crazy and told me to mind my own business. We were in a pub when all this kicked-off; she spat a mouthful of beer into my face, got up, walked out. That was it. I only saw her one more time after that.'

'You thought Carol was an addict?'

'Yes. I blamed myself for not being able to help her. It scared me so much, because I was certain the drink and drugs would kill her.'

'You were only twenty. Something like that is difficult to deal with even when you're older. You shouldn't blame yourself. So . . . Ben?'

'Some time after we split up, I received a letter from her telling me that she was pregnant and I was the father.'

'Carol wanted to see you again?'

'No. She wrote saying that she didn't want financial support from me for the baby, and certainly didn't want to see me again. I tried to find her, but by this time she'd moved out of her flat. Her friends were sick and tired of her erratic behaviour and had given up on her, too. Carol simply vanished into thin air.'

'You say you saw her again?'

'A year after I received the letter, I was on a train as it pulled out of St Pancras Station. I clearly saw Carol standing on the platform. She carried a baby . . .'

'It was definitely her?'

'Oh, yes. No doubt about it.'

'So, Ben has come back into your life?'

'Seems like it.' He didn't want to appear abrupt, but discussing his own son, who he'd only glimpsed for a few seconds all those years ago, had left him shaking inside.

'What I don't understand is how this friend of Ben's knew your phone number.'

'That's easy enough to explain. Ben broke his leg, and a doctor pumped him full of painkillers. Apparently, Ben was talking about me and repeating my name, even though he was only partly conscious. The friend found my website. It has my name and contact details, of course, so they just picked up the phone, and you answered the call at the barbecue this afternoon.'

'We'll need to tell Vicki and Oliver.'

'That they have a half-brother?' He nodded. 'Of course. But I suppose that's the end of the matter. I'm never likely to see him, am I? Ben's never tried to get in touch with me, even though he knew my name and what I do for a living.'

'You don't intend to visit him in hospital?'

'No, Ingrid. All this is just a fluke. A blip in our lives, that's all.'

'I wouldn't try and stop you from seeing him. He's your flesh and blood, after all.'

'No. You, Vicki and Ollie are my family. For I all know, I might not be Ben Darrington's biological father anyway.' His hands trembled as he opened the printer manual again.

Ingrid kissed him on the cheek. 'I'll support whatever decision you make.' She gave a faint

89

smile. 'Now I'll leave you to bring your mummy girl back to life.'

'Ha . . . hardly that. I'm afraid the dead stay dead.'

The night had a deeper darkness here.

'Dark black,' Oliver murmured as he gazed out through the open bedroom window.

He knew his mother would have corrected him, if she'd heard what he'd just said; she'd point out that there's no such thing as *dark black*. The eleven year old knew differently. The night was *dark black* here. Back home in London, night times weren't dark at all. Millions of street-lights lit up the entire city.

Oh . . . but here in Devon it was different. Oliver knew that the grounds surrounding Baverstock Castle were huge. There were forests, fields and hills, and there was loads of desolate moorland. All this land was privately owned. Even the roads hereabouts were private, so there was hardly any traffic. What's more, there were only about ten houses in this part of the castle grounds. And now, at midnight – all was dark, all was silent.

He leaned out, feeling the warm night air on his face. It had been a tiring day. The party had been amazing at the Oldfields' house. He'd loved the water battle. Kids versus grown-ups. Oliver had made sure that his father had been drenched from head to foot. Normally, he'd have been fast asleep at this time, but a nagging worry had taken root inside his head. Earlier, he'd heard a snatch of conversation between his parents. They were talking about a son. However, they'd referred to the son as Ben, and Oliver had realized they were talking about another son of his father's.

'But I'm the only son they've got,' he murmured. 'There aren't any more sons.'

Yet he'd clearly heard them mention someone called Ben Darrington. The notion that a random person could suddenly become his father's new son alarmed Oliver. He found it hard to put into words, but the feeling was of some frightening stranger roughly invading his family. Was this Ben going to push his way into their lives? Would Ben want this bedroom? Would his father like Ben Darrington more than Oliver?

A little horror film played in Oliver's mind. He saw his mother and father standing by the front door. His father hands Oliver a suitcase. 'Oliver, we don't like you any more. Your place is being taken by Ben. We like Ben a lot. He's better than you. Now, go away, Oliver, don't come back.' The door swings open. Oliver's mother and father push him roughly out of the house.

Oliver sees himself begin to cry in the mind-film. 'Where am I going to live now?'

'How should we know?' says his mother in a spiteful voice. 'It's not our problem. You're on your own.'

Yes, just imagination. Even so, Oliver shivered. Those weren't pleasant pictures inside his head. Oliver leaned further out of the window. He glimpsed a prickly, black ball moving across the lawn. The prickly lump was a hedgehog. It moved slowly with a rolling, side-to-side motion.

'Oliver, shall we go night-walking?'

The voice was so close that Oliver flinched with shock. He glanced back over his shoulder, convinced that someone was in the room with him.

'Eyes front, Tolworth.'

Startled, Oliver looked outside again. He realized that a figure stood on a tree branch, which was level with the bedroom window. A pair of eyes burned in the darkness.

'Who is it? What do you want?' Oliver's heart pounded.

'It's me, noodle head.'

'Fletcher?'

'I've come to take you night-walking. Did you know that this area was once a tropical swamp a hundred million years ago? Dinosaurs walked where your house is. If a T-Rex was here right now it could stand on the lawn and its head would be level with your window.'

Oliver blinked with surprise. Fletcher could say such funny things about science and stuff. 'Why are you here? It's midnight.'

'Like I said, to take you night-walking.'

'I can't. I'm not allowed out at night.'

'Frightened?'

Oliver was tempted to lie and deny that he was scared, but seeing Fletcher being ill-treated today at the barbecue had made him feel for the boy. He decided to trust him as a friend. 'I'm a bit scared. After all, you told me about the Egyptian mummies in the castle.'

'What? That they're all dried out? Crispy as cornflakes? Got hooky hands like claws?'

'You said that when people slept that's when the mummies woke up.'

'I'm sorry I scared you, Oliver.'

'And you were weird in the graveyard this morning. You pretended that you could press a button on the gravestone and it would make the coffins come up to the surface.'

'I did, didn't I?'

Oliver's eyes adjusted to the gloom; he clearly saw the boy standing on a branch that was level with the attic window. 'It's a long way down,' he said. 'Careful you don't fall and bust your brains.'

'You know, if I did fall, nobody would *boohoo* over my coffin.'

'I don't want you to hurt yourself, Fletcher.'

Fletcher moved closer, his feet resting on the tree limb while his hands gripped another branch above his head in order to secure his balance. 'Can I tell you a secret, Oliver?'

'As long as it doesn't involve dead people attacking me.'

'No, nothing to do with that. People don't like me. I mean, other kids at school, or even grown-ups who live here. You saw what happened when Mark Oldfield blasted me with the water. I wasn't even taking part in the game. I was eating.'

'Mark shouldn't have done that to you.'

'Thanks, Oliver. I'll tell you another secret.'

'What is it?'

'My dad doesn't like me, either. He says I'm not right in the head. Which is true. My mother liked me. She made me mash and stew with Yorkshire puddings every Sunday. That's my favourite. But I haven't eaten it in three months and three weeks, because my mother's in hospital, dying.'

Fletcher's words had come faster and faster; he was unburdening himself of truths that had been simmering away inside of him.

'I'll be your friend, Fletcher. I won't stop liking you.'

'You will.'

'Won't.'

'Will, because I'm weird. I don't think like other people, Oliver. I get strange thoughts inside my head. I know I look strange as well. And when I say strange things I can't help it. The words just come out of my mouth, and I can't do anything to stop them.'

Oliver retreated back into his bedroom.

'Oliver . . . Oliver? See, I knew you'd stop liking me. You've gone back to bed, haven't you? I'm the kid with the unlikeable bones, aren't I? Bye, Oliver.'

'Wait.' Oliver returned to the window. 'Here . . . catch.'

He threw a red ball cap out to where Fletcher stood on the branch. Oliver could see that Fletcher reacted with surprise as he caught it. There was something else there in the boy's expression. Hope. Fragile hope, but hope nonetheless.

Fletcher asked, 'What's this for?'

'It's my cap. I bought it before we came to Devon.'

'Why did you throw it to me?'

'I want you to have it.'

'Really? But it's your cap.'

'You have it, Fletcher. When you think you're going to be weird, and can't stop yourself, turn the cap around so the peak's pointing backwards.

That's your signal that you're going to say strange, bonkers, nutty stuff, but it'll be OK, I won't mind, I won't take it seriously, because you've sent me a secret signal that you can't stop yourself saying weird stuff, and you don't mean it . . . not *really* mean it.'

'That's a great idea.' Grinning, Fletcher put on the cap; he twisted it so the peak faced backwards. 'Oliver. Spiders will run into your ear and eat your brain.'

'That's it. Just turn the hat around. It's our secret sign. It'll be great.' Oliver paused. 'You were just joking about the spiders?'

Oliver rotated the cap so the peak faced forwards. 'Yes. Although it's a fact that every British spider is poisonous.' He grinned. 'But they're only poisonous to flies, not humans.'

'I'm going to go to sleep now, Fletcher.'

'Maybe we'll go night-walking another time?'

'Maybe.'

'Goodnight, friend Oliver.'

'Goodnight, friend Fletcher.'

Fletcher climbed down from the tree. Even though he vanished back into the darkness, Oliver heard him clearly enough. The boy sang to himself, happy as can be.

There was plenty to occupy John Tolworth's mind as he familiarized himself with the 3D printer in the back room of the cottage on Sunday afternoon. He'd only arrived here a couple of days ago, and hadn't even started work properly, but already life had become that bit more complicated. He hadn't expected that his childhood friend, Lord Philip Kemmis, would be living in the gatehouse – or that he would be clearly deranged. And yesterday afternoon he'd taken one of the most shocking telephone calls of his life. A friend of Ben Darrington, a son he'd never ever met, had called to say that Ben had been hurt in an accident. Was that a hint for John to visit his son?

John didn't know what to think. What appealed to him now was to escape into his work. He'd bought the 3D printer so he could build copies of badly damaged artefacts, including the pottery jars that had once contained the papyri that had been torn to shreds in antiquity before being hurled around the tomb like confetti at a particularly lively wedding. His attempts at modelling yesterday hadn't been especially successful. So he'd attached his laptop again to the printer, downloaded new software, then plugged in the memory stick that Samantha Oldfield had given him. This contained a detailed CAT scan of the young female mummy. The restoration team had named this anonymous corpse Amber on account of the amber earrings she'd been wearing in her coffin. Although three thousand years old, Amber was still in a reasonable state of preservation, thanks to sophisticated mummification techniques and the arid part of the world where she'd been buried, resulting in only the faintest traces of moisture being present in the tomb that would cause decay.

The 3D printer worked by melting a thin strip of plastic; then, using information contained in the computer record of Amber, it slowly built up a 3D model. The key word was *slowly*. This print job had been running for hours. Inside the closed compartment, a printhead would be engaged in what would resemble an elaborate dance as it laid down layer upon layer of plastic in incredibly thin strips.

John sipped his coffee. The machine hummed, clicked, whirred. Inside that cabinet the magic should be working – hopefully. If it did work properly, the printer would create a detailed 3D model of Amber's head. He'd used a program created by the preservation team that should present the girl's head as it was in life, with the ravages of death and centuries spent in the grave airbrushed out (as it were). When he lifted the model out of the printer he should see something approximating the head of a living girl. Of course, it would be in a single colour, the colour of the plastic used in the process. He'd need to paint in the lips, eyes, and so on, to produce a lifelike model.

John finished his coffee while trying patiently to let the printer do its work. Should he be tempted to lift the lid of the printer compartment – something which he'd done before – in order to glimpse what was taking shape inside, the temperature would fluctuate, resulting in yet another failed attempt to produce a good-quality model.

Then, at long last, he heard a *ping*. John nodded with satisfaction. Time to see what his resurrection machine, as Ingrid had named it, had produced.

'OK, family, enter my laboratory.' John Tolworth spoke jokingly. 'It's time to unveil my creation.'

97

Ingrid, Vicki and Oliver filed into the back room of the cottage. On the table an object stood beneath a white cloth. John intended to make the reveal a dramatic one. He was proud of what he'd achieved.

'So it worked, then, Dad?' asked Oliver. 'The three-D printer?'

'Worked perfectly, Ollie.'

'Can I print something? Like a gun or a penknife?'

'You're not having a penknife,' Ingrid said firmly, realizing where her son's line of conversation would take them. 'Knives are dangerous.'

Vicki folded her arms. 'Will this take long?'

'Do you need to be somewhere in a hurry?' Ingrid spotted a hidden agenda.

'Might go for a walk.'

'In the hope of bumping into our handsome, teenage neighbour?'

Vicki's eyes narrowed with anger. 'Don't start that again. I'll see who I want, when I want. I'm sixteen. I'm not your little girl any more.'

'OK, OK.' Ingrid raised her hands. 'I'm only joking.'

John attempted to bring his family's focus back to the object on the table. 'This will only take a minute.'

John explained how the printer worked. Oliver's expression was one of fascination. Vicki, on the other hand, yawned. Ingrid politely listened.

'What I've done,' continued John, 'is produce a copy of the head of one of the female mummies from the castle.'

'Cool.' Oliver tried to peep under the cloth.

John held the cloth in place. He was pleased with the results of his test and wanted this to be a surprise for his family. He told them all about Amber, adding, 'I've used modelling paint for the hair and lip colour.'

Vicki's patience evaporated. 'OK, show us the flipping thing. I want to go outside.'

Oliver lowered his head so he'd be eye-level with the model. 'Show us the mummy of doom, Dad.'

'OK, family, I introduce you to Amber.' He whipped back the cloth with all the flourish of a conjuror, revealing the amazing result of his magic trick.

Ingrid blinked in surprise. 'John . . . really?'

'Wow, Dad.' Oliver grinned. 'That's really cool.'

Vicki's eyes locked on to the plastic face that was the colour of butter. The expression on the model's face was calm, even serene. John had painted black eyebrows and black hair. The lips were red. Eyes were dark brown. The high cheek-bones were especially striking. Vicki glanced at her father then back at the plastic reproduction of the dead girl's face. She clenched her fists. 'If this is your idea of a joke, Dad, it's not funny.'

'What joke?' John shook his head, puzzled. 'I'm not playing any kind of joke.'

'This!' Vicki jabbed her finger at the plastic head in fury. 'You're sick in the brain, Dad. It's me! Why did you give that thing my face?'

Ingrid gave John a very cool and very direct look. 'Tell me, John, did you deliberately play a trick on our daughter?'

'No.'

'She's sixteen years old. You scared her.'

'Vicki seemed more angry than scared.'

'You shouldn't have made the model of the dead girl look like her.'

'I didn't, I swear.' John paced the back parlour. The plastic head stood on the table, regarding them with that serene gaze. 'I simply used the computer generated image of Amber to print this model of the head.'

'Didn't you look at the face when you painted in the lips and eyes? Didn't you notice that it resembles Vicki?'

'Resembles?' He picked up the head. 'It only resembles our daughter if you apply your own imagination . . . I mean, does it really look like Vicki?'

'Yes, actually, quite a lot like her.'

'I don't see it; neither does Oliver.'

'See the shape of the lips, the nose? The model has the same almond-shaped eyes . . . those high cheekbones are the same. Come on, John, I know you like having fun with us; you can tell me if you tweaked the program to make the Egyptian girl's face more like Vicki's.'

He replaced the head on the table. 'I wouldn't do something as cruel as that. What I planned to do was produce models of all the mummies' heads, the idea being that visitors to the exhibition could see what the family were like when they were alive.'

'A rather morbid "before and after" display.'

'That's what interests the public. But, no, I would not produce a model of a corpse's head then make it resemble my own daughter. That would be distasteful, to say the least.'

'Absolutely.'

'Perhaps what Vicki is identifying is some shared ancestry traits.'

'My grandmother was Indian, John, from the banks of the Ganges, not the Nile.'

'OK.' Taking a deep breath, he sat down. 'How do I persuade Vicki that it wasn't a joke, and that by sheer coincidence she happens to resemble a sixteen year old from ancient Egypt? Because I'm sure that whatever I say will only make her angrier.'

'Give her a couple of hours to cool off.' Ingrid smiled. 'If she enjoys herself in the company of handsome Jason from next door, she'll probably forget all about looking like someone who's been dead for thousands of years.'

'Now you're pulling my leg, aren't you?'

'Just a little bit. OK, hide Amber in a cupboard before Vicki comes back.'

Taking a walk to clear his head seemed a good idea to John. It was a little over an hour since he'd revealed the model of the mummy's head produced by the 3D printer, and he couldn't forget how Vicki had accused him of playing a cruel trick. John considered himself playful, and not averse to pranking, but he would never produce what was, essentially, a replica of a corpse and manipulate its features in order to make it resemble his daughter.

He left Ingrid to read her book in the sunshine. The surroundings really were idyllic. Here they were in their own private realm. The castle grounds were off-limits to the public at large (at least for now; when the restoration was completed, visitors would be invited back). This countryside seemed so remote from the outside world. Apart from the castle and the gatehouse, there were just a few cottages, housing employees of the company that now owned the castle, and this stretch of Devonshire landscape.

He walked up the lane. The Oldfield family occupied the nearest house to the Tolworths. This is where the rumbustious barbecue took place yesterday, along with the water battle between parents and children. John saw the oldest of the Oldfield sons, Jason, pushing Vicki on a rope swing attached to a tree. Every time Vicki swung back, seventeen-year-old Jason whispered in her ear. She laughed out loud – a laugh that was almost delirious with happiness. John couldn't help but smile. He also felt a huge wave of relief sweep through him. He'd expected to find her sitting by herself on the hillside doing some teenage brooding – seeing the copy of herself in plastic had shocked her. In fact, she'd been furious. However, instead of seething with rage right now she hooted with joy.

Jason spoke a few words to her before dashing back to his house. At that moment, Vicki spotted her father. She scrambled off the swing, suddenly more like an excited seven year old than a young woman.

'Dad . . . Dad.' She was breathless and so happy her eyes sparkled. 'Jason's asked if I'll go to Lynmouth with him. Can I go, Dad? His mother's taking us in the car. I want to go, Dad. I can, can't I?'

He grinned with the sheer pleasure of seeing his daughter so happy. 'I don't see why not. I'll mention it to your mother.'

'Jason's really nice. He plays in a rock group. He says they're really good and they're going to be in a battle of the bands on television.' Her words came out in a rush. 'He's going to download some of their songs on to my phone.'

'I'm glad you've found a friend here. I was worried you'd be lonely.'

'Oh?' She looked shyly down at the ground. 'I like it here.'

'Are you coming back to the house now?'

'Jason's gone to get some ice cream. I thought I'd just hang around here for a bit.'

'Useful he's got the rope swing, then? Ideal for hanging around.'

His dad-style joke bypassed her. His daughter already gazed in the direction of the Oldfield house, waiting for the reappearance of her new friend. *Or should that be boyfriend?*

John smiled. 'I'll see you later.'

'Uh, OK . . .'

'I'm just going for a walk. Sorry about the model of the head.'

She waved at Jason as he stepped from the house, carrying two bowls.

'Sorry about the model looking like you, Vicki. It's just coincidence. I said to your mother that—'

'Hmm? It doesn't matter, Dad. Jason's back.'

'I'll see you later, then.'

103

'Yes. Bye . . . Wait, Dad. Promise me something.'

'Promise you what?'

'Don't mention Jason to Lee back home.'

'Is Lee your boyfriend?'

Vicki shrugged. 'Yes and no. Sort of. Promise you won't tell Lee about Jason.'

'I wouldn't dream of telling Lee. We'll keep Jason a secret.'

'Thanks, Dad. Love you.' Those words were unexpected enough. Vicki had stopped saying 'Love you' to her parents since she was twelve. Even more surprising was what came next. She kissed John on the cheek. 'Bye.' She walked nonchalantly back to Jason, who'd set the bowls down on a picnic table.

'You're just like your mother,' he murmured to himself. 'You like to be in control.'

He continued along the lane, where he came to a bridge that crossed a stream. Oliver and the strange boy, Fletcher Brown, were throwing sticks into the water.

John asked, 'Doing anything interesting?' He noticed that Fletcher wore a red cap. Although he couldn't be certain, he thought it was the same one that his son had bought before they left for Devon.

Oliver spoke with glee. 'There's a dead fish floating in the water.'

'Trout.' That's all that Fletcher said.

John wondered if Fletcher had taken his son's cap. However, Oliver appeared to be enjoying Fletcher's company. Oliver threw a stick at the dead fish. It missed.

The boy laughed. 'Nearly. I'll get it next time.' He turned to look at John. 'Fletcher's got a penknife.'

'Swiss Army knife,' Fletcher uttered in that wooden manner of his. 'Three blades, five tools. Stainless steel.'

'Can I have a Swiss Army knife, Dad?'

'Ollie, just imagine asking your mother that question. What do you think her answer would be?'

'It's not fair.'

'I let Oliver use the knife, Mr Tolworth.'

'Perhaps that's not a good idea, Fletcher. Oliver's only eleven.'

'Did you have a Swiss Army knife when you were eleven, Mr Tolworth?'

'That's neither here nor there. Knives can be dangerous.'

'Philip Kemmis didn't cut his hand off with a Swiss Army knife, did he? Something else was responsible for him losing his hand.'

'I don't know the circumstances of the accident,' John said. Even as he spoke, a vivid image burned inside his head. It was of Philip all those years ago, just minutes after they crept into the mummy room in the castle tower and the lights went out. The ten-year-old John Tolworth had run downstairs. Philip had joined him a few moments later. Something had happened to Philip . . .

The noise the stream made as it poured over rocks vanished. He stopped hearing the birdsong. Shivers ran through his body. A sensation like insects crawling across him hit him so forcefully that he shuddered and stepped back; it felt like he was going to fall.

105

'Can I have a penknife, Dad? Dad . . . Dad? Answer me.' Oliver scowled. 'It's not fair that I can't have a knife. I bet you had one when I was your age.'

Fletcher's eyes fixed on him. 'Mr Tolworth. Struck mute. Horror does that. People witnessing horrific events, or recalling horrific events, can suffer muscle spasms that affect limbs and even vocal chords, meaning that they are mute, meaning they cannot speak. Muscles lock tight and do not function.' For some reason Fletcher turned the hat round so the peak pointed backwards. 'Experiencing a horrific incident can even freeze the muscles of the mind. Memory goes into paralysis. It does not function. Someone might see a terrible accident, yet the mind locks the memory away beyond recall. The witness might have blood on their clothes, but they still insist that the accident never happened. The mind protects itself from psychological harm by forgetting.'

Oliver laughed, as if Fletcher was doing some kind of comical routine.

John found he'd frozen there on the bridge. He couldn't move, couldn't speak. *I'm having a brain haemorrhage*, he told himself with a sense of dread.

Fletcher picked up a stick. He and Oliver were laughing; they clearly hadn't noticed that John's entire body had seized up. Fletcher turned the red cap around so the peak jutted forwards.

The world came rushing back, and everything returned to normal in a heartbeat. Taking a deep breath, John checked his hands; they trembled a little, that's all. Perhaps the summer's heat had

106

affected him? He said, 'Have a good time, you two. I'll see you both later.'

'Goodbye, Mr Tolworth.' Fletcher didn't look at him as he spoke. His focus stayed on the dead fish, caught in the weeds at the side of the stream.

'Bye, Dad. You won't tell Mum about me using the penknife, will you?'

'Don't worry, Ollie. It will be our secret.'

John continued along the lane. Already, he rationalized that the strange 'episode' was due to the heat, that's all. What preoccupied him now was the word 'secret'; it flitted around the inside of his head; a butterfly of a word, alighting on one memory then another in quick succession. He stepped over a line of ants, marching across the road. Secrets. He'd promised his daughter that they'd keep Jason's existence a secret from her boyfriend back in London. After that, he'd told Oliver that they'd keep the fact he'd been playing with a penknife secret from his mother. *Secrets. Everyone has secrets. Isn't that what Fletcher had told Oliver? Does Ingrid have a secret? Does Samantha Oldfield have a secret?* He recalled her sultry manner, those erotic glances. He glanced up at the hilltop. There, standing amongst those strange rocks that resembled soldiers, was a solitary figure. He recognized the figure as Philip Kemmis immediately. *What's your secret, Philip? What happened to send you insane?*

Philip walked along the skyline – he looked like a man with an urgent need to be somewhere else; a man to whom secrets attached themselves like a shadow.

John paused at the edge of the stream. He gazed

107

down at his own face reflected there. 'What's your secret?' he asked his reflection. A forced smile appeared on his face. 'But I don't have any secrets, do I?'

At that moment, he thought about his first son. He'd never even told his own wife that Ben Darrington existed. *A secret son*, he thought. *Secrets don't come any bigger than that, do they?*

Night-walking. That's what Fletcher Brown called it. Fletcher had climbed the tree in the back garden and tapped on the attic window with a stick; Oliver Tolworth had woken to see the boy looking at him. Did all people from Devon climb trees after midnight? Oliver suspected they didn't. What the nocturnal tree climbing indicated was that Fletcher wasn't like other boys. *Come to think of it*, thought Oliver sagely, *Fletcher probably isn't like anyone else in the whole wide world. He's a strange kid, alright.*

Going outdoors at the dead of night without his parents' knowledge or permission was wrong. Oliver, however, didn't want to appear like a wuss to his older friend. So, within moments of Fletcher doing the rappity-tatt thing with a stick on the window pane, Oliver quickly pulled on jeans, T-shirt and sandals and headed downstairs and out the back door. Everyone else was asleep in the house. Silence ruled the warm summer night. Oliver couldn't hear a thing.

Fletcher clambered down the tree to join Oliver on the lawn. 'Ready to go night-walking with me?' he asked in a loud voice.

'Shush. You'll wake everyone up.'

'Frightened?'

'If my mum and dad wake up, they'll kill me.'

'They'll be angry because they love you and would be concerned for your safety.' Fletcher stated this fact in a strangely mature way. 'My father, on the other hand, doesn't care a fig whether I'm safe in bed or not.'

'Really?'

'Even though I'm his son, I scare him.'

'Keep your voice down! I don't want my mum and dad to wake up.'

'They might not wake up . . . They might not be *able* to wake up right now.'

Those words troubled Oliver. 'What do you mean?'

'Listen, I'll tell you a secret.' Fletcher's face became strangely skull-like in the starlight; a white oval with two shadows where the eyes should be. The boy wore the red cap that Oliver had given to him. 'Sometimes people here go into a deeper, special sleep. When people in these houses are in that special sleep, nothing can wake them. You could shout in their ear, or jab a fork into their face, and they wouldn't feel it. Nor would they wake up.'

'You're talking weird again, Fletcher.'

'I'm telling the truth. Only I know about the special sleep. When they sleep like that it's like they're dead.'

'You're supposed to turn the cap around when you're saying weird stuff, so the peak points backwards.'

Fletcher spoke like he was a trance. 'The special sleep doesn't affect me. That's because my brain's different to everyone else's. When the special sleep makes everyone in those cottages unconscious, I, Fletcher Brown, am immune.'

'You're saying strange stuff again, Fletcher. Are you trying to scare me?'

'I'm warning you what will happen.'

'Will this special sleep affect me?'

'It might. If it does, you'll fall asleep like that.' He clicked his fingers. 'Don't worry, if you pass out tonight I'll catch you, so you don't fall and hurt yourself.'

'I'm going back home.'

'We're night-walking.'

'But you're doing that thing again – trying to frighten me. That's bullying.'

'Want to have a go with my Swiss Army knife?'

To Oliver's surprise, he realized they'd walked further than he thought. They were in the lane that ran up through the trees to the castle. Oliver felt shivers. *Have I been sleepwalking? I don't even remember walking out of the garden.* The starlight was bright enough to make out the dark outline of the castle. The huge building seemed so ominous and menacing as it sat there on the hill. Oliver remembered his mother saying that castles were built with the intention of intimidating local people. A threat in stone. A promise of hurt if the people didn't obey the lord of the castle.

'I don't believe in magic sleep,' Oliver told Fletcher. 'You've made it up to scare me.'

'Here, take the knife. I've sharpened its blades today.'

The cold steel felt reassuringly heavy in Oliver's hand. It annoyed him that Fletcher said these

110

strange things, but maybe that was just Fletcher's way? Perhaps Oliver would get used to his idiosyncrasies. Meanwhile, he had an opportunity to handle the amazing knife with its foldaway blades; that alone made Oliver more forgiving of his friend's quirky behaviour.

Fletcher put his hand on Oliver's shoulder. 'Look . . . mice.'

Five, no, six mice scurried across the lane in front of them – little splodges of pale fur in the gloom. Quick as a flash, they vanished beneath a bush.

Fletcher said, 'At night you see more animals. I can show you where the foxes play in the forest.'

'I can't go far. What if my mum and dad wake up and find that I've gone? They'll go ape.'

'Magic sleep.' Fletcher turned the cap around, their secret code for when he was joking, or doing one of his peculiar, wacko things. 'Magic sleep conquers all.' He grinned, then turned the hat back around so the peak faced to the front again.

They continued along the lane. Oliver decided he'd go to see the foxes before returning home. A breeze flowed through the forest. The sound seemed to mimic respiration; a sense that gigantic lungs inflated then deflated.

A dark shape raced out of the gloom.

'Fox,' Fletcher whispered. 'There's another one. Two, three, four foxes. They're running this way. Something's scared them.'

Oliver stared as the foxes ran by; they seemed too frightened to even notice the pair of humans standing there in the starlight. Their eyes glinted with terror. Oliver shuddered. What kind of predator would make foxes run away like that? More animals rushed by, all running in the same direction. Rabbits, mice, rats, badgers, stoats, hares.

'I don't like this,' Oliver whispered. 'Something bad's happening.'

'I couldn't agree more. Something wicked this way comes.'

The breeze blew harder, making a whooshing sound in the treetops. Oliver suddenly felt very cold, because a figure had appeared on the lane in front of them.

Twenty yards away stood a tall figure. Very thin, very still and very strange. It didn't move, yet something did move on its arms and legs and torso. Oliver clearly saw that strips of cloth fluttered in the breeze. They streamed outwards, all in the same direction, like pennants or small flags on a pole. The figure still didn't move, and the rounded shape of its head didn't seem right to Oliver. In fact, it was very wrong. More skull than head.

Then Oliver saw why. The figure stepped forward in their direction. Light from a street lamp fell on this lone night-walker. And the light illuminated a ruin of a body. A shrivelled face, with eye sockets that held darkness and nothing more; a hairless head, with holes in the scalp that revealed bare skull; arms as thin as bones; feet that clicked when this monstrosity walked – the sound of one bone clicking against another.

This man is dead. He is one of the mummies from the castle. Oliver knew that simple, irrefutable fact. His hands clenched into fists as terror screamed through him. The penknife in his hand hurt his palm, even though the blade was safely shut away inside the steel body of the knife. The pain was due to the sheer pressure he exerted on the object.

'It's the mummy,' Oliver muttered to Fletcher. 'It's alive.'

'I told you . . . I said that when people sleep that's when the mummies wake up.'

The tall figure, wrapped in bandages, walked towards them. The eyes, which weren't eyes but holes in the front of the face, appeared to be locked on to Oliver's own face. He realized that although this nightmare man didn't possesses living, human eyes it saw him nevertheless. Oliver could hardly breathe; his throat grew tight. It felt like he'd been holding his breath for a full minute. *Breathe*, he told himself. *Breathe!*

But breathing was beyond him. Moving was beyond him. He wanted to scream but couldn't even utter the slightest of croaks.

Fletcher thumped Oliver's arm. 'Run!'

Fletcher darted away into the shadows. Oliver, however, couldn't move so much as a finger. That's when the mummified corpse began to move faster. Oliver watched, appalled, as the face grew bigger the closer it got. Starlight revealed jagged cracks in its face. The head appeared to be encircled by a metal headband. After three thousand years in an Egyptian tomb, the man's lips had shrivelled; they'd shrunk back to form an everlasting snarl. Oliver saw its teeth; he glimpsed the dried member that was its dead tongue.

Oliver knew then he would be killed by the

mummy in this lane in Devon. He'd hear his own bones break; perhaps he'd glimpse his blood running out of gaping wounds. Even though he was only eleven years old, he knew that his death would be agonizing. And there would be terror . . . absolute terror.

The mummified corpse loomed over him, a gigantic totem of broken skin, bones, fluttering bandages; there were criss-cross strips of linen over the chest, through which some of the naked bones of the ribcage were clearly visible; there was an overwhelming impression that a dry shell of muscle and skin enclosed its skeleton.

Oliver felt a painful jolt as the dead thing crashed into him. Instead of falling, however, the boy realized he'd been picked up. The man – what had been a man long ago – had picked him up in its arms. It carried him along the lane, running at a furious speed. Trees blurred past. Oliver couldn't scream. He lay limp in the tight grip of dead arms. The face was no more than ten inches from his. He looked into the empty pits of the eye sockets – it was like looking into the pit of a grave. There was darkness there, a frightening darkness that seemed to whisper promises of terror and dead things to Oliver. The monster carried him away into the night. He didn't know where they were going. He certainly didn't know what would happen to him when they finally arrived at their destination, or exactly what the mummy would do to hurt him.

At last, Oliver found his voice. 'My name's Oliver Tolworth. I'm Oliver. Please don't hurt me. I'm Oliver.' Whether it was to establish some human connection by identifying himself, or something else, Oliver didn't know. Instinct told him to keep saying his name aloud to the monster. Perhaps it's harder to slaughter a person you know the name of? Oliver didn't know. All he could do was to keep repeating his name as this dried-up, bandaged thing carried him.

'I'm Oliver Tolworth. My name's Oliver. I'm just a kid.'

The arms gripping Oliver held him even tighter. The ruined face filled his field of vision. The empty eye sockets, the open crevices in the skull. Oliver could even see beard stubble on its jaw.

'My name's Oliver . . . Please don't kill me.'

Fletcher Brown arrived home long after midnight. His father slept soundly, not even knowing that his son had been night-walking. Fletcher took off the red cap that Oliver had given him. 'I'm sorry, Oliver,' he whispered to himself. 'I told you, didn't I? When people sleep, the mummies wake up. You're dead now, Oliver, and that's the end of that.'

He went to his room and sat on the bed. In his hand was the penknife that he'd picked up in the lane. Oliver had dropped it when he'd been attacked. Fletcher was sad for the boy, and he was sad to be by himself again – friendless. He saw his own life thirty years from now. Returning to a house where he lived alone. He'd watch television, eat a meal, then lie down and go to sleep. To his neighbours he'd be the strange man. The peculiar guy that people crossed the road to avoid. But that's what nature had done to him. His brain was different to everyone else's.

'Oliver's been killed by a mummy from the castle. That's a fact of life.' Fletcher could do nothing to change what had happened. 'I wonder what Mr and Mrs Tolworth will do when they find out that their son is dead?'

Oliver lay there. Sunlight pierced the gap in the curtains, creating a brilliant white line on the opposite wall.

His mouth was dry. His hands were sore; his head was full of the strange and frightening dream he'd had the night before. He remained lying in the same position on his back, vivid images erupting inside his mind. The dream had been incredibly vivid – frighteningly vivid. He dreamt he'd gone night-walking, as Fletcher called it. He and Fletcher had walked along the lane in the middle of the night. Fletcher had teased him again with some strange story about people falling into a magic sleep, saying that they couldn't be waken whatever you did to them, whether shouting in their ear, or, as Fletcher suggested, sticking the sharp points of a fork into their face.

Oliver shuddered as he remembered what happened next in the dream. An old Egyptian mummy had appeared in the lane. It had picked him up and then run away, carrying him. Now, that was weird . . . heck, nightmare weird. Oliver still felt pangs of fear when he remembered that dried-out face with crusty holes where the eyes should be.

He remembered telling the mummy that he was Oliver Tolworth, believing it might somehow save him from being killed by that dead husk. Funny

116

. . . it worked, because, after a while, the mummy had stopped running and had put Oliver down.

Oliver hadn't wasted a second. He'd dashed back home. He'd run so fast that he'd lost his balance and gone down – *bang*! – hard on to the ground, scraping his hand. Well, that's what happened in the dream, anyway. Oliver continued to lie there in bed. He watched an insect flying through the light coming through the gap in the curtains. Its wings seemed to turn to gold as it flew from the shadows into the light. Oliver had experienced plenty of worrying nightmares before. The trick was to keep telling himself it was only a dream. When he put his hand to his mouth to try and stifle a colossal yawn, though, he realized how sore his hand was. He held his hand out into the shaft of light piercing the curtains. Red scratches covered the palm of the hand. What's more, it was dirty. The scrapes on the skin were of the kind he suffered when he fell while running.

He whispered to himself, 'I was running in the dream. The scratches weren't there yesterday, were they?'

Twelve

John Tolworth made an early start for work that Monday morning. The rest of his family were still in bed, but then they had no need to get up just yet. This was a holiday for them. He was the only one with commitments today. After

117

munching through a bowl of cornflakes, he decided to put his morning tea into a thermal cup; it would be pleasant to stroll through the meadows to the castle, sipping his drink and listening to birdsong as he did so.

He'd just filled the kettle when his phone signalled a call. Not recognizing the number, he answered with a simple, 'Hello.'

'Uh . . .' grunted a male voice in his ear.

'Hello?' John repeated.

'Mr Tolworth?'

'Yes.'

'This is Ben Darrington.'

John's heart missed a beat. Ben Darrington? His son. *My secret son, at that.* Although, strictly speaking, he was a secret no longer. Ingrid knew about Ben now.

'Hello, Ben.' John spoke clearly, although it almost seemed as if someone else spoke on his behalf. 'What can I do for you?'

There was a pause. Ben Darrington had stopped speaking, perhaps not knowing what to say next to his father who, after all, he'd never met.

'How's your leg?' John asked.

'Not that good . . . Ahm, I'm sorry to ask this. The doctor is discharging me from hospital today. I've got nowhere to live. What's worse, because of this busted leg I can't walk properly, at least for a while, anyway.' John heard the stranger that shared his DNA take a deep breath, as if having to force himself to ask a tricky question. 'Mr Tolworth, you could say I'm homeless. Can I stay with you?'

* * *

118

John Tolworth had planned to make an early start for work that Monday morning. After taking the phone call he realized he'd be late, and on his very first day, too. *Talk about making a good impression*, he told himself despondently as he climbed the stairs to wake his wife with what would be startling news.

John imagined Ingrid flying into a berserk rage. *What's that?* Ingrid would yell. *Bring your son – your SECRET SON – here to live with us? No way! Not ever! Not in a million years.*

Gently, he woke Ingrid. She unfurled herself from the vast white sheet of their king-size bed. She was still so relaxed from the deep sleep that her face seemed prettier and younger than he'd seen it in years. Her dark eyes glinted in the light filtering through the blind.

'Changed your mind about work today?' She smiled. 'Are you coming back to bed?'

'Ingrid. I don't really know how to begin breaking this news to you. But I've just had a phone call from Ben Darrington.' He took a deep breath and simply plunged in, telling her that his son by another woman from over nineteen years ago would be leaving hospital today, and would be homeless.

For a moment, she regarded him with those dark, exotic eyes that never failed to remind him of paintings of queens from ancient Eastern kingdoms. He could almost see the machinery of her mind through those eyes as she processed and carefully assessed what he'd just told her about Ben.

'Homeless? His mother is still alive, isn't she?'

119

'Reading between the lines, or rather listening between the lines, it seems as if Carol Darrington is still as emotionally erratic and unreliable as she was when I knew her all those years ago. She's backpacking in Thailand, possibly with her latest boyfriend, who's only just been released from prison.'

'Prison? What did he do?'

'Ben didn't say. Although he did sound tense when he spoke about his mother's latest love interest.'

'Love interest? That's a quaint way to say "boyfriend". John, don't tell me you're jealous?'

'No, of course not.' Talking about an ex-girlfriend to his wife, even if the girl had vanished from his life over two decades ago, embarrassed him. 'The bottom line is that the mother gave up her home to go travelling. Ben had left his student accommodation, because he planned to do some summer job or other that came with a room. Of course, he can't take up the job offer now, and all his friends are either back home, or simply don't want to have to look after someone with a broken leg for the next six weeks.'

'I see. Ben's faced with a real problem, isn't he?'

'Of course, he can't stay here with us,' John decided suddenly, realizing what he was asking of his wife. 'Ben's a stranger. We've never met him. There's nowhere for him to sleep, either.' He pulled the phone from his pocket. 'I'll call him back and tell him to find somewhere else to stay.'

But John underestimated Ingrid's compassion and tolerance. Her wisdom constantly surprised him – he was just about to be surprised all over again. 'John.' She leaned forward in bed to take his hand as he sat beside her. 'John, he must come here to stay with us.'

John started to protest.

'No, hear me out.' She gently squeezed his hand while looking at him with a serious expression. 'Ben is your son. Don't you think your decision to turn him away, when he clearly needs someone to help him, will come back to haunt you in the future?'

'We don't know what he's like, Ingrid. He might be repulsive, argumentative, disruptive.'

'Then again, he might be lovely. He's also your son. He exists because of you.'

John felt humbled by his wife's sensitivity. What's more, he felt a needling sense of guilt, because he'd expected her reaction to be one of fury and a complete rejection of Ben. All too readily now, he recalled how she'd always devoted herself to her pupils at whichever school employed her. There were late-night calls from desperate children who had no one else to turn to, or perhaps no one they trusted more to help them in times of crisis, whether it was a teenage girl discovering she was pregnant, or a child whose parents had fought to the point that blood had been spilt. Whatever the problem, Ingrid calmly went about finding the solution. Even so, John couldn't envisage Ben Darrington living under the same roof as his family.

He shook his head. 'Carol might have lied to me. What if I'm not Ben's biological father?'

'You'll know the moment you see him.'

'Blood being thicker than water?'

121

'You'll just know. Instinct will tell you whether he's your flesh and blood.'

He could see that Ingrid wholeheartedly wanted to give Ben a home for at least a few weeks. *Maybe she's seen something incomplete in me*, John told himself. *Does she think that I'm missing out on an important part of my life, because I've never met Ben?*

Ingrid smiled – one of those deeply sympathetic and completely genuine smiles that John found so touching. 'John, it'll only be for a few weeks. Give Ben this chance to get to know you. Think how important it could be for him. He'll be meeting his dad. Think how excited and how scared he'll be right now. He'll be imagining what it'll be like to meet you. His heart will be pounding away like crazy.'

'Mine's doing the same.'

'Then you'll phone him?'

'Yes, after work tonight.' He saw the way she looked at him. 'He'll be on tenterhooks now, won't he?'

'Absolutely. He's waiting for one of the most important phone calls of his life.'

He leaned forward, kissing her on the lips. 'As ever, you're the wisest half of this relationship. It would be cruel to keep Ben waiting.'

Ben had made the call – one that John realized was important to him, too. He'd never even seen a picture of his son. All that he had to form an image was the voice. And that voice sounded in his ear right now. A good voice, he decided. Well-spoken. Not harsh. John suddenly found himself imagining a boy opening presents at

Christmases and birthdays. Presents from his mother, and from uncles and aunts, perhaps, but never one with 'From Dad' on the label. The image of a little boy reading the gift labels flashed through his mind in less than a second, yet it had such a powerful impact on John. So much so that he couldn't speak for a moment.

'Hello?' repeated the voice in his ear. 'Mr Tolworth?'

'Don't . . .' John took a deep breath; he found it hard to construct even the simplest of sentences. 'Don't call me Mr Tolworth. There's no need . . . I'm John . . . so, call me John. OK?'

'OK, John.'

John could hear the tension in Ben's voice. The nineteen year old must have been absolutely terrified as he waited for an answer to the question he'd asked just twenty minutes ago. 'Ben?'

'Yes?'

'You're more than welcome to stay with us. Give me the name of the hospital. I'll come and pick you up.'

'There's no need for that Mr Tolworth – sorry . . . John.' The voice speeded up, and it developed a wobbly quiver due to sheer relief and happiness. 'Some friends of mine from university are going down to Devon for the surfing. A place called Woolacombe?'

'Woolacombe, yes, I know it.'

'They'll drop me off at your house. Is this evening OK?'

John's first meeting with his son wasn't what he expected. A van, with surfboards strapped to the roof, pulled up at the house. There were no side windows in the van, so the first glimpse that John had of his son was when a head covered with curly hair appeared out of the back of the van as the door swung open: the stranger vomited copiously on to John's feet.

'I'm sorry. I'm sorry.' The youth retched again. More vomit spurted from the mouth with the force of a hosepipe. Wet splashing sounds accompanied hot liquid drenching John's feet. 'God, I'm sorry. I . . . ugh.'

The driver, a man of around twenty or so, quickly climbed out of the van. More young men emerged from the passenger door and the back of the vehicle. John grimaced. As well as the unpleasant stench of hot puke, there was a powerful smell of booze. Clearly, his son had spent the journey drinking until he made himself sick.

Ingrid, Vicki and Oliver had put on clean clothes and had stepped towards the van in order to greet the mysterious Ben Darrington. Vicki and Oliver, of course, had been told that Ben Darrington was coming to stay – and that he was their father's son. That had been difficult news for them to digest. Now Vicki and Oliver had been splashed by what the young man's stomach had so vigorously rejected.

'I'm sorry,' Ben muttered as he wiped his mouth. 'I shouldn't have had so much.'

'Don't worry.' Ingrid smiled at him. 'That's not a problem. What is important is that you're here. We've been looking forward to seeing you, haven't we, John?'

'Yes . . . of course.'

Ben's student friends grabbed his arms and hauled him out of the back of the van. Ben's leg was encased in a yellow fracture cast that extended from his ankle to his hip.

'We'll help him inside,' one of them said. 'Then we'll get out of your way.'

Ingrid whispered to Vicki, 'Towels and a bowl, please. The bowl from the sink.'

'I'm really sorry about the mess.' Ben made it through the front door before heaving again and dousing the rug.

The man's arrival confused Oliver Tolworth. The eleven year old knew that Ben Darrington was his father's son, making Ben Oliver's half-brother. Ben wore a bright yellow cast on his leg. People had written all kinds of stuff there, most of it rude. There was no time to discuss what was happening, though; Ben was spectacularly throwing up over everything.

There was no angry shouting, everyone was terribly polite. Somehow the people that had brought Ben here in the van with the surfboards got him indoors. The downstairs room at the back of the house that had once been used to house Dad's new printer had been turned into a bedroom. Ben managed to hobble (with pauses to puke on to the floor) into the room. His mother spread towels on the mattress. Vicki put the plastic sink bowl on the floor beside the bed. After that, Ben flaked out on the bed with his arm over his face.

'I'm sorry . . . I've made a mess.' That's pretty much all the drunken man said.

125

Vicki whispered to Oliver, 'We find out we've got a half-brother, now we find out he's also a drunk. He'll steal all our money to spend on booze.'

The man on the bed grunted and wiped his face with the pillow. This stranger appalled Oliver. That sense of horror of the drunken man, who'd invaded their home in such a rude way, was mixed up with what happened last night when Oliver went night-walking with Fletcher. He tried to rationalize what had happened when he'd seen the mummified corpse. However, he couldn't remember properly now, other than that the figure covered in bandages had rushed towards them. Then everything got confused. He couldn't make sense of it all. Although, it was only a dream, wasn't it? Oliver couldn't decide if what had happened last night was real or not. And now this . . . A man called Ben Darrington had arrived. Oliver's father was also Ben's father. That horrified Oliver, too. Why had his world gone so topsy-turvy?

Oliver heard his dad murmur to his mother, 'Remember, we can't be sure that Ben is really my son.'

'Just look at him,' whispered his mother. 'Look at all that curly hair and the shape of his face: the resemblance between the pair of you is obvious. There's a photograph of you from when you were nineteen, and you look exactly alike. You don't need a DNA test to prove that you're his father.'

Now that Ben had emptied his stomach, he was much calmer. He rested his palm on the top of his leg that was encased in the cast and winced.

The man who'd driven the van entered the room carrying a bulky rucksack. 'These are Ben's worldly possessions,' he said cheerfully.

Oliver's dad thanked the man and leaned the rucksack against the wall.

'Mr Tolworth,' the man said, 'I'm sorry that Ben's in this state.'

'I was a student once,' said Oliver's dad. 'Don't worry.'

'No, no, it's not Ben's fault. We didn't realize that Ben had been given strong painkillers at the hospital. We thought we were helping when we gave him cranberry juice to drink.' The man gave an embarrassed shrug. 'We put a lot of vodka in the juice. You know, sort of anaesthetic; the bumps in the roads were sheer bloody torture for him.'

Oliver's mother smiled. 'We understand. You were doing your best to help your friend.'

'Yeah, it wouldn't have been fun listening to him groaning like a wounded donkey for the whole two hundred miles.'

'Well, Ben's here now,' said Oliver's mother. 'We'll take care of him.'

His mother gave Ben a T-shirt and shorts that belonged to Oliver's dad. Oliver wondered when his possessions would start being handed over, too.

'Dad . . . Dad . . . I'm scared.'

John Tolworth climbed out of bed the moment he heard his son cry out. Enough moonlight filtered through the blinds that he could clearly saw the open door to the corridor which extended through the centre of the old house. Oliver's bedroom was in the attic directly above this bedroom.

'Dad . . . Dad . . .' Oliver's call changed to sobbing; such a broken-hearted sound. John hurried along the corridor to the staircase that led up to the attic room. 'Dad, I'm scared. I don't want to see it any more . . .'

John ran up the stairs. 'It's OK, Ollie, I'm here.' He opened the door to Oliver's room. The windows were open. A breeze blew the curtains. The branches of the tree that grew close to the house tapped at a window pane. An urgent noise that sounded like bones tapping against the glass.

'Dad . . .'

'Oliver, what's the matter?'

The boy was so scared that he lay in bed with the sheet over his face.

'Dad, I'm frightened.'

'Don't worry, I'm here.' John quickly crossed the room to the bed. The breeze sent the curtains flapping wildly. Branches clattered against the window, and the winds made their own weeping sound as they blew around the roof.

'Dad. I can't see! Where are you?'

The small figure lay absolutely still under the sheet, entirely covered by it. The boy must be so frightened that he daren't move. John felt a surge of dread, wondering if Oliver had suffered some kind of fit.

'Dad!'

'It's OK, I'm here.' He pulled back the sheet. His heart froze when he saw what lay there. The blood roared in his ears, and the gales outside

128

rose to a piercing scream . . . or had he screamed? He just didn't know. Because lying there, still and lifeless on his son's bed, was a mummified corpse wrapped in bandages. Its face was cracked and dried-out from thousands of years in a tomb. The eyes, however . . . The eyes were plump spheres that were glistening and wet. Those were living eyes; they stared up at John with an expression of absolute horror.

'Dad? What's happened to me?'

John's entire body convulsed. He realized he was sitting up in his own bed. The blood running in his veins felt so cold that he shivered. A sensation like spiders crawling up the bare skin of his neck took hold of him. He ran his fingers over his neck to brush away the insects, but there were no spiders there.

That was a hell of a dream, he told himself with a shudder. *A mummy in Oliver's bed? That was just horrific. Vivid, too.* The image of the corpse lying there on the mattress had burned itself on to his brain. When he lay down and closed his eyes to try and sleep again he was haunted by memories of the skull on the pillow; that and those eyes: the glistening, plump eyes that bulged from their sockets. The eyes were alive. He could imagine himself touching them, and feeling how wet they were, just like living eyes.

Ingrid turned over in her sleep. There in the darkness, he moved his hand towards her and felt the bandages that wrapped the dead husk lying beside him. Flinching, he caught his breath before forcing himself to place his hand on the hip of the . . . corpse? No. The fabric pressing against the palm of his hand wasn't the dusty wrappings of a mummy; what he felt there was Ingrid's nightdress – her warm and very much alive body was just as it should be. She sighed in her sleep. He sat up in bed again in order to check that Ingrid did, in fact, lie beside him, and that no ghoulish substitution had taken place.

He experienced a surge of relief when he made out her face in the gloom. Yes, Ingrid, wonderful Ingrid, fast asleep. His imagination had replaced her with a desiccated hag. *Good God, that had been a vivid nightmare.* Maybe it's a dad thing, but even though he realized he'd only dreamt that his son had been either transformed into an Egyptian mummy, or been replaced by one, he couldn't sleep until he'd checked that his family were all OK.

The clock on the bedside table revealed it was one in the morning. After leaving the bedroom, he closed the door behind him so as not to disturb Ingrid. He switched on the light in the corridor, which gave him enough light to see by without waking everyone else in the house. First, he checked on his daughter, Vicki, in the next room. She lay fast asleep, her phone on the bedside table – her vital link to her social life. Next up, he checked on Oliver in the attic bedroom.

His imagination wickedly told him that he'd find a mummified body lying there on his son's bed. Nope . . . his son lay there. He slept deeply too, the bedding thrown to one side due to the warmth of the summer night. His bedside table had already become cluttered – hand-held games, chewing gum, birds' skulls, and a papery object that appeared to be the sloughed skin of a snake. John began to feel more relaxed now he'd been able to dispel the unease generated by the nightmare. Yawning, he headed back downstairs to his bedroom. However, at the door, he paused.

He thought: *I've still to finish checking my family*. That's when the reality struck him hard that he'd acquired another family member, and a close blood relation at that: a teenage son. Padding down to the ground floor, he opened the door to the back room. Glimmers of light from the kitchen made Ben Darrington's face shine. He breathed deeply as he slept. John felt strong emotion pierce him. Was this instinctive recognition that the stranger was his child? Or even a sudden burst of love for a son he'd never met until yesterday?

John had decided that Ben Darrington would merely be a visitor who'd stay with them for a while before going back to university when his leg healed in a few weeks. Now John realized that perhaps he was starting to bond with this young man that resembled him so closely. They had the same unruly hair, which was a mass of recalcitrant curls that could defy any comb known to man. When he looked at Ben's face it made him recall his own face when he looked in the mirror as a teenager. They were father and son alright.

John Tolworth found himself staring at the stranger who seemed so uncannily familiar. *I don't know the date of his birthday*, he told himself, feeling guilty, though he knew he couldn't possibly be responsible for this lapse. Ben's mother had never given him any information about the child.

131

I don't know what interests Ben. What his hobbies are. What course he's studying at university. I don't know if Ben is even likeable. He might be arrogant, irritating, boring, self-obsessed, selfish . . . I know nothing about him.

But that wasn't true, John realized. Even though Ben was asleep, his face suggested that here was someone who was pleasant, even sensitive. What's more, John knew that Ben must be feeling vulnerable. His mother was emotionally capricious (John knew that from when they were together as girlfriend and boyfriend). Possibly, Carol still took illegal drugs. He also knew that Ben was homeless, as well as being at least temporarily disabled due to the broken leg. John doubted if Ben had much in the way of money. After all, he was a student. John had no concerns about providing accommodation here and food; he could also give him some cash. Should he also contribute to university fees, and living expenses?

'It's going to be an unusual summer,' he murmured to himself on leaving the room.

Just how unusual he didn't know, but when he glanced through the glass panes in the front door he began to suspect that the summer would become even stranger, perhaps frightening, for standing at the end of the driveway was a figure. The moonlight revealed that the man, who was still as a statue, was none other than Philip Kemmis, John's childhood friend . . . *who's not only lost his hand but his sanity*, John thought. He realized that thought had elements of brutality as well as flippancy; however, there was a whole lot of truth in there, too.

John looked out at the haunted face of the man standing there in the lane. The man stared back at John with burning eyes. John suspected that Philip would rush to the door and start pounding insanely on the woodwork, just as he'd done with the car when they first arrived here, scaring the Tolworth family half to death. John noticed that his childhood friend wore a green dressing gown over jeans and a shirt. On his remaining hand, a black leather glove. The stump left by the missing hand was concealed by the dressing gown sleeve.

At that moment, Philip touched the skin beneath one of his eyes, and then pointed at John. A gesture that clearly meant, *I see you.* Even more worryingly, it might mean, *Watch out. I'm keeping an eye on you. Get ready for what I do next.* Abruptly, Philip swept away along the lane. The dressing gown flared out like a cloak, giving the impression that he was a king from a Shakespeare play. A tragic king. A doomed king. And one capable of drawing innocent people into this man's ongoing tragedy.

Yes, John understood that this was going to be a strange summer. He began to suspect, even fear, that it would be a troubling one, too.

The next day John continued work in the castle. He'd been given his own room, where he'd set up his laptop, scanner and 3D printer. John had run tests on the scanner by copying pages from a magazine that he'd torn to pieces. The software enabled him to piece together the fragments on the computer screen in seconds. The software had the sophistication to identify shapes of fragments and match them accurately as if the machine was a jigsaw wizard. Reassembling the ripped-up sheets of papyrus would be much more demanding, though. John anticipated that the next few weeks would involve plenty of intensive work.

'Coffee time, co-worker.' Samantha Oldfield sashayed into the room, her eyes twinkling in that flirtatious way of hers.

'Sounds good to me.' He yawned.

'A wild night on the tiles?'

'Nothing as exciting as that. I didn't sleep well.'

'You probably still need to acclimatize to our Devon air. Soon you'll be sleeping like a kitten. Here, careful, it's hot.' She handed him a cup of coffee.

'Thanks.'

'If you can spare five minutes, I'll introduce you to the rest of the team.'

'I thought I'd met everyone yesterday.'

She waggled her fingers and made ghostly *whoo-whoo* sounds. 'I'll introduce you to your deceased co-workers.'

He smiled. 'You treat the mummies as co-workers?'

'Oh, believe me, John, even in death, they'll be working to draw the money in. Our Egyptian family will be the star exhibit when the castle opens to the public.' She beckoned him with that provocative smile. 'Follow Samantha to her chamber of ghoulish delight.'

He laughed politely at her play-acting. She left the laboratory and crossed the corridor to a room that bore the sign 'DANGER! KEEP OUT!'.

'It's the old sign from the tower,' she explained.

'We decided to put it on the door to discourage any unauthorized nosy parkers from meddling with our darling mummies. Even sneezing on their poor, dead flesh would play havoc with our research.'

Her hand swept downward across a row of switches. Brilliant lights came on, illuminating a line of grisly figures. Four lay on their backs on tables. The fifth sat on an imposing chair with arm rests and a high back, resembling a throne. All of the mummies had been partially unwrapped. A few strips of cloth remained around arms and legs, and criss-crossed a torso here and a face there. Plenty of bare mummy flesh was visible. John knew that in years gone by 'mummy unwrapping parties' were extremely popular. Crowds would pay to watch the bandages being teasingly peeled off for that first glimpse of a face that hadn't been seen for two thousand years or more. It might be said that a mummy unwrapping party was the archaeological equivalent of a striptease.

'Wow.' John stared. 'Finally, I get chance to meet them . . . in the flesh.'

'Here they are, frozen in time. We've halted decay the best we can, and we've repaired damage caused by rats, mice and downright neglect over the last hundred years.' She walked along the line, indicating each body in turn. 'This is the mummy of the teenage girl, which we've named Amber. The smallest mummy is of a boy aged between ten and twelve, who we've nick-named Ket; a knife was found tucked alongside him in the coffin.'

'A weapon to take into the afterlife?'

'Probably. Next up, a youth in his late teens.

135

He's called Bones. Then we have Isis. Of course, the names are just our inventions, enabling us to differentiate one mummy from the other. When you've put the papyri back together, perhaps we will have documents that nicely confirm that we have, in this room, a king and queen.'

John shuddered when he reached the last of the mummies. The male figure sat on the chair. Its lips had shrivelled back, exposing the teeth in an eternal snarl of anger. The skin was flame red in colour, adding to the impression that this figure was the essence of fury. Of course, the reddening of the skin would be caused by salts used by the embalmers to preserve the flesh. One of the most striking features of the mummy's skull was that it appeared to be wearing a headband. Made of greenish metal, it ran around the entire skull just above the eyebrow line.

Samantha noticed that he was particularly interested in the strip of metal encircling the skull. 'We're not sure whether the headband is some kind of adornment, or a minimalist crown that the man wore when he was alive, or whether it was placed there after death as part of a funerary rite. Then, this has to be one of the most mysterious interments I've ever seen. And take a look at this oddity.' Samantha bent down to gaze into the dead face. 'See? The eyelids are closed. There's no shrinkage of the eyeballs. They haven't sunk inwards, so it looks as if Kadesh is just sleeping.'

'Kadesh?'

'Our name for the mummy until you can reveal the actual one this gent was known by.'

'Are the results of the DNA tests back yet?'

'No, but we're hoping they will prove that this is a family related by blood.'

'It's unusual for an Egyptian to be buried in a sitting position.' Shivers ran up his backbone as he, too, examined the dead features. And, yes, the man really did appear to be merely sleeping. However, time hadn't been kind to the face; cracks in the flesh revealed bare cheekbones, and part of the jaw was denuded of flesh.

Samantha whispered, 'When people sleep that's when the mummies wake up.'

'What made you say that?'

'Oh, it's something the servants use to say when the castle was home to the Kemmis family. They claimed that the mummies would prowl the corridors when everyone else was in the land of nod. Several maids claimed that when they woke up they found dust on their mouths. You see, they believed that Kadesh had crept into their bedrooms and kissed them on their lips when they were asleep. Super creepy, huh?'

'A collection of mummies like this would lead to all kinds of stories being invented.'

'You don't believe that when we sleep the mummies wake up?'

'Do you?'

'I have to admit that these mummies do walk into my dreams when I'm asleep.'

John remembered last night when he'd dreamt that a mummy lay under a sheet in his son's bed.

Samantha went on, 'In fact, I dream about them nearly every night. Once I woke up and . . .' She touched her lips before rubbing her fingertips together as if they were covered in dust. 'I'm just a romantic, aren't I? Dreaming that an Egyptian king returns from the dead to kiss me when I'm sleeping.' She smiled. 'Perhaps stories about being kissed by mummies are ones for the psychiatrist rather than the archaeologist?'

'Egyptian mummies are potent figures. Collections of mummies in museums are what visitors make a beeline for. It's hardly surprising you dream about them.'

'Sometimes the dreams aren't so nice.' She shivered, gooseflesh puckering the skin on her bare arms. 'I have nightmares about this one, the adult female corpse, which is believed to be the mother. I dream that she stands outside my house at night. She calls up to me. I can't understand the words, but she seems to be begging for help. She's terrified, panicky, beside herself; really, really frightened that something terrible will happen. But what?' Samantha shrugged. 'That's the mystery, because I don't understand the language.' She shuddered again. 'Dreams, huh? Sigmund Freud could have written a book about mine.'

Despite the woman's normally cheerful and decidedly sexy come-hither nature, John saw that memories of those dreams had really got under her skin. The images she saw inside her head troubled her. He noticed a light box on the wall; clipped to it were a number of X-ray photographs.

'Are these of all your mummies?'

'They are. You can see that Isis still wears several rings on her fingers under the bandages. The internal organs are still present, which is unusual, of course, because the embalmers usually removed those and put them in jars, which would then be placed in a different part of the tomb from the body.'

'This is a highly unusual burial,' he said. 'It doesn't conform to the ancient Egyptian norm at all, does it?'

'In fact, it's so mysterious as to be out-and-out weird. No internal organs were removed; the adult male was entombed in a sitting position; and there were no names on the coffins or on the walls of the tomb. One thing any self-respecting Egyptian would never do is go to the grave anonymously, because that would hinder their prospects of a happy afterlife. In fact, their name-less spirits would be inclined to tragically roam the earth, or so the Egyptians believed.'

'Then such a burial might be punishment for the family?'

'Possibly.'

He took a swallow of coffee. 'I should get back to work. I want to copy the first batch of papyrus fragments today.'

'Sorry, John.'

'Sorry for what?'

'A couple of days ago I was just a bit too mischievous by suggesting that our family of mummies here were similar to your family.'

'I guess they are, age-wise.'

'I was teasing you.' She did seem genuinely regretful. 'It's my nature. I can't resist giving people's chains a yank.'

'Don't worry about it. I knew you were joking.'

'I was also inaccurate, as you rightly pointed out.' She waved her hand to indicate the mummies. 'There are five here. You are a family of four.'

He stared at the five corpses in front of him
– a mother and father, perhaps, with three children. Suddenly, he had the feeling of standing
on the edge of a cliff and looking down such a
long way, while having the frightening sensation
that he was beginning to topple forward.

'Samantha, you were right, though.'

'Pardon?'

'They do resemble my family.'

'Now, who's joking?' She laughed. 'John,
Ingrid, Vicki, Oliver. Four people, not five.'

'You don't know this, but I have another son.'

'Oh?'

'He's called Ben Darrington. He came to stay
with us yesterday. I've never seen him before.
He's nineteen, pretty much the same age as Bones
here.' John felt light headed. 'You see, he's
broken his leg and can't look after himself; his
mother's travelling overseas.' He looked at
Samantha. She appeared stunned by what he'd
told her. 'We're a family of five, after all.'

'What did you say about him breaking his leg?'

'Some kind of accident. I don't know the details,
other than he broke his leg in three places here.'
He patted the side of his thigh. 'Is there something
significant about him breaking his leg?'

The woman appeared to be in shock. Even so,
she stammered out, 'No. Not at all.' She took a
deep breath and tried to laugh off the sudden air
of tension in the room. 'Well, it was still ridiculous of me to compare your family to this one.
Apart from a slight coincidence of ages.'

'And physical build, I should say.' He wondered
whether he should tell Samantha about the 3D

140

model of Amber's head, which the printer had constructed, and which resembled his daughter so closely.

'Just random chance; superficial similarities – happens all the time.' Samantha waved her hand at the X-rays. 'Besides, take the adult male. You're nothing like him.'

'He was the same age as me when he died. Late thirties or so.'

'Ah, take a closer look at the X-ray. What do you see, or more accurately, what don't you see?'

'One of his hands is missing.'

'Precisely. Which means he's not like you.' She laughed. 'Though why we're having this bizarre conversation, I don't know. It's not as if you and your family are living replicas of the mummies we have here. The adult male, after all, is missing a hand. You have both your hands. Look.' She abruptly grabbed his hands. For a moment, she looked into his eyes as she squeezed his hands tight.

John could have sworn that she was silently pleading with him not to continue the conversation. At that moment, also, he realized an important truth. *Samantha is frightened of these bodies. No . . . it's more than that. She lives in dread of them.*

She released her grip, whirling away as she did so, to point at Kadesh in the chair. 'The stump where the hand has been severed is still wrapped in plenty of cloth, but the X-ray shows the hand is missing. It must have been amputated at least a number of months before his death, because there are signs of the wound healing. But Kadesh here has one hand, while you have two.' She walked briskly – perhaps even gratefully – out of the room.

John looked at the bandaged figure sitting there on the throne. The dead man with one hand. Beyond the seated figure was a large window that looked out over the grounds of Baverstock Castle. John saw a figure pacing back and forth across the driveway. He recognized the figure as Philip Kemmis. The living man with one hand.

Thirteen

Midnight. Fletcher Brown climbed the hill to where meadow turned into moorland heather. Here, black rocks stood like soldiers waiting for the start of a battle. Fletcher wore the red cap that his friend Oliver had given him. The twelve year old had spent so much time outdoors at night that starlight was enough for him to see by. His father slept soundly, not that it bothered Fletcher whether the man was awake or not, because his father didn't care if Fletcher was at home or roaming the countryside. Fletcher knew that his father didn't like him. He often overheard his father saying to people, 'That boy of mine, he's not right in the head.'

Fletcher understood that he wasn't like other boys of his age. He found it difficult to make friends. Heck, he even found it difficult to have conversations with other people. He could tell they saw something they didn't like in his behaviour; they would make their excuses and leave.

If it was other boys, they might shove him and punch him before they left him alone – they didn't trouble themselves with anything as subtle as excuses. Whatever adults or children did in order to avoid him, the message was all too clear: *Go away, Fletcher. We don't like you. We don't want to speak to you. You're strange.*

Fletcher had learned to embrace the strange. He took pleasure in being different. When people looked up at night they saw stars. Fletcher, however, knew that stars were suns like the one that shone down upon the Earth. Yet those other suns were a vast distance away. Their light might take thousands of years to reach this planet. And that light of theirs might fall on planets that circled those distant stars. Alien eyes might use the light to see their own strange worlds.

Fletcher walked along the crest of the hill, picturing bizarre life-forms on those faraway planets. From up here, he could see the outline of Baverstock Castle. A little closer were the cottages on the lane that ran through the woods. That's where Oliver lived with his family. Oliver's parents were nice. They'd been kind to Fletcher. Not like the Oldfield family, who shunned him; their son, Mark, liked to hit Fletcher in the face.

Fletcher moved amongst the tall outcrops of rock, those dark stones that resembled a gathering of warriors on the moor. He continued along the hill, intending to find the family of foxes that lived beneath thick gorse bushes. The vixen had had cubs a few weeks ago. Fletcher liked to watch them emerging from beneath the bush to play in the starlight.

He approached the clump of bushes, moving as quietly as he could so as not to scare the foxes away. It seemed to Fletcher that the stars had begun to shine brighter. Points of light above him burned out of the blackness like the eyes of animals from the shadows of the forest. He had a sudden sense that the world around him – no, the entire universe – had experienced an abrupt surge of energy. A breeze sprang up, one fierce enough to make bushes hiss violently. His teeth tingled. There was a strange electric taste on his tongue. His muscles tensed, the way they did when he knew a bully was about to punch him. The twelve year old turned round, confused and even frightened (strange, because he never felt fear when night-walking); tonight was different, however. The hill became a menacing place. The rocks that haunted the moorland seemed on the point of jolting into life before they attacked him.

Fletcher walked faster, wondering why he felt this way. His father said that Fletcher wasn't right in the head. Did his father speak the truth? Was he entering a new phase of insanity? Fletcher's heart pounded. The grass, stones, bushes, and even the bones of a dead sheep seemed to be alive with energy that sent silvery sparks shooting into the air.

I'm going mad, he told himself with a jolt of fear. *Dad's right. Something's wrong with my brain.* He ran in panic. He didn't know where he was running to, but he had an overwhelming need to run away from . . . from . . . from what? He didn't know what he fled from – only that he had this gut-feeling he was in danger . . . that someone wanted to attack him, to hurt him, make him cry out . . . make him die.

He found himself on a track on the other side of the hill. There, in the starlight, he made out a white box-shaped vehicle. A camper van had been parked facing out over a valley. It was a beautiful lookout spot for walkers, though the camper van shouldn't have been parked there. The twelve year old knew that all this was private property. The driver of the camper van must have sneaked in along some back lane in order to park for free. It was a beautiful, elevated position, some two hundred feet above the valley floor, giving wonderful views by day of fields and woodland.

The electric tension in the air made Fletcher jumpy and fearful. A fox darted from the under-growth, startling him, making him yelp in fear. The animal seemed more frightened than him and sped away into the night. Gales roared across the hillside, making it look as if invisible claws ripped at the long grass. Birds, disturbed in their roosting places, flew past, screeching in fury.

Then Fletcher saw him. The figure walked purposefully along the track. Starlight illuminated that gaunt totem of dried-out flesh. He clearly saw bandages fluttering in the breeze. The reddish skin almost appeared to glow – a fierce, angry red – the colour of danger. He made out a greenish metal band around the skull of the mummy. Fletcher had seen it before on visits to the mummy collection in the castle. Fletcher knew the identity of the figure. This was Kadesh.

Fletcher now understood why the world had

turned so strange in the last few minutes. He'd sensed an uncanny force crackling through the air. The mummy had caused that. Its presence, and the very fact it moved like a living human being, offended nature. It distorted the laws of life, because a dead thing had been animated again, just as it had when it had carried Oliver Tolworth away. *Poor Ollie, poor dead Ollie . . .*

The mummy strode in the same way an angry schoolteacher would stride towards the back of the class where a child was being badly behaved to an infuriating degree. There was a vengeful purpose in that walk. Its body language radiated a burning need to inflict punishment. The creature was angry. It wanted to fight. Fletcher understood that much. And he saw that the figure was headed for the camper van . . .

Fletcher knew that when the mummies woke up, people sometimes entered a magic sleep. They couldn't be woken, no matter how hard you shouted or shook them. *How* Fletcher knew this, he had no idea. Often he wondered if he suffered from delusions. People certainly believed he had bizarre ideas. Then, everyone thought that Fletcher was strange in the head. At that moment, Fletcher wanted to believe it, too, and that the mummified figure walking along the track was pure hallucination, because if this monstrous apparition was real, then his life was in danger. He sensed total menace radiating from Kadesh. Its body seemed to glow with pure aggression, just as the stars glowed because they were worlds of fire.

Fletcher got ready to run back home. Yet he

paused, because he understood a worrying fact. 'The mummy's going to attack the people in the camper van.' He'd murmured the words aloud, feeling his blood run cold. 'It's going to kill the people in the van.'

The mummy was perhaps a hundred yards from the vehicle. It walked quickly, yet Fletcher knew he could reach the van first, hammer on the door, try to wake the people and get them to safety. He dashed down the slope to where the van was parked, facing out over the valley. Just beyond the front of the vehicle the ground sloped away sharply, down to a stream that glistened like a line of tears. Fletcher reached the van. He hammered on its aluminium door at the back with both fists.

'Wake up! It's coming to get you. Wake up!' He bashed hard at the metalwork. A frantic drumming sound. A sound that should have been loud enough to wake any human being. *When the mummies walk, you can never wake people up. They fall into a special kind of sleep. Nothing can wake them, it's impossible.* That's what Fletcher had told people in the past; of course, they'd reacted with contempt to his statement, considering him to be crazy.

He glanced back along the track. The gaunt man was fifty yards away. Bandages fluttered from the body. Little pennants attached to dead bones.

'You've got to wake up!' Fletcher kicked the sides of the van. The booming sound was immense. Even so, nobody stirred inside. There were no angry shouts of: *What the hell are you doing out there?* 'Get out of the van! Get away from here! He's coming!'

The mummy's pace was relentless. Now it was thirty yards away. Fletcher could even hear its feet crunching on the gravel – a munching sound; the sound could have been teeth crunching up bone.

'Wake up!'

Fletcher ran to a side window. Because the night was so warm, the window had been left open. He pushed back the blind in order to look inside. Straightaway, he saw a man and woman lying in the double bed that had been made up from the camper van's seats. They were dead to the world.

'Wake up! Hey, wake up! Look what's out here!'

They didn't even stir. The couple continued to sleep, their breathing rhythmic, faces relaxed. A small white dog lay at the end of the bed. The animal didn't stir, either. The occupants of the van seemed to be in some kind of coma. Whatever Fletcher did, whether yelling at the top of his voice, or bashing his fists against the van, didn't disturb them.

These people would sleep through a hurricane. They'd also sleep through what happened next. Fletcher knew something would happen. And that something would be horrific.

Fletcher glanced back along the track. Twenty yards away, the frightening apparition moved ever closer. Its eyes were closed, yet it seemed to stare right through the metal walls of the van and see its sleeping occupants.

Fletcher Brown could do nothing more to wake the couple. With one last desperate lunge, the boy flung himself at the open window. Reaching in, he grabbed hold of the sleeping dog and pulled the animal out of the van. It didn't stir in his arms as he ran back up the hillside, panting, gasping, sobbing. 'I tried, I really tried; it's not my fault.'

The towering figure of Kadesh reached the back of the camper van. For a moment it paused. Strips of cloth fluttered in the breeze. It raised its face to the stars, as if to feed on their light – to draw energy from those distant suns far out in space. The metal headband glinted. The eyelids of this dead-alive man remained closed.

Then Kadesh moved. With a calm sense of purpose, it reached out. Its palms rested against the back of the van. Kadesh pushed . . . pushed hard. Despite the fact that its parking brake must have been on, the camper van moved forward; perhaps the force of that shove had disengaged the brake. Whatever the reason, the wheels turned freely. The nose of the vehicle dropped downwards when it crossed the lip of the slope. A moment later, it freewheeled down the hill, quickly gathering speed, until it bounced and lurched violently, before smashing through bushes.

Fletcher watched the vehicle, containing the sleeping man and woman, slam into a tree trunk with an enormous crash. The dog still slept in his arms. It hadn't stirred once.

Fourteen

Ingrid, wearing a white T-shirt, shorts and sandals, walked into the kitchen where John sat at the table eating breakfast. Sunlight turned the lawn a dazzling green, even though it still wasn't eight o'clock. The weather looked set for a perfect summer's day.

Ingrid poured herself a cranberry juice from the fridge. 'I've just been listening to the local news,' she said. 'There's been a terrible car accident just a couple of miles away from here.'

John swallowed a mouthful of cornflakes. 'Those narrow roads can be tricky.'

'No. It's not the usual kind of road accident. A couple were sleeping in their camper van when it rolled away during the night, taking them over the edge of a hill. They were both killed.'

'In their sleep?'

'Seems like it. The bodies were found in nightclothes, and the camper van's bed had been set up.'

'The brake must have failed.' He grimaced. 'It just shows, doesn't it? The Grim Reaper is an opportunist.'

'Their dog survived. There wasn't a mark on it. Police found the animal sitting beside the body of the woman. I can't stop thinking about it.'

He glanced up; her expression told him that she was seeing the smashed-up van in her mind's eye. 'Try not to dwell on it, Ingrid.' He poured some cornflakes into a clean bowl for her. 'What are your plans for today?'

'After you go to work, I thought I'd potter around the garden for a while. Later, I'll set up the barbecue. We could eat outside tonight.'

'Good idea.'

She sat down opposite him. 'At some point I need to buy Oliver some more flip-flops.'

'He's got a new pair.'

'They fell apart. It looks as if he's run a marathon in them.'

A light knock sounded on the kitchen door. The face that appeared round the door managed to be both unfamiliar yet strangely familiar at the same time. Ben had his mother's dark eyes, yet the shape of the face and the unruly mass of curls were just like John's when he was nineteen.

'Uh, sorry to interrupt.' Ben did sound genuinely uneasy at coming into the kitchen while they were having a conversation. 'Good morning . . . thanks for the cereal and juice. I'm sorry about making a mess in the house on Monday, Mrs Tolworth. Me being sick all over the place. The painkillers were stronger than I thought, and I hadn't realized my friends had put vodka into my drink.'

Ingrid stood up quickly to take the bowl and glass from his hand as Ben hobbled into the kitchen, using a crutch to balance himself. The cast on the leg clattered against the door. Clearly, he was in pain and found walking difficult.

Ingrid said, 'Thank you, but you needn't have brought the bowl back. I'd have collected it from your room later.'

'I don't want to be needy, Mrs Tolworth, you shouldn't be running around after me.'

'Ben,' she said firmly, 'let's be clear on certain points. You have hurt your leg; it's no trouble for me to collect a bowl and a glass from your room. And I insist you call me Ingrid.'

He grinned. 'OK, thanks, Ingrid.'

Ingrid smiled warmly. 'And this is John, of course, unless you prefer "Dad"?'

John glanced at her in surprise. He'd never expected that Ben, long-lost son or not, would call him 'Dad'.

'No disrespect,' Ben said politely. 'Using the word "Dad" would be a bit odd. I've never called anyone that before.'

'Call me John. After all, you're an adult now.'

'Cheers, John.'

John realized that Ben must have been anxious about meeting his biological father for the first time. Their first encounter hadn't been straightforward, or what could be described as mutually satisfactory, because Ben had vomited copiously on to John's feet. Yesterday evening, John had tried to have a conversation with Ben when he'd come home from work; however, the painkillers he'd taken were so strong that he'd been too drowsy to speak, or even follow the thread of what John had been saying. This morning was the first time they'd been able to speak properly.

Ingrid pulled out a chair. 'Would you like to sit down, Ben, if you can manage it?'

'Thanks.' He hobbled to the chair. With the help of John and Ingrid, he managed to lower himself down. 'Sorry. I'm sure I'll be more

152

mobile in a day or two. I just need to get used to this cast on my leg.'

'Take your time,' John told him. 'The main thing is to give the bone chance to heal.'

'I broke it in three places.' He glanced at each in turn, perhaps guessing more information was required. 'I fell down some steps outside a pub.' He flushed with embarrassment. 'You're right, alcohol was involved.'

John realized that his son – his new nineteen-year-old son – was quite a shy person. He clearly hated putting people out.

'We want you to feel at home here,' Ingrid told him, smiling. 'Treat the place as if you've lived here years.'

'It's a great-looking house. I mean, look how old it is. Ceiling beams. Stone walls. And so in the middle of nowhere. I didn't notice much on the way here. In fact, I hardly knew my own name, but all those fields, woods, and hills. That blows my mind. It's like a desert . . . only instead of sand there's heather . . . or does that sound an odd comparison? The painkillers are strong enough to send me a bit loopy at times.'

John smiled. 'It's a beautiful part of the world. We're only going to be here for a few weeks. I've a short-term contract, and the employer's provided this house.'

Ben nodded. 'You're working at Baverstock Castle, and you're involved with restoring Egyptian papyri.'

'That's right. How did you know?'

'I read your blog, so I know you specialize in virtual reconstruction of artefacts.' Ben continued

153

enthusiastically, 'A couple of years ago my mother finally – *finally* – gave in and told me your name, so it was easy to Google you and find your website. Every now and then I check out your blog.' He paused. 'Sorry. It sounds like I'm stalking you.' He suddenly appeared uncomfortable about revealing his interest in his father. 'What you do is really cool. I'm studying archaeology at university myself.'

Ingrid patted Ben's hand. 'It's perfectly understandable that you'd want to discover more about your father. After all, you'd never met him. You're bound to be curious.'

'Thanks. It was strange seeing his photograph on the website. I'd never seen a picture of you before, John. Weird.'

Ingrid laughed. 'Yes, he is a little weird, but lovable, too.'

'Sorry, I mean weird to see a picture of someone who resembles me. A bit like looking in a mirror, and . . .' He tried to find the right words. 'I don't know . . . just made me feel strange inside. There's my dad, wow. And I've never met him.'

John smiled. 'We'll have plenty of time to get to know one another.'

'Thanks. Oh . . . and finding out that I've a brother and sister. That's so surreal . . . Good, too. I think it's great that I've got this new family I never knew I had.'

John didn't want to appear too gushing, nor did he wish to appear aloof. *But what's the right balance?* 'We're all in unknown territory.' He spoke in a friendly way to put Ben at his ease. 'But I'm sure we'll get along together.'

'Mr Tolworth? Sorry, I mean John.'

Ingrid gave Ben's hand a reassuring squeeze. 'You don't have to keep saying "sorry". We're easy-going people.'

'Right. OK.' He nodded, smiling. 'It's just going to take some getting used to, isn't it? I mean, for everyone? Especially for your own children. They've suddenly got a big brother who they didn't even know existed.'

'They'll be fine,' Ingrid reassured him.

'Hey, I saw what you'd done with a three-D printer.'

'Oh?' John wondered what he was referring to.

'I found the model in my room. You've made a copy of your daughter's head. Looks neat.'

'No, that's not Vicki.'

'Oh? It looked like her.'

John suddenly had the cold sensation of dead men's fingers crawling down his back. 'There's a collection of Egyptian mummies in the castle. I used a computer program that created an image of how one of the mummified females would have looked when she was alive.'

'Really? Wow. That's such a coincidence, isn't it?' Ben was astonished. 'I could have sworn that you'd made a three-D copy of your daughter's head.'

John and Ingrid exchanged glances. John remembered how freaked out Vicki had been when she'd seen the reconstruction of a dead girl's face that so closely resembled her.

Ingrid clearly decided it was timely to change the conversation. 'Tea or coffee, Ben – which would you prefer?'

* * *

155

Samantha Oldfield stood outside the castle's main door. Her arms were folded, and she wore a worried expression on her face.

John walked towards her. He was keen to process another batch of the torn papyrus fragments, but he guessed from her expression that work might be delayed today. 'Morning, Samantha,' he said. 'Is something wrong?'

'A bloody break-in,' she fumed. 'I found the door wide open when I arrived here ten minutes ago.'

'Oh no! Anything stolen?'

'Greg's gone to check. He's told everyone to stay away . . . He doesn't want our fingerprints and DNA contaminating the place before the police get here.'

'Damn it, there's all our equipment in there.'

'And our priceless mummy family. If they've been damaged or stolen, we'll be in so much trouble.'

'Hardly our fault, is it, if there's been a robbery?'

'Want to bet? Our employers will decide we should have been sleeping in the laboratories, guarding the mummies with our lives – especially if it's proved that they are Egyptian royalty. Damn it, John, we're in the shit. Our careers will be blighted. We won't work again.'

'Surely, it won't be as bad as that?'

'Want to bet money on it, John? Do you really want to?' When she noticed a figure striding up the driveway, she groaned. 'Oh my God, this all we need: the local madman.'

Philip Kemmis hurried up the driveway towards them. He wore the green dressing gown over his day clothes. The man's eyes flashed wildly; his expression was one of absolute dread. John had to admit the man did look deranged. He wore black leather gloves – one of which covered the artificial hand.

'Have you heard?' Philip shouted. 'Have you heard what happened?'

'Yes, there's been a break in,' John said.

'No! About the two people camping up on the hill. They're dead. They've been killed.'

'The runaway camper-van?' Samantha nodded. 'I heard it on the news this morning.'

'A terrible accident,' John added. 'They died in their sleep.'

Philip thundered, 'Accident be damned! They did it! Them, in there!' He strode past them to the doorway.

'Hey!' Samantha blocked his way. 'You can't go in there.'

'I'm going to drag those things out here and burn them.'

John shook his head in bewilderment. 'What things?'

Samantha answered for the man: 'The mummies. He's done this before. He blames the mummies for causing all kinds of mischief. Isn't that right, Philip?' she asked with a contemptuous toss of her head.

'I'll break them to pieces. Then I'll burn them.'

'You'll do no such thing.' Samantha held out her arms to stop him going further.

Snarling, the man lunged at her. He grabbed her with one hand while he used the other arm, with the artificial hand, to push her aside.

157

'Let go of me, you lunatic!'

John seized Philip by the collar of the dressing gown and pulled him away from Samantha.

'I'll report you to the police.' Samantha stabbed her finger in his direction. 'It's time they put you away. You're always causing trouble. Enough, OK?'

Philip raged: 'Don't try and stop me. I'll drag those monsters out here, smash them to pieces . . . I'm going to burn them to ashes!'

John tried to simply hold the man still, with the intention of calming him down, but it didn't work out like that. It turned into an exhausting tussle. Philip Kemmis had plenty of muscle. He pushed John, almost toppling him on to his back. John recovered his balance, and soon he and his old friend circled each other, both pushing and being pushed by the other. Samantha watched with a mixture of bemusement and shock.

'Calm down, Philip,' John panted. 'You'll get into trouble with the police.'

'What does that matter to me? I'm in trouble with life in general. I've been crippled with trouble since I was eleven years old!'

'I'm not letting you go until you calm down.'

'You won't stop me burning those damn monsters. They took my hand from me. Last night they killed an innocent man and woman.'

'It was an accident.'

'Let go!'

'No!'

'I'll burn the castle down, if need be. I'll wipe those things off the face of the earth.'

'Philip, listen. You were my best friend once. Remember? When I lived here, we had such great times together. You were eleven. I was ten. We spent all day roaming the countryside. Fishing, riding bikes, firing that air rifle you had.'

'Please, John. I've been wanting to do this all my adult life. I picture myself piling those husks into a mound, pouring petrol all over them, then setting them on fire and watching them burn.' Tears ran down the man's face. 'Let me kill them once and for all.'

'They're already dead, Philip. They're just bits of bone and skin. They've been dead for over three thousand years.'

Philip hissed, 'You wouldn't say that if you'd seen what I've seen.'

At that moment, Greg appeared at the doorway to the castle. 'What's wrong? Is that man causing trouble again?'

'Everything's OK, Greg,' John called back over his shoulder, even though he still gripped Philip. 'A misunderstanding, that's all.' He turned to face his old friend and whispered, 'I'm going to let you go now. Just walk back down the drive.'

'I'll burn them!'

'No, go home. If you don't, Greg will bring the police here. You must know what that will mean. They'll take you away, and you'll probably be put into a secure psychiatric unit. Understand?'

Philip nodded. 'OK.' He took a step backwards. 'Promise that you'll meet up with me later? I need to talk to you.'

'As long as you don't cause trouble now, I promise. We'll talk as much as you want.'

Philip gave a curt nod before marching briskly away in the direction of the gatehouse.

Greg came up to John. 'Goodness gracious. What on earth did he want?'

'Oh, it's nothing, Greg. I think he'd got himself upset over something.'

'I've got the telephone number of his social worker; perhaps I should call them?'

'No need for that, Greg. He's calmed down now.'

'OK,' Greg said doubtfully as he watched the figure in the dressing gown striding away.

Samantha joined them. 'What's been taken?'

'Oh, there's been no break-in.' Greg smiled. 'False alarm. There's a glitch with the new electronic locking system. The doors popped open by themselves last night. In fact, they did so at precisely eleven twenty-two, according to the computer.'

Samantha shook her head, clearly annoyed. 'Greg, the new electronic locks are supposed to be state of the art. They're designed to keep everything secure in there, and you're saying the computer unlocked the doors for no reason?'

'I'm afraid so. Rather embarrassing, isn't it?'

'I'll say.'

John was puzzled. 'Samantha, you said the door was open, not just unlocked?'

'It was open. Wide open.'

Greg shrugged. 'When the lock mechanism disengages there's nothing to keep the door shut, no bolts or anything like that. It was breezy last night as well.'

'You're saying the wind blew the door open?'

'It must have.'

Shaking her head, she went inside.

'Don't worry,' Greg said. 'I'll call out the technical people. They'll soon have the doors fixed.'

'Are you sure that someone hasn't tampered with the locks?' John asked. 'Isn't it worth checking the CCTV recordings at the time the doors opened?'

'Ah, even though the cameras have been installed, we're still waiting for the wiring to be finished. We won't have video surveillance for a few days yet.' Greg put a brave face on things and clapped his hands together. 'At least we can carry on with our work as usual.'

Today's a day of surprises, John told himself when he returned home and saw what was taking place on the back lawn. *First we find that the castle doors are opening by themselves, now this.* He stood there on the patio and watched the scene in front of him. The early evening sun blazed down. Ben Darrington sat on a lawn chair, his leg, in its cast, resting on a plastic crate. Standing a dozen paces or so away were Oliver and Vicki. The three skimmed a frisbee to each other. They were laughing, calling out jokey comments, and generally having a wonderful time.

Ingrid stepped out of the house to join him on the patio. 'They've been like this for over an hour,' she said. 'It's uncanny . . . It's like they've known each other forever.'

'They are blood relations. Perhaps there's already an instinctive bond.'

He watched Ben try to catch the Frisbee from where he sat in the chair, all but falling from his seat. Oliver and Vicki laughed when he play-acted

161

falling with exaggerated waves of his arms. They rushed forward to grab a hold and help him back into the chair.

Ingrid smiled. 'I can't stop watching them. I mean, I literally can't take my eyes off them as they're playing. Our family has just grown from four to five. Isn't that a sort of miracle?'

'It should feel strange,' he told her, 'but this feels perfectly natural.' A surge of emotion filled him. 'It's good though, isn't it?'

'It makes me happy to see them. Oliver enjoys being with Ben. I think there's already some hero worship going on.'

'Vicki's getting on well with him, too. I thought she might have been a bit stand-offish.'

Ingrid smiled. 'I've noticed something unusual, though.'

'What's that?'

'For the first time in months, Vicki seems at ease with herself . . . almost content.'

'You mean, she hasn't had one of her prickly moods when she contradicts everything you say?'

'In a nutshell, yes. I haven't seen her so relaxed since . . . well, I don't know when.'

Ben noticed John. 'Hello. Had a good day at work?'

'It's been alright. I've got plenty done.'

'Maybe I could tag along at some point and see what you're doing?'

'Sure.'

'Ollie.' Ben skimmed the Frisbee back. 'Over to you. Watch out, I've put a bomb on board!'

Oliver caught the Frisbee, pretended it exploded, then hurled himself back on to the grass, laughing at the top of his voice.

Ingrid whispered, so only John would hear, 'Your new son is here to stay, isn't he? He's already part of our family.' With that, she returned to the house.

Ingrid didn't seem unhappy with her observation. In fact, she was relaxed, too, in the way mothers are when all their children are safely at home. John watched the three at play (getting his head around the fact that there were now *three* was becoming easier); a moment later, he stepped into the kitchen where Ingrid busily prised apart frozen beefburgers.

'Would you light the barbecue, John?' she asked. 'I want to make a start on cooking these, because Oliver has asked Fletcher over.'

'I mustn't forget the most important job of all first.'

'What's that?'

'This.' He put his arms around her and kissed her on the lips.

'Mmm, that's nice. Thank you.'

'Can I get you a drink?'

'There are bottles of water in the fridge. I'll have one of those, thanks.'

'Where did we put the lighter fluid?'

'It's on the table next to the barbecue.'

'Take one last look at my eyebrows, Ingrid. I always end up incinerating them when I light the charcoal.'

'I've put the extra-long matches on the table, too. Use those. But even so . . .' She beckoned him closer. 'Bend down.' She kissed his eyebrows. 'There. Magical protection. They won't get burnt off now.'

'Thank you, my dear.' Chuckling, he headed back outside.

The frisbee match was in full swing. For the next couple of minutes he found himself part of the game. Everything merged so pleasantly and seamlessly – the warm evening sunshine, the smell of grass, the birdsong, the encircling rampart of greenery that was the forest, his children's laughter. *This is the perfect thing to come home to,* he told himself with a powerful sense of satisfaction.

At last, excusing himself from the Frisbee game, he headed to a flat area where the barbecue and garden table stood, and he glanced up at the sound of a voice.

Samantha Oldfield stood at the garden gate. 'I don't know whether to shout "cooee" or not,' she said. 'My mother used to holler it to attract people's attention. I always thought it so uncouth.'

'Hello, Samantha.'

'I come bearing news. May I enter the Tolworth domain?'

'Of course. You have an open invitation to come over anytime you wish.'

'Thank you.'

'You say you come bearing news?'

'Yes, Greg has organized a staff outing for our families on Saturday.'

'Sounds good.'

'He's hiring a bus to take us all to Hele Bay. There's a nice beach there and a couple of lovely pubs.' She approached John, while taking a keen interest in Ben at the same time. 'That's your long-lost son?' she whispered.

He nodded. 'Ben seems to be settling in well.'

'I'll say. They look like they've known each other forever.'

'Those were Ingrid's words exactly.'

'Golly, John. He looks just like you. Same hair. Same shaped face. From this angle it could be you.'

'Although a much younger me.'

Her eyes twinkled in that flirty way again. 'You don't look old enough to have a grown-up son.'

'Bizarrely, I'm pleased that he broke his leg, otherwise I might never have met him.'

'Ah, coincidences can have such profound consequences.' Samantha watched Oliver scramble up a tree to retrieve the frisbee. 'I met my husband when I bumped into an old friend who I hadn't seen in years, who then suggested we go to a tapas bar together to catch up. I'd never been in a tapas bar before in my life. It was there I met Tom. He was playing in a flamenco band. Ten months later we were married.'

'You're a believer in coincidences, then?'

'They happen all the time, don't they? Though I prefer the word "synchronicity", which is the scientific name for coincidence. Synchronicity involves a series of apparently unconnected events that come together with significant consequences.'

'Such as thinking about an old friend at random, then suddenly getting an email from that friend moments later?'

'Synchronicity would be more sophisticated than that. For example, you've been worrying over some problem. You then think, apparently

165

by chance, about an old friend you've lost touch with, who then emails out of the blue, and what they say in the email, apparently at random, helps you solve your problem.'

He squirted inflammable liquid on to the charcoal. 'Do you think there's some kind of synchronicity going on with the mummies and my family? After all, you said that they – we – resembled one another in stature, age, gender . . .'

He shrugged, not taking what Samantha was saying particularly seriously. He didn't believe in the so-called powers of newspaper astrologers, clairvoyants or fortune-tellers, so he wasn't going to leap on the *yes-I-believe-in-synchronicity* train anytime soon. 'Do you think I should treat the coincidental resemblance between the mummy family and my family as important?'

'There *are* striking similarities.'

He lit the inflammable fluid. Fortunately, his eyebrows escaped being scorched. 'But what are you getting at, Samantha? Are you saying that ghosts, or saints, or gods are trying to send me a message of some sorts, because they made five people who died in Egypt thousands of years ago resemble . . . loosely resemble, at that . . . five people who are alive in this part of Devon today?'

'Loosely resemble, you say?' She gripped his elbow. 'Remember the mummy of the boy who died when he was a teenager? The one we call Bones?'

'You already told me the name.'

'You never asked *why* we called him Bones.'

He shrugged. 'OK . . . why?'

'His thigh bone had been broken in three places.

166

Remember that number: *three*. There are tell-tale signs that the break occurred just a short time before death, because the fractured sections of thigh had begun to knit together again. Which part of Ben's leg is broken, and in how many places?'

'Ben's thigh bone is broken. It's broken in three places.'

At that moment, Ben recalled the head produced by the 3D printer: a perfect reproduction of the head of the mummified girl the restoration team called Amber. The face of the plastic model was uncannily similar to Vicki. A cloud passed over the sun. A sudden coldness spread over John's skin. The cold went deep into him. It went into his bones. It went into his heart. The DNA results from the mummified corpses would arrive soon. What if . . . no . . . he didn't want to ask himself, '*What if?*' This similarity between the dead and the living had begun to prey on his mind.

Samantha, meanwhile, said her goodbyes and left the garden. John placed the mesh grill on the barbecue. He found himself glancing at Ben; he had three breaks in his thigh bone, just like the mummy they called Bones. His gaze wandered to Vicki. She resembled the 3D model of Amber. Now he found himself staring at Oliver. In his mind's eye, he couldn't help but overlay the image of the mummified boy's face over the face of his living son, trying to identify similarities.

John inwardly recoiled from the gruesome image that his imagination created – a merging of an ancient face, frozen in death, and the pink, smiling face that belonged to his son.

* * *

Philip Kemmis sat on a bench near the gatehouse where he lived. He wore a long-sleeved white shirt and black jeans. John Tolworth had decided that he'd keep his promise to talk to his child-hood friend, so, after the barbecue, which had been cheerful and light-hearted, John had told Ingrid that he intended to call on Philip. She knew that they'd been friends long ago. Even so, she'd warned, *'If he begins acting strangely, or becomes aggressive, leave – don't try having a conversation with him.'*

John murmured to himself, 'I'm here now, as I promised. Let's get this over with.'

For the sake of their old friendship John would give Philip the courtesy of spending some time with him. The man was clearly mentally disturbed. However, if his behaviour remained at least rela-tively normal then John would listen to what Philip had to say, even if it was the product of some peculiar fantasy.

John walked along the path through the trees.

The moment Philip saw John approach he stood up. He wore black leather gloves – one would be on the living hand, the other on the artificial hand. Philip spoke crisply in those upper-class accents that John remembered so well from three decades ago. 'I had a distinct feeling you'd come over this evening.' He appeared in control, showing no signs of the agitation or even downright terror of earlier in the day when he'd stormed up to the castle, wanting to burn the mummies.

'Hello, Philip. How are you?'

'As you can see, old chap, I'm not raving like an inmate of Bedlam. How are you?'

'Fine, thanks.'

'If you're in the mood for a walk, John, I'd like to show you something that you'll find interesting.'

'Are you sure?'

'Don't be concerned that I might pounce on you, clawing at your throat. Ha!' His eyes were glittery, and he spoke quickly.

John would use the word 'hyper' to describe the man. He appeared elated; his movements were so fast that it was almost like watching film of a man on fast-forward. Even so, he did appear to be . . . to put it bluntly: sane. 'OK,' John told him. 'We'll take a walk.'

'There's a good hour before sunset; that gives us plenty of time.'

'What should I call you?'

The man laughed. 'What did you call me when we were boys?'

'Philip.'

'Then what do you want to call me now? The Mad Hatter? Crazy Man? I've been a good fellow, John, I remembered to take my medication after that minor kerfuffle this morning up at the castle. Apologies for that. Forgiven?'

'Of course – but you inherited your father's title, didn't you? You're a lord.'

'Call me Lord Kemmis, if you wish; it's a mouthful, though.'

'OK, Philip.'

'And good to meet again after all these years.' He held out his left hand: the living hand.

John shook it. 'Good to meet you again, Philip. When I applied for the job at the castle I realized

169

that it had new owners, so I never expected to find you living in its grounds.'

'I hate it here. But I could never leave.' He didn't elaborate. 'You're here with your new family, and you're working in my old home. Life plays curious tricks, doesn't it?' Instead of waiting for a reply, he nodded at the steep path that they climbed. 'Goodness, do you remember how we used to cycle down here? Like we were riding on rockets! Ha! It's a wonder we didn't break our necks.'

John tried to stop himself, yet he glanced at the glove concealing the artificial hand.

Philip noticed what John was looking at. 'No, I didn't lose the hand in a cycling accident. Ho! And there's the tree where we had the rope swing. We played for hours on that, didn't we? Ah, just up there to your right, John; it's a steep climb, I'm afraid. It'll be worth it when I show you the astonishing discovery I made this afternoon, though.'

They continued uphill to where the meadow gave way to a vast expanse of moorland. Even though the sun hung low in the sky, the temperature was still formidable. John felt a bead of perspiration run down his face. Philip, on the other hand, strode tirelessly uphill.

Philip showed no sign of being out of breath when he began speaking. 'My parents planned for me to complete my education at public school. After that, I'd either go to university or join the army, depending on my proclivity. Of course, the accident put paid to that. It wasn't so much the severing of old Mr Hand here.' He held up his arm as he walked. 'Nerves suffered more than flesh. My parents sent me to an establishment in Denmark where the children of the upper echelons of society go if they are misfiring mentally. While I was there, my father sold the castle and its grounds to an investment company. You might remember our family were broke – on the verge of bankruptcy, in fact. One of the terms of the sale of the castle was that my family could continue to live in the gatehouse rent free in perpetuity. After my parents died, I had the place to myself. I also have enough cash in the bank to live in a modicum of comfort, providing I don't eat more than two meals a day. Ah, look, you have a good view of the sea now.'

John shielded his eyes against the sun. He made out a strip of blue between land and sky that was the Bristol Channel. He asked, 'Don't you have any family?'

'You mean married with kiddiewinks?' He shook his head. 'When I approach, ladies flee. Women are good at seeing this above my head.' He reached up into the air above him. 'The black cloud that hangs above me wherever I go.' Philip noticed John's expression. 'A metaphorical cloud. An aura of despondency. Nay, an air of doom haunts me.' Philip still spoke in an oddly cheerful way. The medication, perhaps?

'What is it that you want me to see?' John asked.

'Almost there.' Philip marched towards the hilltop. 'Saw your website, John. You use computer software to restore damaged archaeological finds.'

'That's why I'm here. What I've been hired to do is piece together the shreds of papyrus that were found in the Gold Tomb.'

'God help you, there must be thousands of the bloody things. Turn left here. Watch out for our serpent friends, they're all over the hill. One sank its fangs into Fletcher Brown last year. Of course, adder bites are rarely lethal, but they do sting to high heaven.'

If anything, Philip was like the old Philip from boyhood. John remembered the posh voice, the idiosyncratic phrases, and that he could be so damn bossy at times.

They crossed the brow of hill. Black rocks protruded from the heather; they always reminded John of soldiers waiting for an order to attack. A long, thin shape moved across the path in front of him; it was one of the snakes that Philip had warned him about. He paused until it had slithered away under the heather before moving on. He hoped that Oliver wouldn't venture up here; even so, he decided to warn him that there were venomous snakes in this part of the world. Ahead of him, Philip Kemmis walked swiftly with a straight back, the aristocratic air all too apparent.

A moment later, Philip stopped and pointed. 'There,' he said. 'Do you see the oak at the bottom of the slope?'

'The one with the white mark on the trunk?'

'That's the one. The camper van hit the tree last night, ripping off the bark at the bottom.'

'You wanted to show me the scene of an accident?'

'No, not exactly, though you'll realize the

172

significance of the accident after I show you what I've found.'

'You know something, Philip? I'm going to go back home now.' John suspected that the accident excited the man in a ghoulish way. Perhaps Philip would show him splashes of the victims' blood on the ground, which would be in bad taste, if not downright sick. John didn't want to poke around the site of a tragedy that had claimed the lives of two people.

Philip didn't appear to have heard what John had said about returning home; he crouched down in front of a bush that was little more than knee-high.

'Philip, I'm going home. I'll see you later. Goodbye.'

'No!'

'I'm not interested in gawping at the aftermath of accidents.'

'Wait, there's something here you must see. I found it this afternoon.'

'What is it?'

'Take a look for yourself.'

Warily, half-suspecting Philip would pull some weird trick, John leaned forwards to look at the gorse bush with its spiky leaves.

'Do you see what's there?' Philip asked.

'Just a tiny piece of cloth.'

'Is it familiar?'

'No.'

'Look closer.'

John crouched down in order to examine the fragment of cloth that was no bigger than a postage stamp. The fabric was grey, with a loose weave that revealed the individual strands. The fragment was ragged at the ends, torn rather than neatly cut.

Philip nodded. 'You know what that is, don't you?'

'It looks like, but . . . No . . . It's not possible.'

'Go on, John, tell me where it's from.'

'It appears to be a piece of cloth from one of the mummies. How on earth did that get up here?'

Philip looked him directly in the eye as they both stood up straight. 'John, do you remember the night when you stopped overnight in the castle? You'd have been ten. I was eleven. You'd asked to see the mummy collection that was kept in one of the tower rooms.'

'I think I remember something or other . . . exploring the castle, going up into the tower and such. It was a long time ago, though. It's all very hazy.'

'No, you don't consciously remember all the details, do you? Not everything that happened to us. You locked the memory away due to the shock you suffered that night.'

'What shock? Nothing happened that shocked me.'

'Oh, but it did, John.' Philip spoke with quiet authority. 'We climbed up into the tower. We went into the room where the mummies were kept back then. They were covered with sheets. When I—'

'That's not a piece of the mummy's binding.' John pointed at the scrap of cloth caught on the bush. 'It can't be!' John felt hot, breathless, he was shouting the words. 'You put it there for a joke, or to make me think—'

174

'Think what, John? That the mummies fail to obey the rules relating to death?'

'It's just a scrap of old bed sheet. And nothing happened regarding the mummies in the tower!'

'Try to remember, John.' Philip spoke softly. 'We went into the room, and I turned on the light. The mummies were under sheets. I began to remove the one from Kadesh that sits on the chair. The light went out.'

'Oh, God . . . oh no.' John's heart pounded. His mouth flooded with a horrible metallic taste. He'd have fallen if Philip hadn't caught his arm and steadied him.

'You ran downstairs, John. Later, I followed you into the corridor. You turned to me and you asked . . .'

'*Philip! What happened to your hand?*' John clutched his throat as if in a desperate attempt to stop the torrent of words erupting from his mouth. 'Your hand . . . I remember! That's where you lost your hand. There was blood pouring from your wrist. There were strips of torn skin hanging down. Oh God, I'd never seen anything like it before.' Purple flashes appeared in front of his eyes. He knew he was close to passing out, there on the hilltop. 'How the hell could I forget something as terrible as that? Until a moment ago, I'd have sworn on my family's life that it had never happened. Now I can see you in my mind's eye. You're walking slowly towards me . . . There's blood . . . Your wrist is in such a mess . . . like raw meat.'

'I lost my hand in the room with the mummies. I pulled back the sheet that covered Kadesh. The

175

light went out. Then someone grabbed my hand. After that I felt pain like . . . well, pain beyond any comparison I can make. What separated my hand from my wrist? I'm not sure. I couldn't see, on account of the darkness. I believe, however, it was teeth. My hand was bitten off.'

Blood thundered in John's skull. His entire body felt strangely stiff, as if some evil magic was turning him to stone. Shock, he reasoned. He found himself shaking his head as he repeated, 'To forget what happened? It doesn't make sense.'

'It makes perfect sense. You were ten years old. The human mind often protects itself by sealing away traumatic memories. My mind didn't hide away the memory of what happened to me; that is why I had a nervous breakdown and was sent away to a psychiatric institution in Denmark. The memory of what happened to this . . .' He twisted the artificial hand clad in the black leather glove, separating it from the wrist with a click. 'The memory of what happened to this ruined my life. I couldn't function properly after the attack. I couldn't attend school. No woman looks at me twice. I'm the man everyone avoids. They say I'm insane.'

John stared at his childhood friend. He saw tragedy in his eyes. The events of that night still haunted him. The gruesome and terrifying memory still ate into his bones and his mind like acid eats into flesh. At that moment, Philip Kemmis spoke lucidly. A powerful sense of calm radiated from him. It was as if he'd been waiting all his adult life to speak these words, and now that the time had come he'd found the inner strength to speak clearly. He seemed incredibly focused – totally in control of his emotions and thoughts.

'John, listen carefully to what I say next. When the light went out in that room thirty years ago, I was attacked. Some *Thing* in the room detested the intrusion. It attacked me. And that *Thing* was Kadesh that sits in the chair. The creature, for want of a better description, bit clean through my wrist in the darkness. My parents said later that I suffered a freak accident. I know better.' He pointed at the shred of cloth caught on the gorse bush. 'That same mummy walked up here last night. A piece of its wrapping was torn off by a thorn and left there. Then the creature pushed the camper van, containing two sleeping people, over the edge of the hill.'

'Why?'

'That three-thousand-year-old corpse is absolutely determined to protect the other four mummies. It will ruthlessly defend them. Anyone who comes here is seen as a threat. Therefore, that vile husk will attack living people.'

John felt unsteady on his feet. The shock of remembering how his injured friend had looked all those years ago confused his thoughts. Some part of him realized that he should be loudly refuting what Philip told him. Yet just to close his eyes for a second brought back the vivid image of his friend, with shreds of torn skin hanging from his wrist.

Philip continued, 'For years I've seen visions of the mummies. They have the power to superimpose images of their faces over living people.

177

When I see a man or woman walking by the gatehouse I often see them wearing the withered face of one of the mummified corpses. When you arrived here in your car I saw you driving what appeared to be a car full of ancient mummies – yet they were dead and alive all at the same time, if you understand what I mean.'

'That's why you struck the car? You thought my family were mummified bodies.'

'I tried to warn you, John.'

'You were hallucinating.' Yet even as he said those words he couldn't bring himself to believe them. All too vividly he recalled Samantha Oldfield telling him how his family resembled the mummy family in the castle. The one called Bones with the broken thigh-bone, just like Ben. The 3D model of the head that resembled Vicki. John backed away from the bush with its shred of cloth that had once been pressed to dead skin.

Philip said, 'The real reason I brought you here is far more important than showing you that piece of mummy cloth. I brought you here to warn you. The mummies have started walking. Your family is in danger. If you don't leave now, they will be destroyed.'

Ten minutes to eleven at night. The lamp on the bedside table cast a soft glow over the bedroom. Ingrid's naked body gleamed with the same rich hue as dark honey. She yawned, stretched – the way her body lengthened during that sensuous stretch gave a wonderful shape to her breasts, something that only rarely failed to send tingles of desire through John. Yet fail it did tonight.

John was utterly preoccupied with the conversation that he'd had with Philip Kemmis this evening. John still continued to struggle with the truth: that he'd been in the castle tower with Philip thirty years ago when Philip's hand had been . . . what, exactly? Torn off due to a freak accident? Bitten off by one of the mummies? Despite not accepting the notion of such a bite from a corpse for one moment, he found himself imaging those ancient teeth of a dead man, crunching through the skin, tendon, muscle and bone of a boy's wrist. A bitter taste flooded his own mouth. His blood ran cold, yet he felt his hands become clammy with perspiration.

Ingrid pointed at one of her breasts. 'Look at this, John. A mosquito bite; the thing itches like crazy. Would you like to rub on some cream for me?'

He stared at the red mark on her smooth skin without answering.

'Hello? John, did you hear me?'

'Uh? Yes.'

'Then will you?'

'Will I what?' He blinked, realizing that he'd been so fixated on what happened in the castle three decades ago that he hadn't, in fact, heard her question. 'Sorry, I was thinking about what Philip said to me tonight.'

'How did it go?' She slipped on the T-shirt she'd be wearing for bed and climbed in beside him.

'Uh, not well. He's clearly mentally disturbed.'

'I'm sorry to hear that. You were good friends, weren't you?'

'When we were boys we were inseparable. We spent hours together, either fishing, or riding our bikes up on the moors.'

'It must be hard to see him in this state.'

'The loss of his hand seems to be the root of it all. Not long after the accident, his parents sent him away to a mental hospital in Denmark.'

'They sent him away? Like he'd become an embarrassment to the family?'

'They'll have thought they were doing the right thing.'

'Did Philip tell you about the accident?'

'No. He didn't want to discuss it. The memory's probably too painful for him.' John wondered why he'd lied to her. *Maybe this doesn't seem the right time*, he thought. *I'd have to tell her the whole story about staying with Philip when he lived in the castle with his parents, and how we sneaked up into the tower where the mummies were kept.* However, for some reason, he found it difficult to fully accept that something bizarre had happened to him, too, because he'd suppressed the memory of Philip emerging from the spiral staircase at the bottom of the tower with his arm bleeding from the wound at the end of his wrist. Those mental images sickened him as much as they alarmed him, and he didn't feel ready to reveal all this to Ingrid yet. He knew he would in the next few days, preferably in the bright light of day. Of course, he wouldn't repeat Philip's assertion that one of the mummies had torn his hand off with its jaws when the lights went out. Surely, that must be some bizarre, if decidedly gruesome, fantasy that had developed later as the

180

boy's mind had crumbled due to the trauma of the accident.

Ingrid, bless her kind heart, chatted about inviting Philip over. Once again, this golden-hearted woman wanted to rescue someone in distress. John had watched her do exactly this dozens of times before when her students had suffered some tragedy or other.

Memories of that horrific night continued to rebound inside his head though. Now he understood why he'd felt so strange when he'd seen the castle for the first time in years a few days ago. And those strange episodes of dizziness and anxiety he'd had recently were all explicable. *The suppressed memory was beginning to break out: it was trying to erupt into my conscious mind.* Once again he felt panicky – the emotion he felt was that of a ten year old who'd just seen his friend step through a doorway after having his hand ripped off. John realized he needed to divert this alarming train of thought, so he changed the subject.

'When we go to Hele Bay on Saturday . . . I wonder if we could somehow get Ben on to the bus. The cast runs from his ankle to the top of his thigh so it won't be easy. It doesn't seem right to leave him here, though.'

Ingrid smiled. 'That's such a sweet thought. Yes, we should take Ben with us.'

'He seems fairly mobile on crutches. I think he'll manage OK, and there are pubs in Hele Bay where we could eat.' John felt the muscles in his chest relax; his heart stopped pounding, and its rhythm became less frantic. 'I'll take a picnic, though, just in case it's not easy for Ben to reach the pub.'

'Make him one of your chicken curries. They're lovely to eat cold, especially if you put lots of raisins in. Oh, I noticed that Ben likes reading on his phone. We could treat him to some new e-books.'

'Tomorrow, I'll ask him for his bank account details. I'll transfer some cash to his account so he can buy some more. Do you think fifty pounds will be enough? No . . . I'm being stingy, aren't I? I'll make it a hundred pounds. Ingrid . . . what do you think to a hundred? Ingrid?'

He glanced at her. A moment ago, she'd been wide awake. Now, she lay there with her eyes lightly closed. Her chest rose and fell slowly.

'Ingrid, are you awake?' *Silly question*, he thought. *She's fast asleep.*

John turned on to his other side so that he could reach out and switch off the lamp on the bedside table. He managed to reach perhaps half way. Suddenly, however, he felt odd. His arm felt so incredibly heavy. Even though he tried, he couldn't lift his head from the pillow. For a moment, he froze in that position. The lamp shone on his phone and on his wristwatch. The time was just five minutes after eleven. A light breeze made the curtains undulate – a ghostly movement. He heard his own respiration; his heartbeat seemed to have slowed to a ponderous thud with long intervals of silence in between. John had just enough time to experience a surge of surprise. *I've never felt like this before . . . what's happening? Why can't I move?*

The next moment he became submerged in a deep, dream-filled sleep where his ten year old self asked the boy with the dripping wrist: '*Philip. What happened to your hand?*'

At six minutes past eleven, Philip Kemmis paced through the rooms in his home. He heard the television in the adjoining apartment. Philip felt an explosion of rage. *How can I sleep with that bloody cacophony?* Philip knew full well, however, that it wasn't the sound of a TV drama booming through the wall that bothered him; it was the same old thoughts that haunted his every waking moment. The memory of something sharp piercing the skin of his wrist thirty years ago when the light went out. The white hot eruption of pain. How he was engulfed in terror when he was attacked in the darkness. Then he'd entered the living nightmare that was the Danish madhouse. He gave a harsh laugh – a sound full of distress and absolute despair, rather than a reaction to something humorous. When he looked at ordinary men and women, as they went about their business, he watched as the mummies superimposed images of their own dead and ravaged faces on the living faces. So many times he'd pass an attractive woman in the lane, only for her face to be transformed in front of him into a mask of dead skin, shrivelled eyes, and lips that had dried so much that they'd shrunk back to expose her teeth in a vicious snarl.

Hallucinations, his doctor said.

'Hallucinations be damned,' he muttered angrily to himself as he paced the lounge. 'And how will

I ever sleep with all this noise?' He pounded on the wall that separated the two apartments. 'Hey! Turn that damn thing down, will you? It's keeping me awake!'

The clock on the wall told him it was eight minutes past eleven. The television sounded louder than ever. A booming noise monster in its own right. The screech of tyres from a car chase blasted through the walls. The heroine screamed constantly. Drums thudded, guitars were howling. Yet, at that instant, Philip stopped his restless pacing.

His mouth fell open as the muscles in his jaw went slack. With a huge effort, he managed to reach an armchair, where he flopped down.

'But I'm not even tired,' he managed to utter before falling into what seemed a vast emptiness where even his own anxieties that constantly gnawed on his nerves could not reach him.

Nine minutes past eleven. In the apartment next door, Fletcher Brown walked past the table where his father sat. The man rested his head on his arms, which lay flat on the table. His father was dead to the world. He slept soundly despite the loudness of the television. The noisy car chase on-screen didn't disturb the man. He didn't even flutter so much as an eyelid when the girl in the film screamed in horror.

The news about Fletcher's mother tonight had been bad.

'She's slipping away from us,' his father had told him. 'Your mother doesn't even know I'm there when I sit by the bed.'

His dad wasn't interested in what Fletcher had to say. Instead, he'd simply told Fletcher to go to bed. Fletcher had to bottle up his emotions. His mother might be dying, but his dad didn't appear to care one jot about Fletcher's feelings. Dad had switched on the television, turned up the sound, and tried to lose himself in the story.

His father now slept soundly. Fletcher put on his boots and went outdoors. The night was warm. Moths flew around the lamp fixed to the gate-house wall.

Fletcher ran. He wondered if he'd be able to release the sadness he felt for his mother if he could yell and cry. But he rarely showed any sign of emotion. His blood felt hot enough in his veins to the point it hurt him – the scalding flood actually stung the inside of his body from head to foot. All he could do was run and keep running, in the hope that exhaustion would cool his blood; then, perhaps, like his father, he could sleep.

Even though he was just twelve years old, he understood that sleep was a blessing at times of grief like this. Sleep allowed an escape from reality. Sleep could help heal emotional wounds. Fletcher knew full well though that sleep would elude him. He'd be condemned to remain awake with his worries.

Fletcher ran along the forest path. Enough star-light filtered through the branches to reveal the way. The eyes of animals glittered at him from the dark. Bat wings whispered through the air above his head. He glimpsed a fox with a dead blackbird hanging from its jaws. Fletcher ran and ran, hoping to outrun the sadness he felt for his

185

mother. Of course, he never could quite run fast enough. The memory of her thin face lying on the pillow in the hospital ward gnawed away at him persistently – agonizingly.

Opening his eyes, Oliver Tolworth gazed up into the darkness. He felt wide awake. When he realized he couldn't get to sleep again he checked the luminous dial of his watch. The time stood just before eleven thirty.

'Sleep,' he told himself.

Nope . . . not working. He pushed back the sheet and sat up in bed. By touch alone he found the light-switch on the bedside table. *Click.* Light flooded the bedroom. Deciding to get a drink of water, he climbed out of bed. It had been so warm lately that when he got water from the bathroom it was tepid and had an unpleasant dusty taste so, deciding to help himself to nicely chilled water from the jug in the refrigerator, he went downstairs. Everyone else in the house seemed to be fast asleep. The door to his parents' bedroom was partly open, and he noticed that the bedside lamp had been left on. What's more, his dad slept with his arm out of the bed as if he'd fallen asleep as he'd attempted to switch off the lamp. That looked funny. Oliver grinned and headed downstairs, where he could hear the slow, rhythmic breathing of Ben Darrington from further along the corridor.

Oliver couldn't get over the fact he'd suddenly got a new brother out of the blue. A grown-up mystery brother, at that – one he'd never met before. *Heck, I never even knew he existed at all,*

Oliver told himself with a renewed sense of amazement that this stranger had suddenly appeared here at their house.

Curiosity tugged Oliver, pretty much like someone tugging a dog on a leash. In no time at all he stood outside the back parlour that had been converted to Ben's bedroom. He gently eased open the door. Of course, the stupid thing gave a loud creak that would make anyone wake up with a furious yell. Oliver froze there, the corridor light spilling across Ben's bed, lighting up his face. Ben, however, slept soundly. Oliver padded across the floor to look down at the teen-ager. The face was so much like Dad's, Oliver realized. Ben had the same mass of bristly curls as both Oliver and his dad. Ben was a stranger, but then he didn't look like a stranger, or even seem like a stranger. Oliver liked Ben. It felt like he'd known Ben for . . . well . . . forever.

A rucksack leaned against the wall. That was Ben's bag. Oliver felt the irresistible tug of curiosity again. He didn't question himself if this was wrong or not. It just seemed an OK thing to do. He wanted to find out more about his new brother. Oliver stealthily approached the ruck-sack. He opened the top to find lots of clothes. They weren't folded well; in fact, they weren't folded at all. *Students*, Oliver thought. *They're always messy, aren't they?* He checked a side pouch. A phone in a case; scuffed and scratched. A wallet, with a couple of banknotes and a student union card. Ben peered at the ID photograph. Ben's hair looked like a funny bush on his head. There were pens in the side compartment, old train tickets, timetables, a dice, gum wrappers. Messy students.

Oliver picked up the heavy – hugely heavy! – rucksack in order to put it back where he'd found it. When he put his hand against the yielding fabric at the bottom he felt a square shape. Once more he felt the tug of curiosity. The square shape was probably nothing much, but Oliver reasoned that, in a way, he was paying Ben a compliment by taking an interest in his possessions. He opened up the rucksack again, wormed his hand down between the messy cram of T-shirts and jeans and stuff until he reached the bottom. With a great deal of tugging, he managed to pull out a plastic box of the kind you might put sandwiches in. He pulled off the lid.

'Wow.'

Whether it was the *Wow* Oliver uttered he didn't know, but Ben stirred. Oliver tensed, waiting for angry accusations about invading privacy. All Ben did, however, was sigh as he turned over in bed. His eyes remained closed. Soon his respiration returned to normal.

Oliver stared at what he'd discovered in the plastic box. Wrapped in clear plastic was white stuff. One poke of his finger told him that the plastic bag, which was about the size of a bag of sugar, contained white powder.

'Drugs,' he uttered. 'These are drugs.'

He stared at the white powder with a mixture of dread and astonishment. He'd never encountered drugs before in real life, but he'd seen them often enough on television. When he looked at this bag of white powder he could almost feel its badness – it had an aura of crime about it. Quickly, he put the lid on the box and stuffed it back down to the bottom of the rucksack. He replaced the rucksack where he'd found it, confident that Ben wouldn't notice that it had been disturbed.

Oliver trembled. Just seeing drugs in real life felt wrong – like something he could get into trouble for. He pictured police cars stopping outside the house. He'd even touched the bag with the white powder inside, which, to him, seemed a million times worse than just seeing it. His mouth had gone dry. He really did need that drink of ice-cold water now.

Swiftly, he padded out of Ben's room to the kitchen. He took the jug of iced water from the fridge, poured himself a glass, then, raising the glass to his lips to take a drink, his eyes went to the kitchen window. A figure stood on the other side of the glass. The kitchen light revealed it perfectly. He saw a metal band around the forehead of the skull. The eyes were closed. Cracks in the dry face resembled fracture lines on a planet devastated by some horrendous catastrophe.

The mummy's eyelids slid back, revealing eyes that were plump and bulging and white and glistening – big, staring eyes with brown irises and fierce black pupils.

The glass fell from Oliver's hand. He slowly backed away. The husk of a creature vanished from the window. A moment later, the handle of the back door moved downwards. Then slowly, silently, with no sense of hurry, the door was

189

opened from the other side. Oliver watched in horror as the mummified figure stepped into the kitchen. Those bulging eyes fixed on him – fierce eyes, angry eyes.

The mummified figure walked slowly across the kitchen towards the door that led into the rest of the house. Strips of cloth criss-crossed its chest. The metal headband it wore on its head gleamed beneath the kitchen light. The creature's eyes were unblinking – a fixed stare of hatred and utter fury. This was the same mummy that had grabbed hold of him when he'd gone night-walking with Fletcher. The mummy had seized him and run with him, like it intended to carry him away. Now it was back.

Oliver couldn't take his eyes off this gaunt invader. He glimpsed naked bone through cracks in the skin. One hand had been stripped of its fabric wrappings to reveal individual fingers and fingernails that gleamed like mother-of-pearl. The other arm looked shorter – what's more, the end of the limb still bore its wrappings of ancient cloth. The effect was bulbous – almost as if an attempt had been made to make the arm into a weapon; a club to break the skulls of this creature's enemies.

With a dreadful sense of inevitability, the monster walked through the kitchen. Grey strips of cloth hung down from the body, which was part skeleton. The mummified corpse had a sense of purpose. It was here to do something – and that something would be bad. Oliver knew that. The monster was here to hurt his family. Perhaps even to kill.

Oliver backed into the fridge door. The bump was enough to snap him out of that almost hypnotic state of fear. He darted through the doorway and raced upstairs, yelling at the top of his voice. 'Dad! Wake up!' He charged into his parents' bedroom. 'Wake up, there's something in the house! Dad?'

His mother and father slept soundly. The bedside light remained on, illuminating their relaxed faces and closed eyes. Oliver stared at them both in shock. *What's happening? Why aren't they waking up? I'm shouting as loud as I can!*

'DAD! DAD! IT'S COMING UP THE STAIRS!' Indeed, he heard the slow thud . . . thud . . . thud of its feet as it climbed. Any moment now, it would step through the door. That dead husk of a thing would be inside his parents' bedroom.

'Dad!' Oliver put both hands on his father's chest and pushed hard, trying to shake him awake. 'Dad. It's getting closer. You've got to wake up . . . please . . . open your eyes!' He yelled until his throat burned. He shook his mother, too. She didn't move, didn't even so much as murmur in her sleep.

'Why don't you wake up?' Tears ran down his face. 'Why don't you wake up?' He was so scared now. The boards on the landing creaked as the corpse neared the bedroom. 'Please, open your eyes NOW!'

At that moment, he remembered what Fletcher Brown had told him. He'd said that the mummies in the castle could make people sleep – a magic sleep that they couldn't be woken up from. Fletcher had said that when this happened you could shout in their ears, scream in their faces, pull their hair, shake them until their teeth rattled, yet it would be impossible to wake them. Oliver had thought that Fletcher had been telling him a story to try and scare him. *But it's true*, he told himself with absolute dread. *The mummies can make people sleep. They do something to their minds so it's impossible to wake them.*

Oliver stopped yelling at his parents to wake up. He took a step back from the bed. His father lay there on his back, his arm extended towards the bedside light as if he was already dead. His mother lay on her side, her eyelids closed. She looked so vulnerable there. Neither his mother nor his father could do anything to prevent themselves from being attacked in their own bed – that special, safe place. A bed is that deeply personal refuge from the world: a secure nest of soft pillows, mattress and duvet, where people surrender consciousness to sleep. Even though they don't know what is happening around them, they trust they will remain safe and unharmed in the comfort of their own bed. The monster was going to violate that safe refuge.

The mummy entered through the doorway. Eyes bulging from its head, it stared at the two sleepers. They were vulnerable, helpless; they couldn't fight to protect themselves; they couldn't run away. Oliver knew that they'd lie there fast asleep, and that this nightmare of dry skin and bone could do whatever it wanted to his parents. The mummy walked slowly towards the bed. Strips of bandage dangled from its arms. Its upper lip had shrunk after all those years in the tomb

– it formed a permanent snarl, exposing a line of glinting teeth.

'Mum. Dad. Please wake up.' Oliver knew that he made a last forlorn plea.

They didn't stir: dead to the world.

Dead . . . Oliver knew that within moments the intruder would kill them. Oliver closed his eyes for a second, breathed deeply, and knew what he must do.

Opening his eyes again, he stood in the mummy's path. 'No,' he said in a clear voice. 'I won't let you hurt them.'

The nightmare man approached . . . closer and closer.

'You won't touch them. I won't let you.' Oliver lifted both hands, ready to push the thing back, although he couldn't prevent the attack. This grim figure could break him apart as easily as if he was made out of twigs. The creature moved closer. Those blazing eyes fixed on his mother as she lay sleeping. It seemed fascinated by her face.

'No! You mustn't touch her.' Oliver added in sheer desperation: 'It's not allowed. *You* are not allowed to touch her.'

Then something strange happened. The mummy looked down at Oliver, as if noticing him for the first time. It took hold of his chin and lifted his face so it could examine the features closely. For a moment they stayed like that, the corpse holding Oliver's chin as it stared into his face.

Then it was over, as simply as that. The gaunt figure turned and walked out of the bedroom. Oliver heard the sound of its feet going downstairs. After that, silence.

The next thing he heard was Dad saying, 'Ollie? What's the matter? Don't you feel well?'

Oliver turned round to see his mother and father sitting up in bed; he saw their expressions of concern. Oliver opened his mouth, ready to explain exactly what had happened tonight, how the house had been invaded by someone that had died thousands of years ago, but the room began to spin; he dropped to the floor like a stone before he could utter a single word.

Fifteen

They filmed the man being tortured. DVDs of this gruesome and violent footage would be distributed to the gang's drug mules and underlings to demonstrate that disloyalty would result in brutal punishment. Films such as this ensured employee obedience. The victim's wrists had been tied to a bracket set above his head in the cellar wall. The man being tortured was in his early forties, and he'd been stripped to the waist so that the figure in a red hood which completely covered his head and face, save for two eye holes, had access to his bare chest and stomach.

Methodically, the hooded figure touched the man's exposed skin with the end of an electric cable – this thick, black wire was plugged into a control box that would deliver a painful jolt, but not a lethal, heart-stopping shock. Blue fire arced from the exposed copper strands at the end of the cable; the bolt of electricity plunged into the man's flesh with a loud *CRACK*! The victim convulsed. A piercing scream erupted from his lips, his knees sagged and the nylon cord dug into his wrists. The man's jaw dropped open in a slack way, as if he was surprised by the pain of the electric shock.

The torturer in the red hood poured a bottle of water over his victim's head to revive him somewhat before the next round of punishment. The man was dazed. He extended his tongue to lick at the dribbles of water running down past his mouth. His thirst burned his throat. He needed that water. That cold liquid tasted so good.

The torturer grasped the black cable and applied its tip to the man's roving, pink tongue. CRACK! A flash of blue fire. Smoke pouring from the tongue smelt the same as overcooked bacon. The man jerked his head back so violently that he smacked his skull against the brickwork. His expression of agony intensified. Blood streamed from the cut in his scalp. Crimson flooded down his neck, over his shoulders and chest. Those shoulders began to heave as he sobbed.

A second man stepped from the shadows to the camcorder mounted on a tripod. He zoomed in on the man's suffering face. Tears glinted in the basement lights. Blood painted crimson stripes down his chest. Here was a man who couldn't take any more pain. He'd reached his limits. Shaking, sobbing, bleeding, he began to choke out words. A blister had formed on the tip of his tongue. The electric shock also caused it to swell, making speech difficult.

However, he desperately needed to talk in order to stop them inflicting any more pain. 'I haven't got it any more. The coke's safe . . . I didn't give it to the police. I haven't told anyone about you. I'm sorry . . . It's just a misunderstanding, OK?'

The hooded man moved the end of the cable until it was just a couple of inches from the tip of his victim's nose.

The man, tied to the wall, shuddered, anticipating the agonizing heat of electricity if the live copper strands should touch his nose. 'There's no need to hurt me any more. I'll tell you what you want to know. Anything.'

The man who operated the video camera extended his hand in a gesture that invited the torture victim to speak.

'It's all there. I haven't used any of the coke . . . I haven't sold so much as a gram.' The man took a deep breath. 'I persuaded my girlfriend's son to keep it for me. His name's Darrington . . . Ben Darrington. Have you got that? Ben Darrington. He's staying with his father in Devon. I don't know exactly where, though. You've got to take my word for that. I don't know the address.'

The torturer didn't take his victim's word. He pressed the exposed copper wires to the man's chest.

Once . . . twice . . . three times . . . three blue flashes filled the basement with light. The screams were so loud that they seemed to penetrate the bricks in the walls and pierce the dirt to the ends of the Earth.

Sixteen

The scanner hummed as it photographed precisely one hundred fragments of papyrus. The ancient documents that had been consigned to the Gold Tomb three thousand years ago had been torn into pieces that were no larger than postage stamps. Most of the fragments bore markings in ink. These would be the hieroglyphs that the Egyptian scribes had written on the papyrus, an early form of paper made from reeds harvested from the banks of the Nile.

John placed the fragments of papyrus between sheets of glass to hold them still. After that, he laid this glass sandwich on the scanner and repeated the process, photographing the shreds of ancient paper. The computer program ran as he carried out this task, automatically piecing fragments together wherever it could – an electronic jigsaw wizard tirelessly and expertly working to produce virtual copies of entire documents.

John managed to keep his mind on his work. Though, in truth, he repeatedly recalled what had happened last night when he'd woken up to find Oliver standing there in the bedroom with such a strange expression on his face. The boy had then flaked out, losing consciousness for a worrying dozen seconds or so. He and Ingrid had put him on the bed where he soon woke up – but those twelve seconds had been long ones. Both he and his wife had been incredibly worried. John had picked up the phone ready to call an ambulance. However, within a minute, Oliver seemed almost back to normal. OK, he was confused for a while, and appeared to be muddling a dream he'd had with reality. He'd kept saying, '*I saw it walk into the house. It was in here with you. I stopped it hurting you, Mum. I stopped it. I really did. Smell the air. You can smell that the mummy was in here with you.*'

Just for an instant, he thought he'd caught a musty smell of something old. But when he'd inhaled again he could smell the lavender growing outside in the garden. The odour of dust couldn't have been there after all. Oliver was sweaty, dishevelled. Ingrid interpreted this as the boy coming down with a fever and concluded he had been tossing and turning in bed. She gave him paracetamol, washed down with a drink of water.

Later, as John had tucked his son back into bed, Oliver had murmured, '*I didn't dream it, Dad, I didn't . . . The mummy was here in the house. He wore a metal band around his head.*'

John checked the computer screen. The expensive software worked its magic. Already the computer had connected images of the papyrus fragments together. There were still thousands of pieces to go. This was a start, though, and a promising start at that. In some cases, five or six fragments had been joined together, enabling John to make out lines of hieroglyphs, that archaic writing of the Egyptians formed from pictures of snakes, dogs, temple flags, and seated men, along with lines, circles and other symbols.

He glanced at his phone, tempted to call Ingrid to find out how Oliver was. When he'd left this morning Oliver had been in a deep sleep. He hadn't woken his son. After all, as the saying goes, sleep is the best medicine. John had rested his palm against the sleeping boy's forehead. The skin felt warm rather than hot, so perhaps the fever had begun to ease off. Oliver had probably picked up some bug or other. Even so, he wondered if they should visit a doctor to have him checked out. Once he'd heard someone jokingly say that an anagram of 'parent' is 'I'm always worried'. It was one of those nonsensical jokes that all parents could identify with, and it carried a generous portion of truth. *We are always worried*, he thought. *We worry when our children go to school for the first time. We worry when they look unwell, or are troubled by some secret problem or other.* John resisted the urge to call Ingrid just yet. He'd wait until lunchtime. Of course, she'd be keeping a close eye on Oliver. If there were any indications he was becoming ill she'd call him immediately.

Returning to the computer, he emailed images of the reassembled papyrus fragments to a hiero-glyphs expert for translation. It was important at this stage to make sure that the computer software hadn't randomly connected pieces of the docu-ment. The purpose of this task was to repair the damaged documents in order for linguistic experts to read what was written there and to translate ancient Egyptian into English. These examples would serve as a useful test.

After he'd hit 'send' he went to grab a coffee

before starting on the next batch of papyrus confetti (because that's what the mess of scraps resembled).

Samantha stood by the coffee machine, sipping from a mug. 'Bloody mummies,' she said.

'I beg your pardon?'

'I slept like I'd entered the land of the dead myself last night. But all I did was dream that one of our bandaged brethren walked to and fro past the house.' She shuddered. 'I'm sure one night I'll look out and see the whole bloody lot standing there – our entire mummy family will come to visit me. I tell you, if the salary wasn't so damn good here, I'd pack my suitcase and go back to Oxford.'

Ben received a text on his phone. He touched the screen and read what was written there.

Hey! I need that stuff I gave you to keep for me. URGENT! URGENT! Text me your address. I'll collect it from you today.

The text was from Micky Dunt, his mother's boyfriend. Ben hated the man. Micky Dunt was a low-life thug. He'd only been released from prison a few months ago after serving ten weeks for assaulting a train conductor. Micky had tried riding the train for free. What Ben's mother saw in the guy he couldn't even begin to understand.

Ben thought: *No way is Micky coming to this house to spoil what I've got here. I like the Tolworth family. They've been kind to me. Bringing Micky here would be like bringing a plague rat into the house.* Deleting the text, Ben switched off the phone and lay back on the bed. 'Get stuffed, Micky,' he said out loud. 'You're not going to ruin my life the way you ruin Mum's.'

The first tantalizing fragments of translation arrived. John called Samantha from the laboratory where she'd been examining X-rays of Amber, the mummy of the teenage girl.

'I knew you'd be keen to see this,' John told her. 'Grab a chair by the computer and I'll show you what we have so far.'

Samantha grinned with excitement. 'Names? Confirmation that we have a mummy king in our castle? The story of how a family ended up in the tomb with no names?'

John chuckled, amused by her unbridled enthusiasm. 'Hold your horses, girl. All I did was send random samples of text that the software put together. This is going to be a Humpty-Dumpty of a job.'

They sat down at the computer. John clicked on a file, bringing up images of hieroglyphs. Beneath the ancient text were lines of print in English, the expert's translation.

John scrolled down through the file. 'This is rough and ready, warts and all. What we have here is basically a test-run to prove that the software isn't randomly connecting all those little bits of papyrus and producing a jumble of text that the translator can't make head nor tail of.'

'You're telling me that the text is gibberish?'

'On the contrary, we're getting some terrific results with the first batch of samples.' He smiled at her, pleased that his hard work hadn't been for nothing. 'The software has correctly matched up a lot of torn documents. The hieroglyphs on the restored papyrus – albeit in virtual form – do make sense. Look.' He pointed at the screen. 'This section of hieroglyphs appears to be part of a letter; it says, *I am travelling from the land of mountains to . . .* something, something, that part's missing. *Soon my head will lie upon your breast so that I might hear the drumbeat of your heart. This will be of great pleasure to me.*'

'A love letter home. How delightful.' Samantha's eyes sparkled.

'There are more fragments that talk about the length of a journey in days, and about sailing along the Nile. There is also a list of foodstuffs, such as bags of grain, onions, honey, spices, wine, dried fruit.'

'Provisions for a journey?'

'They might be. Either the library found in the Gold Tomb focuses on travel, or by sheer chance I've scanned in the fragments of a smaller body of work devoted to this particular letter writer's adventures abroad.'

'Time will tell when you've pieced together more of the text. Any names yet?'

'No names. But I haven't checked a second batch of translation yet. I knew you'd want to see for yourself that the software was working.'

'Thank you, John.' She smiled, pleased. 'That's most considerate. In fact, I was like a kid the day before Christmas this morning, knowing we should get some results today.'

'I'll read through the rest of the translation now

and give you a shout if there's anything of interest.'

'Oh, John, you know you shouldn't keep an eager girl waiting.' She gave one of her sexy winks. 'Show me all you've got . . . now. Please? Squeezie pleazie?'

He laughed. 'I wonder what the Egyptian hieroglyphs are for "squeezie pleazie"? OK, we can take a look.'

'Together? Reading translated glyphs side-by-side is so intimate, don't you think?'

Just flirting, he wondered, *or is she really sending out signals?* Not sure what to think, he clicked on the second file. 'Ah,' he murmured. 'This is a translation of the biggest chunk of papyrus that the computer's been able to reassemble so far.' He scrolled down the symbols that had been pieced together by the software until he reached a note from the translator. 'This is a preliminary translation of the letter.'

Samantha frowned. 'Another letter written in hieroglyphs?'

'Shouldn't it be?'

'No. Excuse me if this sounds patronizing, John, because I don't know how much you know about ancient Egyptian written records.'

'I know hardly anything. I'm the techie side of things.' He patted the scanner.

'Hieroglyphs were a type of writing used for formal declarations, laws, sacred books; they were painted on to tomb walls, etched into temples and statues. Someone writing a letter three thousand years ago wouldn't use cumbersome hieroglyphs, they'd write the message in a simpler form called Demotic. This was more like writing as we'd understand it.'

John shrugged, not sure what she was driving at. 'This letter on-screen was written in hieroglyphs.'

'Which suggests it isn't the actual letter that was sent from person A to recipient B. Instead, someone was making a copy of letters using formal text. This correspondence was intended to be preserved for all eternity in a tomb. These letters were so important that someone – perhaps the very people in the tomb – decided that the letters should accompany them into the afterlife.'

'If they're so important,' he began, 'then let's see what information they wanted to preserve forever.'

Samantha leaned forward. He could hear her respiration and feel the light tickling sensation of her breath against his face as she read what was on-screen – and what she saw made her glance sideways at John in astonishment.

John read the translation of the ancient letter himself. He soon realized that someone had sent a heartfelt warning to an individual who faced extreme danger, only they hadn't realized it yet. John read the warning for a second time, which was presented in a form that was almost poetic as it was ominous.

My friend, my brother,
You who travelled to the Western horizon in search of me when I was lost in the great sea of dust. You who saved my life when all considered me beyond reach. Pay heed. Beware, my friend, enemies are

moving ever closer to you. Beware. Make ready your weapons. Sharpen your arrows, restring your bow. The cruellest of enemies approach. They are like lions in the night that will tear a child from the arms of its sleeping mother. They are like a scorpion in your bed. They are as savage as the demon in its cave. Beware, my trusted and loyal friend. Be ready to fight for the lives of your wife, your sons, your daughter. Your enemy longs to feast on vengeance as the glutton feasts on meat. You will—

John said, 'According to the translator, the rest of the letter is still missing.'

'Even so . . . that's one heck of a warning. Whoever the letter was meant for certainly would have realized that the bad guys were coming and he should get ready to protect his family.'

'And for some reason the warning letter was copied on to papyrus then put in the tomb for safe keeping.'

'That was the intention, but it didn't work out that way. The letters weren't safe, were they? Otherwise you wouldn't be putting them together again.'

John gazed at the screen and shivered. Had the breeze coming through the window turned colder, or was it because he'd read the letter containing that ominous warning? In his mind's eye, he saw the Egyptian reading the recently-arrived letter then rushing to a doorway all those centuries ago to stare out at the desert, expecting to see 'the enemy' approaching his home. The family in the tomb: were they victims of 'the enemy'? Hadn't the man's bow and arrows been enough to save them?

A cold tingling ran across his body. Icy fingers reaching out from the grave to caress his skin? A touch of death? A morbid notion to be sure, yet it remained with him as, once again, he read the line: *'Beware, my friend, enemies are moving ever closer to you.'*

That afternoon Ben Darrington sat on a chair on the patio. He made sure he stayed in the shade, otherwise the heat irritated the skin under the cast that ran the full length of his leg. His younger brother (*Funny thinking the words 'younger brother'*, he thought) had stayed in bed all day. He'd have liked to chat with Oliver, but stairs were as formidable as Mount Everest with this cast on. Ingrid had assured Ben that Oliver had only picked up a bug, as likely as not one of these twenty-four-hour things, and that he'd feel a lot better soon. His teenage sister (*Hey! I have a sister!*) was smooching with the seventeen-year-old boy next door. Ben had glimpsed them laughing and exchanging kisses as she sat on the rope swing beneath the big oak tree. Ben still marvelled that he had a brother and sister; OK, half-brother, half-sister. He'd always believed he was an only child until a couple of days ago. His mother had told him nothing about his father. His mother tended not to talk about families, or cherish stability. He'd grown up admiring her as some kind of rebel, who lived by her own rules. A free spirit. One of life's natural-born adventurers.

That's before he'd discovered that she had an insatiable appetite for drugs. Yeah, he'd smoked cannabis. He'd eaten magic mushrooms (and hallucinated that his shoes had turned into crocodiles). His mother, however, loved cocaine. He thought about the plastic container in his bag that held what must be fifty grand's worth of coke, and wondered if it had been destined for her own consumption – that amount of cocaine would burn her two nostrils into one big, ugly mono nostril.

He squeezed that unpleasant image of disfigurement from his mind and allowed his gaze to settle on a rabbit that had hopped from under a bush on to the lawn to nibble a dandelion leaf. *This is a good place*, he told himself. *I'm unlucky enough to break my leg, and then I'm lucky enough to end up here with such a nice family.*

He listened to birds singing in the trees. A pair of yellow butterflies performed a delicate dance around each other as they flew across the flower beds. *Yup, the Garden of Eden*, he told himself. The e-book that he was reading on his phone drew him back into the story. Survivors in a jungle adventure were being pursued by a Zeppelin airship that fired machine guns at the hero . . . His phone made a chug-chug sound. He exited the e-book to see an ID pic of Nat Silvers, who was on the same course as him at uni.

He answered brightly: 'Nat! How's it swinging?'

'Swings good, amigo. How goes it with the leg?'

'Not too bad . . . Having said that, it feels like ants are feeding on the bone where it's broken, but they say it prickles like that when the bits of bone are fusing back together.'

'Uh, sounds unpleasant.'

'Doing anything good today? In fact, doing *anyone* today?'

'I live in hope. Hey, Ben, I don't want to worry you . . . but . . .'

'Now you are worrying me.'

'Something weird happened today. That guy your mother knows came to the house. He wanted to go into your room.'

'Did you let him?'

'Heck, no. I know you hate the guy. I told him that you weren't living there any more and had given the key back to the landlord, which is the truth, isn't it?'

'Sure is, Nat.' Ben felt a stab of anger. Why was his mother's boyfriend wanting to get into his old room at the student house? Ben didn't trust Micky Dunt one little bit.

'Ben, I don't like to bother you with something like this, what with your leg, but this guy wanted to know where you're staying in Devon.'

Ben pictured the plastic box full of cocaine in his bag. He should never have agreed to keep it for Micky, but Ben's mother had got all tearful when he said he wouldn't. *Damn it, I should have said no. I could be in trouble if the police find out.* Of course, he'd kept the existence of the drugs a secret. He hadn't even confided in Nat, who was one of his best friends.

Ben said, 'Did Katy give you the address of my dad's place down here?'

'No. It's probably a good thing, too.'

'Why's that?'

'This guy turned nasty – I mean, totally nasty – when I told him I didn't know where you were staying. He started pushing me back down the hallway, like he was thinking about beating the address out of me.'

'Jesus Christ, Nat, he didn't hit you, did he?'

'No, but, man, he was blazing angry.'

'Micky's a thug. He spent time in jail this year for attacking someone.'

'He looks the sort. A real knuckle-dragging cave man.'

'You can say that again.'

Nat's voice became more thoughtful. 'There was something odd, though.'

'Odd? How?'

'After I told him that I didn't have your address, he yelled at me, like I'd stolen his life savings or something. The more he yelled the more I got the impression he was scared . . . in fact, terrified. Before long he was begging me for your address, like he's desperate to find you.'

'He's probably made my mother angry and wants to use me to get round her; you know, put a good word in.'

'Do you want me to pass on your address if he comes back?'

'Heck no. Micky is hell on earth waiting to happen. I don't want to even set eyes on the bastard.'

'After seeing him today, I feel the same way.'

'You should call the police. Tell him he threatened you.'

Nat paused for a second. 'Hmm, no. I'm going

209

up to my grandparents' place in Scotland tomorrow. I'll be away for three weeks. If he comes back here, there'll be no one home.'

'Cheers, Nat. Thanks for letting me know about Micky.'

'Oh, just one more thing. Micky must have made someone mad.'

'How so?'

'Someone's beaten the crap out of him; his face was all bruised. There were blisters, too, like he'd been burnt with a cigarette lighter or something.'

'I'm sure he deserved what he got,' Ben said and meant it.

'OK, I'd best go and pack for Bonnie Wee Scotland. See you soon, Ben; take care of the leg, drink lots of cider, limp after some girls.'

'Yeah, I'll do plenty of that. See you soon, Nat.'

'Ciao, Ben.'

Ben sat there thanking his lucky stars that Micky hadn't got hold of this address. The last thing he wanted to see was that slug's repellent face here in Devon.

John hurried home after work to check on Oliver. He found Ingrid sitting with the boy in his bedroom. Oliver answered when John asked him how he was feeling. He still seemed tired, however; his face was flushed, and he had an air of being preoccupied with something that worried him.

Ingrid tried to reassure John. 'He does seem much better. He's had plenty of fluids, and about twenty minutes ago he ate a sandwich.'

'I'm sure he's on the mend.' John cheerfully ruffled the boy's hair. 'You'll be back to normal

210

tomorrow. But if you're still feeling under the weather we'll have a trip to the doctor's; that sound good to you, Oliver?'

Oliver nodded. His face remained expressionless, which made John a little uneasy.

John asked, 'You've no aches or pains? You don't feel sick?'

Oliver shook his head. 'Something happened last night. I can't remember what it was. It did, but I don't know what.' He lay down on the bed to stare up at the ceiling.

He can't remember what happened? John now remembered what had happened in the castle thirty years ago. The night that Philip lost his hand in a terrible accident. John had suppressed the memory of his friend's bloody wrist. *Is Oliver suppressing a memory, too?*

Ben Darrington was reading his e-book in the garden, so he was already holding the phone when the call came through. He checked the screen. *Micky calling.*

'No way,' Ben grunted. 'I'm not taking a call from you, you low-life bastard.'

He ignored the call, leaving Micky to be directed to voicemail. At least the creep didn't know where Ben was staying. Ben intended to keep it that way. There wasn't a chance in hell he'd tell Micky where he was staying. In fact, Micky Dunt could go to hell as far as he was concerned.

Ben went back to reading his book. The sun had moved across the sky, and the shadow from the tree no longer gave him shade, but Ben hadn't bothered to move his chair. The heat felt good on his face. He relished its power. Ever since he'd broken his leg he'd either been cooped up in hospital or had been lying in that gloomy back room in the Tolworths' house. Being outdoors in the sunshine felt like being liberated from a prison cell.

More calls had come through from Micky Dunt. He ignored them all. He'd even covered the screen with his hand so he couldn't see the caller photograph. That was one photo and contact he'd delete. *In fact*, he thought, *this is the perfect time.* He picked up the phone from the patio table at the same moment another call came through. He saw his mother's photo appear on-screen. For a moment, he thought of not answering. But his mother was in Thailand. What if she was in trouble and needed him? He took the call.

'Hello,' he said, wondering if there was a problem; after all, it must be the middle of the night in Thailand. 'You OK?'

'Hello, Ben,' said his mother. 'It's lovely to hear your voice. How's your leg?'

'On the mend. Isn't it late over there? I mean, after midnight or something?'

'That doesn't matter. I just wanted to give you a call.'

'Is there something wrong?'

'No, no, everything's alright here. It's hot, though. Like a sauna. Like . . . phew!'

Ben heard her voice slurring. Drink? Drugs? Both? Crap. Yes, both. He knew his mother's habits only too well. 'Are you sure nothing's wrong? You've got a hotel for the night, haven't you? You're not having to sleep outside?'

'No. Don't worry about me, sweetheart. I'm stopping with friends.'

'You have friends out there? In Thailand?'

'I'm fine, baby. They took me to a banquet tonight. Fish on skewers, all kinds of things . . . but . . . that's by the by. It's Micky.'

'Uh . . . I thought you'd mention him.'

'I'm fond of Micky.'

'He's a bastard. He hits you.'

'That's all in the past, Ben. Listen. Micky's worried. He doesn't know where you are.'

'I'm stopping with my father and his family.' *Best not tell my mother where I am*, he told himself. *She'll only tittle-tattle to Micky.* 'They're looking after me while my leg heals.' He brushed away a fly that scurried up the cast.

'Oh? John Tolworth? That's lovely, really lovely, Ben, I'm pleased.' Again, slurring. 'Micky wants to visit you.'

'I bet he does.'

His mother kept her voice sweetly pleasant. 'You've got something of Micky's. You know the – the *thing* that he asked you to keep safe.'

'Get to the point, Mother. You mean, Micky wants his drugs back.'

'Yes, he needs them, like, *now.*'

'He'll get them back in a few weeks when I can move round again on my legs.'

'No, Ben. This is important. He needs the *thing* now.'

'Thing! Drugs. Coke. Nose candy. That's what you're referring to.'

'Don't use those words. Stick with *thing*, OK?' She sounded breathless, like she was scared all

213

of a sudden. 'You don't know who might be listening.'

'Like the police?'

'Ben, this is important. Tell me where you're staying. Micky will pick up the thing you're keeping for him.'

'No way. I'm not telling Micky where I am. I won't tell you, either.'

'Please, Ben. You don't know what's happened.'

'I know that Micky steals from you, and he's stolen money from me. If you hadn't burst into tears when I said I wouldn't hide the drugs for him, I'd have told the bastard to piss off.'

'Ben. Oh, please, Ben. Micky's in trouble. The coke isn't his. There are people who want the drugs back. They're ever such bad people, do you understand? They've hurt poor Micky. If he doesn't give the coke back to them they're going to kill him. I know they will. They've tortured and murdered before. Tell Micky your address, or he'll end up dead, and – and I don't want him to die.' She began sobbing.

Ben listened with a mixture of horror and disgust. How had his mother wound up with such a loser as Micky Dunt?

'Please, Ben. Give him the coke back. If you don't, they'll kill poor Micky. Tell me your address . . . you've got to, baby. Please—'

Ben couldn't take any more and ended the call. He sat there, feeling so upset by his mother's pleading that he felt sick. But this time, he resolved not to let his mother's tears make him do something stupid; he wouldn't tell Micky his address. It might put the Tolworths – his new family – in danger, not to mention himself.

'Ben, you shouldn't sit in the sun for too long. You might make yourself ill.'

Ben swivelled his head to see John Tolworth emerging from the house. Ben's nerves were in shreds. He hated the fact that his mother was distressed, but – *Christ!* – he wasn't going to help Micky-shithead-Dunt.

John said, 'I could help you into the shade.'

'I'm alright here.'

'The sun's strong today. I thought—'

'Don't give me orders! Damn well stop telling me what to fucking do! OK?'

'OK.' John physically recoiled from Ben's yell. 'Only trying to help out, Ben.'

'I'm nineteen. I know what I'm doing. If I want to sit in the fucking sun, I will!'

'OK.'

'So don't you ever – ever! – give me orders!' Abruptly, Ben stopped shouting. He closed his eyes, took a deep breath, and realized he was shaking.

John said, 'I'll leave you in peace.' He walked across the patio in the direction of the house.

Ben called out, 'John, I'm sorry.'

John stopped and turned to face Ben.

Ben shook his head, feeling angry with himself. 'Sorry. I had a call from my mother. Well . . . you know . . . not good. When I talk to my mother it's always the same. Difficult.' Ben realized he wasn't expressing himself clearly, but his mother had that effect on him. She got him so tensed up, he wanted to punch something, yell, spit in Satan's eye – anything to release the unbearable

215

tension that hurt every muscle in his body. *Now I've blown it with John. I swore at him. He'll tell me to leave.*

John, however, didn't storm back to the house. He walked across the patio and sat on a low wall beside Ben. 'If it helps,' John said with a heartfelt note of sympathy, 'Carol, your mother, made me feel the same way. It was a long time ago, of course. I was young, and I loved your mother. I cared about her. The trouble was, she did things in her life that frightened me.'

'Drugs?'

John nodded. 'I tried talking to her, because I genuinely thought the world of her. But I didn't seem to be able to make Carol see how much I cared, or how worried I was, because she was putting that poison into her body. Whenever I tried to raise the subject of drugs she either wouldn't listen, or got angry.'

Ben sighed. 'You know, it could be me saying the same thing. I care about my mother. But what she does . . . taking drugs, boozing at nine in the morning . . . it frightens me. It scared me back when I was kid, and she'd be off her head when I came in from school.' He grunted with the pain of remembering. 'One Christmas morning I woke up so excited that the day had finally come. I'd have been ten or eleven. I went downstairs and found that my presents had been unwrapped and left by the back door. Of course, this mystified me, so I went up to my mother's bedroom. She lay in bed with a man I'd never seen before. I couldn't wake her. She'd vomited down herself. The guy woke up, got dressed, went downstairs, and began stuffing my presents back into the Santa sack. I stood there, just five feet from him, watching him do it. I mean, what could I do to stop him? I was a kid. The guy left the house with my presents and never came back, but there were others just like him. Now my mother's in Thailand. I think she's there because her boyfriend, a thug called Micky Dunt, has made her go. It's something to do with drugs, I know it is. He's probably using my mother as a drugs mule, and . . . and . . . when she calls I get so uptight, so wound up, I can't speak to her for more than thirty seconds without wanting to scream at her. Why has she fallen for a loser like that? Why won't she wake up and realize that I care about what happens to her? And what if the police catch her when . . .? Uh . . . sorry. I can't . . . Damn, damn, damn.'

Ben closed his eyes again, feeling himself tremble so violently that his body seemed in danger of shaking itself to pieces. An arm went around his shoulders. Suddenly, he felt a powerful hug. The sensation bewildered him. He remembered the rare occasions he'd visited his mother's father: his grandad used to hug him like this. Ben took a deep breath. When he opened his eyes John had sat back on the wall again.

John spoke gently. 'Ben, if you want to talk about your mother to me, then we'll talk. If you don't want to talk about her, that's fine, too. I'm here though. I'll listen.'

Ben didn't know what to say or do next. For a full minute, he sat knowing he should say something. John's care . . . his compassion . . . had left Ben floundering. Knowing he should do

217

something, he held out his hand. Smiling, John shook it.

'Thanks,' Ben said. Then a moment later added, 'Thanks . . . Dad.'

Micky Dunt pulled on a pair of latex gloves in the back yard. After that, he gained entry to the student house where Ben Darrington had rented a room by squirming through the kitchen window, which had been left open. Micky would have preferred to leave this particular bit of housebreaking until after dark, but the guy who owned the cocaine that was, theoretically, still in Micky's possession wanted his drugs back. *And one guy you don't mess with is Karl Gurrick,* Micky told himself with a shudder. *Gurrick, king of the local mobsters. Even the police don't tangle with Gurrick.*

Micky stood absolutely still in the kitchen. He could smell bacon that had been cooked here earlier. The frying pan stood on the hob; fat from the bacon had begun to solidify and turn white as it cooled. This, and the fact Micky could hear the sound of a TV, proved to him that one or more people were still in the house. *Another one of those bratty students?* Micky wondered. *A bratty student like Ben Darrington?* He loathed Ben, only tolerating him because he was screwing the kid's mother.

As Micky stood there, listening for signs of movement in the house – especially sounds that would suggest someone was heading in the direction of the kitchen – he saw his reflection in the glass panes of a wall cupboard. Bruises, his face was dappled with them. Even worse were the

218

burn marks from the electric cable that had been used to torture him. The circumstances that led to his body getting blistered to hell and back by that sadist in the cellar infuriated Micky Dunt. It should have been so easy, right? But, no, it wasn't – the plan had all gone to shit. It started off well. Micky had cut a deal with Gurrick. Gurrick had paid upfront for two kilos of coke. Micky, along with Carol Darrington, had taken the ferry to Rotterdam, contacted the dealer, bought the two kilos of coke, then they'd smuggled it back through customs at Hull. The problem was that the police had started taking an interest in Micky. They'd searched his house when he'd been away in Rotterdam. So, what to do? What to do? Micky couldn't keep the drugs at his house, because the cops were likely to come busting their way in again (Micky was well known to the police; he'd got convictions for drug-dealing in the past). So, Micky had come up with the simple solution. He'd persuaded Ben Darrington – with a little help from Carol – to stash the drugs for a few hours until Micky could arrange a meet-up with Gurrick. But then the stupid kid had broken his leg. Before Micky could retrieve the stash from Ben, the kid had vanished. All he knew was that Ben had gone to stay with his father. The big problem was that nobody knew exactly where Ben Darrington was staying.

The even BIGGER problem was that Karl Gurrick suspected that Micky had pulled a scam. That is, Micky had persuaded Gurrick to hand over a heap of cash for drugs that didn't exist – or did exist, but Micky had lied about not being able to pass them on to Gurrick. The mobster was furious. He punished his drug mules who didn't deliver, or who tried to cheat him by pretending they had to dump the coke, or heroin, or whatever they were carrying, because the police were chasing them. Gurrick hurt anyone who cheated him, or failed to do their job to his satisfaction. The guy was a tyrant. He enjoyed burning bare flesh with a live cable. Micky could vouch that burns caused by electricity were agonizing.

He ran his blistered tongue over his lips and flinched at the pain. There'd be more torture to come if he didn't get that coke delivered to Gurrick soon. So, time to find out where the kid was staying and grab the coke. Micky would also deliver some torture of his own on Ben Darrington's body. Ben had jerked Micky around – made life more difficult for him. If Ben had given his address when Micky had phoned him, then he wouldn't be risking jail by breaking into this house.

Micky moved as quietly as he could. He left the kitchen and found himself in a big hallway. Typical student accommodation, scuffed paint-work on the walls from bikes being leant against them. In fact, there were a couple of bikes standing against the wall at the far end. A noticeboard by the front door displayed leaflets for music gigs, bike repairs, takeaway menus, bus timetables. How considerate of those bloody students to tell each other where they could get their crappy bikes repaired or buy the cheapest pizza.

Micky growled with anger. Students! Ben Darrington thought he was so superior to Micky. The kid looked down his nose at him. 'Well, I'm boning your mad bitch of a mother,' Micky grunted.

The sound of the TV grew louder. Audience laughter, bright and bouncy music. A game show, probably. Micky's plan was simple: break into Ben's room (because he suspected the other student had lied to him when he said that Ben didn't live here any longer). With luck, Micky would find the address where Ben was staying. 'I'll show the bastard what torture is,' he snarled. A blister on his tongue burst, flooding his mouth with a vile taste.

Just then, a door opened in front of him. Micky darted to the wall, pressing his back against it. He'd expected to see a young kid emerge from the room, one of the students that lived here in their poxy rooms. But what Micky saw was a man of around sixty with lots of white hair tied into a ponytail. The guy had turned right when he'd exited the room; he faced away from where Micky pressed himself against the wall, so he hadn't seen the intruder.

Micky remembered the searing pain of electricity blazing from the end of the cable into his skin. The smell of burning. The convulsions. The sheer mind-blowing agony. Gurrick would do that again to Micky if he didn't deliver the coke. Hell, the sadist would torture him in many other inventive ways, too. Micky's predicament was desperate. He'd have to do whatever it took to find Ben's address, otherwise the consequences would be unthinkable. Micky padded up behind the man, grabbed him by the white hair, and smashed his head against the wall. He pounded the guy's skull against the brickwork again and again. When the body went limp he allowed the man to drop to the floor. *Good, out cold.* Micky's instinct told him to check his victim's room first. You never know, there might be someone else in there who needed taking care of.

Sure enough, there was a game show on television. Luckily, there was no one else in the room. Micky noticed a desk with a computer. There were charts on the wall with a list of rooms that either had the words 'let' or 'not let' beside them. Ah, so Micky had clobbered the landlord. He quickly checked a cork board on which were pinned notes, picture postcards, unpaid bills, and a list of students boycotted by other landlords for not paying their rent or smashing up their rooms.

Then . . . BINGO! A square of paper had the name '*Ben Darrington*' printed neatly across the top. Below that was this message: '*Mr Oates. If you need to contact Ben he's stopping with his dad throughout August.*' An address in Devon followed.

Groans sounded from the hall. Mr Oates was waking up. Micky checked the drawers in the desk. He found a wallet containing cash; the wallet went into Micky's pocket. Then he left the room, pausing only to stamp on Mr Oates' head.

He had the address. His spirits were rising. He'd get those drugs back, and Gurrick would be pleased with him. There'd be no more torture. In fact, Gurrick might be so pleased that he'd invite Micky to join his gang of mobsters. There'd be a chance of earning some big money, at last, being part of a drugs cartel.

The thug grunted with satisfaction. 'Watch out, Ben. I'm coming to get you.'

'I'm going insane!'

John Tolworth glanced up as the woman strode into the lab where he'd been carefully placing shreds of papyrus on to a sheet of glass. 'Good morning, Samantha,' he said. 'Have the CAT scan people turned you down again?'

'No – worse! Far worse!'

'Oh?' He put another sheet of glass over the papyrus fragments to hold them in place. 'So you're insane,' he said cheerfully, in an attempt to raise a smile on that worried face of hers. 'Are you going to tell me what drove you insane, or are you going to keep me in suspense?'

'The mummies!'

'You've not been dreaming about them walking past your house again?'

'No, worse. This is real life.' She held out a bare wrist that extended from beneath her blouse sleeve. 'Pinch me, John. Give me a good, hard nip.'

'You're not turning into a masochist, too?'

'Nope. I just wanted to check that I wasn't dreaming.'

He gave the back of her wrist a gentle nip. 'Are you awake? Or am I in your dreams?'

'I wish. Well, I'm awake and haven't dreamt the weird thing that's happened to me.'

'So, what's wrong?'

Samantha folded her arms and scowled. 'Am I, or am I not, an osteoarchaeologist?'

'A bone expert? Yes, unless you forged your credentials.'

'My God, I worked so bloody hard for my qualifications. I can name every bone in the human body. Give me a femur and I can identify the anchor points for muscles and tendons. Put a human skull into my hand, and I will give you the person's age at death, their sex, their lifestyle. I can read teeth like you read a book. And now this happens.'

'What happens?'

'Oh, heck, better to show than tell. Wait, I'll be right back.'

John watched Samantha stride out of the room – she looked like a beautiful blond huntress in pursuit of prey. Her body language radiated ferocity and purpose. Still puzzled by her outburst, he picked up the papyrus fragments, in their sandwich of glass panes, and put them on the bed of the scanner. He double checked that the hieroglyphs on the scraps of ancient paper faced downwards. Satisfied, he closed the lid of the scanner, returned to his computer and initiated the scan. Through the castle window he saw Oliver and Fletcher. They were flying a kite on the meadow that stretched between here and the gatehouse. John was pleased that Oliver seemed to have recovered from the fainting fit a couple of nights ago. Ingrid was right after all; Oliver must have picked up one of these twenty-four-hour bugs. The boy seemed perfectly fine now. He watched as his son laughed when the kite plunged from the sky, nearly hitting Fletcher on the head. John laughed too, taking pleasure from the fact that Oliver was enjoying himself. Come to think of it, all his family were in a good mood. John now automatically included Ben as part of the family. He liked Ben a lot. *That's a hell of thing, isn't it?* John told himself. *A son I've never met before arrives just days ago and already I feel as if I've known him all my life. There must be something in that saying about 'blood being thicker than water'. Ben is my son, and it feels right to call him my son.* John sincerely hoped that Ben would stay in touch when his leg had healed and he was back at university. John wanted to be Ben's father. He wanted shared times together. Maybe holidays, birthdays, and to be there in the audience when Ben graduated from university. *OK, that won't be for some time yet, and there will be—*

Samantha's voice crashed into his train of thought: 'John? Can you spare a couple of minutes?'

'Sure, just give me a moment to start running the program on this latest scan.'

'OK, meet me in the mummy chamber in five minutes.'

Samantha wore an odd expression – one of triumph, as if she'd suddenly realized someone had been duping her, but now she'd rumbled their nefarious scheme. *Strange,* he thought. *What on earth has she discovered?* John opened the program and set it to work on the latest scan. Immediately, the scanned images of the jagged pieces of papyrus began a spinning dance on-screen as the software attempted to match up the edges. This was like watching the invisible hands of a jigsaw genius at work. The software analysed the uneven edges, rips, and protrusions of the fragments, then attempted to match up the thousands of scanned pieces. It successfully connected three pieces in less than ten seconds. A hieroglyph symbol representing a wide open eye appeared. The program was working its magic. All being well, he'd be able to email another section of Egyptian document to the translator this morning. They were making headway at last. The library of documents and letters found in the Gold Tomb had, finally, begun to reveal their secrets.

Leaving the program running, he headed to the mummy chamber, wondering just what Samantha had discovered that would have such a powerful effect on the woman.

Samantha stood by the seated mummy, the adult male that had been given the name Kadesh by the conservation team. She brandished a transparent sheet of plastic that was perhaps twelve inches by eighteen inches.

'This is what has sent me insane,' she declared furiously. 'This bloody . . . stupid . . . bewildering X-ray.'

John tried to appear unperturbed by her anger. 'Why? What's wrong with it?'

'Just take a look.' She pushed the top part of the X-ray under a clip on a light box on the wall. 'Tell me what you see.'

'You're the bones expert, Samantha.'

She took a deep breath. 'Humour me, John. Please . . . now, what do you see?'

'OK.' John looked closer. 'The X-ray of the mid-section of a body. Lower ribs, arms, hands, spine, pelvis, hip bones.'

'Hands plural.'

'Yes, I can see arms ending in a right hand and a left hand. Is this an X-ray of one of our mummies?'

'Yup. Do you know which mummy?'

John read what was written at the bottom of the X-ray transparency. 'Kadesh. It can't be.' He turned to look back at the seated mummy. 'You told me that one of Kadesh's hands had been amputated before he died.'

'Yes, I did, didn't I? Because the X-ray I showed you clearly revealed that one of the hands is missing.'

'So when was *this* X-ray taken?'

'Back in 1955.'

John looked again at the mummy sitting on the chair. He could see the left hand clearly enough, because that had been unwrapped. The arm with the missing hand remained heavily bandaged, making the end of the arm appear bulbous; what's more, the ancient Egyptian embalmers had covered the end of the arm with a black substance. It wasn't at all easy to tell, simply by looking at the limb, if there was a hand under there or not. Until the body was X-rayed, archaeologists must have assumed that the mummy possessed two hands. John turned back to the X-ray. 'So which X-ray is the correct one?'

'Both.'

'Don't be ridiculous.'

'I might be going crazy, John, but don't call me ridiculous.' She laughed to make her riposte appear light-hearted, yet there was real tension in her voice. 'We have recent X-rays and CT scans, which clearly show that Mummy Kadesh is missing his right hand. Furthermore, the stump

227

where the hand was severed reveals clear signs of a long period of healing before death took place.'

'Let me get this straight. The 1955 X-ray reveals that Kadesh had two hands. Later X-rays and scans show he only has one?'

'Yes.' The woman was angry as well as mystified. 'How can a three-thousand-year-old corpse simply shed a hand that was wrapped in strips of linen then coated in bitumen? Who could reach through those wrappings –' she pointed at the bulbous end of the arm where the stump was concealed under fabric and thick, black tar – 'and not only reach inside the mummy's bandages, and remove the hand that existed in 1955, but also make it appear as if the bone, where the hand had been severed, had begun to heal?'

'That's not possible.'

'I know. That's why I'm going out of my bloody mind.'

'I'll tell you what it is – it's a bloody mistake.' He smiled. 'Those are old X-rays; the labels will have got mixed up. This one with the two hands must be another mummy.'

'No. The position of the leg bones show that the mummy is in a sitting position. The only mummy sitting down is Kadesh. The others are laid flat.'

'This old X-ray is smaller than recent ones. Perhaps those aren't hand bones and finger bones. Might they be just random marks on the negative?'

'John, give me some credit. I earn my living studying skeletons. Those are hand bones! I can identify individual components of the hand. See?

Those parallel white lines in the image are the metacarpal bones, and the little white dots are the triquetral, lunate and scaphoid, just where they should be near the wrist. All the phalanx bones of the fingers and thumb are intact. In short, the X-ray clearly reveals both a left hand and a right hand.'

John shook his head. 'Samantha, think about what you're saying here. You are claiming that Kadesh is undergoing internal transformations: impossible ones at that.'

'I could prove that Kadesh lacks a right hand today, but it would mean taking a scalpel to the coverings on the stump and cutting away the bitumen and the bandages. It would be like opening up a walnut to see the kernel inside.' She gave a shrill laugh. Tension again. 'Of course, the owners would never allow it. Too destructive.'

'Couldn't the addition of an extra hand in the old X-ray be a practical joke?'

'Who would do that, John? Morcover, why would they do that?'

John shrugged. 'Here's another possibility: the mummies have been lying in the castle for years. Visitors probably stole bits of them for souvenirs.'

'But the stump is encased in a hard shell of bitumen and linen. It would be like stealing the kernel out of the walnut without breaking the shell.'

John shrugged again. 'Where there's a will there's a way.'

'Even if they could extract the hand without damaging its coverings, how could they fake the signs we see on CAT scans of the stump naturally healing when Kadesh here was still alive?'

'There'll be a simple explanation. A prank, or a mistake. Perhaps there was a fault with the CAT scan.'

'A simple explanation, you say?'

'Yes.'

'Then find me a simple explanation for this.' Samantha gently eased back the sheet that covered the mummy called Amber. This was the corpse of the teenage girl.

John looked into that dead face, which seemed so serene. Though whether she was serene at the moment of death was debatable.

Samantha picked up a pencil. 'After I identified the discrepancy between the 1955 X-ray of Kadesh and later X-rays and scans, I took a closer look at our mummy family.' She pointed with the pencil. 'Look here. What do you see?'

John found the process of examining the corpse's head unsettling. He could smell the spicy aroma it gave off. In ancient Egypt, spices were used to mask the odour of death.

'What am I looking for?' he asked.

'There, at the hairline, a small nick in the skin.'

'I see it.'

'It wasn't there before.'

'How can you be sure?'

'John, these mummies have been scanned, mapped, photographed, you name it. There are meticulous records going back decades that describe their physical appearance and their state of preservation.'

'I don't see what you're driving at.'

'That nick in the skin would have been recorded, just like her amber earrings were recorded, and there is a list of every mole, freckle, and mark on the body.'

'Mummified corpses still deteriorate. That split could have happened recently. Decay and nothing more.'

She took a magnifying glass from a drawer. 'Look closer. The cut on the scalp occurred just before death. There are remains of a scab in the cut.'

'You're saying that Amber suffered that wound just hours before she died?'

'Yes. What's more, I'm stating categorically that the cut on the scalp doesn't appear in any photograph or forensic drawing of the head and face.'

'Samantha, you are starting to worry me.'

'I'm worried, too, John.'

'What you are suggesting sounds crazy to me, and it will sound crazy to other people too if you decide to repeat those claims.'

'I'm a scientist. I observe. I am morally and professionally obliged to reveal the truth of my findings.' She nodded at the mummies. 'And what I have discovered is that at some point since 1955, the mummy known as Kadesh has lost a hand, even though the wrappings haven't been disturbed. And, recently, the mummified female called Amber has acquired an injury to her scalp, which must have occurred just a few hours before her death.'

'I'll pretend we never had this conversation, Samantha. Repeat what you've told me to any other member of staff and they'll report you to our bosses. They'll fire you.'

'I repeat, I am a scientist. I'd stake my professional reputation on this fact: the mummies are undergoing a physical transformation. And it's nothing to do with decay. These corpses are acquiring physical characteristics they NEVER had when they were alive.'

The drive to Baverstock Castle in Devon would take four hours, if he didn't stop en route. The address of his destination lay there on the passenger seat. Already, boredom drove Micky Dunt to begin talking to himself. 'I'm coming to get you, Ben Bastard Darrington,' he muttered as he sped along a motorway flanked by fields of corn. 'I'm going to make you suffer for messing me around. Oh yes, suffer you shall, old son.'

Micky had left the car's radio on; he'd already heard news reports of a Mr Jonathon Oates being left in a coma after being attacked in his own house.

'Good. If you're sleeping you ain't talking, Mr Jonathon Oates.' Micky pictured Oates lying in the hospital bed with a tube up his nose, and the *beep . . . beep . . . beep* of monitors. The mental image encouraged Micky to feel even more optimistic. The cops couldn't link Micky to the attack on the guy. 'I wore gloves,' he told his reflection in the rear-view mirror. 'So, no fingerprints. Mr Oates never saw my face, either, before I bashed his bloody head in. Even if he wakes up he can't describe me. Nice one, Micky, you are a genius.' He grinned at the mirror. Straight away, he saw that the blisters on the end of his tongue had filled up with pus again. 'Ack! Like grapes they

232

are . . . like a bunch of green grapes. Pus grapes. Bastard.'

Karl Gurrick had caused those – the sadist had burnt Micky's tongue with an electric cable. He didn't blame Gurrick though; who he really blamed for his injuries was Ben Darrington. If Ben had got one of his student mates to hand back the drugs to Micky when he'd broken his leg then none of this would have happened. Gurrick would have got the drugs he'd paid for. There'd have been none of that torture in the basement. Micky snarled at his reflection in the mirror, 'But no, it's that cretin, Ben Darrington, that got me into trouble with Gurrick. And who wants trouble with a mobster? Ben thinks he's better than me. Always looks down his nose like I'm shit on his shoe.' Micky got angry with his own reflection; this was developing into an argument. He drove even faster as his temper flared, sounding the horn at any other motorist that got in his way. 'Let me tell you, Ben Darrington, you student snob, I'm not some low-life crap. I studied the viola for six years. Six years! Not the violin, mind, but the viola. My mother played flute in an orchestra. Mozart, Mussorgsky, Bach, Wagner – the whole bloody lot. I could have played in an orchestra, too. There I'd be, in a suit and tie, with a viola tucked under my chin, bowing the strings, making music. Ha!' He stabbed his finger at his reflection. 'You didn't think I went to a posh school, did you, Ben Darrington?' And now he really did see Ben's face in the mirror, not his own bruised features. 'I'd got what it takes to be a brilliant viola player, but I didn't want to do what *Mother* told me. I'm a free spirit. I do what I want! OK?' He lashed at the mirror, breaking it.

Micky had got into drugs when he was fourteen. He'd sold his viola and bought enough gear to take him to the freaking Moon and back. Micky laughed. He remembered when he was that shy and polite boy in a school uniform. That had all changed in his teens. He fell in love with those magic chemicals. He found great friends in a gang that bought and sold drugs, and smashed up stuff for a laugh. Michael Dunt's life changed. He became Micky – hellraiser, drug-taker, jail-bird. 'But it was all my choice. Now Ben Darrington has caused me a lot of inconvenience. Inconvenience? He's been taking the piss. I'll get my coke back. Then I'm going to make him suffer, the way he made me suffer.'

Micky took one hand off the wheel as he blazed along the motorway. He reached over, pulled down the flap of the glove compartment, and nodded with approval at what it contained. There, resting on a yellow duster, was a pistol. The weapon gleamed a metallic blue colour. Beside it was a clear plastic bag containing twenty bullets. The gun had cost him plenty this morning. However, this mission to retrieve the stash of coke mustn't fail. Taking a gun would ensure success. Nobody would dare stand in his way when they saw that pistol in his hand.

'Watch out,' sang Micky Dunt. 'Hell's coming to Devon. Watch out, Ben Darrington. Hell's coming your way!'

* * *

234

Oliver Tolworth walked alongside Fletcher Brown. They were heading back to the gatehouse where Fletcher lived with his father. The strange man, Philip Kemmis, occupied an apartment in another part of the gatehouse. Oliver hoped they wouldn't see Philip. The man was frightening. *Crazy insane, more like*, Oliver told himself. *He ran up to our car when we arrived and started bashing it with his hand . . . or had he bashed it with the arm without the hand?*

Fletcher carried the kite they'd been flying. Suddenly, he asked, 'Why are you worried?'

'How'd you know I was worried?' Oliver asked.

'I'm good at reading expressions. So, what's worrying you?'

'I hope we don't see that mad man who lives at the gatehouse.'

'Philip? He's alright. He's just different, like me. If someone's different, it worries people. It can scare them as well. Are you scared of me?'

'Not any more.'

'Good.' Fletcher studied Oliver's face. 'You'll be worried about the mummy, too. You've seen Kadesh walk. He carried you away. For a while I thought you were dead. I was sure he'd have broken every bone in your skeleton and smashed your skull. And he's been in your house, hasn't he?'

'Don't say that.' Oliver went cold inside. 'I told you, it was a bad dream. Everything about Kadesh is bad dreams.'

'Then we had the same bad dream, because I saw what happened the night that Kadesh picked you up and ran along the lane, carrying you.'

235

'I told you about my nightmare; you're just pretending that you were there. You like messing with people's minds.'

'I'm sorry, Oliver. You didn't dream about Kadesh, because I've seen him walking before.'

Oliver shuddered, too scared to talk. The sunlight had been roasting hot, but now it felt like he stood in a massive deep freeze.

'I like you, Oliver,' Fletcher continued in sympathetic tones. 'Remember what I just said? About being able to tell what people are thinking just by their expressions?'

Oliver managed a nod. For some reason he felt like crying.

'I can tell stuff from people's faces. But there's another thing I can do. It's hard to explain. It's like the world around us has an expression – all the trees, and grass, and rocks, and dirt, and buildings – to me, they're capable of expressing emotion. I don't see it, as such, with my eyes. I sense it. But when I look at those trees down there, and the wall by the road, and even that old gatepost, they seem to be expressing emotion.'

'Expressing emotion?' Oliver echoed. Fletcher had an odd way of using grown-up phrases. Of course, he sort of seemed grown-up in some ways. Even though he was only twelve, he had the eyes of a man . . . an old man at that. Fletcher's appearance was different to that of other boys, too. He had those thick, black eyebrows. He rarely laughed or joked around like other kids. Sometimes, Oliver thought that Fletcher had a hobgoblin face.

Fletcher continued speaking in a quiet voice, almost as if he was murmuring to himself. They were on the grass at the side of the road that led from the gatehouse to the castle. Only, it felt as if they stood far away from this place. Like it was a million miles away. Like Fletcher had spirited them away to another planet and Oliver saw the world where he lived from some huge distance. At that moment, he felt fear twist his heart. What if he couldn't go back to the world where his family and friends lived? What if he continued to live in Fletcher's strange domain? This felt like a dream – and a strange dream that he couldn't wake up from.

Fletcher seemed to have been speaking for hours. Those softly spoken words of his floated in Oliver's skull. Fletcher was claiming that he could read the expression on the face of the world. He said that every plant, tree, stone, house, road, fence – everything – was capable of revealing emotion.

'I've been able see the mood of rocks, and trees, and furniture, and even the hills over there, since I was little. It's like the world knows what will happen in the future and it tells me by wearing an expression on its face, even though there is no actual face. Six months ago, I looked out of the window and saw that the world had a sad face, and that's when I knew my mother was going to die before my dad told me that she was dying.'

Oliver stared at his friend. He felt like a character in a film who'd had his mind taken over by an alien. He could see Fletcher, he could hear him, yet he couldn't speak or move, or run away, and he longed to run back home right now; this was frightening. Just then, he realized that Fletcher would break some news . . . some really bad news.

Fletcher glanced around at the meadow and the trees. There was sunlight, although the shadows cast by the sun seemed to dominate the landscape right now. Oliver saw the shadows of telephone poles squirm over the grass like black snakes, their bodies oozing with venom. Shadows cast by trees were the shadows of bunched fists. They spread over the ground towards Oliver, threatening him with violence. The shadows had become as dangerous as monsters.

Fletcher spoke in that calm voice: 'Do you know what I see on the face of this world that surrounds us? I see fear. The trees, and stones, and plants are frightened for us. Everything you can see for miles around is scared, because we're in danger. Everyone who lives here is in danger. Something is coming that will hurt us.'

'The mummies . . . Is it the mummies?'

Oliver blinked; he realized he stood outside the front door of his house. How did he get here? Just a moment ago, he stood on the driveway that led up to the castle. And where had Fletcher gone? Fletcher had been talking to him just a moment ago.

Oliver Tolworth sensed that something strange and frightening was happening to him. Just what, though? He couldn't explain it, only that there was this intense feeling that things were changing. Was he changing? Was the world around him being transformed in some mysterious and alarming way?

Fletcher's words came back to him, shimmering, echoing . . . haunting him, as if they were spoken by a ghost: *Everyone who lives here is in danger. Something is coming that will hurt us.*

That evening John Tolworth returned home to find Ingrid worrying about Oliver.

'He's not ill again, is he?' John asked.

'No, but he's quiet and withdrawn.' Ingrid frowned. 'Fletcher's the cause of it. I don't know if they've been fighting or if Fletcher has been teasing Oliver, but Oliver just clams up if I ask him what he and Fletcher have been doing.'

'They were flying the kite this morning. I could see them from the lab window.'

'Did they look to be getting on OK?'

'They were having a great time. It's probably just some spat.'

Ingrid nodded. 'Maybe. I'll give him a couple of hours then talk to him again.' Her face suddenly hardened. 'But if I find out that Fletcher's been bullying our son I'll go straight up to the gate-house and tell his father what I think.'

'Don't go in with all guns blazing. They'll probably be friends again tomorrow.'

In her finest schoolmistress tones, she declared, 'I shall monitor the situation. But, if necessary, I will take further action.'

'My God, you're a formidable woman.' He kissed her. 'I'm sure you'll become head of the United Nations one day.'

OK, a weak joke, he told himself, but it did the trick. Ingrid laughed and began to relax. 'Vicki's in the garden with Jason.'

239

'You think there's something going on with our handsome teenage neighbour?'

'Oh yes, I suspect that romance has raised its pretty head.'

John followed Ingrid into the kitchen where she began rinsing a bowl of tomatoes. 'They're both teenagers,' he said. 'They live next door to one another. We shouldn't be surprised.'

'When it comes to teenage romance I'm not surprised by anything. There's beer in the fridge.'

'I'm ready for one. How about you?'

'Go on, then. I'll share your can.'

'Share?' He wrinkled his nose. 'It's been thirsty work slaving over a million pieces of papyrus.'

'OK, give me a full can.'

'Aye, aye, captain, two beers coming straight up. Where's Ben?'

'He's doing his best to get some exercise. He went hobbling down the lane on those crutches. Ollie's gone with him.'

John opened the beers. 'While he's out, I'll get some of my things from his room.'

'I thought you'd moved all your stuff out when we made up the bed for Ben?'

'I left the model of the head in there that I'd made using the three-D printer.'

'Don't remind me about that.' She sipped her cold beer with a heartfelt *mmmm*. 'I still haven't forgotten how you painted it so it looked like Vicki.'

'Not deliberately! OK, I'll go grab the head now.'

'Go grab the head?' She smiled. 'I hope that isn't a euphemism.'

Laughing, he kissed her on the lips, tasting the

bitter tang of beer. 'Ask me to repeat it again later when we're in bed.'

'Kinky.'

'Oh, and after *grabbing the head*, I'll check my emails.'

'Work? You're allowed to switch off, you know?'

'I'll be ten minutes. There should be more translations coming back soon.'

'You're making progress?'

'It's going better than I thought it would. The software's accurately piecing together images of shredded papyrus. The expert we're using is translating the hieroglyphs, so we're starting to build up a picture of the people in the tomb.'

'Do you know their names yet?'

'No. They'll have to remain known by their nicknames for a bit longer yet.'

Ingrid began slicing the tomatoes. 'Right, get your work done, then spend some time with me, OK? I like your company.' Her eyes twinkled. 'I might even sit on your knee in the garden.'

'That's guaranteed to give Vicki the abdabs!'

John retrieved the model of the head from the downstairs back parlour that now served as Ben's room and took it into the lounge. He couldn't help but recall what Samantha had told him about the 1955 X-ray of Kadesh, which revealed that the mummy had two hands, and then the mystery of subsequent X-rays, which indicated that the mummy's right hand was missing. John knew that this couldn't be possible. There had to be a mix-up with the X-ray photographs, or that some practical joke had been played decades ago.

After her revelation about Kadesh, Samantha had then made the equally surprising claim that the mummy called Amber had a cut on her scalp at the hairline, which had never been noticed before. What's more, the injury had occurred before death because scab material could be identified in the wound.

Remembering what Samantha had told him about Amber prompted him to check the head produced by the 3D printer. He looked into the beautiful, albeit plastic, face of what had once been a lively, *and alive*, sixteen year old. The lips were pink, the eyes open, the hair black as coal. He'd applied the paint, and yes, subconsciously, he'd given the model the same hair colour and skin tones of his daughter. True, there was *some* similarity. But could it be that Vicki and Ingrid's side of the family had descendants that originally came from North Africa, or even Egypt itself? That would account for the superficial resemblance. Despite himself, he found his heart beating faster as he checked the hairline, half-expecting to see a duplicate of the wound that Samantha had found in Amber's scalp. He held the head up to the light streaming in through the window. Smooth skin, a black fringe painted on to the plastic . . . but no mark indicating a wound. Then, did he really expect that the plastic head would have acquired an injury since it emerged from the printer? No, he did not.

He glanced about the lounge, hunting for a place to put the head until he could retrieve it in the morning before taking it to the lab. He found a space in the corner of the room behind an armchair where he could tuck the copy of Amber's head out of sight (he didn't want to annoy Vicki by leaving it on view; the reproduction of the face had freaked her out the first time she saw it). That done, he went upstairs, switched on his laptop in the bedroom, and sat on the bed to check his emails. He heard laughter from outside. Glancing through the window, he saw Vicki and Jason as they sat together on a garden bench. They clearly enjoyed being together. The way their eyes were fixed on each others' faces suggested that love might be in the air.

Turning his attention back to the in-box, he saw an email from the translator in London. Quickly, he read the lines that had been translated from Egyptian hieroglyphs to English.

My friend! My brother! He who gave his life to defend the lives of those whom I love, I praise you. I venerate your memory. The days we spent together hunting ibex in the great sea of sand live in my heart, just as strongly as they did when we rode forth. The wine and the honey cake—

(Translator's note: part of the document is missing here; however, fragments suggest that the writer is recalling youthful adventures with a friend.)

I grieve for your death, I grieve for the deaths of my own loved ones. I therefore vow to house your body in a fine tomb of golden walls with my—

(Translator's note: part of document missing.)

—so that you might continue to protect them for as long as the world shall live. I will prepare a testament of the wrongdoer's crimes and place it with you, so that the gods might read of your heroic fight and self-sacrifice.

There were more pieces of text that referred to lists of foodstuffs and weapons that might have been a record of items sealed inside the tomb with the mummies at the time of burial.

John fired off a short email thanking the translator, and then he went downstairs. He helped Ingrid in the kitchen. He mixed flaked tuna with mayonnaise before returning it to the fridge. Outside, there was still laughter in the garden.

'Just imagine if they decided to get married,' he said to Ingrid. 'The Oldfields would become part of our family.'

'I don't know if I'd like the idea of Samantha being family and prowling around you all the time. She really is beautiful – men's heads turn when she walks by.'

'My eyes are firmly on you.'

'Cheesy.' She wafted a fly away from the salad.

Just then the laughter outside stopped. John clearly heard Vicki exclaim: '*Shit!*'

Parental instinct signalled that there was trouble. John and Ingrid rushed outside to find Vicki holding a frisbee in one hand, while clamping the other to her forehead. Jason put his arm round her shoulders while watching her with eyes that were big and round with concern.

'Damn tree.' She swiped a branch with the

244

frisbee. 'Look how sharp the end is. It went and stabbed me. See? It's cut my head. I'm bleeding.'

The evening sun flooded the landscape with light. Even Micky Dunt had to admit that this was an astonishing part of the world. He'd used satnav to reach a country estate called, according to the sign at a road junction, Baverstock Castle. He'd ignored the warning: 'GROUNDS CLOSED TO THE PUBLIC. PRIVATE ROAD ONLY. TRESPASSERS WILL BE PROSECUTED.' Micky had driven along the private road to within a quarter of a mile of the address he'd taken from the unfortunate Mr Oates. The route had taken him over moorland that had masses of weirdly shaped rocks. Micky knew that it wouldn't be wise to simply drive up to the house where Ben was staying with his father; therefore, Micky left the road for a dirt track that led into a forest. After a couple of hundred yards, driving along the bumpy lane, he parked the car in a small clearing surrounded by thick bushes. Good. The car couldn't easily be seen. Of course, this operation required secrecy. He didn't want anyone noticing him or the car, because soon the police would be investigating one hell of a crime. Micky sure as hell didn't want to be linked to what would happen to Ben Darrington in the next few hours.

Before leaving the car, Micky slipped the handgun and bag of extra ammo into a rucksack. After that, he headed into the forest. He held his phone in one hand, using the navigation app to take him to where Ben had hidden himself away.

Micky saw a castle through the trees. It was a huge stone building complete with battlements and towers. The castle wasn't his destination, though, and soon he saw the place he needed to find. Standing alongside a lane were half a dozen houses surrounded by trees. These were isolated homes, miles from the nearest village. Good. Micky liked what he saw. These houses were a long way from other people and, more importantly, the police.

Voices nearby startled Micky. Not wanting to be seen, he dropped to a crouch behind a bush. What he saw coming along the lane both surprised and delighted him.

'This is going to be so easy,' he murmured, pleased. 'The patron saint of mayhem is smiling on me today.' The patron saint line amused Micky so much that he had to push his fist against his mouth to prevent himself barking with laughter.

There, in the evening sunlight, walking along the lane that ran through the forest, were two figures. One, a boy of about ten or so. The other, a guy of nineteen. That guy was none other than Ben Darrington. The student lurched along awkwardly, using crutches. The yellow cast that enclosed the full length of his leg was plain to see. *Jesus Christ*, thought Micky, *wearing that thing on your leg must be torture in its own right. Ha . . . and just think, Ben, you inconsiderate bastard, there'll be more torture to come.*

The lane would bring the pair to within twenty feet of where Micky concealed himself. He unzipped the rucksack, pulled out the pistol, clicked off the safety catch, then settled down to wait. His prey approached slowly on account of Ben's condition, the crutches tapping against the ground as he heaved himself forward. Despite the effort, and probably the pain of moving the broken leg, Ben smiled as he chatted with the boy: the pair enjoyed each other's company. The boy pointed at squirrels running up a tree trunk, and both paused to watch the animals.

Micky whispered to himself, 'Keep walking, guys. Just a bit closer. Then I'll step out and say hello.' Micky curled his finger around the trigger. The weapon felt as heavy as a brick in his hand. In the ammo magazine were eight bullets. On pulling the trigger, the bullet would speed from the muzzle at five hundred miles per hour – that was as fast as an airliner. *Just imagine the damage a bullet travelling at that speed would do to the human body.* Micky allowed his imagination to supply bloody images of that bullet smashing into Ben's chest. 'Pow,' Micky breathed with satisfaction. 'Ben, I screwed your mother. Now I'm going to screw with you in an entirely different way.' He grinned, pleased with his cool sense of humour.

Micky waited behind the bush. Sunlight filtered down through the trees. A yellow butterfly flitted in front of him. Ben and his little friend were walking again, coming this way, getting closer. Any moment now . . .

'Oliver . . . it is Oliver, isn't it? Ahoy there!'

The voice of another man encouraged Micky to dip his head lower so that he wouldn't be noticed. Carefully, he parted the branches of the bush so he could see. *Damn it!* A guy on a bicycle rode up to the pair then stopped. Wearing a white shirt, with a blue necktie, he was dressed for the office rather than a bike ride. Not that it was his choice of clothes which annoyed Micky Dunt. The arrival of the stranger complicated things. Micky had intended to step out from behind the bush, aim the pistol at Ben, and then demand the return of the very valuable consignment of cocaine that he knew was in Ben's possession. Now this . . . Another person arriving on the scene had ruined his plan.

It got worse. A car drove slowly along the lane. It, too, stopped. The driver, a woman with blond hair, began chatting to Ben and his group. The woman soon drove off; however, the guy on the bike dismounted and all three began walking back in the direction of the houses. Another guy, aged about forty or so, emerged from one of the houses and came to the end of the drive. He waved a greeting at the three in the lane. After that, he stood there, waiting for them to join him.

Micky clicked on the safety, put the gun back in the bag, and retraced his path back to the car. *Not yet*, he told himself. *Too many people about. Wait until the sun goes down. Strike then . . .*

Philip Kemmis perspired as he hurried towards the gatehouse. He'd been walking for miles in the hope he would exhaust himself, which might permit him a good night's sleep. The problem was he'd forgotten to take his medication with him, the pills that helped keep his anxiety under control. Now that anxiety came blazing back with a vengeance. His heart beat faster. He panted

248

hard as he rushed along the path. Vines that climbed up the branches of a bush suddenly had the appearance of venomous snakes. He heard vicious hissing. Out of the corner of his eye he saw snake heads dart at him, their jaws open wide, revealing glinting fans. When he spun round to look at them the snakes weren't snakes at all, they were simply vines that swayed in the warm breeze. *Should have taken my pills*, he thought. *Hallucinations are flaring up again.*

He moved faster along the path. From the corner of one eye, he glimpsed dark figures in the shadows that watched him – they were potent with menace. They wanted to hurt him. Of course, when he twisted his head to look at them directly, those still figures became tree trunks again.

'You're not real,' he snarled as he caught sight of the dead husk of a woman; for a second he saw bandages fluttering from her arms and head. He stopped and stared at the creature, his heart pounding so hard that it hurt.

No . . . there was no mummy there. It was just an old gatepost. He knew that his anxiety levels had gone nuclear. What Philip's doctor referred to as 'your old trouble' had exploded back into his head. Philip's right hand began to throb painfully. It felt as if the bones in the hand were being crushed one by one; an agonizing sensation. Yet he had no right hand. An accident, his parents had told him, just a freak accident. Philip knew the truth, however. He knew alright.

He groaned with pain. Clutching the stump at the end of his right arm, he stumbled towards the gatehouse door that led to his apartment. The puckered skin at the end of the wrist stump hurt so much, like it had been plunged into boiling cooking oil.

Philip clawed at the door handle and entered the hallway. In every doorway inside the apartment, he glimpsed bandaged figures in the shadows. Dried-out corpses. Strips of cloth formed criss-cross patterns across their chests. Even though the eyes were lifeless, they did see him. He sensed it. Those dead eyes gazed into his soul and saw his terror.

Philip somehow made it into the bathroom. He swung back the door of the wall cabinet. Grabbing a blister pack of pills, he popped out two, the prescribed dose . . . choking, gagging on the hard pills in his throat, he nevertheless managed to swallow them. For good measure, he took two more. He cupped his hand under the cold water tap and gulped a few mouthfuls of water to make sure the pills went down his throat into his stomach. Sighing, relieved to have taken the medication, he closed the cabinet door and saw what stared back at him from the mirror.

Kadesh looked into his eyes. Philip couldn't see his own reflection. There was only Kadesh, the mummy. Philip saw the band of metal around the top of the skull. The eyes were closed.

With shocking suddenness, the eyelids slid back. Philip stared into the mirror; he saw two plump, living, glistening eyes in the dead face. They glared with absolute ferocity from that ruin of dried skin that had broken open in places to reveal the bone underneath. The lip curled back, exposing the monstrosity's teeth.

From shrivelled lips came a hiss: 'Be ready
. . . be ready.'

Philip threw himself back against the bathroom
wall, covered his face with his remaining hand,
and screamed as loud as he could.

The screams from the adjoining apartment rever-
berated through the living room.

Fletcher's dad yawned. 'His Lordship's in good
voice.' Picking up the TV remote, he thundered
at the wall that separated the apartments, 'Shout
louder, I don't think you've woken the dead yet!'
Fletcher's dad pressed the volume control, making
the TV louder, in an attempt to drown out the
sound. 'God help us, living next door to a
madman.'

Fletcher knelt in front of a coffee table. The
TV cop drama boomed loudly enough to make
the toy soldiers he was lining up on the table
wobble. Fletcher was too old to play with these
plastic soldiers – his mother had bought them for
him years ago as a surprise gift when she worked
as a cleaner up at the castle – but he had taken
them out of the tin from under his bed to remind
him of the time when his mother had been a
healthy and cheerful woman. Just twenty minutes
ago, the hospital had telephoned to say that Mrs
Brown had taken a turn for the worse. The doctors
couldn't wake her. Respiration had become
laboured. Fletcher viewed this decline in his
mother's condition with equanimity. He did not
feel sadness. The fact that his mother was dying
was simply that: *a fact*. He viewed her failing
health dispassionately. Fletcher realized that

251

some might think him cruel, but he knew he wasn't like other people. Emotion rarely affected him. He often told himself those rocks out on the hillside felt more emotion than him.

It hadn't concerned him particularly when their neighbour, Lord Philip Kemmis, had started screaming thirty minutes ago. Every few days the man would have screaming fits. OK, this one was louder and more prolonged than usual, but neither Fletcher nor his father were perturbed by it. If anything, his dad was annoyed by the shouting.

Even though the TV blasted out sound at full volume, Fletcher could hear some of the things that their neighbour yelled: '*Get out of my house! I did not give you permission to enter this room!*' The voice still had its customary posh tones, although Fletcher could hear the man's terror.

Earlier, Fletcher had told Oliver that he could sense emotion in objects such as trees, rocks and buildings. This morning he'd sensed their dread – when he looked at the faces of the plastic soldiers, they wore expressions of dread, too. Now Philip Kemmis expressed terror and dread in the way he screamed.

His father shouted above the sirens on TV, 'Fletcher! I might have to go out tonight! If the hospital phones again about your mother, I'll go over there!'

Fletcher pulled the last soldier from the tin. 'My mother's going to die tonight.' The world around him emoted dread. These walls wore an expression of anguish, or so it seemed to him. Then, Fletcher could see what nobody else could

252

see. Oh, people would laugh and be scornful if he told them that walls, trees, fences, toys, cars, furniture and just about everything else could sense the approach of an ominous event. *They say I'm insane*, he told himself, *but I known that objects express emotion. They detect what will happen in the future and react accordingly. This time they reflect the impending death of my mother.* He knew his thoughts would seem oddly precocious to people . . . or just downright odd.

His father stirred himself from his own thoughts. Once again he shouted over the din of the television, 'If the hospital telephones about your mother, I'll drive over there and sit with her. I don't want you to come. You stay here. Play with your . . .' He waggled a finger at the toy soldiers. 'Just lock the door after I've gone and stay indoors. Don't go out walking when it's dark.'

Fletcher repeated what he'd said a moment ago: 'My mother's going to die tonight.'

His father didn't express surprise at the statement. He'd got used to his son's peculiar behaviour over the years. 'Yes,' he said matter-of-factly, 'she probably will.'

Fletcher Brown finished lining the toy soldiers up in front of him on the coffee table. In the apartment next door, screams had given way to a kind of moaning, as if their neighbour's terror had exhausted him. At that moment, the telephone rang. Fletcher's dad killed the sound on the TV as he took the call.

'Yes? Alright. I understand. I'll set off now.'

Fletcher placed his arm flat on the coffee table and slowly swept the toy soldiers, which his

253

mother had bought him, into a waste bin that was half full of pizza crusts, cigarette butts and orange peel.

His father stood up. 'I'm going to the hospital to see your mother. Remember, lock the door, and stay at home.'

This seemed like another world to Micky Dunt. He was used to living in cities. The countryside here in Devon unsettled him. Too quiet, for one. Also, all this greenstuff, the plants, trees, grass, and miles of moorland, seemed a chaotic jumble compared to neatly ordered urban streets and buildings.

Micky sat in the car waiting for night to fall. Already, it had become gloomy here in the forest clearing. Above him, streaks of red cloud could have been savage claw marks running across the sky. He took the time to check that the gun operated smoothly. He unloaded it and loaded it again with those shiny, gold-coloured bullets. He'd have liked to fire the gun. The weapon was new to him; he'd only rented it from a guy this morning. However, he knew if he fired the gun it would make a heck of a bang. In a silent wilderness like this, the noise would be heard for miles. No . . . he decided he couldn't risk taking any practice shots. The air was so warm that he lolled back in the driving seat with his legs hanging out through the open door. The only moving things were animals. He'd not seen a single person come anywhere near the car. There were squirrels though; they'd startled him by scampering over the vehicle's roof, with a skittering sound. Rabbits had come out of the long grass to stare at him. It was like he was an intruder in their world. More animals had emerged from the shadows to stare at him – stoats, foxes, rabbits, squirrels, mice, badgers. They'd stared like they disapproved of his presence here. Micky Dunt sensed them resenting his presence. That expression in their staring eyes annoyed Micky. Even made him a bit paranoid. Those creatures were hostile. They didn't like him. He'd have loved to kill a couple of them with the pistol – show them who's boss, but, again, that *BANG* would send out a signal to people in the castle grounds that there was a gunman somewhere close by. Micky needed to remain out of sight. An invisible assassin. He didn't want people giving his description to the police. The bruises on his face would be as obvious as the flashing light of a beacon.

So Micky Dunt waited. He didn't wait patiently, but he waited.

As the sun went down, Micky checked his emails. One had come through from Karl Gurrick, the mobster who'd sent him here to retrieve the cocaine that Micky had entrusted to Ben's care. The email simply said: '*Just a friendly message to ensure your fealty.*' There was a link to a website. Micky knew better than to ignore such web-links from this ruthless gangster; there might be an important message for Micky on the website. There was . . . of sorts . . . The link took him to a video. Micky watched footage of two masked men beating a sweaty, black-haired guy with baseballs bats. The black-haired guy screamed and shouted what seemed to be some words of Spanish. Micky noticed a photo of a young girl stuck to the wall behind the guy. The two masked assailants stopped smashing the guy's face with bats. One reappeared with a shotgun and blew the victim's head to pieces. The hair was no longer black.

Micky had seen videos like this before online. They were used by gangsters to reinforce the loyalty of their own employees. Sometimes they were copied to disk and posted to border guards, custom officers and police – anyone who the gangsters wanted to intimidate into turning a blind eye when a consignment of drugs, for example, came through a border checkpoint. Probably, the little girl in the photo on the wall was the daughter of a cop or border guard. Micky knew that the use of these torture-murder videos was particularly prevalent on the US–Mexico border. Boy-oh-boy. You didn't need subtitles or voice-overs to explain that the kid in the pic would get the same treatment if her border-guard father or mother didn't ignore the packets of white powder in the drug mule's suitcase. 'And they say nature is red in tooth and claw.' Micky enjoyed a sadistic chuckle.

He glanced up to see a pair of eyes staring at him. Damn it. He nearly jumped out of his skin. 'Clear off.' He waved his hand, and the owner of the eyes, a sheep, trotted back into the shadows and disappeared.

A chirp told Micky he'd got a text. He opened it up. Oh shit . . . it was from Gurrick, and this was what it said: *I'll make you an offer of fealty.*

Do this to earn back my trust. Film torture of Darrington. Email to me by tomorrow morning at latest.'

'Fealty? What the crap does fealty even mean?' Micky shook his head. This was getting seriously heavy. Gurrick not only expected him to retrieve the stash of coke, he also demanded that Micky film himself beating up Ben Darrington. The torture video would be used by Gurrick to bolster his status in the criminal underworld. It would also be a way of Micky winning back Gurrick's trust. 'Fealty? Fealty? What does he mean by that?' Micky googled the word. Ah . . . he began to understand when he read the definition. Fealty was a pledge of allegiance. In medieval times, men pledged an oath of loyalty to their local lord. Fealty was a solemn pledge to serve the lord, remain loyal, and woe unto the dude who broke their oath of fealty. If they did betray the lord, or failed him in some way, there would be consequences. No doubt violent and bloody consequences.

Micky Dunt understood what was going on here. He'd been given a chance to repair his relationship with the vicious gangster Karl Gurrick. If Micky failed to return the drugs and make that torture video, then Gurrick would punish Micky – and probably in such a way that the high-voltage cruelty of a couple of days ago would seem just about as painful as being tickled with a feather. Micky knew he'd have to hurt people tonight. What's more, he'd have to take explicit footage for his new lord and master. There's nothing like the use of terror to guarantee obedience.

* * *

Shadows crept into the garden. The setting sun had left a splash of vivid red on the horizon. Despite the night closing in, the air remained so warm that nobody felt inclined to go indoors just yet. John brought Ingrid her lime tea to her where she sat on a lounger on the patio. He perched himself on a low wall beside her and sipped his coffee. Ben Darrington hobbled along on crutches to make sure that Oliver didn't burn himself as he lit citronella candles dotted about the garden on the tops of ornamental walls and tree stumps.

Ben had comfortably slipped into the role of big brother, offering advice to Oliver, while keeping a watchful eye on the way the boy handled the matches. 'Don't point the matchstick downward too much,' Ben said. 'It'll burn up too fast and toast your fingers.'

Oliver laughed. He was enjoying the attention of the brother he never even knew existed until a few days ago. 'Is this better?'

'Yes, that's better, Ollie. Don't let the flame get too close to your fingers. Blow it out and light another match.'

Oliver called out, 'Dad, can we light the big lantern hanging from the tree?'

'I don't see why not. Though you might want to let Ben light that one for you.'

'It's OK,' Ben said. 'I'll lift Ollie up.'

Ingrid smiled. 'Just don't go hurting your leg. Oliver is heavier than he looks.'

Oliver and Ben chatted happily to one another as they made their way across the lawn to where the lantern dangled from a branch six feet above the ground.

Ingrid stretched out comfortably on the lounger. 'We've been here nearly a week.'

'Time's flown.'

'Do you like it here?'

He nodded. 'It's hard to think of anywhere more beautiful and quiet.'

'Hmm, quiet. Addictive, isn't it? When I think of that constant din of traffic going by our front door in London it makes me want to stay here forever.'

'You'd miss teaching at school.'

'I could transfer to another school down here.'

'What? A sleepy, rural schoolhouse with a dozen pupils?'

'Yes. Lovely.'

He grinned. 'You thrive on solving other people's problems. A quiet little school would drive you crazy with boredom.'

She reached out to rest her hand on his knee as he sat there beside her on the wall. 'I could take up lots of hobbies. Crafting, fell-walking, baking.' She winked at him and whispered, 'Alfresco nudism.'

'Now, that is something I would love to see.' He picked her hand up from his knee and kissed it. 'Would you like a glass of wine later?'

Smiling, she shook her head. 'I'm fine with this.' She took another sip of her tea. 'You go ahead and have a glass if you like.'

'I might have a beer later.'

In a relaxed way, Ingrid watched Ben lift Oliver up to light the lamp in the tree.

'Don't drop any lit matches on my head,' Ben joked. 'Because it'll make me flaming mad.'

Ingrid chuckled. 'He's even got your talent for cracking dreadful jokes.'

'A chip off the old block, eh?'

'Yes, absolutely.' She glanced at John. 'You don't want Ben to disappear out of your life, do you?'

'In a few weeks, he'll be going back to university.'

'But you will stay in touch with him, won't you?' Her expression told John that she did sincerely want Ben to remain part of their family after the summer in Devon was over.

John smiled. 'Yes, of course I will.' He heard voices in the lane. 'Ah, here come the lovebirds.'

From out of the gloom came Vicki and Jason. They were holding hands, although as soon as they entered the garden they quickly let go, as if they'd be embarrassed if anyone commented on the hand holding.

Oliver brandished the matchbox. 'I lit the candles. Citronella keeps bugs away.'

Vicki quipped, 'I wonder if you can get candles that keep scrotty little kids away?'

Despite the remark, the mood was a pleasant one. Everyone exchanged a friendly, 'Hi.'

John invited the new arrivals to help themselves to cold drinks from the fridge. 'Non-alcohol ones, Jason,' he added, 'otherwise your mother will be coming over here on the warpath to take my scalp.'

Jason laughed, while keeping his eyes locked on Vicki's face. *Smitten*, thought John. *I hope the relationship doesn't lead to complications.*

Ingrid asked, 'Vicki, how's your head?'

'Oh, it was just a scratch. Stupid branch. It shouldn't have sharp bits.'

Jason's expression was one of concern as he said, 'Sit down, Vicki, and I'll get you a drink.'

Her eyes twinkled. 'Thank you, Jason.'

'You've taken the plaster off,' Ingrid pointed out. 'You should have left it on for tonight at least.'

'Why do I want to walk around with a great, big plaster stuck to my forehead? I don't want to look like an idiot.'

Ingrid's sharp eyes focused on her daughter's face. 'You've covered the cut with make-up as well, haven't you?'

'That red mark on my forehead made me look like Frankenstein.'

For a moment, John thought that Ingrid would correct their daughter, explaining that Frankenstein wasn't the monster, but the man who'd created it. Thankfully, Ingrid didn't go down that route, which could easily have triggered a mother–daughter argument. If anything, Vicki appeared happy to bask in handsome Jason Oldfield's presence. She allowed him to position a chair for her on the patio, and she sat down.

Ah, happy families, John thought. *I hope it lasts.*

Micky Dunt found the ideal place to keep watch on the house where Ben Darrington was staying. He'd tucked himself amongst trees on a hillside, confident that nobody could see him. The house stood in a quiet country lane with a smattering of other properties nearby. Micky had taken a peek a few minutes ago and seen, to his relief, that only two houses appeared to be occupied right now. Micky had assumed, on hearing that Ben had gone to stay with his father, that it would be just the two of them in some remote cottage in the Devon countryside. A kid with a broken leg and one guy would be easier to handle than a whole bunch of people. However, a bunch of people is what Micky Dunt saw right now.

He had a perfect view of the back lawn. Candles were burning, giving out plenty of light now the sun had set. A man and a woman sat on the patio drinking from mugs. Ben Darrington had been helping a boy light the candles; it was the same kid Micky had seen earlier in the lane. Just minutes ago, another couple had arrived. They'd been holding hands as they walked along the lane. They'd also been kissing one another as they walked. Though a stronger word than kissing would be more apt – 'snogging' was better. The pair had snogged each other's faces off.

Micky was ready for tonight. He'd brought the gun in the rucksack. Also in there were rolls of gaffer tape for binding hands and feet together. In addition, he'd helped himself to several wicked items from the car's tool kit: pliers, a screwdriver with a very sharp point, a card cutter (that, also, had a sharp blade), and a claw hammer. Hammers are perfect for breaking finger bones. He'd also charged up his phone from the car's cigarette lighter. Gurrick had ordered him to film some physical mayhem tonight, and that's exactly what Micky planned to do.

The sky had turned from blue to black. The

red smudge on the horizon, where the sun had vanished, faded away. Bats flitted above the trees. A dog barked in the distance – a shimmering sound that just sort of ghosted through the forest. An eerie sound, for sure.

Micky checked that the gun was the first thing within reach in the rucksack. Good, all loaded and ready to go. The main problem now was the number of people down there at the house. He counted six; he hoped they weren't fixing to have a garden party.

The teenage couple left the patio and disappeared into the house. So maybe they lived there, too. That meant there'd be a house full of people. Even so, nothing could deflect him from what he needed to do tonight. Micky knew that Karl Gurrick would be waiting impatiently for news that the valuable consignment of cocaine had been retrieved. Micky didn't want to keep the gangster hanging. There'd be painful consequences for Micky if Gurrick became annoyed.

Micky watched and waited. He snarled with frustration when he spotted a figure on the lane. This was a tall, blond woman. She strode like she was on a life-or-death mission. *Yup, just my luck. She's going to the house, too.* The woman hurried in the direction of the people on the lawn like lives depended on it.

Samantha Oldfield arrived like a tornado in human form. She rushed into the back garden where John and Ingrid sat talking. Ben balanced himself on crutches, while Oliver showed him the screen of a hand-held computer game.

Samantha seemed to explode into their presence, waving her arms, and shouting, 'I'm getting out, and you should, too!'

Everyone in the garden stopped whatever they were doing and stared at this woman with the flashing eyes and heaving breasts.

John stood up, wondering what the hell was going on. 'Samantha, what's wrong?'

'You know what's wrong. So you'll do the sensible thing – pack yourself and your family into the car and drive!'

Ingrid swung her legs off the lounger and stood up, too. John felt his heartbeat quicken. One glance at his wife's expression yelled out loud and clear what she was thinking.

The blond woman took a forceful step towards John. Abruptly, she lost her balance and had to steady herself using the wall of the house.

Ingrid said, 'Samantha, perhaps you should sit down.'

'As you so rightly notice . . . yes! I've had a drink.'

A skin-full of drink, John told himself. *She's wasted.*

Samantha stood up straight in that odd, stiff-backed kind of way that people adopt when they've had too much alcohol, as if to say, *Look, I can stand up straight. I'm sober.* Samantha swayed, despite straining hard to appear dignified. 'Yes, I've had a drink,' she repeated in a forceful voice. 'You would drink, too, if you'd made the discoveries I've been making over the last few days.'

'What discoveries?' When Ingrid asked this question she gave John a very direct look.

264

'Discoveries that would shock you, Ingrid . . . shock you to the core.' Samantha stepped sideways to keep her balance. 'You wouldn't believe what I've shown to your husband.'

'Wouldn't I?' Ingrid's mouth twitched angrily. 'Why don't you tell me all about it, Samantha?'

John got ready to catch Samantha if she lost her balance completely.

'Listen . . .' Samantha pointed at all four of them in turn – Ingrid, John, Ben and Oliver. 'Leave while you still can. Get away . . . get right away from here. I'd say the same to our other neighbours in the lane, however . . . however, they're either away from home on holiday, or otherwise absent . . . the . . . the summer school thing . . .'

'Perhaps you should go home,' John suggested. 'We can talk about this tomorrow.'

'No, John.' Ingrid glared at him. 'I want to hear what Samantha's been showing you.'

Ben put his hand on Oliver's shoulder, encouraging him to return to the house so as to prevent him from hearing something embarrassing about his own father.

John threw up his hands as his patience gave out. 'Samantha. Don't do this. You're mistaken about the mummies.'

'The mummies?' Ingrid's eyes widened in surprise; she clearly hadn't anticipated that Samantha's revelation involved mummified bodies.

'Hasn't John told you? Well, he should have done.' The woman surged on: 'Those mummies up at the castle are changing . . . transforming

. . . transmuting. The mummy called Kadesh used to have two hands. Now he has one hand. The other has *pfftt*.' She fluttered her fingers to suggest a hand vanishing into thin air. 'The girl mummy, Amber, has just acquired a cut to her head. It wasn't there twenty-four hours ago. The injury, however . . . however! . . . occurred just before death, three thousand years ago. The mummies' physical characteristics are being altered.'

Ingrid shook her head, baffled. 'Dead bodies are changing?'

'Yes, Ingrid, they're changing.'

'Changing into what?'

'Changing into you! All of you!'

When Ingrid heard this, her jaw actually dropped open in shock. 'And you told John that this was happening?'

'Yes.'

Ingrid turned to John. 'Why didn't you tell me?'

'Because it's impossible,' he said as calmly as he could. 'For some reason, Samantha is getting herself worked up over ideas about the mummy collection.'

'This woman gets you alone in the castle and confides her innermost thoughts to you?'

'Yes, but it's not what it seems. It's a mistake or a practical joke from years ago. The mummies *aren't* transforming.'

'Oh, but they are!' Samantha lurched forward to grab John's arm.

'John.' Ingrid's voice rose in surprise. 'Samantha is frightened. She is absolutely terrified. Look how she's shaking.'

John could feel the tremors running through the woman's hands as she desperately held on to him: the same desperate grip as a shipwreck survivor clinging to floating wreckage.

'Listen,' Samantha hissed. 'Ingrid . . . John . . . the mummies are changing into your family. Amber is just like your daughter, Vicki. There's a – a mummy we call Bones. His thigh bone is broken in three places. Just like Ben's. There is the mummified body of a little boy – Ket. He and your son, Oliver, resemble one another so much. Same bone structure, same height, same age.'

Oliver heard this clearly enough. 'Dad?' he shouted. 'Is she saying I'm going to be dead like that Egyptian boy, too?'

'No, Oliver.' John pulled Samantha's hand from his arm. 'Samantha's only joking.'

'But it's all true!' she said. 'Amber is Vicki. Ben is Bones. Ket is Oliver. You, Ingrid, are Isis. Look . . . look . . .' She dipped her hand into her pocket and managed to pull a stick of chalk from those tight jeans. 'Look . . . watch this.'

John said, 'I think you should stop this now.'

Samantha ignored him. 'Watch.' There, in the light of the candles and lanterns in the garden, she drew two parallel chalk lines across the patio slabs. Above one line she wrote *Mummy family*. Above the second line, running parallel to that, she chalked *Tolworth family*. 'Now watch.' She quickly blazed white lines to form a giant asterisk. 'This asterisk is what I call the event. The "event" isn't far away. It's soon. Keep watching as I extend the two lines. See how I'm making them converge? This indicates that, as time goes by, the mummy family and the Tolworth family are gradually coming closer together. Resemblances between the two families – alive and dead – are becoming more noticeable. The mummies are developing your characteristics.'

Ingrid stared at Samantha. 'Are you claiming we're . . . what? Twins in time? Doppelgängers? Clones of one another?'

'Give it another day or so and you will be identical.' Samantha's voice rose in triumph as she realized Ingrid had, at last, grasped the explanation. 'What's more, I believe those mummified corpses will have the same finger-prints as you. They will even have identical DNA to yours.' Samantha threw the chalk down so emphatically that she nearly toppled forwards after it. John caught hold of her, steadying her.

At that moment, Vicki and Jason stepped out of the house. They clearly only had eyes for one another and barely noticed the bizarre scene of the drunken Samantha being kept on her feet by John.

Samantha nodded. 'Ah, here we have Amber, also known as Vicki.'

Oliver suddenly gave a piercing yell. 'She's trying to scare us! She's saying we're going to die and be wrapped up in bandages like mummies!'

Ben gently ushered Oliver to the house. 'Come on, mate. We'll find something to watch on television.'

When they'd gone, Ingrid hissed, 'Well, you did a fine job of scaring my son.'

'I'm a scientist,' Samantha retorted with as

268

much dignity as she could muster. 'I am compelled to tell the truth.'

Jason seemed to notice the presence of Samantha for the first time. 'Oh, hello, Mum. Vicki cut her head on the tree tonight, but you can't see the mark, can you?'

'Ha!' Samantha let out a yell of triumph. 'Told you! Told you, didn't I?' She pointed at the chalk lines that grew closer together as they approached the EVENT asterisk. 'Convergence. The mummified body, Amber, forms a cut on her head. Tonight Vicki has cut her head. And I am certain it will be in the same place at the hairline. Do you understand what I'm telling you? The Tolworths are becoming the mummy family, and the mummy family are becoming the Tolworths. Convergence!'

'You're forgetting something.' Ingrid adopted the voice of cold logic. 'You claim . . . drunkenly, I might add . . . that the Tolworths are becoming identical to the mummies in the castle.'

'It is the truth.'

'But John isn't like Kadesh. John has two hands.'

'Correct, John Tolworth does have two hands. But he . . .' She pointed at a figure in the shadows. 'But *he* only has one.' Samantha beckoned. 'OK, Philip, you can join us now. Help me convince the Tolworths to get away from here. They've got to run. And to run like all the monsters and devils of hell are chasing them . . . with the intention of ripping them apart!'

Light from the candles and lanterns illuminated the garden, allowing Micky Dunt a clear view of

269

events taking place down there. Micky couldn't hear what was being said, but something dramatic was occurring. A blond beauty had turned up; she'd talked while making lots of impassioned gestures. She appeared to be drunk – swaying, staggering, occasionally shouting, sometimes even hanging on to a guy for support. She'd pulled an object out of her pocket – a pen? Too far away to be sure. Yet she'd used whatever it was to draw or write on the paving slabs. Another woman was annoyed by the blond's antics. That woman had shook her head a lot and argued with the visitor.

Now another man joined the party. He was tall, serious looking; he reminded Micky of a judge walking into a courtroom; very upright and dignified. All these new arrivals complicated the situation for Micky. He wanted to go down there and make Ben Darrington hand the cocaine over. But how could Micky simply stroll into the garden with five people down there, and two more in the house? OK, he had eight bullets in the gun, but he doubted if he could hold them all at gunpoint while he got to work on Ben Darrington. Karl Gurrick had demanded that Micky film some torture-porn, too.

Despite the problems that Micky was facing, he found himself drawn into the drama unfolding down there in the back garden. It looked as if things were getting even more interesting. The tall, silent guy held up one arm. Even from way up here in the trees, Micky could tell that the guy's right hand was missing. Micky wished that reality had a volume control. He wanted to up the sound and hear what those people were saying to each other. He guessed it was getting more fascinating by the moment.

Philip Kemmis emerged from the darkness to stand in the light cast by the candles. John saw that despite the way he stood up straight, the man's eyes had a wounded quality, as if he suffered intense pain – though that wouldn't be physical pain. John knew that the man had never recovered emotionally, or mentally, from the mystery accident that cost him his hand.

Ingrid shook her head. 'You tell us to . . . What was that you said? To run like all the monsters and devils of hell are chasing us? Intent on ripping us apart! My God, Samantha, what's wrong with you? It can't just be because you're drunk, is it?'

'No, Ingrid. I am here to warn you to get away! To flee! I'm warning you, because I like you, I like John, I like your family.' Swaying unsteadily, she looked from face to face in the garden – Ingrid, John, Vicki, Jason and Philip.

John looked in the direction of the house. Ben and Oliver sat on the sofa in front of the TV. Ben was shooting glances back at the drama unfolding in the back garden; he must be wondering what the hell was happening to his new family.

Philip spoke in a formal way. 'Good evening.'

Samantha nodded at the new arrival. 'Philip, thank you for coming.' She pointed at the lines she'd chalked on the patio. 'I've been explaining how the mummy family and the Tolworth family are converging. They grow more alike, physically, every day. It is all beyond coincidence. This is destiny.'

Vicki was clearly alarmed. 'Is Samantha saying we're going to turn into Egyptian mummies?'

Ingrid snorted. 'Samantha is drunk. She should be home in bed.'

Samantha disagreed: 'Nope, I'm not drunk *enough*. I'm scared about what will happen when the mummies eventually become identical to you all.' She stamped her foot on the asterisk chalked on the slabs. 'When that happens, the "Event" will occur.'

Jason was bewildered. 'What event?'

'The big event, Jason, my dear . . . an event with fatal consequences.'

'Mother, you *are* drunk.'

'I wish I was totally pissed. I wouldn't feel as scared as I am now.' She beckoned Philip. 'Come on over. Tell everyone what happened to you back when you were eleven.'

Philip stepped on to the patio. Moths flitted out of the darkness above his head. In the candlelight, they resembled sparks of fire. John looked into the man's wounded eyes and felt a cold, cold dread seeping through his own veins. John knew what was coming. He didn't want to hear those grim words again.

Philip spoke in a calm voice, telling them, simply, what happened to him that night thirty years ago: 'I went up into the castle tower. The mummy collection was housed in a room there back then. John accompanied me.'

'Dad was there?' Vicki's expression was one of astonishment.

'John lived with his family in the castle grounds. John wanted to see the mummies. I obliged. I began to remove the sheet that covered Kadesh, the mummy that sits on the chair. That's when the light went out. We were plunged into total darkness, couldn't see a thing. All black. Absolute black. Within seconds, I felt something grip my wrist. I know what gripped me were jaws. Then there was a pain of such intensity that I can't begin to describe its magnitude. Teeth bit through the skin, veins and bones of my wrist.' He looked at each person in turn. 'Kadesh bit off my hand.'

Ingrid turned to John. 'Did you see any of this?'

'No. As Philip said, it was completely dark. Philip shouted for me to get out. I ran down the tower steps and returned to the main part of the castle. When Philip came down I saw . . .' John couldn't finish the sentence. Instead, he found his eyes drawn to Philip's arm that ended in a stump, not a living hand.

Ingrid took a deep breath. 'Samantha, if you're claiming that Kadesh is somehow one and the same as Philip, why did Kadesh attack him?'

'A reflex action. Besides, as I've said, the transformation process is gradual. Thirty years ago Kadesh still had two hands. He hadn't yet begun the metamorphosis into Philip.'

'Samantha. Please go home.' Ingrid pointed at the driveway. 'Just go! I've had enough of your deluded fantasies about time twins, clones, and portents of doom.'

Philip's expression was grave. 'Listen to Samantha. She's an intelligent woman. She is telling the truth. After you've heard her out, put your family in the car and drive away. Never come back. You're in danger here.'

Ingrid pointed again. 'You can go, too, Philip. Good night.'

Philip said, 'Samantha, tell them about the translations of the Egyptian documents.'

Samantha nodded. 'John, as you know, has been reconstructing ancient documents. We've received the first translations of the hieroglyphs, and they show that an Egyptian family experienced a terrible tragedy in 1000 BC. A mother and father lived with their three children on the banks of the Nile. The father had an enemy who'd travelled a long way to exact revenge, or simply to attack them. We haven't discovered the assassin's motive yet. For some reason, the father was prevented from protecting his family. Instead, his friend tried to do just that. The father's enemy arrived, and there was a terrible . . . event. The friend attempted to protect the family but failed. The mother, daughter and two sons were killed. The friend died, too. The father buried his family in the Gold Tomb, together with a written record of the murders. His friend was embalmed and placed on a chair to keep watch over the mummified family, and to protect them in the afterlife. At some point, tomb robbers broke in and destroyed the papyrus letters in the adjoining chamber. What happened next is conjecture, but I believe the mummy that we call Kadesh came to life, killed the tomb robbers, and resealed the tomb from the inside before resuming his place on the seat. And there he sat, guarding the family of his friend for the next three thousand years.'

Ingrid's eyes burned. 'Samantha, you've had sex with my husband, haven't you?'

274

John gasped, '*What?*'

Philip retained his composure. 'Listen to me, Ingrid. For years I've seen mummies – they have a way of projecting their faces on to people I meet. The face of Isis is superimposed on to your face now. I can see strips of binding material around your neck. Vicki wears the mummified face of Amber. When I look through that window into your house I don't see Ben and Oliver, I see Bones and Ket. To me, they are mummified dead people with dried-out faces and eyes that have sunk into their skulls. Their bodies are wrapped in bandages. They have the dust of the tomb in their hair. I know you see them as living people – I, on the other hand, see dead flesh.'

Ingrid lost it. She covered her ears with her hands and screamed, 'Enough! This isn't about death, this isn't about dead Egyptians. This is about sex! Samantha's trying to disguise her indiscretion with my husband by inventing fantasies about mummies being transformed into my family!' She pointed at Samantha. 'You've got drunk, and you've recruited this lunatic.' Her eyes flashed at Philip. 'You've recruited him to back up your lies, because the poor devil doesn't know any better. Yes, I believe he sees mummified corpses when he looks at us. That's because he's mentally ill!'

'Samantha and I haven't done anything wrong,' John protested. 'I've never touched her. She's a colleague!'

'So?' Ingrid turned on him. 'When did working together prevent people from getting naked together?'

275

Vicki burst into tears. Jason immediately began to comfort her.

Philip went on in that calm voice, 'Please, John, I care about the safety of you and your family. Please leave here tonight. You see, I can't take any more. When I look into a mirror, I don't see my reflection. I see Kadesh.'

'Go! Get out!' Ingrid went truly ballistic. She hurled herself at Philip, shoving him backwards. 'This is my home! You've tried to frighten my family. Just go!' She turned around, grabbing Samantha by the arm. 'You, too! Get out!'

John could only stare in shock as his usually self-composed, ultra-rational wife wrestled with Samantha on the patio. When Samantha refused to move, Ingrid grabbed handfuls of that blond hair and dragged the woman along the drive.

'I haven't had sex with John,' Samantha grunted. 'I'm only trying to help. I'm—'

'Go home, sober up. Don't ever come back on to my property again.' Ingrid tugged so hard on Samantha's hair that she yelled in pain.

Everyone followed as Ingrid hauled Samantha to the gates. At that moment, a car roared up. John saw Tom Oldfield, Samantha's husband, behind the wheel. The youngest Oldfield son, Mark, sat in the back seat. He stared out in horror as his mother was cruelly dragged towards the car.

Philip walked alongside John. He watched what happened, saying nothing. He still maintained that air of weary dignity, yet there was such pain in his eyes. 'Leave, John,' he whispered. 'While you still can.' He walked away into the gloom.

276

Meanwhile, Tom sprang from the car. John thought he'd join in the fight. John had a mental image of the Tolworths and the Oldfields throwing punches at one another. However, instead, Tom snatched his wife from Ingrid so violently that it left strands of Samantha's yellow hair in Ingrid's hands.

Tom panted, 'I'm sorry. I've never seen Samantha like this before. God help her, I think she's had a nervous breakdown. She drank half a bottle of brandy when she came home from work. I thought she was in bed. I'm sorry. I can't apologize enough.' He bundled his wife towards the car.

Samantha yelled, 'We're leaving here right now! You should do the same!'

Tom managed to get Samantha into the passenger seat. 'She insisted I pack suitcases. We're going to stay with friends in Barnstaple. I'm sorry. I never even realized she'd left the house.' He began to shout, 'Jason, get in the car. Jason!'

'I want to stay with Vicki,' Jason protested.

'Please get in the car, Jason. We'll sort this out later.' Apologizing again, Tom closed the door, shutting his wife in. When Jason was in the back seat, alongside his terrified brother, Tom drove away, headlights blazing into the darkness.

Samantha opened the window. 'Leave, leave! The Event is coming. The mummies are changing into you!'

After the shouting, the anger, and the mayhem, there was silence as the Oldfields' car vanished into the night.

For a moment, nobody said anything. Then Vicki erupted. 'It's not fair! You've done all this to stop me seeing Jason, haven't you?'

Ingrid was trying to catch her breath after tussling with Samantha. 'Don't be ridiculous. This is nothing to do with you and Jason.'

John added with some heat, 'And it's certainly nothing to do with me having an affair with Samantha. I haven't touched the woman!'

Vicki stormed into the house, and Ingrid gave John a hard stare before following her indoors. John shook his head. He stood there by himself on the driveway and wondered how on earth he'd convince Ingrid that he'd done nothing wrong.

'Oh, wow,' Micky said, chuckling. 'That was amazing. I wish I'd filmed it.'

The back lawn was illuminated by candles and lanterns. He'd witnessed everything. The shouting, the arm waving, then the two women brawling. That was so frickin' cool. Of course, he didn't know what had caused the argument down there; he couldn't hear actual words from this distance, but what a show! That had beaten television drama. Even from way up here, he could tell that the dark-haired woman had wanted to kill the blond. Then the car had turned up, the blond and the teenage kid had got in, and the car had gone roaring away like it was being pursued by cops. Micky shook his head in astonishment. He only hoped the next stage of the drama tonight, the one he was just about to initiate, would be half as exciting and, well . . . **VIOLENT.**

* * *

Fletcher's dad had explicitly told Fletcher to stay indoors while he went to the hospital. Fletcher didn't obey the order. He left the gatehouse apartment and walked along the drive in the direction of the castle. He sensed electricity in the air tonight. Something would happen. He was sure of it. Stars blazed in the sky, and Fletcher told himself that each and every one twinkled with anxiety. Even the stars flashed a warning to those on earth who knew how to interpret the signs. But Fletcher walked confidently through the darkness.

When he approached the big main doors of the castle he saw they were wide open. There were no lights on inside. Fletcher had watched the men installing electronic locks on these doors a few days ago. He knew that the doors could be locked and unlocked by a computer inside the castle. Now the doors were very much unlocked; they yawned open, like the doors of a tomb in a horror film.

He saw something, else, too. The mummies walked. He made out the silhouettes of five figures in the distance – five slow-moving figures that had strips of cloth hanging down from their limbs. The mummies had left the castle, and Fletcher knew that people would die tonight.

Everyone's gone nuts. Crazy, shouting, fighting nuts. That's the conclusion Oliver had reached as he sat watching television with Ben while the grown-ups yelled outside. Just five minutes ago, Mr Oldfield had driven away with Mrs Oldfield, Jason and Mark.

Oliver worried about what was happening. Was his family going to move into different houses? He'd got friends whose parents had split up. Was this happening to his mother and father? The shouting had been so violent and frightening.

'It'll be alright, Ollie,' said Ben, sitting on the sofa beside him, the leg in the cast stretched out. 'Everyone argues.'

'I've never heard Mum and Dad argue like that before.' He could hear his mother stomping around in the bedroom upstairs now. Vicki was in her own bedroom. She'd run upstairs crying and saying stuff about her mother trying to stop Jason from seeing her. 'Why do people sometimes act like their brains have gone wacko?' asked Oliver.

Ben shrugged. 'It's human nature. Often we get angry with the people we care about.'

'I hate this. If families like each other they should stay friends and not yell.'

'I couldn't agree more. Just wait until tomorrow; everything will be back to normal again. People will be smiling and happy.'

'I don't want you to leave, Ben. I like you. It's great having a big brother.'

'Cheers, Ollie. Don't worry, I'm not going anywhere. We're going to the coast tomorrow, aren't we? We'll play frisbee on the beach, and you can try out your mask and snorkel in the sea.'

'I haven't got a mask and snorkel.'

'In that case, I'll buy you one.' Grinning, he ruffled Oliver's hair. 'You can swim out and catch a shark.'

Oliver laughed. Even so, he still felt worried.

He remembered only too vividly that Ben had that packet of white powder in the bottom of his rucksack. Oliver wasn't so naive to believe that powder was sugar, or soap powder. *Drugs.* Just thinking the word made Oliver shiver. *Drugs are illegal. If the police know that Ben's got drugs, they'll take him away. He'll go to prison. Those drugs could be the reason that he leaves us.*

'Where you going, champ?' Ben asked.

'To get a drink of milk. Want one?'

'Why not? Cheers.'

Oliver went straight to Ben's room at the back of the house. Ben, being in the lounge, wouldn't realize where he'd gone; he certainly couldn't follow easily with that busted leg, either. Oliver's mother and sister were upstairs. His dad was outside in the garden, sitting all moody and bad tempered on a patio chair. Oliver couldn't make everything all right with his parents, but he could keep Ben safe from being caught with the drugs, and getting arrested and thrown into a cell. Oliver didn't hesitate. He unzipped the rucksack, dug his hand down inside, and pulled out the plastic box containing the bag of white powder. After that, he darted upstairs to his bedroom. Carefully, he tucked the plastic box, with its evil contents, under his bed.

Minutes later, he returned to the lounge with glasses of milk and sliced cake on a tray.

Ben used a ruler to scratch an itch down inside the cast. 'I was beginning to think you'd gone to bed.'

'I couldn't find the cake. Mum had hidden it at the back of the pantry.'

'Hey, dude. We're eating stolen cake. That makes us partners in crime.' Laughing, Ben high-fived Oliver.

Oliver laughed, too. If anything, he felt a massive sense of relief that he'd had the good sense take the drugs from Ben and hide them away. Tomorrow, he'd dump those drugs in a pond out in the forest.

Micky Dunt read the text from Gurrick. *'I want my property. Confirm you have it back. NOW!'*

Micky didn't reply to the text. However, he knew the time had come to act. If he didn't retrieve the coke from Ben Darrington, Gurrick would soon be threatening Micky with the kind of punishment that would make even a medieval torturer turn queasy. 'Time to go, Micky.'

He headed down through the trees towards the house where he knew Ben was staying. At least some of the people had left after the fight in the garden earlier. As far as he could tell, there was a woman and a teenage girl in the house, along with a young boy and Ben. Even from here, he could see the only guy left at the property. He sat on a chair on the patio. The light from the candles and lanterns illuminated him clearly enough. And that guy was the only serious obstacle to Micky taking control down there. Ben, with his busted-up leg, couldn't offer much in the way of resistance. And apart from Ben, there was only the woman, the girl, and the little kid.

Micky checked that his phone was in a side pouch of his bag. He'd been ordered by his mobster boss to film torture in the house. Gurrick wanted gruesome footage to post on the web, proving that he wasn't a guy to be messed around. The police wouldn't be able to link the footage to Gurrick, but Gurrick's associates and rivals would be told that he'd orchestrated the torture vid and had made sure it was uploaded as a lesson to others. *Yup, phone fully charged, good to go.* He pulled out the handgun. Fully loaded, too. Micky's trigger finger started to tingle. Already, he could imagine aiming the pistol at someone's head, then using that tingly finger to pull the trigger.

The obvious first step was to destroy the guy on the patio. If he was removed from the equation, then holding up the rest of the household, retrieving the drugs, then filming someone being hurt – screaming-puking-eye-bulging hurt – would be straightforward.

In the event, the first part of the plan worked out surprisingly well. Micky padded up the drive and crept to where the guy sat on the patio chair; he was staring into space, his mind on other things. Micky slammed the pistol into the side of the man's head. He just gave a funny-sounding grunt. After that, he flopped sideways on to the ground.

It was after eleven o'clock at night. Nobody had told Oliver to go to bed. What's more, he didn't feel like going to bed. He felt all strange and worked-up inside and didn't know whether he wanted to shout swear words or cry. Oliver stood by his chest of drawers. He scratched its shiny woodwork with a coin. He knew he was damaging it by covering it with scratches, but he didn't care. He was angry with his parents for behaving like they were spoilt kids.

Suddenly, he heard his name being whispered.

'Ollie . . . Ollie, it's me.'

He glanced back at the open window. 'Fletcher? What is it?'

Just beyond the open window, he could make out the twelve year old in the gloom. He stood on a branch in the big tree that grew close to the house. Fletcher wore the red cap that Oliver had given him. Fletcher walked along the branch, arms extended to keep his balance. He grabbed on to the window ledge and leaned forwards so that his head was in the room. 'Ollie, I came to warn you.'

'Warn me about what?'

'It's the mummies. They're walking. I saw them heading this way.'

'I don't care.' Oliver spoke angrily. This evening's events had upset him badly.

'You should, Ollie. The mummies are *walking*. I know something will happen tonight. I can see it. Everything – the stars, the rocks, the trees, the walls of this house – they've all got a worried expression.'

'You're stupid, Fletcher. You say stupid things all the time. I'm sick of you lying about the mummies walking.'

'Ollie, you've seen them walk. Kadesh picked you up and almost carried you away.'

Oliver threw the coin at Fletcher. It missed the boy's head by an inch. 'My parents have gone wild with each other. I'm worried they might split up, and you come here telling me stories!'

'It's not a story. The mummies have left the castle. All of them are walking. I've seen them.'

Tears ran down Oliver's face. 'It's not fair. I liked it here, now it's all spoilt.'

Fletcher's manner was quietly sympathetic. Somehow he seemed so grown up tonight. 'Tell me what's wrong, Oliver.'

Oliver sat down on the bed. It all came pouring out – all the worry, the fear, the distress. He told Fletcher that Mrs Oldfield had come into the garden. She'd been acting weird, saying that somehow the mummies were turning into the Tolworth family. Oliver couldn't understand properly what she'd said. 'She kept using the word "convergence",' Oliver explained. 'She said that my family were like those mummies, and that we were getting close to an "event". She kept saying that something bad will happen to us soon, and that we should leave here while we still can.'

'Mrs Oldfield is right. Something will happen. I don't know what it is, but I know that the mummies from the castle are involved. You know it too, deep down. You told me that Kadesh came into the house. You know the mummies walk, and they have a way of making people sleep when they do.'

Oliver had never felt such misery before. 'Could the bad thing be about drugs?'

'Drugs? Why do you say that?'

Oliver told him that he'd found a bag full of white powder in the bottom of Ben's rucksack.

'The police will take Ben to prison if they find out he's got drugs, won't they?'

'Where are the drugs now?'

Oliver reached under his bed and pulled out the box that contained the bag of white powder.

'You've got to get rid of that stuff.'

'I was going to chuck it in a pond tomorrow.'

'If the police come here, they'll have dogs that can sniff drugs out. You've got to get it away from the house right now.'

'It's nearly midnight.'

'It could be cocaine or heroin. Ben would go to prison for possession.'

Oliver shook his head. 'It's late. I'm not allowed out.' Fletcher's expression was so sympathetic that a lump formed in Oliver's throat.

'You've got to be the big man, Oliver. You've got to become the hero. If you want to save Ben from prison then you've got to get rid of those drugs. His fingerprints and DNA will be on the box. The police will use that as evidence in court.'

Oliver shook his head. 'I'm not going out. I daren't; you said the mummies are coming here.'

'Maybe it is something to do with the drugs. Because you're agitated it makes the mummies agitated. You'll be able to relax again as soon as we've dumped that stuff. Then they might just go back to the castle.'

'Do you think I'm turning into a mummy?'

'What? A dead Egyptian?' Fletcher tried to make a joke of it. 'Nah, you're just some kid from London, wearing a stupid yellow T-shirt.'

Despite himself, he laughed at Fletcher's grinning face. 'OK, I'll come with you.'

286

'Climb out of the window, and use the tree. All the house lights are on, and I've seen your mother and sister moving about. If you go downstairs, they'll see you and stop you from coming with me.'

Oliver tugged on his sandals, grabbed his rucksack, stuffed the box of evil white powder into it, and pulled the straps over his shoulders. The drugs were like a curse. He dreaded the idea of the police taking Ben away. He liked Ben and felt safe with him. 'Where are we going?' he whispered as he climbed out of the window.

'I know a place where we can hide those drugs so they'll never be found in a million years. Watch where you put your feet. If you fall, it's a long way down.'

Micky Dunt had spotted the kid in the red cap come scuttling into the garden. Before the kid could notice Micky and the unconscious guy on the patio, Micky had dragged his victim into the bushes where they'd both be out of sight. *Don't want some lousy kid raising the alarm, do we now?* Micky had crouched next to the guy, who was dead to the world. *Kids are weird,* he told himself. *What's this one doing climbing a tree at this time of night?* There was no obvious reason why the kid indulged in nocturnal tree climbing.

Micky heard the kid talking to the younger boy, who was in a bedroom. He didn't make out any actual words, but the younger boy was upset – at one point he started to cry. A little while later both boys climbed down out of the tree before heading off into the forest. *Maybe gone out to smoke a joint?* An entirely plausible notion to

287

Micky, who'd joyously embraced the drug culture when he was still a schoolboy.

The man on the ground moaned. *OK, sleeping beauty's starting to wake up. Time to get busy.* Micky pulled the gaffer tape out of the rucksack. It didn't take long to tape the guy's wrists and ankles together. *Nicely trussed up, completely powerless: good work, Micky.*

The guy muttered something, squirmed a little, and grimaced when the pain of the blow to the skull began to register. He still hadn't come round properly. Grabbing the man's feet, Micky dragged him back on to the patio. He took his phone from the bag. He filmed the man lying there, eyelids fluttering, grunting, a trickle of blood leaking from the head wound across the patio. Micky had started making his torture video. OK, time to recruit some more actors for his production. He chuckled when he looked through the window into the lounge. The woman, the teenage girl, and Ben were there.

'All this is flowing nicely,' he murmured, pleased. He knew his plan was going to work just perfectly. Pulling out the gun, he entered the kitchen by the back door and headed for the sound of voices.

A female (the girl) shrieked, 'I don't care what you do to me. You'll not stop Jason and me seeing each other.'

The older woman came back with, 'Why do you always think that the world revolves around you, Vicki? Other people have issues in their lives, you know?'

Micky had heard Ben's voice often enough to

recognize it now. Ben seemed to be trying to calm the pair down. 'It's none of my business, but isn't it best you sleep on all this tonight?'

Micky clicked off the handgun's safety switch. Smoothly, without rushing, he stepped into the living room.

'Micky?' Ben's expression was one of total astonishment.

The two women gasped in shock when they saw the pistol. Their eyes became so big and round in their heads that Micky half-believed their eyeballs would pop right out.

Micky grinned. 'I'm here to collect my goods, Ben.' He raised the gun, making sure they all saw that the muzzle pointed at Ben's head. 'Do not shout. Do not move. You're all going to do exactly as I say. In a moment, I will tell you to move outside to the patio. Do not try and run away. Otherwise I will shoot. OK? Good . . . Now, Ben, you infuriating bastard, bring me the cocaine I asked you to keep safe for me.' Micky used the pistol to tap the leg cast. 'Come on, Ben. Hop to it.' Micky laughed. 'Hop to it? Ha. Ha. And you and your broken leg.' Suddenly, he grabbed hold of the front of Ben's T-shirt and dragged him to his feet. 'Get my stuff. Go!'

Moonlight revealed the path at the edge of the forest. Oliver Tolworth followed Fletcher; both were running. Oliver could feel the heavy box in his rucksack knocking against the bottom of his back as they ran. There were lots of drugs in the box. To Oliver it seemed as if that evil powder wanted to make its presence felt. *Jab, jab, jab!*

289

The corner of the box was like a finger digging into his spine, hell-bent on reminding the boy that he carried a substance that was as dangerous as it was illegal. Do kids get locked up if they're caught with drugs? Oliver hadn't heard of any school children being jailed, but maybe there were. Imagine, if a policeman stepped out in front of him right now and said, '*You've got something in your rucksack, haven't you? Show me, boy.*' Oliver shivered. He could already hear the clang of a cell door in his ears.

'Here!'

Oliver was so startled by Fletcher's yell that he cried out.

'Nervous?' asked Fletcher.

Oliver nodded. 'I don't want the police to catch us with this stuff.'

'The police never come here.' Fletcher paused. 'Did you see them on the other side of the field?'

'See who?'

'The mummies. All five of them. They're walking towards the houses.'

Oliver couldn't take any more tonight, no more stress, no more emotional overload. 'Stop lying, Fletcher.'

'You noticed them. They're easy to see with the moon being so bright. You're just pretending that they're not there.'

'Stop that shit!' Oliver's face burned with anger. 'Having these drugs in my bag is scaring me. I just want to get rid of them.'

'Then get rid of them.'

'How?'

'We're here.' Fletcher left the path and stamped

on a patch of moss. Instead of his foot making a soft thumping noise, like it should when stamping on mossy ground, it made a loud, hollow-sounding clunk.

'What is that?' asked Oliver. That clunk sounded like a big wooden box being stamped on. Mental images formed inside his head of a coffin buried just below the surface. Once again, searing flashes of panic burst inside of him.

Kneeling down, Fletcher began scraping the moss away. 'It's the top of an old mine shaft,' he explained. 'Years ago they sealed the opening shut so people wouldn't fall down and be killed. The planks are rotten now. It's easy to move them.' Fletcher did just that. Working by moonlight alone, he lifted up a slab of wood and pushed it aside. 'Listen.' He picked up a stone and dropped it through the gap.

A long . . . long . . . time later Oliver heard a splash of water. 'Damn and hell,' he breathed. 'That's a long way down.'

'Nobody will find anything that goes down there. Dump the drugs in it.'

Oliver didn't need telling twice. Quickly, as if there was a danger the white powder would burst into flame and burn his hands to the bone, he tugged the plastic box from the rucksack. He felt the heavy bag of powder slide inside the box. It was as if the drugs were alive in there and trying to find a way out. 'I'll open the bag and tip the powder down.'

Fletcher shook his head. 'No. The breeze is getting up. If the powder is blown on to your clothes, the police sniffer dogs would pick up the scent of drugs on you. Keep everything in the box. Chuck the lot down there.'

Crouching, Oliver pushed the box through the gap. The smell of cold, stagnant water reached his nostrils. He opened his fingers, allowing the heavy box to tumble away into the darkness. A long time later the sound of the splash echoed up the mine shaft. The drugs were gone. He hoped the anxiety he felt would now vanish, too.

Out on the patio, Micky Dunt stared at Ben in disbelief. 'What do you mean it's gone?'

'The box with the coke. I kept it in the bottom of my rucksack. It's vanished.'

'Vanished where?'

'I don't know.'

'Did you tell anyone about what you'd got stashed there?'

'No.'

'How can it have disappeared, then?'

'It just has, Micky. I checked this morning and the stuff was still there.'

'But now it's gone?'

Ben nodded.

'Oh, right.' Micky glared at the kid as he stood there, using the crutch to balance himself. 'I show up, and all of a sudden thousands of pounds-worth of cocaine disappears from your bag. Convenient, huh?'

'I'm telling you, Micky, it's—'

'Shut up!' Micky considered the situation. Here he stood on the patio. The guy he'd knocked out still lay at his feet, ankles and wrists bound together by tape. The woman and the teenage girl stood at one end of the patio, some ten feet from him. Their eyes glittered with fear in the light of candles and lamps dotted around the garden. Just seconds ago, Ben Darrington, the son of Micky's girlfriend, had hobbled out here to tell him that a valuable consignment of cocaine had gone missing from his bag. Shit. What would Karl Gurrick say if Micky phoned him with the news? 'Sorry, Mr Gurrick, Ben Darrington mislaid your coke. You're not at all annoyed, are you?' Gurrick would ignite with rage. He'd chop Micky to pieces. Gurrick would suspect Micky of keeping the drugs so that he could sell them himself and take all the money. Of course, Micky now concluded that Ben Darrington planned to do exactly that. He'd portion out the coke into little plastic bags then sell it to his student friends, while, no doubt, laughing at Micky's misfortune.

Micky aimed the gun at Ben. 'Give me back my drugs.'

'I haven't got them.'

Micky pointed the gun at the older woman. 'Ben, I won't ask twice. I know you're hiding my gear. Give it back.'

'You've got to believe me, Micky. I haven't got that coke. It's gone. Someone stole it.'

Micky strode over to the woman and jabbed the gun into her chest. 'I don't believe you, Ben. But if you're content to see this lady get shot . . .'

The two women gasped in shock.

The older woman took a deep breath. 'Ben. Do as he asks.'

'Ingrid, I'm so sorry. I don't know where they've gone.'

'You brought drugs into my home, Ben. We trusted you. John thought you were wonderful, and now we learn that you're just some drug-dealing piece of shit.' The woman – Ben had called her Ingrid – glared at him in fury, her eyes flashing. She didn't even seem concerned that the pistol was jabbed into her ribs.

'I didn't want to bring them here.' Ben sounded distraught. He hobbled closer to Ingrid. 'I only agreed to keep them for a few days, then I broke my leg. I went to hospital and didn't have an opportunity to return them.'

The teenage girl stared at Ben in astonishment, and Ingrid shook her head in disgust. 'You're *friends* with this man?'

'Micky Dunt? Hell, no. I hate him. He's a thug. He's my mother's partner, but he knocks her around.'

Micky barked out one word: 'Bastard!' He kicked the crutch away from Ben. The kid lost his balance, crashing to the floor with a yell. Micky watched with satisfaction as this individual, who had caused him so much trouble, writhed in pain while clutching the leg cast.

Micky said, 'You will tell me where you've hidden my stuff.' While aiming the gun at the woman, he pulled out his phone, switched to movie camera mode, pressed 'Record', and then he kicked Ben's broken leg. He watched the phone's screen as Ben's face twisted with agony. 'All you have to do, Ben, is tell me where I can find the coke. Then I'll leave.'

That was a lie, of course. In all the excitement, Micky had overlooked one important fact.

These people could identify him to the police. They'd have to be silenced forever. When all this was over, when he'd got the coke safely in his bag, when he'd got torture footage that would satisfy Karl Gurrick, then he'd have to come up with the next part of the plan. Perhaps something to do with a tragic house fire? A situation where the skeletons of a whole family are found in the smouldering ruins. Yes, that would work nicely.

John Tolworth realized that in this terrible situation he had one small element in his favour. The gunman didn't know that he had recovered consciousness. John only opened his eyes by the tiniest fraction. Candlelight revealed the scene. He lay on the patio, his wrists and ankles bound together. His head hurt so much that he wondered if he'd been shot. He recalled Samantha rushing into the garden, breathlessly telling them that the castle mummies were changing. That they were beginning to share physical characteristics with the Tolworth family. He remembered right up to the point where he'd been sitting out on the patio, wondering how he could persuade Ingrid that he spoke the truth – that he'd not had sex with Samantha Oldfield. He'd been brooding over the evening's events; moths had been flying around the candle flames. The next thing he knew he'd woken up on the ground.

He'd clearly heard people speaking. He knew Ingrid and Vicki were there, being held at gunpoint by the crook Micky Dunt. John knew that his wife and daughter were scared, no matter how defiant they sounded when they answered Micky back. John had pieced together what had been said since he came round. Micky had left a significant quantity of cocaine in Ben's care. Micky wanted it back. Ben claimed that the drugs had vanished. Micky had shown no qualms about threatening to shoot John's wife and daughter. Now Ben lay beside John, and he'd been kicked several times. John had been able to make out that Micky held a pistol in one hand, while he used a phone to film Ben. The kicks kept on coming. Ben grunted with the force of the boot smashing into his ribs.

Micky shouted, 'Is this your father, Ben?' He kicked John's hip. 'He looks like you.'

Agony flashed through John's hip bone. He forced himself to lie still, feigning unconsciousness, yet he still kept his eyes open by the tiniest amount.

'You two.' Micky gestured at Ingrid and Vicki. 'Get down . . . kneel . . . hands on top of your heads.'

John tried to watch what happened next without moving his head and without raising his eyelids any further. He didn't even feel the pain in his own head now. What he saw shocked him so much he could hardly breathe.

Micky filmed Vicki as he pointed the gun at her face. 'OK, Ben. Tell me where you put the coke, or I'll blow her head off.'

At that moment, John felt like he wanted to die. He could do nothing to save his daughter. All he could do was lie there and watch her be murdered. He'd never felt so helpless in his life.

It was as if all the bones had vanished from his body, leaving him as useless as a lump jelly.

'You've got to believe me,' Ben panted where he lay beside John. 'I do not have those drugs. OK? Someone stole them.'

'Who?'

'I don't know.'

'Alright, you're to blame for this, Ben. This is your fault. You watch when the bullet goes through her mouth and rips off the back of her head.'

Vicki screamed, '*Dad! Wake up!*'

John would have given anything to be free of these bonds. He'd leap to his feet and beat the thug to death with his fists. Instinct, however, told him to pretend he was out cold. That might just give him a precious element of surprise.

Micky snarled, 'On the count of three I fire.' He positioned the phone so that it filmed a close-up of Vicki's terrified face. 'One.'

Ben wept. 'No, Micky, please.'

'Two.'

Ingrid spoke softly: 'Micky, look at me. I'll do anything you want me to do.'

'Three.'

John closed his eyes tight, waiting for the sound of the gunshot. A long pause. A night bird called. The breeze rustled leaves in a tree.

'*BANG!*'

John's heart convulsed. He almost screamed. A moment later he breathed again. That *BANG* hadn't been the sound of the gun being fired. That had been Micky shouting; the sadist had made them all think that he'd shot Vicki. Micky

Dunt was just playing mind games – OK, they were the cruellest of mind games – and he clearly didn't intend to kill anyone just yet.

'OK, Ben.' Micky pointed the gun at Vicki, Ingrid and Ben in turn. He ignored John, clearly believing him to be still unconscious. 'I'm going to find another way to make you tell me where you've put my property.'

He took hold of Ben's leg in its cast and hoisted it upwards. Ben, lying there on his back, grunted in pain. Micky rested Ben's foot on a chair. After that, he collected a candle where it burned in its holder on the table. Micky positioned the candle so that the tip of the flame licked where the back of Ben's knee was encased by the fracture cast.

Micky filmed the candle beneath the leg. 'So . . . how long do you think it'll take that flame to burn through the cast and start roasting your skin, Ben?'

Ingrid whispered, 'Please, Micky. Stop hurting Ben. We're all frightened.'

'Shut up.'

'Remember what I told you. I'll do anything you want. Why don't just the two of us go back inside the house?'

Oliver Tolworth tried to make sense of what he saw in the back garden of his house. Candles and lamps illuminated the scene. His father lay on the patio, while his mother and sister knelt on the ground. For some bizarre reason Ben lay on his back on the ground with his leg raised, so his foot rested on a chair. A candle had been positioned under his leg. Ben's head rolled from side to side as if he was agitated. His father didn't move at all. Were they playing some kind of joke? A trick of some sorts? Were they all drunk? Oliver couldn't understand what was happening.

One second later he understood perfectly. A man stepped out of the shadows. He held a pistol in his hand, which he pointed first at Oliver's mother and then at this sister. The man was laughing and talking. He was too far away to allow Oliver to make out any actual words. Oliver, however, knew exactly what the man was doing.

Fletcher stood beside Oliver; he, too, stared at the people in the garden.

Oliver was surprised at how calm he sounded when he spoke. 'That man's holding my family at gunpoint. He must have come here to rob us.'

'Why isn't your dad moving?'

'He's not dead.' Oliver spoke more in hope rather than absolute conviction. 'There's tape around his arms and legs: he's been tied up.'

'It's something to do with the drugs, I'm sure it is. This is what happens when drug dealers fall out. Drug wars.'

Oliver started walking down the slope towards the house.

Fletcher caught him by the arm. 'You can't go down there.'

'I've got to help them.'

'What can you do, Oliver? You're eleven years old.'

'I've got to do something. That man might kill them!'

'Look.' Fletcher pointed into the shadows.

299

'They've come to watch. They knew that this would happen tonight.'

Oliver followed the direction of the pointing finger. There, standing in near-darkness beneath the trees, was a line of five figures. Oliver saw that the figures were absolutely still; they didn't make a sound; they stared at the people being held at gunpoint in the garden. Oliver used the word 'stared' in relation to the five. But how could they 'stare'? They had no eyes. Five bodies that were husks of dried flesh, partly wrapped with strips of linen, stood not fifty feet from Oliver and Fletcher. They did not react when the man with the gun laughed and jabbed the pistol into the side of Vicki's neck. When she screamed, the man laughed louder. And what else was he doing? He held a phone in his hand. The way he moved it suggested he was using the phone to film Oliver's family.

Ben gave a yelping sound. He began to squirm. The man filmed the candle burning under Ben's leg. For now, he seemed more interested in what the candle was doing to Ben's leg than terrorizing Vicki.

'He's going to hurt them all, isn't he?' Oliver said with a sensation of dread. 'Then he's going to kill them.'

'I'll call the police,' whispered Fletcher. 'But we'll have to go back home for my phone.'

'Come on, then!' Running as fast as he could, Oliver headed down the path that led to the gate-house where Fletcher lived. Fletcher followed, panting hard. A sense of urgency seemed to pulsate in the air, and Oliver knew with absolute certainty that time was running out. He blanked the mummies from his mind, and the strangeness of them coming back to life and standing there to watch events unfolding in the Tolworths' back garden. What was vitally important now was reaching the phone and making that emergency call to the police.

When they approached the gatehouse, a figure emerged from a doorway in the building. Oliver recognized the figure as Philip Kemmis, the man with one hand. Oliver's heart lurched with fear. What if the man went crazy now and tried to hurt him and Fletcher? The man strode from the shadows into the moonlight. The wrist stump revealed itself as a pale shape. On the other hand, a black leather glove.

'Fletcher.' He held up both the stump and the hand to stop them. 'Is that you, Oliver? What's wrong? Why are you out so late?'

Oliver would have preferred to rush indoors to telephone the police; however, words spurted from Fletcher's lips. 'There's a man with a pistol,' he panted. 'He's got Oliver's family up at the house. He's hurting them. He's making them scream.'

Philip Kemmis started running in the direction of Oliver's house. 'Come with me,' he called.

Oliver protested, 'He's got a gun. We need to call the police.'

Philip stopped dead and looked back at Oliver. 'It'll take the police at least twenty minutes to get here. It could be too late by then. Besides, I've been expecting this for three thousand years.' The man wasn't joking. His expression was set like stone. 'History's repeating itself. Kadesh failed to save the lives of the family that are now mummies in the castle. Now your family are in danger – I must save them. I have to break the cycle.'

Fletcher's voice rose as if he had a revelation of his own. 'That's why the mummies walk, isn't it? Their spirits are restless.'

Philip's eyes gleamed strangely. 'I see it now. I am Kadesh . . . Kadesh is me. Fundamentally, we're one and the same person. I'm being tested again. If I can save John and his family I will be healed, too. I'll be healed in here.' He pointed at his own head.

Fletcher followed Philip Kemmis. The boy's face shone in the moonlight: there was a kind of eagerness there that was more than being simply eager. His expression was one of ecstasy. It disturbed Oliver so much that he didn't know whether to laugh or cry out in alarm. His own emotions were in turmoil. He was afraid for his family. He was afraid of Philip and Fletcher, too. They looked strange – it was as if both had madness inside of them. All this about history repeating itself and Philip's claim that he and that ancient mummy, Kadesh, were actually the same person freaked Oliver out. At that moment, Oliver decided he was the only rational one of the three.

Once again, he tried to reason with the man and the boy as they ran. 'We should still telephone the police.'

'There isn't time,' Fletcher shouted. 'Come on!'

Oliver Tolworth shot a single, wistful glance

back at the gatehouse; that's where he'd find a phone that would allow him to call for help. With a helpless shrug, he realized he must go with Fletcher Brown and Philip Kemmis. They were heading into danger, but what else could he do but follow?

Philip Kemmis had not been as clear-headed as this in years. He was in complete control of his thoughts. 'I know what I'm doing,' he murmured to himself as he ran along the path in the direction of John Tolworth's house. 'This is the right thing to do. You must break the cycle. You have to stop history repeating itself.'

Philip didn't question whether his actions might be regarded as irrational. No. He knew with absolute certainty that Samantha Oldfield had spoken the truth when, a few hours ago, she had explained that he and that dried-out husk of a corpse known as Kadesh were becoming increasingly more alike. *Yes. I am Kadesh, and Kadesh is me. Three thousand years ago an Egyptian family were attacked and murdered by an unknown enemy. Kadesh tried to protect the family. He failed and died during the attack. Kadesh and the family were mummified and buried in the Gold Tomb. Now those mummies have undergone physical changes to the point that they uncannily resemble the Tolworth family. The Tolworths are in danger. A man holds them at gunpoint. History repeats itself. This is the opportunity for me to save their lives and prevent the same tragedy from happening again.*

Yes . . . it all made perfect sense to Philip.

303

Even though his right hand had vanished thirty years ago, he sensed a tingling there – the flesh had gone, but it was as if a ghost hand still remained. The moon shone down through the trees to cast patches of silver on the grass. Where the moonlight didn't reach the ground, the shadows were the darkest Philip had ever seen. Already, the nature of the earth seemed to be changing, just as the mummies were changing. Tonight would be extraordinary. There would be mir-acles. He knew there'd be horror, too, just as there was horror when some unknown indi-vidual had murdered a mother and her three children long ago in Egypt.

Philip glanced back. Both Fletcher and Oliver followed. Instinct told him they must be part of what happened tonight. No matter how violent, how bloody, or whether this sequence of events had fatal consequences.

A smell of burning, followed by a yell. Ben Darrington, lying on the patio, arched his back as the pain slammed into him. Micky Dunt real-ized that the candle had, at last, burnt through the fracture cast, and the intense heat was searing the back of the teenager's knee.

Micky used his phone to film Ben convulsing. *Funny how just a little candle can cause so much pain*, Micky told himself. *Imagine how agonizing it would be if a blowtorch was used on someone's leg.*

'That's enough!' The woman called Ingrid shouted the words. She darted forward, batting the candle away with her hand.

'Hey!' Micky shouted. 'I didn't give you permission to move, did I?'

'I won't let you torture that boy.'

'Boy? He's nineteen, and he stole valuable drugs. I want them back.'

Ben gasped, 'I haven't got them any more. Someone stole them from me.'

'Keep telling me lies, Ben, and I'll keep hurting you.'

Ingrid stepped forward. 'He's not lying. After the way you've hurt him, don't you think he'd have given you the drugs if he still had them?'

Micky sneered, 'All he need do is take a bit of pain tonight. After I've gone, he can sell that coke for a hell of a lot of cash.' Suddenly, Micky felt uneasy. He had a sensation that eyes were boring into his back. He turned round. Ben's father still lay unconscious on the ground. *Come to think of it, though, had he moved?* Micky thought he'd been lying nearer the patio wall. Now he seemed closer to Ben.

Shivers poured down Micky's back. Raising the hand that held the gun, he turned to face the hillside where all those trees were illuminated by the moon. *Wait . . . just for a moment, I thought I saw someone up there. A tall, thin guy, staring in this direction.* Micky got uneasy. Here he was, with four people, in a back garden lit by lamps and a shitload of candles. There was a pool of light, meaning he could be seen holding the gun. Micky felt too exposed. Perhaps there wasn't anyone watching from the woods, but what if someone happened along? Didn't they have gamekeepers and poachers out here in the

305

countryside? What if someone saw him torturing the kid? They'd be sure to have a phone with them. They'd report this to the police.

Micky experienced an urgent need to get indoors and out of sight. What he did next to these people must be done in private. He approached the guy on the ground – the one he now knew was called John Tolworth – and he kicked him in the side of the head. The guy didn't open his eyes, or move (even though he couldn't move much; Micky had taped the man's wrists and ankles together). So, Micky reasoned, he must still be out cold.

He waved the gun at Vicki and Ingrid. 'OK, get Ben inside the house.'

They didn't protest and helped Ben to his feet. Supporting him between them, they helped him into the lounge of the house. There they set him down on the sofa. Micky ordered the women to sit on either side of Ben. Quickly, Micky taped Ben's wrists together with the gaffer tape. Then he did the same to Vicki and Ingrid. He also bound their ankles together in case they decided the time had come to make a run for it.

Ingrid said, 'You won't hurt us?'

Micky clicked his tongue. 'This isn't my fault. It's Ben's here. You persuade him to give me the coke back, then I'll leave.'

Oh . . . but what a gem of a lie. Of course I'm not going to leave them here in one piece so they can tell the police what I've done. There's going to be a fire tonight. A big, big evidence-cleansing fire.

It took some doing, but Micky managed to drag

306

John Tolworth in through the back door. Hauling Tolworth all that way to the lounge, which meant going up two steps, seemed too much like hard work. Micky found an easy solution to his problem. He dragged the unconscious guy across the stone floor and into the larder just off the kitchen. Micky had taped the guy's limbs together, meaning he couldn't move easily. Even so, just to play it safe, he shut Tolworth in the larder, then locked the door from the outside. If the man recovered consciousness he still wouldn't be a problem. What's more, he'd be nicely trapped in the larder when Micky set fire to the house.

As soon as he heard the key turn, John opened his eyes. He knew immediately that he'd been locked in the larder that led off from the kitchen. A small window let in moonlight, revealing shelves of food, bunches of dried herbs, and plumbing pipes running along the bottom of the walls. The kick in the head had been difficult to bear without revealing that he was awake, but he'd managed it. Once again, he understood he had one very small factor in his favour. Micky Dunt thought that John remained unconscious. Now, here was John's chance to do something. But what? He was tied up and locked in the larder. How could he help his family? However, he must do something. Ingrid, Vicki and Ben were vulnerable. John had seen Micky hurting Ben. He knew that Micky wanted those drugs back. What's more, John knew that they could all identify Micky when they reported this to the police. Would Micky simply leave here, knowing

307

that he'd be arrested within hours? Hardly. Micky would have to deal with any witnesses that could testify against him.

John Tolworth opened his eyes fully, straining to adjust to the few beams of moonlight coming through the window. He tried to wriggle free of the tape that held his arms and legs. Nope . . . no way could he break that strong tape. He'd have to come up with some other plan. He scanned the shelves full of cans and packet food, the pipes on the walls, and prayed for inspiration. He needed to act fast.

Micky continued to demand that Ben tell him where the drugs were. Each exhausted shake of Ben's head brought a punch. Each, '*I don't know where they are!*' triggered another outburst of rage in Micky that led to slaps being delivered to all three on the sofa.

'You *will* tell me where they are.' Micky pulled a knife from his pocket and set it down on the coffee table in plain view. 'Because if you don't I'm going to start cutting your face.'

Lying there on the larder floor, John heard Ben cry out. The screams came every few seconds – long, loud, filled with so much pain.

'Do something,' hissed John. 'Think . . . think. What can you see?' His eyes swept the room. 'Shelves, food, vacuum cleaner, stepladder, string, water pipes, shoes, jars, empty bottles, carrier bags . . . Wait, just wait.' He stared at the plumbing fixed to the wall. 'That's not a water pipe – *it's gas.*'

He bent his knees, drawing his taped-together feet up. He bided his time until he heard Ben's next scream echoing throughout the house. That's when John kicked out. The bottom of his feet struck the metal gas pipe – it was old and, hopefully, brittle.

Even though he'd kicked the pipe as hard as he could, he realized he hadn't made so much as a dent. He couldn't kick again when it was quiet in the house, otherwise Micky would hear the noise and investigate. The thug would probably kill John there and then to make sure he didn't try anything else. So when Ben screamed again – Micky was working hard to inflict pain – John kicked out at the pipe once more. The scream covered the sound of his shoes slamming into the pipework.

This time . . . success! The pipe snapped clean in two. Gas instantly jetted from the broken pipe. It didn't just breeze into the larder, it gushed forcefully from the open end of the pipe. In fact, the rush of gas was so powerful that it raised a dust-storm. Bunches of herbs fluttered in that jet of foul smelling vapour. John felt it blast into his face, tugging at his hair. He knew that domestic gas wasn't toxic. Even so, the smell made him nauseous. And although the gas flooding into the room wouldn't poison him, it was inflammable. In a few moments, when enough gas had poured out, all it would require was a spark. That gaseous fuel would create one hell of a fireball.

John struggled into a sitting position. So far so good: now he must find something that would produce the spark which would ignite the gas.

* * *

Philip reached the house where his childhood friend John Tolworth lived with his family. The time was well after midnight. Oliver and Fletcher were with him. Philip put his finger to his lips; the two boys nodded, knowing that both stealth and silence were vital. Philip glanced again at Oliver Tolworth. Just for a moment, the boy's face revealed wide cracks in the skin, shrivelled eyeballs, and tufts of hair attached to a decaying scalp. Instead of clothes, the boy wore the linen bindings of an Egyptian mummy. The moon shone down on a living boy by the name of Oliver Tolworth, but for a few seconds Philip had seen the mummified child known as Ket. Fletcher remained Fletcher, of course. He wasn't part of this strange convergence that was taking place between the mummies from the castle and the Tolworth family. Philip concealed the revulsion and fear he'd felt when he'd seen Oliver take on the appearance of Ket. Of course, Oliver wouldn't have felt any change in himself. Fletcher had noticed no change either. Only Philip saw the mummy's shrivelled face superimpose itself on the face of the living child.

Philip steeled his nerves for what he needed to do next. He carefully approached the house. In the back garden he saw burning candles. There was no one there, but a sudden yell from the house told him where the gunman had taken his hostages. Philip padded in the direction of the lounge window. Before he got any closer he gestured to the boys to stay back. They obediently crouched down in the shadows. Philip knew that all hell would be let loose if the gunman caught sight of them.

He edged his way to the window. The lounge was brightly lit and Philip took everything in with a glance. He saw a youth on the sofa flanked by Ingrid and Vicki. All three had their wrists and ankles bound together. No sign of John, however. A man in his forties held a pistol in one hand and a phone in the other. He struck the youth's head with the butt of the gun. The youth cried out.

Then it happened again: Philip felt strange sliding sensation in his head. When he peered in through the window he saw Ingrid, Vicki and the youth transform in front of his eyes. Suddenly, Philip was seeing three mummified bodies sitting on the sofa. They were from the collection of mummies at the castle that he knew so well; once those husks had belonged to his family. He saw the mummies called Isis, Amber and Bones. The youth was the most horrific of all. Parts of his flesh had decayed away, exposing the ribs and sections of skull around one eye and alongside the jaw. The teeth were fully exposed on that side of the head. The gunman saw nothing amiss with his hostages, though. He jabbed the pistol at the three as he intimidated them. Philip, alone, saw the living people transform into the mummies. The hideous sight was deeply disturbing. Philip bit his lip hard to stop himself from crying out.

What did make him grunt out loud, however, was his own reflection in the glass. He saw Kadesh there. The mummy's eyes were wide open. The eyeballs were glistening, living eyes, which made the dead face even more horrific. The contrast between living eyes and ancient, lifeless flesh was nothing less than an abomination. He gulped in a lungful of air, trying to hold on to his sanity – or what remained of his sanity. When he looked again he saw three living people on the sofa – Ingrid, the youth, and Vicki.

Philip returned to the boys and whispered, 'Stay there, I'll be right back.' He skirted round the house in order to look for John. He glanced in each window in turn. When he reached the kitchen he smelt a powerful odour. 'Gas.'

Surprised, he looked in through the kitchen window. Nobody there. He moved on. He wouldn't have even noticed the tiny larder window if it hadn't been for the incredibly strong smell of gas filling his nostrils. Approaching the window, he realized straight away that the gas was coming from there. He tried to open the small section at the top, where the stench of gas was at its most pungent, but it was held in place by a lock. The window was open by barely an inch. Philip, however, managed to see inside. There on the floor lay John Tolworth. Even though it was gloomy inside the larder, Philip could make out blood on John's face.

Philip whispered through the gap, 'John . . . John. Up here. It's me, Philip.'

John's hands and ankles were bound, too. Even so, he managed to raise his head. Their eyes met, and John's expression of surprise and sheer relief was plain to see. He began talking in urgent whispers: 'Philip! There's a man with a gun. He's called Micky Dunt. He says that Ben has drugs that belong to him.'

'Ben?'

'Ben Darrington. He's my son . . . I can't explain everything now. That guy, Dunt, is torturing Ben. He'll end up killing us, because we can identify him to the police.'

'Don't worry, I'll tackle this Micky. I'll make sure your family are safe.'

'No, you can't. He's got a gun. He'll kill you, Philip. Micky is a ruthless bastard.'

'I'll think of something.'

'I already have.' John nodded at a pipe that was snapped clean through. 'I've broken the gas pipe.'

'I can smell it.'

'Look.' He rolled sideways on the floor. 'I've found a cigarette lighter; it was next to that box of candles.'

'John, what are you planning to do?' Philip stared at the man in horror.

'I'm going to start shouting. When Micky opens the door I'll ignite the gas that's filled this room. It will blow Micky Dunt to kingdom come.'

'You can't, John, you'll be killed, too.'

'I've no choice, Philip. That guy will murder my family soon. I know he will.'

Philip's heart pounded with shock. 'John, the gas won't just burn, it will explode with the force of a bomb. You'll kill your whole family.'

'It's the only way, Philip.'

Philip stared in at the man on the larder floor. Yes, there lay John Tolworth. Thirty years ago, they'd ridden their bikes along the lanes here and they'd fished in the pond. But now Philip saw another man – one that looked like John, but who Philip had seen in another country, in another time, in another life. Three thousand years ago he'd met this man coming into a house made of mud-brick. The man had had a sword in his hand. Philip remembered what happened next with brutal clarity.

'I know you,' Philip hissed. 'I know who you *were*.'

'Don't flip out on me now. I need you to get my family out of the house when I start shouting.' John positioned his fingers so they were on the lighter switch. He took a deep breath, ready to start yelling to the gunman.

Philip hissed, 'Samantha was right. Kadesh and I are one and the same, only we're separated by three thousand years. Your family are clones of the mummies in the castle.'

'Philip, that's insane.'

'No, it's true. At first, I thought that in a former life you were the father of the three mummified children. I'm wrong. You weren't the father. You were their murderer!'

'Philip, stop this. I'm going to call Micky's name. When I begin shouting, get Ingrid, Vicki and Ben out of the house. I'll ignite the gas when Micky opens the door.'

'No.'

'Philip, please save my family. You're the only one who can do that now.'

'No, you are going to kill that family all over again. History will repeat itself.'

Philip sensed that he was becoming detached from the world; he was floating back and back and back . . . he stood in a mud-brick house in a desert at night. Dogs howled. The stars shone

314

brighter than he'd ever seen before. He saw a river in the distance. On the far bank there were temples with gigantic statues standing outside. In this vision of the past, he saw himself block the doorway to the house with his body. He held a spear in one hand. A figure came out of the darkness. Philip saw that the man resembled John, though it was John in an earlier life. The man carried a sword, and Philip/Kadesh knew that this was the enemy, the assassin, the man who had come to kill the family that he, Philip, in an earlier incarnation, was protecting. The man rushed at him, thrusting forward with the sword. Philip fell to the floor. He lay there, blood gushing from a wound in his chest, unable to move as he grew weaker and weaker. He saw everything, though. Four people ran into the room. He saw figures that resembled Ingrid, Vicki, Ben and Oliver. They wore the same type of clothes as Egyptians wore three thousand years ago. The assassin that resembled John walked towards them. He swung the sword faster . . . faster . . . Then the bloodletting began.

'Don't use the lighter,' Philip begged, back in the present. 'You will kill them all over again.'

'I'm sorry, Philip. You are ill in your mind. It's a delusion. There are no such things as time twins, or mummies that come to life.'

'You saw, though, didn't you?' Philip's heart was nearly exploding. 'Thirty years ago, there was enough light coming through the door from the staircase. You saw me pull back the sheet that covered Kadesh. You saw him bite off my hand. That's why you blocked out the memory.

315

You saw exactly what happened when Kadesh attacked me.'

John's eyes became strangely glassy. He seemed to be slipping into a trance. Nevertheless, he spoke in a dead-sounding voice. 'I will count down to zero from sixty. Then, even if Micky doesn't appear at that door, I will still use this lighter to ignite the gas. I'm sure the entire house will be destroyed. I have no choice, Philip. I'm going to do it. Whether you save those people is up to you. But when I reach zero I will detonate the gas.' In that eerie, flat voice he uttered, 'Sixty . . . fifty-nine . . . fifty-eight . . .'

Philip's heart thundered in his chest. *Time's running out . . . It's almost zero hour . . .*

Oliver Tolworth couldn't wait any longer. Screams came from the lounge window. He had to know what the man was doing to his family inside the house. Fletcher followed as he padded through the back door and into the kitchen. Immediately, he smelt a powerful odour. That was gas, wasn't it? Despite the worrying notion that there was a gas leak, he couldn't allow himself to be distracted.

The man's gruff voice echoed from the lounge. 'One last time, Ben, tell me where you've hidden the drugs, otherwise I will start cutting the faces of these two pretty women too. Tell me where you've put the coke, OK?'

Oliver felt an unearthly sense of calm as he pushed open the door. He knew what he must do.

The gunman spun round and pointed the handgun at Oliver.

316

In a clear voice, Oliver said, 'I know where the drugs are. I took them from Ben's bag.'

'OK, kid,' said the man. 'My name is Micky. Tell me where they are.'

'I can't tell you, Micky. But I can show you.'

With that, Oliver turned and ran from the house. He took the path alongside the woods that led to the old mine shaft. Fletcher ran beside him. 'You'd don't have to come with me, Fletcher,' Oliver panted.

'We're friends. We stick together.'

The man with the gun followed. 'This better not be a piss-take,' he growled. 'Or you're going to get the beating of your life.'

The moon shone on the path, lighting their way.

Philip stood at the window. The reek of inflammable gas was almost overwhelming. John Tolworth remained lying there on the floor. In that strange, dead-sounding voice, John slowly counted down from sixty. There was a fatal inevitability about this. Philip knew that in a past life John had killed a mother and her three children. He'd do the same again. History repeating itself. A lethal loop of events. A bloody end to lives that had been lived for a second time three millennia apart. At that moment, Philip knew that in the future this would be repeated by people with different names who, nevertheless, looked like the Tolworths, who in turn resembled the mummified corpses that had been found in the Gold Tomb in Egypt.

Philip begged, 'Please, John, stop. Don't use the lighter. The explosion will kill everyone in the house. Do you really want your wife and children to die?'

John continued, adrift in a world of his own: 'Twenty-six . . . twenty-five . . .'

When he reached zero he would shout in order to bring the gunman to the room. If the gunman didn't appear, he'd still use the lighter to produce a flame. Then – BOOM.

'Twenty-four . . . twenty-three . . . twenty-two . . .'

From somewhere inside the house came the sound of shouting: women and a man yelling as loud as they could. Philip had reached the point of no return. He'd failed to save the family three thousand years ago in that desert kingdom. He might fail this time. But he had to try and stop them from being killed.

He raced through the back door into the kitchen and headed for the lounge. He prepared himself to tackle the gunman and try and get the pistol out of his hand. To his astonishment, he saw that the man had vanished. The three on the sofa all shouted at once.

'Philip! He's gone with Oliver,' Ingrid cried, trying to break the tape that held her wrists together. 'Oliver said he knew where the drugs were.'

Philip dashed back to the kitchen, unlocked the larder door, and entered the gas-filled room.

John lay there, chanting the countdown: 'Eight . . . seven . . . six.'

'John, give me the lighter!' Philip didn't wait for an answer though. He ripped the cigarette lighter from John's fingers. He then turned off the flow of gas at the gas meter. After that, he dragged

John, one handed, into the kitchen. He opened the back door wide, allowing the breeze to flood in and wash the fumes out of the house. That done, he grabbed a carving knife and quickly cut the tape that restrained John. He hurried back to the lounge and did the same in order to release the others. He noticed that Ben was in a poor state. He was covered in blood. There were cuts around his eyes. Even so, Ben struggled to his feet.

Ben shouted, 'Find Oliver. Micky will kill him if he hasn't got the coke.'

'Where did he go?' Philip asked.

All three shook their heads; their expressions were helpless and frightened.

'I don't know,' Ben said. 'Off into the woods somewhere.'

'I'll find him! John's in the kitchen. He might seem odd . . . He's taken a hard knock on the head.' Philip then ran out of the house and into thc night.

Oliver slowed from a run to a walk. *Play for time*, he thought. *The longer it takes to reach the mine, the more time Philip will have to help everyone back at the house. They'll be able to telephone the police. Also, they'll be able to lock the doors, so the man can't get in and hurt them again.*

'Hurry up, kid, I haven't got all night.' Micky shoved Oliver in order to make him move faster.

Oliver glanced sideways at Fletcher as he walked beside him. The twelve year old stared straight ahead, maybe trying to guess what Oliver planned to do next. The bushes at either side of the path seemed ghostly in the moonlight. Their leaves had a silvery glint, resembling staring eyes.

'I told you to hurry up.' Micky pushed Oliver again. 'Where did you hide my stuff?'

'Drugs,' Fletcher announced. 'Call them drugs, not stuff. Cocaine is a toxic chemical that harms the brain. It also helps finance organized crime and terrorism.' The statement was typical of Fletcher Brown: precocious and maybe just a little bit odd coming from the lips of a boy.

'I didn't ask for a moralizing lecture.' The gunman pushed Fletcher.

Fletcher stumbled forward, landing on his hands and knees. 'Ow! You made me hurt my ankle.'

'Stand up.'

'Can't.'

'Stand up.'

'Can't. My ankle hurts.'

Oliver noticed the sideways glance that Fletcher shot him. He understood that Fletcher had deliberately fallen. He was playing for time, too, giving Philip a chance to help Oliver's family back at the house.

Micky jabbed Oliver with the toe of his boot. 'Come on, you little shit, get back on your feet.'

'It really hurts. I can't stand up.'

'OK.' Micky pressed the handgun's muzzle against Fletcher's neck. 'They shoot lame horses, don't they? I'll shoot you.'

'I'll help him, mister.' Oliver grabbed Fletcher's arm and helped him stand. 'Don't shoot him. He'll be alright.'

'Listen, you two, don't mess me around any

longer. Show me where you hid my stuff – *my coke* – or I'm going to start hurting you. OK?'

The fierce expression on Micky's face told Oliver that he was serious. This man had tortured Ben; he'd do the same to Oliver and Fletcher. Oliver nodded. 'This way. Not far now.'

'Good. Now hurry up.'

Oliver walked faster. The path ran between the forest and open pasture. The moon revealed Baverstock Castle on its hill half a mile away. Sheep in the meadow watched the three pass by; the animals' eyes shone brightly. Even they seemed to expect that something shocking would happen soon.

Oliver's feet grew heavier. Despite the man shoving him in the back and urging him to move more quickly, his pace did get slower. Because soon they'd reach the old mineshaft. True, the drugs were there, but they were a long way down at the bottom of the pit. It would take ropes and specialist equipment to reach the drugs. They were well beyond the reach of Micky. Oliver knew that the criminal would get angry – blazing angry, murderously angry. Once Micky realized that the drugs couldn't be retrieved he'd start firing that gun. He would start killing. Shivering, Oliver thought: *I've saved my family. But how can I save Fletcher and myself?*

The area of moss was clearly visible in the moonlight. That's where the slabs of timber sealed the opening to the mineshaft. Rabbits scampered into bushes at the side of the path. Fletcher shot a look at Oliver. The seriousness of that glance revealed that Fletcher knew this

321

was crunch-time. They'd bought everyone back at the house a few minutes in order to give them a chance to call the police. But this was it for Oliver and Fletcher.

When they reached the flat area of moss, Oliver stopped. He might as well tell the truth, he decided. No point in postponing what the gunman would do to them. 'The drugs are here,' Oliver told him.

'Where?'

'There's a hole between two pieces of wood just there.' Oliver pointed at the ground.

Micky went to the spot, dropped to his knees, and scraped pieces of moss away. Straightaway, he saw an opening that was perhaps a foot long by five inches wide.

'Shit. What's down there?'

'It's a mineshaft,' Fletcher told him. He didn't even seem frightened. Like Oliver, he was resigned to whatever terrible thing would happen to them in the next few minutes. 'It's hundreds of feet deep.'

'I threw the drugs down there.' Oliver felt a flicker of triumph. He enjoyed the look of horror on Micky's face. 'It's so deep you'll never get them back.'

'Bastards!' Micky put the gun down on the thick planks that covered the opening to the mineshaft. He began tugging at the woodwork; he actually tried to break through, maybe hoping there'd be a ladder or something that would allow him to climb down and retrieve the cocaine. 'When I've got my stuff back,' he snarled, 'I'm going to put the pair of you down here. Do you hear? This is going to be your grave!'

Oliver didn't have the strength to run. All he could do was watch. Fletcher seemed the same. Both boys were frozen there. They'd done everything they could – now they waited for their punishment.

Oliver allowed his gaze to focus on the trees at the edge of the forest. Four people stood there in the shadows cast by the moon. No, not four people. Those were the mummies from the castle. Oliver recognized Amber, Bones, Ket and Isis. Even though he couldn't see their eyes, they seemed to be watching the man, who still tugged at the planks while cursing and threatening all kinds of punishment. The mummified figures stood there without moving. A breeze fluttered the strips of cloth hanging from their arms and their torsos. There was an air of calm, almost serenity about them. Oliver noticed that the features of the smallest mummified body seemed to alter. Strange . . . just for a moment, Oliver was convinced that he saw his own features there on the face of Ket; almost as if a photograph of his face had been projected on to the front of the mummy's skull. When he looked at the other mummies he saw the heads flicker and change, there in the shadows. He glimpsed familiar faces – they were the ones of his mother and sister and Ben. How could the mummies wear the faces of his family? Then he remembered what Mrs Oldfield had said. Tonight she'd told them that the mummies were changing – they were starting to look like the Tolworths.

Micky snarled, 'It's impossible. I'll never get them back.' He seized the gun and stood up, facing Oliver and Fletcher. 'You've thrown away something very valuable. You've got me into trouble with my boss. Now you two are going to suffer for what you've done.'

A fifth figure stepped out of the shadows.

Kadesh. Oliver recognized the mummy of the adult male. He wore a headband made of metal. The red skin on the mummy's face seemed to glow in the moonlight. It was as if a light shone inside the mummy's skull.

That grim husk took another step forward. Just for a moment, Oliver saw the face transform into that of Philip Kemmis. Then it changed back into the ravaged features of the corpse. The upper lip had shrunk back, forming a snarl.

Micky stared at Kadesh in surprise and laughed. 'You kids playing more tricks? Who have you got to dress up like a jerk from a mummy's tomb? Ha.' The man shook his head. 'OK, stay right where you are. Do not come any closer.' Micky aimed the gun at the figure clad in strips of linen.

Kadesh walked forward; there was a lethal purpose in that stride.

Micky didn't hesitate. Aiming the gun, he pulled the trigger. Those loud bangs hurt Oliver's ears. Flame spat from the muzzle. Once, twice, three times. Bullets ripped into the chest of the mummy; dust jetted from between the bandages.

The man fired again as he screamed, 'You're not real . . . you're not real!'

Kadesh raised the arm that ended in a bulbous shape, not a hand. He swung it down against

Micky's head. The blow was enormous. To Oliver's ears the **CRUNCH** it made was much louder than the gunshots.

The force of the impact knocked the man clean off his feet; the pistol flew from his hand into the grass. Before he could climb upright again, Kadesh picked him up. The man lay almost like a child cradled in its father's arms. But that shocking face didn't belong to a loving parent. Micky opened his eyes, saw that portrait of ruin, and screamed again.

He was still howling in terror when Kadesh walked away into the forest. The other mummies followed. The criminal's yells grew even more terrified and panic-stricken. Oliver still heard the screams, even though he couldn't see Kadesh carrying the man.

Just a moment later, the screams stopped abruptly. Then, silence. Oliver and Fletcher stood there without moving, not knowing what they should do next.

Soon, however, a tall figure stepped out of the forest's shadows, and Philip Kemmis walked forward into the bright light of the moon. He said gently, 'It's all over. He can't hurt you. Come on, it's time you went home.'

Seventeen

The hospital was, even at three in the morning, a world of bustling movement, noise and bright lights. Oliver Tolworth had been examined by doctors. His mother and sister were there in the room with him; they were exhausted and sat holding hands. Nevertheless, they smiled with relief when the doctor announced that Oliver was perfectly fine.

Oliver followed his mother out into the corridor. He looked through a doorway into a room where his father and Ben were lying on beds after receiving treatment for their injuries. Both had bandages around their heads. Oliver thought they looked like Egyptian mummies. There were police officers in the room with them. They asked his dad and Ben questions and made notes in books as they did so.

Oliver ran into the room. His dad hugged him and ruffled his hair. The police stopped asking questions at that point and smiled at Oliver.

His father hugged him again. 'Are you alright, Ollie?'

Oliver nodded. 'The doctor says I'm fine.'

'That's good news.' His dad sounded hugely relieved. 'It's been a rotten night, but we're all going to be OK. Ben and I have got some bashes and grazes. We'll be back to normal in a few days, though.'

Ben reached out from his bed, and Oliver grasped his hand tightly.

'I'm sorry, Oliver,' Ben told him. 'I did something really stupid, and what happened is all my fault.'

'It's not,' Oliver insisted. 'It was that man with the gun. You're not to blame. I don't want you to go away.'

'I've just had a chat with your dad. He's asked me to stop for the rest of the summer, despite what I've done, if you'll have me?'

Oliver hugged Ben, a fierce hug that made the nineteen year old wince. Even though the wounds hurt, he didn't pull away, and he hugged Oliver back. At last, Oliver reluctantly left the room while the police continued their conversation with Ben and Dad.

'The police questioned us, too,' Vicki said.

'But you won't be asked anything tonight,' his mum added. 'They will want a little chat with you and Fletcher later, but there's nothing to worry about. You're not in trouble.'

The police must have thought that Oliver was out of earshot in the corridor; however, he heard one of them say, 'Mr Tolworth, we found the body of a man in woodland. We believe it to be Michael Dunt, the individual who attacked you. He's well known to police and had only been released from prison a few weeks ago . . .'

Doctors and nurses in green scrubs walked briskly along the corridor. There were other side rooms where people were being treated. A lady with long white hair was connected to a machine that bleeped. A drunken youth was trying to get out of bed while a nurse encouraged him to stay put. Just another night in A&E.

A nurse invited them to sit in a waiting room away from the bustle in the corridor. Vicki and his mother sat side-by-side. Oliver lay on the chairs with his head on his mother's lap. After a while, both Vicki and Mum fell asleep.

* * *

Philip Kemmis climbed the hill in the moonlight. When he reached the top, he gazed back down at the dim shapes of the gatehouse and the castle. Beyond the castle, a misty glow revealed where the moon shone down on the ocean. The police had interviewed him about what had happened tonight. They'd told him about the discovery of Dunt's body. Philip had expected accusations that he'd killed Dunt. However, the detective had quite openly voiced her opinion that Dunt, a small-time crook, had arrived here with an unknown accomplice; that there'd been a falling out between thieves and the accomplice had murdered Dunt.

So be it, Philip told himself. *If the police believe that an accomplice killed the man, why complicate things with other explanations? The police wouldn't believe me, even if I told them what really happened. They'd say I'm insane.*

Philip breathed deeply, catching the perfume of wild flowers on the night air. All of a sudden, he froze. He realized he felt different. Ever since he'd lost his hand as a boy, a storm had raged inside his head. That internal storm had tortured him night and day; he'd not been able to think clearly. Everywhere he looked he saw the mummified dead. Now, however, his mind had become quiet. At last the storm inside his head had died away. A sense of peace filtered through him, relaxing his muscles, eliciting a sigh of relief.

Was it too early to hope that his life would change for the better? Maybe. But perhaps this was the beginning of the end of his nightmare. Philip walked down the hill through the moonlight and, to his surprise, he realized that he was smiling.

Oliver stood up, left the room, and walked along the busy corridor. The hospital was immense, and it wasn't long before he found himself heading into a quieter part of the building with dimly lit corridors. He didn't know where he was going in particular. He just felt like walking.

He found one long corridor completely deserted, apart from a lone figure sitting on a chair against one wall.

'Oliver, I thought about you coming to find me, and you did.'

Oliver saw that figure was Fletcher. The boy sat there in the red cap that Oliver had given him. Oliver asked, 'Didn't the police take you home after the doctor looked at you?'

'Yes, but my father brought me back here again.'

'Oh.'

'You see, my mother died tonight.' Fletcher didn't have any expression on his face. He simply gave a shrug. 'It was expected. They've covered her face with a sheet.'

'I'm sorry your mother's died, Fletcher. That's rotten.'

'She'd been ill for months. It wasn't good that she was suffering. She isn't now. It's like she's sleeping.' Fletcher gazed down the corridor; the far end was gloomy. Oliver followed the direction of his gaze. A tall, thin figure stood there in silhouette. 'That's Kadesh, isn't it?' Fletcher asked.

329

'Maybe.' Oliver couldn't be sure – all he could tell was that a tall figure stood in the corridor a hundred paces away. The figure appeared to be looking this way, but it didn't move or make a noise. 'This *is* all over, isn't it? I hoped the mummies wouldn't walk any more.'

Fletcher stared at that mere ghost of a shape. 'I wanted Kadesh to do something for my family. I like to think he's here to take my mother to a place where she'll be at peace.'

Oliver stared into the gloom until his eyes watered. He couldn't see the tall figure any more, and he began to wonder if it had ever been there at all. 'I'd best go back to my mother and sister.'

'OK, Oliver. Thanks for coming.'

'Did you really make me come and find you just by thinking it?'

'You know me by now, Ollie. I'm not like anyone else.'

'Where's your dad?'

'I don't know. There's paperwork, I suppose. The death certificate. Stuff like that.'

Oliver said goodbye and started walking along the corridor. He paused and turned back to look at his friend. The twelve year old sat there by himself in the gloom. He suddenly looked so alone and so forlorn. Even though Oliver was only eleven, he realized that Fletcher would always be alone in life. He wouldn't be able to maintain relationships or marry. Oliver felt, at that moment, as if he'd been given a glimpse of the future, and he saw a grown-up Fletcher forever living by himself in the gatehouse, with its view of the old castle on the hill.

Fletcher gazed down at the floor, already lost in a world of his own.

'Fletcher,' Oliver said, 'I'm going to stay in Devon for the rest of the summer. We'll still meet up every day.'

Fletcher gave a sad smile. 'You won't. Your family will leave as soon as they can. They won't want to live in a house where bad things happened. Goodbye, Oliver. Thanks for the cap.'

'I'm going to tell my mum and dad that I want to stay in Devon. I'll see you tomorrow, and we can go fishing in the big pond.'

Fletcher gave a single nod and returned to staring at the floor. Oliver went back to find his family, determined to persuade them to stay in the house in Devon. He wanted to spend the rest of the summer there with Fletcher.

Vicki stood by the door of the waiting room. 'Ollie, we can leave now.'

'We're going back to the house?'

She shook her head. 'We're staying in a hotel tonight, then we're going back home to London tomorrow. Come on, we're being driven to the hotel in police cars. Ben's coming, too.'

'Wait, I'm going to say goodbye to Fletcher.'

His sister was too exhausted to argue. She just gave a little shrug and leaned on the wall, where she'd wait for him to return.

Oliver ran back along the corridor, pushing open swing doors as he went. He found hospital corridors that stretched into the distance. These were gloomy and silent and completely empty. Oliver kept running. When he called out Fletcher's name, his own voice echoed back. There was no

331

sign of that strange and lonely boy in the red cap and, at last, the corridor took Oliver back to his sister. Oliver knew that he couldn't keep searching for Fletcher, so, with a sigh, he took hold of her hand and they both walked out into the night where his family patiently waited beneath the moon that shone down on this sleepy corner of England.

The police cars arrived that would take them to the hotel. Before Oliver climbed in, he looked up at the hospital and murmured softly, 'Goodbye, Fletcher. When I grow up I'll come back to the castle and visit you, I promise.'